D0122247

Praise for novels by Heidi Chiavaroli
The Orchard House

"As a longtime fan of Louisa May Alcott's *Little Women*, I was eager to read *The Orchard House* by Heidi Chiavaroli, anticipating a glimpse into the life of the author who penned the classic. I got that and so much more. . . . *Orchard House* invited me in, served me tea, and held me enthralled with its compelling tale."

LORI BENTON, CHRISTY AWARD–WINNING AUTHOR OF *BURNING SKY, THE KING'S MERCY,* AND *MOUNTAIN LAUREL*

"*The Orchard House* is a captivating story of sisters, difficult relationships, and the mending of broken hearts. . . . Heidi Chiavaroli has written *Orchard House* with depth and soul."

ELIZABETH BYLER YOUNTS, CAROL AWARD–WINNING AUTHOR OF *THE SOLACE OF WATER*

"With insight into the complexities of female friendship and sisterhood, Heidi Chiavaroli spins a dual tale that is at once rooted in history and solidly contemporary. *The Orchard House* is sure to please historical fiction fans, readers of Louisa May Alcott, and anyone who has ever had a friend who felt as close as a sister."

ERIN BARTELS, AWARD-WINNING AUTHOR OF *WE HOPE FOR BETTER THINGS* AND *THE WORDS BETWEEN US*

"A line from *Orchard House* captures the very essence of this time-slip novel. Chiavaroli did an exceptional job 'giving awareness through the power of this story,' merging the poignant topic of domestic abuse between historical and contemporary. This is a story I had a hard time walking away from, even after reaching the epilogue."

T. I. LOWE, BESTSELLING AUTHOR OF THE CAROLINA COAST SERIES

"I knew from the very first page that this was going to be a special book. Lyric, evocative, and honest, *The Orchard House* is a book meant to be savored."

SUSIE FINKBEINER, AUTHOR OF *STORIES THAT BIND US* AND *ALL MANNER OF THINGS*

"Alcott fans, take joy! Heidi Chiavaroli has brought Louisa's world of Concord to life through captivating characterization in her modern story line, and in her historical timeline through exquisite detail both carefully researched and respectfully imagined. *The Orchard House* is a home for the literary soul."

AMANDA DYKES, AUTHOR OF *SET THE STARS ALIGHT* AND *WHOSE WAVES THESE ARE*

The Tea Chest

"Captivating from the first page. . . . Steeped in timeless truths and served with skill, *The Tea Chest* is sure to be savored by all who read it."

JOCELYN GREEN, CHRISTY AWARD–WINNING AUTHOR OF *BETWEEN TWO SHORES*

"*The Tea Chest* brings two women, separated by centuries, face-to-face with the same question: What is the price of liberty? A master at writing dual timelines, Chiavaroli takes us beyond the historical connection between these two women and wraps them together with a shared spirit."

ALLISON PITTMAN, CRITICALLY ACCLAIMED AUTHOR OF *THE SEAMSTRESS*

"Swoon-worthy romance, heartbreak, and intrigue combine for a thrilling story that will keep me thinking for a long time to come. Bravo!"

AMY K. SORRELLS, AWARD-WINNING AUTHOR OF *BEFORE I SAW YOU*

"*The Tea Chest* is timeless and empowering. Long may Heidi Chiavaroli reign over thoughtful, effortlessly paralleled fiction that digs deep into the heart of America's early liberty and the resonance of faith and conviction she offers as its poignant legacy."

RACHEL MCMILLAN, AUTHOR OF *MURDER IN THE CITY OF LIBERTY*

"*The Tea Chest* is not only a story of America's birth as a nation, but also one that reflects the clamoring in humanity's heart to soar unfettered by the weight of chains that bind."

JAIME JO WRIGHT, CHRISTY AWARD–WINNING AUTHOR OF *THE HOUSE ON FOSTER HILL* AND *THE CURSE OF MISTY WAYFAIR*

"*The Tea Chest* is an enthralling story of beauty birthed from sorrow, hope amid ashes, and healing through pain."

TARA JOHNSON, AUTHOR OF *WHERE DANDELIONS BLOOM* AND *ENGRAVED ON THE HEART*

The Hidden Side

"*The Hidden Side* is a beautiful tale that captures the timeless struggles of the human heart."

JULIE CANTRELL, *NEW YORK TIMES* AND *USA TODAY* BESTSELLING AUTHOR OF *PERENNIALS*

"Heidi Chiavaroli has written another poignant novel that slips between a heart-wrenching present-day story and a tragic one set during the Revolutionary War. I couldn't put this book down!"

MELANIE DOBSON, AWARD-WINNING AUTHOR OF *CATCHING THE WIND* AND *MEMORIES OF GLASS*

"This page-turner will appeal to readers looking for fiction that explores Christian values and belief under tragic circumstances."

BOOKLIST

"Filled with fascinating historical details, Chiavaroli connects two women through an artifact of the past. This heartrending tale will engage aficionados of the American Revolution and historical fiction."

LIBRARY JOURNAL

"Both halves of *The Hidden Side* are singularly compelling, with more of a fine threading between stories than an obvious connection. There is also the shared message that even during times of spiritual darkness, with prayer and hope, forgiveness and new beginnings are always possible."

FOREWORD MAGAZINE

"Chiavaroli's latest time-slip novel does not disappoint. Both story lines are fully developed with strong character development and they are seamlessly woven together."

ROMANTIC TIMES, TOP PICK

Freedom's Ring

"From the Boston Massacre and the American Revolution to the Boston Marathon bombing, history proves the triumph of grace. . . . Evocative, rich with symbolism, honest in its portrayal of human errors, *Freedom's Ring* explores what happens when individuals reach the limit of their own ability and allow God to step in."

FOREWORD MAGAZINE

"First novelist Chiavaroli's historical tapestry will provide a satisfying read for fans of Kristy Cambron and Lisa Wingate."

LIBRARY JOURNAL

"Joy, anguish, fear, and romance are seamlessly incorporated with authentic history, skillfully imagined fiction, and the beautiful reminder that good can—and does—come out of darkness."

ROMANTIC TIMES

The Orchard House

HEIDI CHIAVAROLI

Tyndale House Publishers
Carol Stream, Illinois

Visit Tyndale online at tyndale.com.

Visit Heidi Chiavaroli's website at heidichiavaroli.com.

TYNDALE and Tyndale's quill logo are registered trademarks of Tyndale House Ministries.

The Orchard House

Designed by Jacqueline L. Nuñez

Edited by Caleb Sjogren

Published in association with the literary agency of Natasha Kern Literary Agency, Inc., P.O. Box 1069, White Salmon, WA 98672.

Scripture quotations are taken from the *Holy Bible*, King James Version.

For information about special discounts for bulk purchases, please contact Tyndale House Publishers at csresponse@tyndale.com or call 1-800-323-9400.

ISBN 978-1-4964-3472-2 (HC)
ISBN 978-1-4964-3473-9 (SC)

Printed in the United States of America

26 25 24 23 22 21 20
7   6   5   4   3   2   1

To Mom.

*Thank you for not only giving me your beautiful poems for
this story, but for always believing in this dream for me.*

I love you.

Acknowledgments

As I sit down to write this thank-you note to the many beautiful people who have had a hand in this novel, I am once again overwhelmed by the collaboration of such an amazing team.

First, a huge thank-you to my mother, Donna Anuszczyk, for coming to my rescue with the beautiful poems contained within this story. I was an author (one who does not consider herself a poet) with a deadline and in need of poems. More than willing, you graciously gave me your best and amazingly enough, several of them fit my story line perfectly. Thank you, Mom!

Thank you to another one of my big champions, my agent, Natasha Kern. Your belief in my stories means so much to me. Thank you for your faith when things might look a bit bumpy. I learn something from you each time we talk, and I'm so very grateful for your support.

To the beautiful team at Tyndale—my amazingly talented and gracious editors, Jan Stob and Caleb Sjogren, and also to Karen Watson, Elizabeth Jackson, Andrea Garcia, Mariah León, and Jackie Nuñez. I can't imagine a better publishing family to be part of. Thank you for making this writing dream possible.

Thank you to my critique partner, Sandra Ardoin, for keeping me sane. Also to my sweet writing friends who I know I can reach out to whenever this journey feels like a lonely one—Melissa Jagears, Melanie Dobson, Tessa Afshar, and Amy Sorrells.

Thank you to the staff at Orchard House for such an amazing tour and for answering my questions. You made *Little Women* and Louisa May Alcott come alive in an entirely captivating way. I don't think I could ever get enough!

To the many readers, bloggers, and reviewers who are enthusiastic about my books and have taken the time to write a review or give a shout-out, you all rock. Thank you!

Thank you to the three most important men in my life—my husband, Daniel, and my sons, James and Noah—you put up with crazy deadlines, skimpy dinners, and weepy moments. Thank you for always loving me and for giving me the inspiration and support to do this thing I love.

Lastly, thank you to the greatest Author of all, the Author of life and hope. Do with these words what You will.

Dear Father, help me with the love

That casteth out my fear,

Teach me to lean on thee, and feel

That thou art very near,

That no temptation is unseen,

No childish grief too small,

Since thou, with patience infinite,

Doth soothe and comfort all.

LOUISA MAY ALCOTT, AGE 12

CHAPTER ONE

I used to imagine my mind a room in confusion,
and I was to put it in order.

~ LMA

Taylor

CONCORD, MASSACHUSETTS
JULY 1995

Thirteen isn't quite grown-up, but it's old enough for a girl to realize that hope can be a dangerous thing.

The first time I realized this I was no more than four. My mother had dropped me off with Uncle Rob. This wasn't unusual, but this time, she was gone more than two sleeps. Longer than she had ever been gone.

When I asked my uncle when she'd be back, he only shrugged and said, "You better hope soon, kid."

Hope.

I did that a lot back then. Each morning when I woke, throwing my threadbare blanket off my shoulders and rolling off the couch to search the small rooms of Uncle Rob's apartment, but finding the woman in his bed was not my mom.

Each night, when I fell asleep, thinking if I only *hoped* hard enough, and maybe held my breath real tight while I did it, my mother would appear by morning.

But time and time again, hope failed. And still, it seemed, I didn't learn. Not after I found my mom's obituary on Uncle Rob's fold-up kitchen table, where I'd left my precious copy of *Little Women* when I was eight, not after the police came and hauled him off to jail when I was eleven, and not when I found myself in the vicious grip of the foster care system a short time later.

And then, a year ago, the Bennetts took me in. And I found hope again. Only this time it was a fragile, frayed thing—a lot like the toothbrush I had growing up that Uncle Rob never remembered to replace.

Victoria Bennett had been my best friend since we were seven years old, and now she was my sister. Her parents gave me new toothbrushes and Nike sneakers and love as much as they were able. They gave me a chance to go to Jo March Writing Camp at Orchard House, a place Victoria and I had become obsessed with. All those years of immersing myself in the world of Jo March, imagining what it would be like to have a family, to have even just one sister . . . to belong.

And now I was here, in the very room where Louisa May Alcott had written her best-loved classic. In the very house where she had set the adventures of her "little women." Dipping my toe in those dangerous waters of *hope* once again.

I closed my eyes and soaked in the near magic of Louisa's bedroom. Beneath my bent knee and through the thin nylon of my string bag I felt the hard edges of my nine-year-old copy of *Little Women*. In some ways, I regretted bringing it today. Mom had sent it to me that first Christmas after she had left. There'd been no note within, just a thick manila envelope with my name on it, the book naked of any red-and-green holiday wrappings.

The present wasn't really suitable for a girl who hadn't even entered kindergarten. Yet while I knew deep down she had probably grabbed it up as a last-minute thought at some secondhand store, I couldn't help but imagine and hope that she had spent hours pondering the perfect Christmas present for me, that she had wanted me to have this gift and this message—the story of a family that fiercely loved and went through hard times together—even when she couldn't bring about that reality in my own life.

I cherished it more than I ought. Still did. And I couldn't resist bringing it along today. Hoping that the old would somehow make way for the new. That maybe, just maybe, the wounds of my past would be covered over with perfection.

Victoria and I had looked forward to this for months, and I couldn't wait for this moment—the moment when I was certain some grand story would strike my consciousness, when time might cease to exist and the brilliance that had inspired Miss Alcott would descend upon me in a magnificent cloud of glory.

I looked down at what I'd written, more journal entry than inspired glory.

There's something funny about being the one on the outside looking in.

Not funny ha-ha, and not funny strange, because strange means out of the ordinary, and for me, not

*belonging is more normal than out of the ordinary. So
what kind of funny am I talking about?*
 Funny lonely.
 Funny I've-gotten-good-at-hiding-my-tears.
 Funny I-wonder-if-it-will-always-be-this-way.

I hastily flipped to a fresh page, feeling the press of time squeezing tight. I poised my pen over the paper, but nothing came. I peered out the window beside Louisa's half-moon desk, wondered if she'd glimpsed the same elm more than a hundred years earlier.

I sighed and pressed the pen on the page until a small dot of black ink expanded beneath it. A dot, but no words.

A warm hand fell on my shoulder and the scent of mothballs enveloped me as our instructor, Mrs. Hayes, leaned over my shoulder.

"There's no wrong answer in writing, dear. It seems the spirit of the muse was upon you a page back. Perhaps entertain it. You never know where it might lead."

I gave her a small smile but hoped she wouldn't linger. I had only another ten minutes to start my literary masterpiece.

She left, but instead of concentrating on the birth of words, I looked across the room at my best friend, perched in front of the fireplace. Victoria scribbled furiously in her notebook, not seeming to come up for a moment of air. Story ideas seemed as plentiful to her as daffodils in spring, and although most of them involved Zack Morris or a New Kids on the Block love triangle, at least she had ideas—and guts enough to write about them.

I swallowed down my jealousy and forced my pen to move

across the paper, scratching out a sentence that described a beautiful old English house. When Mrs. Hayes told us our writing time was nearing an end, I looked down at the flowery words I'd painted—beautiful, but without character or conflict within sight.

When it was time to file out of the room, I took the last place in line and discreetly ran my hand over Louisa's painted desk. For a fleeting second, the whisper of something extraordinary floated up to me . . . something that felt like possibility and hope and excitement. But before I could grasp it and claim it as my own, it vanished.

I pressed my hand harder into the white paint, searching, willing some trace of talent to seep into my being. If I concentrated hard enough, perhaps I would become someone special, perhaps a gift would be given to me, perhaps I would be able to support myself so that I would never again have to depend on the state or the foster care system, or even the Bennetts, to do so. If I could just find this secret *something*, I knew I would find where I truly belonged.

As the line moved forward, I let my hand fall from the cool wood of the desk. The girls made their way downstairs, their footsteps loud on the ancient staircase. Mrs. Hayes stopped me from following them.

"Please don't be discouraged, Taylor. Do you know that both Louisa and Jo had many false starts and even rejections before finding their voice?"

"They did?" I couldn't help the curiosity that crept into my tone.

She nodded. "Why, one of Louisa's stories was considered so sensational, no one would touch it. But guess what? It's being published—finally—later this summer. Your time will come, dear. Stick with it, and maybe your sister can help you."

My sister.

For the first time I felt something shut down within me at the mention of Victoria. I supposed we were sisters in a sense. And yet sometimes—times like these—our differences seemed so apparent that I thought I was just kidding myself. Maybe it was a lie—me being a Bennett, me pretending I could be like all these other girls here.

For once, I felt a need to reveal the truth and set things straight, or it might wrap its cold fingers around my throat and strangle me.

"She's not my sister," I whispered and followed the rest of the girls down the stairs of the old house.

~~

After we said goodbye to our classmates and teachers, I gave one last look at the beautiful, gabled house. Drapes decorated the sides of each window. A grand old chimney topped the historic house and I reminded myself again how lucky I was to be here, where my favorite book of all time had been written. No matter if the words didn't come today—perhaps they would tomorrow.

Turning, I joined Victoria on the walk back home, skipping over the cracks on the sidewalk, my backpack bumping against me with each jump as I listened to Victoria prattle on about the story she'd started that morning. Her words were as plentiful in speaking as in writing, and I listened with rapt attention as we passed the imposing white colonial that used to be Ralph Waldo Emerson's home.

"I'm sick of writing about surface stuff, you know? Being at Orchard House, it was like I felt Jo speaking to me, telling me about a new kind of story . . . a story she would have written."

I marveled at her imagination, her confidence in her story. Was it because she'd grown up with two loving parents? If I'd been with them from the beginning, instead of living in the house of an absentee uncle, would I have Victoria's surety?

"What's it about?"

She kept walking but I noticed the faraway look that took over her expression. Her blue eyes turned bright and she absentmindedly pushed aside a stray lock of hair. "It's about a girl—I named her Sophia—isn't that the most beautiful name? Anyway, Sophia falls in love with a rich man named Logan, who will only love her if she changes herself. He wants her to cut her hair and only watch football and refuses to let her write her stories because he thinks it's a waste of time and in the end, it's about her finding who she is, not about what some boy wants her to be. Don't you think Jo would love it?"

"Wow. That's . . . good. I think she would love it." We kept walking up Lexington Road, the center of town just in the distance. "How do you come up with all your ideas?"

She shrugged, flung her hair over her shoulder. "I don't know—they just come. Yours don't?"

I shoved my hands in my pockets and concentrated on my feet.

Victoria squeezed my arm. "You've been through a lot. Don't be so hard on yourself, okay?"

I wriggled from her hand. "Stop it."

"Stop what?"

"Stop borrowing lines from your mom."

"I'm trying to help, Taylor."

"Then be my best friend, like you used to be."

Victoria quieted before answering. "I'm trying," she whispered.

I ignored the throb of guilt that pulsed through my middle. I had no right to lash out or be anything but grateful to the Bennetts, and that included Victoria. "I'm sorry. I—I know you want to help."

We were almost to the middle of town, and she stopped walking. "We always said we wanted to be sisters, and now we are. Aren't you happy?"

I was a horrible person. Wretched, as Jo March might say. "Of course I'm happy."

But something was missing. Not on the surface, but right underneath. Something that made me feel like an intruder within the Bennett family, an intruder even on this new life I got to live. On this side of things, I felt that I owed Victoria, that we were no longer equals. And worse, I knew . . . knew that her parents, Paul and Lorraine, had invited me into their family not so much because they loved me, but because they loved their daughter.

Even so, how could I be ungrateful? They'd saved me from the foster care system, a place where young teens like me floundered and flopped until they aged out. At least I belonged somewhere now, if only in name.

"I'm sorry," I said again. My complicated feelings on family didn't matter. What mattered was that I showed my gratitude, that Victoria or her parents didn't ever—ever—regret taking me in. I held out my hand to her and she took it. I squeezed. "Best friends forever, right?"

She squeezed back. "Best friends *and* sisters forever."

We walked, our hands swinging between us. "Now," she said. "To help you come up with your brilliant story idea, I say we reinstate the Pickwick Club."

I laughed. "We're too old."

"Tell that to the March sisters!" Victoria raised a fist in the air, clearly fired up by our day at the Orchard House camp. And when she got an idea in her head, nothing was known to stop her.

We'd modeled our Pickwick Club after that found in *Little Women*, and though neither I nor Victoria had ever read Charles Dickens's *Pickwick Papers*, it didn't seem to matter. Our club had originated five years ago as a simple exchange of short stories and ideas—what some more professional writers would call a critique group. We met once a week in the room above the Bennett garage and encouraged each other in our endeavors, taking turns reading stories. I'd always come up with an idea because I never wanted to show up empty-handed and because Victoria was always willing to help me out when my characters got themselves stuck.

But somewhere along the way we'd stopped our club. Sometime after Victoria had told me that Brad Lincoln had kissed her at our first middle school dance. Sometime after the Bennetts had decided to "try me out" as a foster child. Sometime after boy bands and *Beverly Hills, 90210* had become more the fabric of our lives than a classic nineteenth-century story.

But here, today, it seemed to resurrect itself, and I couldn't say I wasn't happy. This was what I longed for: a return to the past, a return to a simpler time when happiness didn't hinge on a boy's attention or how well—or not so well—my chest was growing, but on the simplicity and pleasure of creating a story.

Victoria pushed me lightly with her shoulder. "Come on, sis. If we're going to be famous authors one day, we need to get serious about our writing. I'm talking meeting more than once a week. I'm talking word counts, critiques, contests." Her clear complexion was flushed, excitement making her ten times prettier. "Why couldn't we start submitting to agents? Dream big, you know? Start reaching for those castles in the air?"

I smiled at the reference. The March sisters often talked of their dreams—their hopes—as "castles in the air."

But it was one thing to have dreams, another to start acting on them. Victoria didn't realize how hard it was for me to bare my words even to her, my closest friend. Yet I couldn't stomp on her enthusiasm. And I wanted to succeed, to find that elusive *something* that had whispered to me from Louisa's desk. "Okay. I'm in."

She rewarded me with a toothy grin. She was getting braces next month. I needed them, too, but I couldn't expect Paul and Lorraine to spend the money.

"Let's start right away!" She ran ahead and I chased after her, the warm air brushing my hair back, my backpack slapping my rear as I pushed my spindly legs forward. We ran past the center of town, past Holy Family Parish and the town hall, past the Colonial Inn and North Bridge Inn, and up Monument Street to the Bennetts' massive, gabled three-story colonial. I remember the first time I saw the home, how I'd come off the bus with Victoria, the note my uncle had written giving his permission for me to go home with my new friend clutched tight in my hand. We'd chosen one another for art partners that day. I remember Victoria telling me over plastic palettes of watercolors that her mom made the best banana oatmeal cookies in the world and how she'd have some ready for us when we came home.

Now I followed Victoria up the driveway and, for the hundredth time, tried to accept what the Bennetts occasionally reminded me: that this was *my* home. *My* driveway.

Victoria held the screen door open for me and I followed her in, grabbing my notebook from my bag before hanging it above the large bench in the foyer. We went into the kitchen, where a plate of fresh cookies awaited, as always.

We grabbed a couple before heading through the back door toward the garage. We traveled beneath the portico, spotted Lorraine in her flower beds, and walked toward her.

"Hi, girls!" Victoria's mother waved and stood, brushing the knees of her pants. "How was camp?" She put an arm around Victoria and kissed her forehead, then, with only the slightest bit of awkwardness, squeezed my shoulder.

I imagined those arms around me in a hug, the light scent of her Elizabeth Arden perfume, all roses and jasmine and cedar, enveloping me in a freshness that matched the flowers she loved so much. Still, at the same time that I longed for them, those gentle arms also frightened me. An embrace was giving part of yourself away, making yourself vulnerable, exposed. An embrace would mean I had that much more to lose. An embrace was risky.

I took a step closer to the garage. My relationship with Lorraine was . . . funny. In this case, funny-strange, because it was definitely out of the ordinary. She'd gone from being my best friend's mom, whom I was distantly fond of, to being my guardian and foster mom, to being the realest mom I would likely ever have. Before her, I knew very little of mothers, and most of that was by way of television shows. Clair Huxtable and Jill Taylor and Maggie Seaver. Where did Lorraine fall into my life? The Bennetts had done so much—attending foster classes, wading through lawyers and state regulations and piles of paperwork—all to adopt me.

But I was thirteen. I seemed to have missed the boat on the proper time period in establishing myself with a new mother. Now, even as I longed for and feared the prospect of Lorraine's arms around me, I realized the impossible awkwardness of the situation. I never invited physical contact with the Bennetts—with anyone. My uncle had never touched me, which I suppose I should be grateful for when listening to the stories of some of the other girls in foster care, and yet quite simply, I didn't understand the world of physical love. Victoria thought nothing of squeezing my hand or slinging an arm around my shoulder, and by now I was nearly comfortable with it. But to initiate such a gesture? To Lorraine, who took me into her home and cared for me? Quite simply, I didn't know how, even if I wanted to.

I stood quiet as Victoria chatted on about our day, gushed about the story she was writing, and told her mom about our plan to reinstate the Pickwick Club.

"You sound inspired. How about you, Taylor? Did you have fun?"

I nodded vigorously. "Very much. Thank you so much. I really am grateful." My words gurgled out like a clumsy, bubbly stream.

She smiled and I noticed how the creases around her mouth and eyes were pleasant on her pretty face. "You've thanked us quite enough, honey. We're glad to do it. Just enjoy, okay?"

I blinked fast. Once, then twice, then looked with longing at the garage. Victoria skipped out of her mother's arms, said we'd be back down to set the table for supper, and pulled me along to race up the outside stairs to the room above the garage.

Victoria's father had finished the space long ago. It had a bathroom, an array of exercise equipment, a pool table, and a small sitting area with a television. I placed my stash of cookies on an end table alongside my notebook and headed to the bathroom. Victoria opened one of the huge windows, sprawled out on the area rug near the couches, and opened her own notebook, the cap of her pen already off.

When I had flushed the toilet, I washed my hands, staring at myself in the mirror. I wasn't ugly, but neither was I particularly pretty—not pretty like Victoria, anyway, who pulled off a fawn-like, alluring quality with her petite frame and dark looks. She reminded me of Winona Ryder. I, on the other hand, was too tall and gangly to pull off anything fawn-like. Giantlike, maybe. Aside from my thick auburn hair, there wasn't much beauty to me.

I pressed my lips together to hide my crooked teeth from the mirror before opening the door but stopped short at the sight of Victoria holding my black-and-white composition notebook, open to the first page. Blood rushed in my ears, a silent whooshing sound that quickly spread to the rest of my body, traveling with tunneling force until it throbbed at the edges of my fingers and toes.

"What are you doing?"

Victoria looked up, something like pain written on her face. "I—I wanted to see where you were headed . . . to help . . ."

I snatched the notebook from her. "You shouldn't have done that." My hot hands gripped the cover of the notebook, their warmth making the cardboard damp. I wanted to take the notebook and run back to the main house and upstairs to my room. I wanted to forget the Pickwick Club and Victoria and even Jo March Writing Camp. But I couldn't. Such a display would make me look spoiled, ungrateful.

And what did I have to be sulking about, anyway? I lived in one of the most beautiful homes in Concord with my best friend—my only friend, really. Her parents were providing for my every need—they sent me to writing camp, for goodness' sake! How many times had I longed to simply visit Orchard House? Now I got to write there.

I hadn't a right to be unappreciative. And there was no place for me to go. Nowhere else I even wanted to go. Uncle Rob wouldn't be out of jail for at least five years. I needed the Bennetts. And I needed them to not regret taking me in. No matter what.

And that started here. With not running back to my room and locking myself in, as I so desperately wanted to do.

Instead, I turned to the treadmill and hopped on, pressed the buttons until I had to run to keep up. Fast.

"What are you doing?"

"Running."

"Why?"

"Because I want to run, but I don't want to run *away*." I

had trouble talking around my breaths, wasn't even sure if my words were true. Sometimes, crazy as it was, I *did* want to run away.

Victoria leaned over the treadmill and pushed the Off button. The belt slowed to a stop.

"I'm sorry you're lonely," she said.

I swiped at my nose, ordered tears to stay put.

"I wish I could help more."

I shook my head. "You do. You have. If I didn't have you, I don't know what I'd do. It's me. I—there's something wrong with me."

She didn't deny it, and somehow that made me feel better.

Without warning, her eyes lit up. She grabbed the curved handle of the treadmill. "That's it!"

"What?"

"Your story. *You.* Oh, I'm so deliciously jealous!"

I scrunched my brow. "What are you talking about?"

She pulled me off the treadmill and back toward the sitting area. "You. How many other thirteen-year-olds know what it's like to be in your shoes? How many of us would want to know? You have something all the best writers have—experience. And the emotions to go with it." She opened my notebook to the first page and jabbed her pointer finger into my neatly written words. "This proves it." She thrust the notebook at me. "Write it. Write your story. Like Louisa did in *Little Women*. Write what you know, and it will be brilliant."

I squinted at her, trying to decide if I should give her words any credence. "Are you just trying to make me feel better?"

"I'm serious, Taylor. Readers want to feel. Make them feel. Write your story and make something good come out of it."

Write my story. Make something good come out of it.

That feeling again—the one I couldn't seem to resist at the same time that it often proved unreliable—stirred in my chest. That hope.

Could Victoria be right? Could there be something of worth in my words? In my experiences?

I dragged in a wobbly breath, scooped up my pen, and sat on the rug. I could do this. Write what I knew. Force good from it.

I thought of my copy of *Little Women* and what it had done for me in giving me a connection to my mother. A connection to a perfect life. Even if it was a last-minute thought from a thrift store, that story helped me.

What if, in writing my story, I could one day give hope to another lonely girl?

I swallowed down the intimidation that came with that thought. I caught Victoria's gaze and we shared tentative smiles. I opened my mouth to say "Thank you" but words wouldn't come. She nodded in encouragement and I focused on putting pen to paper.

Maybe I wasn't so alone after all.

CHAPTER TWO

One must have both the dark and the light side to paint life truly.
~ LMA

Taylor

1997

The dead slept beneath the trees. I wondered at the amount of gravestones, at all the people who had lived and breathed and died in this very town.

I shivered. I never could figure out why Victoria frequented this place, but I'd come here as a desperate way of curing my writer's block. Whenever Victoria returned from time at Sleepy Hollow Cemetery, she would get a writing wind. I wondered what sort of inspiration she found here—if it would strike me in the same way it did her.

The scent of pine wound around me, pulling me deeper into the hidden clutches of the old cemetery. I followed the signs to Author's Ridge, allowed the winding paths and groves of the place to call to me in a way I hadn't expected.

Maybe I needed this. More quiet. More time away from the whispers of the girls in school, more time away from the Bennetts, more time away from Victoria, even. She'd been distant of late, and I couldn't understand why, though I felt it might have something to do with her sitting with Laney Richards at lunch. Them going shopping together, whispering at their lockers in the hall, making plans . . . without me.

I supposed this need for time apart was normal for siblings. And yet, how much of Victoria and me was sister and how much of us was best friend?

I'd come to depend on her too much if I couldn't respect her need to be away from me once in a while. It wasn't her fault I never tried to make other friends, that I felt more at home alone in my room with a good book or a pen and notepad.

I passed the Thoreau family graves and sought out those of the Alcotts. I spotted Louisa's right away, as hers was filled with an array of pens and pencils stuck into the ground, various stones, flowers, and pennies surrounding what was supposed to be her place of rest.

I looked around to make sure I was alone, then sat before her gravestone. *LMA*, it read. *1832–1888*. I didn't really think that sitting here would gift me with some magical writing powers, but I did feel something like inspiration stir within me.

Louisa was a regular woman—once a regular teenager, like me. What made her a great writer? Was it the circumstances of her life? Who her parents and family were? Was it her voracious love of reading?

How could I set forth this thing burgeoning within me,

this passion for words and writing, into a story that would captivate others besides myself?

Despite our regular Pickwick meetings, I hadn't yet finished a story. Despite a plethora of beautifully color-coded outlines and character sketches and even several chapters of four different stories, I could never see the characters through to the end and finish what I'd started. That included the story Victoria prodded me to write that first day at Jo March Writing Camp—*my* story.

I closed my eyes. I didn't pray much, but being in this place where so many lay dead seemed to open up the possibility of the eternal. Of something beyond the hazy hope I'd clung to as a child. Of a greater being carrying those who had gone before me. Of a greater being perhaps willing to carry me.

I exhaled a breath. *Give me words.*

Having never experienced this sort of thing before, I really wasn't sure if this was what one would classify as praying.

When I opened my eyes, my gaze caught upon a folded piece of lined paper, the corner fluttering in the breeze, a smooth stone upon it serving as a paperweight.

The wind beckoned again, pulling at the corner and lifting it up. I caught the heading. *Dear Louisa*, it read.

My curiosity stirred, though I wasn't sure if it was over the fact that someone had felt such a connection with Louisa that they had decided to leave her a message in this spot, or that the handwriting upon the paper looked so very familiar.

I swallowed, looked around me again. It wasn't right, invading this sacred place, snooping on another's personal thoughts. And yet whoever had left it had done so in this vulnerable place. They must have known it was susceptible to being seen.

I could look quickly, read just a sentence or two. Maybe this was the answer to my prayer of a moment earlier—an inspiration for a story.

Dragging in a deep breath, I grasped the paper before I could change my mind. One part was slightly stuck on itself and it snagged when unfolded. I carefully pried it open. A small piece of the word *and* had cemented itself to the opposite side of the page, where it was stuck, backward upon other black letters.

I let my eyes scan the page, tried to ignore the pinch of guilt as I realized with certainty the identity of the handwriting, which there could be no mistaking after so many Pickwick meetings. What had Victoria written to Louisa? Did she really think that Louisa—wherever she was—could listen to her, help her even?

I read.

Dear Louisa,

This week was crazy. I slept over at Laney's the other night. We've been hanging around together a lot. Mom came to my room last night, reminded me not to forget about Taylor.

How could I? She's always there. Like, always. It wouldn't be so bad if she'd try to have her own life, her own friends, but she doesn't. I hate that she depends on me so much, you know? Sometimes . . . well, sometimes I wish we could just go back to being friends. Not sisters.

The words, written clear as the blue waters of Walden Pond, blurred before my eyes. I'd felt Victoria pulling away for some time now, felt it might even be normal on some level. But regretting that her family adopted me, that we were sisters? How could I move forward with that knowledge?

I didn't want to read more, and I did. Like the time I found my mom's obituary on Uncle Rob's table, I kept reading. Knowing there was hurt here for me, yet unable to keep away from it.

I know you understand—you felt that way about May, didn't you? It's tough to feel you have to take care of another person all the time. In many ways I guess I know what it's like to be an older sister.

I made the mistake of complaining to Mom last night. She admitted that having Taylor has been an adjustment and not always easy, but then she reminded me that we took Taylor in for me, that we were all doing a good thing in helping her. That without us, she would very likely be stuck in the foster care system, an orphan until eighteen.

At least I get a break when I go to Laney's. We went to the movies, too. Eric and Phil met us there. Laney and Phil sat in the very back and made out most of the time. Eric held my hand and pulled me close during a scary part, and when I felt his face on the top of my head and looked up, he kissed me.

I've never been kissed before. Like really kissed. It was strange and wonderful, but at the same time a little disappointing. I always thought my first kiss would be in a more romantic place. Will Smith fighting aliens from taking over the world wasn't exactly what I had in mind.

But maybe it will make me a better writer. Maybe now I can write a kissing scene. Only I'll have to make it a little more enticing than the real thing, I guess.

I'm excited about my newest story, though Taylor doesn't seem to like it as much as Long Gone. *Thank you for letting me leave you my thoughts.*

Yours,
Victoria

I refolded the paper carefully and replaced it beneath the stone, cold over my sister's innermost thoughts.

And did Mom not feel so differently?

"She admitted that having Taylor has been an adjustment and not always easy . . ."

Was I a burden to her also?

I blinked away tears. I had thought that maybe, in time, I would come to feel a part of the family, but how would that ever be possible if the family resented me?

Victoria and I had been best friends, and now she didn't even tell me about her first kiss?

I tucked my knees up to my chin and let the tears come then. I'd never felt so lonely. Not even when Mom left that day when I was four, not even when they took Uncle Rob to jail and I had no one.

Because there was something worse than being lonely without anyone—being surrounded with people you loved and finding out they didn't feel the same about you.

CHAPTER THREE

*Annie and John may be married in June . . . I am full of woe for I think
it's a very "tryin" thing to have men come and fetch away a body's relations
in this sort of way.*

~ LMA

Taylor

2001

I shivered beneath the sudden chill of the late July night
and pulled my button-down sweater over my shoulders. The
steady thrum of the live band from inside the restaurant
poured out of Main Streets Cafe to the patio tables on the
alley where I sat with my date.

Victoria was the one who had encouraged me to go
out with Anthony. He was a friend of a friend, and in a
weak moment I'd agreed to the blind date. We'd gone to
see a movie—*Pearl Harbor*—incredibly historic, incredibly
romantic, incredibly tragic. I wanted to go home and wallow
in the story or perhaps dissect the themes with Victoria, but
when I'd tried to ask Anthony what he thought of the tragic
ending, he'd shrugged off my words and started talking about
the war scenes.

The waitress placed two ginger ales in front of us, and a steaming plate of nachos between the two of us. Anthony took a metal flask discreetly from his pocket and poured it into his drink before gulping it down. He held it up and it glimmered against the restaurant lights. "Want some?"

I shifted on my seat and shook my head. "No thanks."

He leaned toward me, his crisp blue eyes making me feel something not entirely unpleasant. "I bet you've never even had a drink."

I almost told him he was wrong, but only so he'd think I was sophisticated, mature. But the words would have been a lie, and really, what did I have to prove?

I chose not to answer, grabbed a nacho instead. Anthony leaned back in his chair and studied me, letting my silence go. "You have nice teeth."

I didn't see how he could notice with nacho bits and cheese sauce in my mouth. I swigged some ginger ale. "Thanks." I *was* grateful for my teeth. The Bennetts had treated me as much like their own daughter as Victoria, including paying for braces and now college. I would never be able to repay all they'd done for me.

Victoria and I had had our ups and downs since that day I found her letter to Louisa at Sleepy Hollow. Our relationship could be as fickle as New England weather—warm and full of sunshine one day, frigid and icy the next. I had come to accept that this was what being sisters was about. Deep down though, I believed there *was* something real that bound us—maybe not blood, maybe not even simple friendship, but a tender sort of love I was still coming to understand.

I supposed that's what being family was about. Going through the hard and the messy, even the ugly at times, but knowing that this group of people was *yours*. That you belonged. No matter what.

At least that's what I told myself, what I tried and even longed to believe. Doubts were normal, of course, but the Bennetts had stuck with me through thick and thin. If they were going to abandon me, certainly they would have done so by now.

So why did I still feel like I was always balancing on a knife's edge?

Anthony and I chatted about mundane things over dinner. Anthony's batting average. Anthony's classes. Anthony's part-time job as an intern for an advertising company. He emptied the flask over the ice in his glass and began getting louder. A quarter of the way through dinner I decided that I didn't need another date with this guy to tell me he wasn't my soul mate.

He moved his chair closer to me. The scent of alcohol on his breath reminded me of Uncle Rob, and my stomach churned at the thought of my absent uncle. He'd been out of prison for a year but had never tried to make contact with me. I shouldn't let it niggle as it did.

Anthony slid his hand into mine. I sat, suddenly frozen, unsure why the small contact undid me. Probably because, as always, physical touch terrified me. And this man was quickly beginning to disgust me.

Why then couldn't I bring myself to pull away?

His fingers clung to mine beneath the table, where half of a fish taco sat on my plate. His thumb hung off the end of my hand and I felt it heavy on the fabric of my jean skirt, where it stroked at first tentatively, then with more surety.

"I have my own place, you know." The warm scent of alcohol mixed with onions fanned my face. "We could go back there if you want."

Adrenaline surged through my limbs, and I stood. Anthony's hand dropped. "I have to use the bathroom."

He wiggled his eyebrows, undeterred. "I'll be waiting."

I scooped up my purse and went inside the restaurant. The band played to a crowded room, and I knocked on the single restroom door. When I heard no one's protests, I slipped inside and locked the door. I looked up at the ceiling and closed my eyes.

Help.

It wasn't a prayer, really. Or maybe it was. If some otherworldly being could help me in this moment, I was all for it.

This wasn't the first time I'd found myself with a pushy guy. I wasn't sure exactly what quality I possessed that drew this type—was it a neediness they saw? Was it something I was searching for, first in the Bennetts, then in my writing, now in a different sort of relationship?

I needed to get out of here.

I dug my hand through my purse for my flip phone. I could call Victoria. She'd show up, smooth things over with Anthony, and take me home.

I listened to the hollow ring in my ear. It went to my friend's voice mail, and I groaned. I remembered Anthony's thumb rubbing my thigh, the abrasive action making me feel so very small.

I threw my phone back in my purse. My gaze landed on a sign on the back of the door.

To Guests at Main Streets:

Are you on a date with someone new? Are they not the person you were expecting? Here at Main Streets, we want everyone to have a pleasant experience and that includes the company with whom you're dining. If you are feeling uncomfortable on your date, please ask your server or the bartender for an angel latte. A manager on duty will come out and help you remove yourself from the situation.

I released a sigh that was part surprise, part relief. An angel latte. An angel. That's what I needed. Maybe Someone *had* heard my prayer.

I shook my head, imagined myself going to the bar and doing as the paper instructed. I'd feel like such a loser. No doubt I'd made too much of Anthony's actions.

I pulled back my shoulders. I wasn't a baby. I didn't need a manager to help me. I didn't need Victoria, and I didn't need an angel. I could handle Anthony myself. I'd been handling myself my entire life—one tipsy man shouldn't bowl me over.

I raised my chin and returned to the patio. Anthony stood, wavering over the table, a small wad of cash in his hands. I reached in my purse for my wallet.

He swatted my wallet away. "I got it. Don't worry about it."

"I—I'd like to go home now." I offered him a twenty and

felt dirty doing so. Why was it that I would have let him pay if we'd had a nice time? If I didn't plan on ditching him now?

He blinked. "You don't want to hang anymore?"

I shook my head, still holding out the cash.

He swore at me. "I don't need your money."

"I'd feel better." I offered it again, and he shoved me away. The diners looked at us with skewed glances, which seemed to further annoy Anthony.

"Let's go." He grabbed my arm, dragged me into the alley that led to his parked car.

I tried to wiggle from his grip but was unsuccessful. "You're drunk. I'm not driving home with you."

He laughed at me. "I can handle my liquor better than you might think." His hot hand still clasped my wrist. My mind churned.

"I forgot something in the bathroom," I said.

He sneered at me. "No, you didn't."

"I did. Please, Anthony. I'll be right back."

"Promise?"

I nodded, not feeling guilty for the lie and knowing he would have been able to see through it if he wasn't already two sheets to the wind.

He loosened his grip. "Go ahead, and when you come back, I'll take you home."

I slid my arm from his fingers and walked back into the restaurant. I wondered if Anthony saw me at the bar through the windows. I wondered if he would come in and make a scene. I half hoped he would, for then I wouldn't have to explain myself. Although wasn't that the entire idea behind the angel latte? Not having to explain oneself?

A woman in her midtwenties with red hair handed a drink to an older gentleman in a Red Sox cap. She turned to me. "Can I help you?"

I looked toward the door. No Anthony. "I—I heard you have angel lattes here?" This was stupid. I was stupid to get myself in this predicament in the first place.

For half a second, she looked confused, and I thought about running back outside, running toward the Bennett house. But then realization seemed to dawn over her features. "Oh—yeah, we do. One second."

She went into the kitchen and came out a moment later with a tall man with dark whiskers on his face. He wore a black Main Streets T-shirt that strained against the muscles on his arms. A dish towel sat on his shoulder. He couldn't have been much older than Anthony, but I thought he would be enough to intimidate my date.

The bartender gestured toward me, and the man came out from behind the bar, taking the towel off his shoulder and wiping his hands on it. He nodded at me. "Hey, I'm the manager here. Someone giving you trouble?"

I glanced out the window, but I couldn't see into the dark. "He was. Maybe—hopefully he left. He was drunk. I didn't want to drive home with him."

His mouth tightened. "The waitresses are supposed to be on the lookout for problems like that."

I shook my head. "It wasn't her fault . . ."

His face softened. "No worries. Where is he?"

"In the alley, just past the tables. Blue shirt on."

I hovered near the door as my "angel" approached Anthony. I saw my date roll his eyes and scowl at him.

The manager spoke, his body language calm. I watched as Anthony held up his hands, palms out, his busy mouth running a mile a minute. The manager pointed away from the restaurant, and Anthony spat some angry word, then left.

I ducked back inside the restaurant, waited for the manager to come in. His tall frame filled the door.

"Thanks," I breathed.

"No problem. Do you need me to call a taxi for you? Where do you live?"

I told him. "I can walk home, but I really appreciate your help."

"My shift's over in ten minutes. I can bring you home if you'd like."

I wavered. I'd just been wondering if I was inadvertently promoting my neediness to men—I didn't have to wonder with this one. He knew my neediness; I'd asked for his help.

"I go right by your house, but if you feel more comfortable, we can pay for a taxi. I don't think you should walk home this time of night."

I swallowed down my nerves. I just wanted to get home, bury my head under the covers, and forget this entire mess had happened. No, scratch that. I wanted to tell Victoria what a loser her "friend of a friend" turned out to be.

"I don't want to be any trouble . . ."

"Not at all." He smiled for the first time since I saw him, and it softened his well-cut features in a way that made him look like Ben Affleck and put me at ease. "Just give me a couple minutes to finish up in the back, okay?"

"Okay . . . thanks." I sat on the patio, listened to the hum of the music within, the clatter of glasses and plates, the thrum of conversation. Was it wise to allow a stranger to take me home? Before tonight I would have said no, but I trusted something about this guy. Still, I'd never been the best judge of character. Why should I begin to trust my instincts now?

"Ready?" He had keys in his hand and a Tufts University sweatshirt on.

I stood and followed him to the alley.

"I'm Will, by the way."

"Taylor." We walked another minute. "Thanks again. I feel kind of lame. When I saw that sign on the back of the restroom door, I felt like there really was an angel watching over me."

He grinned, and I caught the flash of straight teeth beneath a streetlamp. "I like to hear that. One of the waitresses had a bad dating experience last year. We decided to come up with something that might help out girls in a tough situation." He unlocked the driver's side door of a beat-up Ford truck, reached in, and unlocked the passenger side.

I climbed in. Or rather, tried to climb in.

"Sorry for the mess. Wasn't expecting company." He pulled a pile of textbooks and folders toward the console.

I sat down and buckled. "School?"

"Engineering." He backed the Ford out of the parking space.

"Nice."

"Yeah, should beat working nights at this place, anyway. You in college?"

I pulled my hair over my shoulder, glad he didn't think I was in high school—I was often told that, despite my height, I looked younger than I actually was. "Yes. Emerson."

"What are you studying?"

"Journalism." When it became apparent there was little I could do with an English degree besides teach, I decided to put my desire to write behind a more practical endeavor. I could write my fiction stories on the side, and if I was successful, maybe one day I could leave the news world altogether.

"Sounds exciting."

"I hope so." Victoria thought it would be, anyway. Sometimes I wondered if I didn't just follow in her footsteps for the sake of not being alone. My journalism plan wasn't really mine—it was Victoria's. But I loved to write more than anything else, and despite our ups and downs, I loved my best friend and sister. Where would I be without her? It made sense that we would continue down the same path.

"Are you doubting your major? You can always change, you know. I started off in computer science. Switched sophomore year. Best thing I ever did."

The beam of headlights shone into the truck and I squinted over at Will as discreetly as I could. "No, I love to write. I can't imagine doing anything else."

"Then . . ."

"You're a little pushy, you know that?"

He laughed, a pleasant, deep sound that echoed in the darkened car. "I've been told that before."

I sighed. "Maybe . . . I guess I'm not crazy about chasing after news stories. It sounds exciting—Victoria, my sister, is nuts about it. But I'm kind of a stay-in-the-background girl, you know? And I don't know if I have enough guts to push for the best stories."

"Sure you do."

"Excuse me?" What did he know about me?

"Well, you had enough guts to manage to shake off that dirtbag back there. Maybe you're not giving yourself enough credit."

"If I had enough guts, I would have been able to handle him on my own."

"Hey, asking for help sometimes takes more guts than going it alone."

I let the conversation drop. I didn't want to search for compliments, search for something that wasn't there.

But there was a new thought—asking for help took guts. I must be one gutsy girl then, because I basically lived the last quarter of my life on charity.

I closed my eyes. I had to stop this. Rachel, my current therapist, said so, and I said so. I was not charity to the Bennetts. Maybe at first, but not anymore. I was family.

I pointed to the next drive. "Right there. The big yellow one."

He pulled into the drive and I gathered my purse. "Thank you so much. For everything." I opened the door and the interior light of the truck shone on us, making me feel more exposed than before.

"My pleasure. I'm glad I could help. Maybe I'll see you around again sometime?"

I smiled, glad for the millionth time that Mom and Dad had invested in my teeth. "Yeah, I'd like that." I closed the door and walked around the truck but turned at the sound of Will's voice.

"Hey, just thinking . . . I might not see you around

sometime unless we plan a sometime. You think you want to plan a sometime?"

My heart beat faster. Was this just some damsel-in-distress draw for him and some knight-in-shining-armor draw for me? More than likely, he would eventually be disappointed. Maybe I would, too. There was definitely something . . . different about him. He was kind, no doubt. But there was this confidence or control he had about him that unnerved me. Why, though? Because I didn't possess it or because I felt it was there, hiding something unseen?

I blew out a long breath. Anthony had rattled me, that was all. The ten minutes in the car had been innocent enough. And he was obviously a good guy—going out of his way to make women feel comfortable where he worked, a devoted student, and definitely not bad to look at. What was the harm?

"Um . . . yeah."

"Yeah?"

I laughed. "Yeah."

He reached in the console, tore off a piece of notebook paper and searched for a pen. "What's your number?"

I gave it to him and thanked him again, watched as he drove off, an unexpected angel in a beat-up Ford.

CHAPTER FOUR

I remember the dear little "Pickwick Portfolio" of twenty years ago,
and the spirit of an editor stirs within me.

~ LMA

Taylor

I CLEARED MY THROAT as I entered Victoria's room. My sister
sat on the bed, her Dell laptop on her crossed legs, fingers
flying over the keys. She didn't look up. I swear, she could
write in the middle of a hurricane with debris and livestock
flying around her.

I cleared my throat again.

She blinked and glanced at me, her mind still tangled in
the words on her screen. She came back to reality slowly—
she always did. "Taylor . . . hey. How did it go?" She closed
her laptop, scooted to the end of her flowered bedspread.

"The date part? Horrible."

She groaned. "You didn't like him?"

I quickly recapped the events of the night, and by the
end, she had fallen back on her bed, her long arms spread
out behind her, a faraway look in her eyes. "Oh, you have
all the luck!"

I lowered myself to her bed. "Luck? I was scared. I think it could have turned ugly."

"But it didn't. Someone was watching over you."

"I—I suppose. Why didn't you answer your phone?"

She scooped it up. "Oops, sorry. I meant to charge it earlier. Lost track of time."

For the hundredth time I tried not to envy her ability to turn off the real world and enter the world of a story.

"You could have called the house, you know."

"I know. I just . . . I didn't want Mom to know." It didn't matter how much my parents did for me, it seemed I would forever be trying to ensure I wasn't inconveniencing them in some way, making sure my debt didn't go deeper. I didn't want Mom and Dad to ever regret all they'd done for me.

"So . . . is he cute? This Will guy?"

"He's—" I let a breath of air pass my lips and a smile crack my mouth—"really cute. He seems like a gentleman, too. Studying engineering at Tufts, a manager at Main Streets . . . I guess we'll see if he calls."

"He'll call." Victoria grew pensive, staring into space. "I'm sorry about Anthony. If I'd realized . . ."

I waved my hand through the air. "It all worked out."

"Yeah, but if anything happened to you . . ."

We'd had some rough months the first couple of years I came to live with the Bennetts. There was no question in my mind that Victoria would always be my best friend, but I think it was sometimes still hard for her to fully share her parents with me. She'd been an only child. To gain a sister so suddenly wasn't easy.

But we'd made it through. Mostly because we didn't

have a choice. In many ways, like real sisters, we were stuck together whether we liked it or not.

I never did tell her that I found her letter to Louisa, that I'd seen additional letters since at the Alcott burial ground but, although my curiosity tempted me, had never ventured to open more.

"I'm glad it all turned out right. I never would have forgiven myself."

I didn't like this fear, the wild look that came into her eyes. I knew her imagination was getting the better of her, as it always did.

I placed my hand on her arm. "I'm fine. It's all okay, right?"

She sniffed, and her eyes cleared. "Yeah. Thank God."

I wiggled out of my sandals and tucked my legs under me. "Do you think there really is a God?" I couldn't help but think about my bathroom prayer, the answer in the most unlikely of places—on the back of a restroom door, the angel it had brought forth.

"Absolutely," she said.

"Why are you so sure?"

She shrugged. "I don't know . . . I think it's some sort of inherent knowing within me. Like God's the One who gave me this creative desire to write, you know?"

I nodded. I'd never thought of it that way.

"I haven't really thought about Him much deeper than that, though," she said. "But I always remember how Louisa called Him a 'friend' in *Little Women*. That stuck with me."

We sat silent for a minute, and it wasn't uncomfortable.

After all these years, there was in fact no one I felt more comfortable to sit in silence with.

She suddenly nudged me with her foot. "Impromptu Pickwick meeting?"

I grinned. "Sure." We hadn't given up our regular Pickwick meetings since that day at Orchard House. We'd grown both in age and as writers, and so our meetings grew with us. They weren't always tranquil, either. Constructive criticism—and sometimes not-so-constructive—wasn't easy to take from your sister. But beneath one another's encouragement and critique, we not only grew thick skin, we became better writers. I trusted Victoria with my words, and I knew she felt the same way with me.

She handed over her laptop and a chill raced down my spine at the quote heading the first page.

A time will come when you will find that in gaining
a brief joy you have lost your peace forever.
A Long Fatal Love Chase, LOUISA MAY ALCOTT

I scrolled to the next page, the start of her story. I savored the words, dark against the white screen. They breathed life into new characters, and I hadn't even moved to the next page when I realized what Victoria had done with one of Alcott's lesser-known stories. My friend's writing was nothing short of brilliant, the characters she drew with words and sentences leaping off the page.

When I finished the chapter, I stared at the screen. "It's magnificent."

"You really think so?"

"A modern retelling of Louisa's most recently discovered story? Absolutely." Alcott had written *A Long Fatal Love Chase* in 1866 after a trip to Europe, but it was considered too audacious for a nineteenth-century readership and wasn't published until 1995, the very same year Victoria and I had attended Jo March Writing Camp. We'd gobbled up the story, even as we found it impossible that it was composed by the same woman who'd written of four sisters with their castles in the air and Pickwick meetings and boy next door.

"The good?" she asked. This was our routine, right to the point. Encouragement. Critique. Encouragement.

"Your modern-day Rosamond—Charlotte—she's perfect. I love her already and understand why she's drawn to Blaze."

"The bad?"

"I think if you tied in a little more of her background, we'd feel even more for her. Other than that, wow."

I set down her laptop and she hugged me. "Thank you, thank you, thank you!"

"I'm excited to read the rest."

"I find it hard to believe you're not sick of my Alcott obsession yet. I don't know why I can't seem to let her go."

"She lived and breathed in this very town. She impacted so many young girls—still does today. I don't think it's weird that you're drawn to her. That *we're* drawn to her. Maybe there's a reason."

What I didn't say was that of course Victoria was drawn to her—she had created a sort of god in her mind with not only her obsession, but her letters and secrets spilled out to a woman who had been dead for more than one hundred years. I didn't think it was healthy—and yet there was no way of admitting how I knew without revealing my own transgression at Sleepy Hollow Cemetery that long-ago day. And healthy . . . who was I to claim to know anything about mental health? My own tattered copy of *Little Women* still sat prominently on the top shelf of my nightstand, my one connection to the mother who didn't want me. The mother I couldn't seem to release despite Lorraine's tangible care and love.

"Thanks, Taylor. I don't know what I'd do without you."

I winked at her. "Lucky for you you'll never have to find out. If you didn't notice, you're kind of stuck with me."

She rolled her eyes. "How's your story coming?"

I scrunched my face. "I've been busy working . . ." I worked with the kids at the summer recreational program. It wasn't my first choice for a job, but between that and my weekend work scooping ice cream at Bedford Farms, I had saved up a good amount of money. While I could never pay the Bennetts back for all they'd done for me, I could at least ensure that I got a good start once I was out of college. That the time and money and efforts and love they poured into me didn't go to waste.

"Come on, Taylor. I can't do this without you. We said we'd both finish a book this summer. What's your word count so far?"

I pressed my lips together. "Does the title page count toward that?"

"Taylor Lynn . . ."

"Okay, okay. I haven't written anything."

"Pickwick meeting tomorrow night. You're supposed to have twenty-five hundred words for me."

"Do you ever think you might take this stuff too seriously?" My words were met with an expression of stone. "Guess not," I breathed.

She threw a pillow at me.

"I'm waking up at 5 a.m. tomorrow. Getting it all done before my shift at Bedford. I'll have those words for you— though I'm not promising they'll be great."

I didn't want her to expect too much. *I* didn't want to expect too much. Her words had always been better, more prolific. And from the moment she won the Orchard House short story contest for youth at the age of fourteen, I'd always known that nothing I came up with would be half as brilliant as what she put on the page.

"You better start praying for another angel," she said as I headed down the hall to my own room.

I grinned back at her, but her words lingered as I went into my room and closed the door. Thoughts of Anthony, then the sign on the back of the Main Streets restroom door, then Will, fluttered in and out of my head.

An angel.

Could there be a story there?

~~

The next morning after I'd squeezed out a thousand words, I heard tension in Mom's voice as I came down the stairs, so I huddled against the wall, not wanting to interrupt the conversation.

It only took a minute of eavesdropping to know they argued over me.

"You shouldn't have set her up with him, then." Mom's matter-of-fact voice.

"I didn't *know* he was an idiot, Mom. Besides, Taylor's a big girl. She took care of herself." Victoria's defensive one.

"All I'm saying is it wouldn't hurt you to think a little bit about your sister once in a while. She doesn't make friends as—"

"I cannot believe this." Something slapped—almost as if Victoria had raised her hands up, then let them fall against her legs. "She's *nineteen*. Why do you always treat her like she needs protecting? If I didn't know better, I'd have a hard time guessing who your *real* daughter was."

She stomped out of the kitchen, practically ran into me. Rolled her eyes and let out a long breath, shook her head, and continued up the stairs.

I stood at the threshold of the kitchen, staring at Lorraine. "I'm sorry," I said, not even exactly sure what I was apologizing for. For existing, maybe?

Her shoulders slumped in defeat. "You are *both* my real daughters. She didn't mean that."

I pressed my lips together, nodded. I knew she didn't. At least, I thought I knew.

Lorraine came over to me, placed a kiss on my cheek. I realized then how I'd stopped flinching over her touch long ago, how I welcomed these moments, even. "Pancakes?" she asked.

"Sure."

~~

Will did call. We went out and had a great time. Then he called again. And again. I skipped one Pickwick meeting, then another. I stopped writing.

Something else happened, too: Lorraine started pulling away from me. It was so gradual, I thought at first I was imagining it—a subtle shift in the foundation of our relationship. It was little things—like a petering out of morning hugs, a coffee date with Victoria that I hadn't been included in.

At first, I thought I was just too involved with Will. Too involved with my own life. But when I heard Victoria and Lorraine laughing together downstairs one morning, I felt suddenly empty. I convinced myself it didn't matter so much. I was growing up. I was falling in love. Separation was bound to come sooner or later.

I pushed aside the hurt. And I clung instead to Will.

On our fifth date Will took me into Boston for a gondola ride on the Charles River followed by Shakespeare on the Common. When the crowd thinned, we walked beneath the stringed lights of the Public Garden, the distant scent of food vendors competing with that of lavender and hydrangeas.

We stopped over Lagoon Bridge to glimpse the graceful leaves of weeping willows shimmering in the moonlight, the Swan Boats parked until dawn called them forth again.

"You ever think how we would have never met if it weren't for your date that night? That maybe we never would have met if it wasn't for that restroom sign?" he asked.

I smiled, studied his handsome profile all in pockets of light and dark, the stars hanging in a canopy above him.

He was beautiful. Perfect. And I was more than a little starstruck that this beautiful, perfect thing had happened to *me*.

"Yeah, I do," I said. "All the time. I even thought about

calling Anthony and thanking him for being such a jerk that night."

Will laughed, and the low rumble warmed my insides. He had his hands loosely folded over the railing of the bridge, the blanket we'd used for the Shakespeare show on the Common tucked beneath his arm. He stared at the slight ripples in the water below us. "I want to tell you something, Taylor, but I don't want to scare you off and I don't want you to feel like you have to say it back."

My brain suddenly felt low on oxygen, as if I were swimming in a bowl of pea soup. A heavenly bowl of pea soup.

He licked his lips. "I guess I just want to make sure you know how I feel about you before we both go back to school . . ." Usually he was the epitome of confidence; I'd never seen him so nervous, so unsure of himself. This was a different side of the man I was coming to care for. "Guess I'm no Shakespeare, huh?"

I laughed, but it came out tight, full of anticipation. *You're perfect,* I wanted to say.

"I love you, Taylor."

His words hung in the star-studded night and I sank into them, let them linger sweetly within my spirit. I placed a hand on the bare muscles of his forearm until he looked at me, for he'd spoken into the water until that moment.

One corner of his mouth was tucked up into a question mark, and I couldn't take my eyes off of it. Then, slowly, he tilted his head to mine.

We'd kissed before, but it was nothing like this. The entire world fell away and nothing mattered except the two of us.

The heavens seemed to open up, to transport us to a place that could only be found in the presence of someone you love.

The kiss deepened, and I felt the intensity of it, of him. His hands tightened on my arms—almost too tight—but I ignored the slight twinge of pain. This was someone who wanted me fully. I felt vulnerable in his arms, but at the same time I felt safe. At home. And I never, ever wanted to leave.

We parted, and I was surprised to find tears at the corners of my eyes. He saw them and brushed them away. "So I know I said you didn't have to say anything, and you don't, but . . . you like me too, huh?"

I laughed and nodded. I'd never told anyone—anyone— that I'd loved them before. Even when my mom told me she loved me, right before she left me on Uncle Rob's doorstep, I had been too busy crying to say the words back. Uncle Rob never was one to talk of emotions, and although Lorraine had told me multiple times, the most I'd been able to push out was a "You too." Never the full three words.

Now, though the thought of saying them caused more than a little anxiety, I felt that I must. I was baring myself, but I also felt sure of the worth of it. Like I stood at the edge of a grand cliff, and all I needed was to make the leap for all to be right with the world forever.

I jumped.

"I love you too, Will."

He exhaled a large breath, and again I marveled that someone could care for me to this extent, that how I felt about them could mean so much to them.

~~

That was the beginning of the most magical two years of my life.

Will filled something within me I didn't know was empty. Or maybe I did know. Beneath the blossoming possibilities of our relationship I felt, for the first time, as if I completely belonged. As if I was out of the shadow of who I had been all my life. An orphan. A foster kid. Victoria's sister. Paul and Lorraine's daughter—the one who would never be their *real* daughter.

I latched on to the identity of being Will's girl, Will's love. And I couldn't get enough. I wanted to be with him every spare minute. Victoria and my parents seemed happy for me. And while Victoria showed some disappointment that we didn't share as much as we used to, I felt her pulling away too. Accepting all too easily what seemed to be our fate—to grow apart and go our own ways. She busied herself with writing and school and time with Mom and the planning of her future.

The horror and tragedy of 9/11 had her organizing a fundraiser to benefit the victims' families. I was too busy convincing Will not to join up to help. When she finished her novel, I offered to read it, but she never handed it over to me.

Other than that, all seemed well enough.

Until it wasn't.

Until the day all my castles in the air fell without warning. Until the day hope dried up and withered.

Until I came home from my last class of senior year, anticipating a night of celebration with Will, and found the man

I loved leaning over my petite sister in front of the doors of the Bennett garage, his hands gently at her slim hips, his mouth on hers.

I sat in my Toyota Corolla, blinking over and over again, certain I was seeing things.

But the vision didn't disappear.

Instead, I watched as the kiss deepened. I remembered that beautiful kiss I'd shared with Will on Lagoon Bridge nearly two years earlier, and a thousand others since then.

We'd been planning our future, planning our lives together. He hadn't proposed yet, but he'd hinted at marriage more than once.

And all of a sudden he was kissing my best friend. Kissing my sister.

I thought about pushing the gas pedal hard enough to propel the Toyota forward, to completely do away with the cause of my pain. Instead, I laid on the horn, blaring so loud it made them jump apart.

I didn't stop. Again and again I honked. Again and again until their mirrored looks of surprise and confusion turned to guilt. Again and again until tears streamed down my cheeks.

I managed to put the car in park and stumble out of it. Will's hands were on me. "Taylor, honey, I'm so sorry. We didn't mean—"

I slapped them off me, pushed at him. "Get *away* from me."

Through my tears, I saw Victoria, and she looked almost as hurt as I felt. I couldn't make sense of it, but right then I didn't care. I just wanted to get away.

For good.

Against Mom's many protests, I packed everything I could fit in my suitcase and loaded it into my Corolla. I was done with it all. People said you could count on them. They said they would love you forever. But you could never really know they would. Never really trust they would.

You could only hope.

And hope, as I'd known for a long time, wasn't all that dependable.

I couldn't stay. There would always be hurt here. There would always be betrayal.

Will chased me around the house as I packed, saying words I didn't hear. They became distorted in my mind. Felt like threats. I tuned them out, and finally he just stopped talking. And then he was gone.

Victoria didn't approach me and an insatiable urge to punish her possessed me. With my Toyota packed, I went to her room and into her closet, grabbed her softball bat from the corner and approached her laptop, sitting on her desk.

The initial hit was satisfying, but each hit after became less and less so. Still, I wanted to believe she had stories she hadn't backed up. I hoped she would cry long and hard over all her work.

When I was done, I threw the bat beside the laptop.

I didn't have to behave anymore. I didn't have to earn the love of the Bennetts. I was leaving. Immediately.

I drove around aimlessly waiting for the bank to open the next morning so I could close my account for good.

Maybe I never belonged here in the first place. Maybe this was how it was always meant to be. Me, on my own. An orphan.

After I took out all the money I had—six thousand dollars—I drove west until I couldn't keep my eyes open any longer. Then I checked into a motel, where I discovered all the things I'd forgotten at the Bennetts' house: the stuffed puppy I'd had since I was three; the medal I won for a race I'd won sophomore year of high school; maybe most devastating of all, my beloved copy of *Little Women*. But starting over meant leaving it all behind, right? I slept a few hours before driving again.

My cell phone rang continuously, and without giving it much thought, I threw it out the window in a field a couple hours outside Des Moines.

I didn't stop driving until I reached the Pacific Ocean. At that point, I wondered if everything had been a misunderstanding—if quite possibly things could have been made right if I had stayed.

But I was the one who had been wronged. If Will still loved me, he'd have to find a way to make it up to me. He'd have to search me out, stop at nothing, just like in the movies. The same went for Victoria and for Mom and Dad.

Only life wasn't a movie. And happy endings weren't a guarantee.

More than once I picked up the phone to call Mom, but then I'd remember the last couple of years, how she'd pulled away from me, had likely been trying to make things fair between her two daughters, but had ended up choosing Victoria over me.

But life wasn't fair, and if I hadn't learned that when my birth mom left me at four, I sure had learned it now.

CHAPTER FIVE

There is no easy road to successful authorship; it has to be earned by long and patient labor, many disappointments, uncertainties, and trials.

~ LMA

Johanna

September 8, 1863

Dear Miss Alcott,

I am writing on behalf of Mother and myself to thank you for the precious gift you've given us in sending us so much bounty—not only the ring Mother had given John upon his departure into the army, but a copy of your Hospital Sketches, *in honor of our dearly departed. We count it a blessing to receive one of the three copies you gifted to your "soldier boys." More than once, Mother has called you an angel—first to our John and now to us.*

I recognized your letter right away, for it was the same hand that wrote the last letter John sent to us, received too late.

I read Hospital Sketches *aloud to Mother and George for the last four evenings by the fire, not without tears. As you can imagine, it is difficult to hear of our John's last days, but we thank God over and over again that he was in the tender care of your hands.*

Mother has requested I send along her best for your continued recovery from the typhoid. You have served our country as well as any soldier, and we realize the personal sacrifices you have made. I am sorry your service ended too soon for you. My cousin suffered the same illness last year and I know what sorrows it can bring forth. We are glad to hear you are recovering.

You say you are a writer of stories and feared we would take issue for the fictionalization of some of John's story in your desire to protect his likeness. Please do not give it another thought. We are so very proud of our John's bravery and will forever treasure and hand down the copy of the book you've given us to all the generations that come after.

And still, Mother, George, and I long for more. Though we realize we are being presumptuous, we can't help but ask for any last tidbit of John you may give to us. Did he tell you of his time in battle? Captain Schrock wrote that he did not initially know how grave his situation, and you confirmed that for us in Sketches. *Mother is driving herself mad thinking of possibilities both in battle and in John's last days, and while I realize the truth may be worse than her imaginings, I have told her I would ask.*

Please, Miss Alcott, we realize you've already given us more than we've a right to ask and yet we boldly ask for more so that we may finally put our John to rest. We know you were with him and took care of him, and for that we are thankful. Do not spare us—tell us all you know so George and I may better honor our dear brother, and so Mother may honor her son. Many times it feels as if memories and stories are all we have left.

Sincerely,
Johanna Suhre

September 23, 1863

Dear Johanna,

I was not certain whether I would hear back from you, and I am so very glad I did. Our Concord company is to return home tonight and the town is in as wild a state of excitement as is possible for such a dozy old place to be without dying of brain fever. Still, I find I cannot succumb to the celebration—won only by the sacrifice of those like your brother—until this letter is off.

Presumptuous as it may be, I confess that your John had become very dear to me in the short time I knew him. I still think of him often. His strength of character and bravery in the midst of the impossible will, I am quite certain, stay with me forever.

His was the best letter I wrote home, for even dying royally, his simple dictation was more heartfelt than the rest as he tenderly bequeathed you and your mother to George.

The reason Hospital Sketches *has become so successful is because of John. He is the hero and the praise belongs to him. He is what draws readers—the face of courage in the midst of adversity, unassuming and innocent but full of warmth and nobility. Quite simply, your brother, a common blacksmith from my understanding, was the finest gentleman I've ever been privileged to meet.*

To go very near death teaches one the value of life. And though I believe wrestling with the typhoid has taught me the immeasurable worth of this, it was in ministering to the wounded souls at the Union Hotel Hospital and of doing the most noble thing one may be called to do in life—sharing another's suffering—that I have truly come to glimpse the beauty of life, your brother being the highest example of which I speak.

To honor your family—and John—I will recount a more personal story of him for you here. I pray it does his memory honor. I hope it is an accurate reflection of the fine man he was.

The truth is that I was deeply impressed by your brother before ever I laid eyes on his tall form, fine face, and serene eyes. To be honest, I was at first intimidated by this stately looking man. A friend of his, who came in with the first group, could not stop praising him, saying John insisted that others more tragically wounded than himself (as if being shot in the lung were a small thing!) be first evacuated from the field station at

Fredericksburg. As a result he came in a few days later than the other men.

Among three or four hundred men in all stages of suffering, disease, and death, your John, my prince of patients, stood out. It was more than the way he silently bore his pain. There was a peace and grace about him. I meant what I said in Sketches—that no picture of dying statesman or warrior was ever fuller of real dignity than this blacksmith. And yet he worried for you, your mother, and for George. When I asked him why he'd gone to war when you all so very desperately needed him, he simply stated, "I wanted the right thing done, and people kept saying the men who were in earnest ought to fight. I was in earnest, the Lord knows! But I held off as long as I could, not knowing which was my duty—my family or my country. Mother saw the case, gave me her ring to keep me steady, and told me to go, so I went."

I must admit he grew in my estimation another tenfold for his answer. The only time I saw his peace waver was at the thought of you all not being provided for.

John was struck twice in the breast, with one piercing his lung. It was only after you were informed of his whereabouts that the hospital matron found a third wound under his shoulder. I feel as if this is not to your benefit to know, but I do as you request and spare no details. He fought bravely, advancing with his division though the wounded men lying at his feet begged him not to. In the cold dark, he ran out of ammunition. His injuries soon followed.

During the night, squads were sent to recover those who had been wounded, and still the Confederate sharpshooters were relentless. Wounded himself, John ushered a comrade to the gates of eternity with all the grace and peace you can imagine of him.

He was evacuated to the east side of the Rappahannock but gave up his place in the convoys in deference to others. I have an inkling he would have done this even if he realized how grave his injuries were, which he did not.

I felt the most worthy thing I had done during my time as a nurse was hold his hand during the probing, bathing, and dressing of his wounds. He never asked for anything except for me to help him bear his suffering, and even that he did not forthright ask, but only happily agreed to after I suggested it.

Under his plain speech and unpolished manner I saw a noble character, a heart as warm and tender as a woman's, a nature fresh and frank as a child's. In some hidden part of him, it seemed he had learned the secret of contentment.

My feelings for your brother are so very tender and complicated. For when I stood by his bed, straightening things up, and when I felt him softly touch my gown, as if only to assure himself of my presence, my heart near overflowed. With what, I am still uncertain. I am not a mother, and yet I felt very much a love I imagine a mother to feel. I am not a wife, and yet I felt very much a love I imagine a wife to feel.

I spent an hour each evening with him and tried to gain a broader picture of his life in his pained whispers.

"Do you ever regret that you came, when you lie here suffering?" I asked.

"Never, ma'am; I haven't helped a great deal, but I've shown I was willing to give my life, and perhaps I've got to; but I don't blame anybody, and if I was to do it over again, I'd do it. I'm a little sorry I wasn't wounded in front; it looks cowardly to be hit in the back, but I obeyed orders, and it don't matter in the end, I know."

My heart near broke in two when he finally asked me the dreaded question.

"This is my first battle; do they think it's going to be my last?"

I hated to answer, but I could not dishonor him with lies. "I'm afraid they do, John."

After the surprise settled in, then did acceptance. "I'm not afraid, but it's difficult to believe all at once. I'm so strong it don't seem possible for such a little wound to kill me."

At his request, I wrote George for him then. I knew of his love for you all when he gave George charge of you and your mother. I only wish your response had arrived in time.

The rest I have told completely in Sketches. He only made one cry before the first streaks of dawn ushered him into eternity. He never once loosened his grip on my hand, and in death, he lay serenely waiting for the dawn of that long day which knows no night.

Johanna, I pray this settles your mother, though I am not sure it will. I contend it is better to think on John's life, rather than the circumstances surrounding his death.

Perhaps you would write them down and recall them—both you and your mother—and share them with me. I admit I am curious to know all there is to know of my prince of patients, this brave soldier who represents the honor for which we all should strive.

Send me your stories of John, and in doing so, we will both reflect on him better, I think, and do his memory the utmost honor.

This has been quite a long scribble, so I will leave you now, in anticipation of your next letter.

Respectfully yours,
Louisa May Alcott

February 18, 1865

Dear Louisa,

It is odd to sit and start a letter without a John story, as Mother and I have come to call them over these months of our correspondence. We truly have racked our brains trying to think of more, but I think they have all been exhausted and have done their duty in bestowing honor upon my brother. Thank you for allowing us to soften our grief in sharing a piece of him with you this past year. Stories most certainly seem to have healing powers, and I wonder if that is not why we are drawn to them?

How does it feel to have a novel published? I admit to being a tad envious of such a wonderful accomplishment and can't wait to read Moods.

Mother improves with the warmer weather. George courts Mary Little, and I think there will soon be a wedding. I have had no serious suitor—oh, I know, I know . . . "liberty is a better husband than love," but how can you be so sure if you have not known love? And while you have your writing which at least earns some, I have no means to support myself, save for a meager income with my sewing. A kind boy named Bryant persists in courting me, though I cannot seem to think of him as more than a friend. I do not mean to complain, but neither do I look forward to living beneath George and Mary's roof. Is it so bad to want to break away? To find a place to belong that sings within my soul?

Enough of that. I am thankful for your friendship, Louisa. Even so, I realize you are busy, and so now that we have exhausted John's stories, I wish to release you from any responsibility you feel toward our family, including these continued letters. Indeed, you have gone beyond what we could ask or imagine in your kindness.

I look forward to reading your novel.

Your friend,
Johanna

April 18, 1865

Dear Johanna,

I've been meaning to write but news of Lincoln's death has rendered me melancholy for the last few days. I pray we can, as a country, cling to his message all the more. I pray we can indeed go forth "with malice toward none" and with "charity for all to bind up our nation's wounds."

It is odd to see such a strange and sudden change in our nation's feelings, for we were only just enjoying a state of grand jollification over Richmond being taken. I was witness to the great procession in Boston. Colored men marched in it also, one walking arm in arm with a white gentleman, and I exulted thereafter.

On a lighter note, I am happy to report that I no longer wear a wig but appear on all occasions with a fine flowing crop. If shaving my head kept my fever at bay, then I am glad Marmee and Papa allowed it, but admit that losing all one and a half yards of my one beauty was quite a strike to my vanity. But never mind; it might have been my head, and a wig outside is better than a loss of wits inside, don't you think?

You speak of "breaking away." If it can be dutifully and wisely done, I think girls should see a little of the world, try their own powers, and keep well and cheerful, mind and body, because life has so much for us to learn and young people need change. Many ways are open now, and women can learn, be, and do much if they have the will and opportunity.

Change of scene is sometimes salvation for women who outgrow the place they are born in, and it is their duty to go away even if it is to harder work, for hungry minds prey on themselves and ladies suffer for escape from a too-pale or narrow life. That being said, I have a peculiar proposition for you if you wish to take flight from the nest.

Due to my nursing experience, I've been asked to accompany a young, ailing woman on a yearlong trip to Europe. While I am a bit hesitant, I cannot think to turn down such an offer. With May off to Boston for art classes and often vacationing upon Clarke's Island, and Anna busy with her own brood, we are in need of some help over here at Apple Slump—ahem, I mean, Orchard House.

Mother can still manage but could use the help. Our little Portuguese girl, Maria, was ill last spring and has not returned to work since. We could pay you a fair sum to keep house, cook, and clean. Perhaps this does not seem a better opportunity than living in your brother's home. If so, please dismiss it altogether. But if some part of you wishes to come to Concord, perhaps start building your own castles in the air, and you don't think you will miss your mother and George altogether too much, perhaps you will accept this offer.

Write as soon as possible and I will send fare for your transportation if you are agreeable to this plan. It would be wonderful to meet you, as I've come to admire the woman I have known only through letters.

I plan to leave in July and would like to settle things well before my departure, if you find it suiting. The decision is yours. I only think it may be wise to try out your liberty before you try out love.

Yours,
Louisa

CHAPTER SIX

Whatever we can do and do well we have a right to,
and I don't think any one will deny us.

~ LMA

Johanna

CONCORD, MASSACHUSETTS
JUNE 1865

I grasped the handle of my tattered valise in one hand and pulled my hat onto my head against a gust of New England wind with the other. As I descended the train's platform, I looked for Louisa, though I hadn't the slightest idea of her appearance.

Stepping away from the platform, I rested my valise on the ground and inhaled the earthy scent of horse mixed with that of the coal burning aboard the train. I felt for Mother's ring hanging at my neck. John's ring. I allowed my thoughts to settle on my brother. In his last letter, he'd given me and Mother over to George's care. What would he think of me traveling so far from home? Of my search for . . . what? Adventure? Experiences? Somewhere to set this passion for words free from a place outside myself?

For the millionth time I wondered about the lady who had cared for my brother in his last days. The lady who, by all accounts, seemed to love my brother and to some extent, he her. The enigma of a lady who claimed that liberty was better than love.

"Johanna?"

I dropped my hand from my neck, twisted to see a tall, rather aged-looking woman. I tried to hide my disappointment. Though I knew Louisa was older than me, I couldn't help but imagine a beautiful vision in a nursing uniform beside my brother. And while I knew her head had been shaved in a desperate attempt to keep her fever down whilst she suffered the typhoid, I'd expected . . . something different. The tall woman before me with snapping gray eyes seemed more aging aunt than sweet friend.

I tried to recover quickly, though the pinched expression on Louisa's face suggested I failed. "Louisa—" I held out my hand—"it's so good to be with you."

And it was. My fanciful expectations were not important. This woman offered me an avenue out of my poor farming life. She offered so much more. Imagine—Massachusetts! And Concord at that. The very place where literature and education and writing came alive. I thought of the papers in my valise, tucked carefully between petticoats and corsets, of the many scribbles of poems written upon them. Poems born of a place deep within me that longed for release. Could anything come of them here in Concord?

Louisa's expression softened, and I glimpsed eyes alive with fire—with the very spirit I saw in her letters. "I am glad you've come, Johanna. Here, I have a carriage waiting."

She introduced the driver of the carriage as John, her older sister's husband. He packed away my valise and we climbed into the carriage.

Once we were settled, John lightly tapped the horses' withers and we pulled away.

"We are not far from here. How were your travels?"

"Quite well, though I admit I felt a bit anxious without an escort."

Louisa smiled, and I noted the lines around her mouth and at her eyes. "You did well." We were quiet a moment before she spoke again. "I am not what you expected."

I floundered for words but came up short.

"The typhoid aged me in ways I did not expect. I went to Washington a topsy-turvy young girl. In many ways, I woke from the fever an old woman. I may not have gone to war as a soldier, but perhaps I've done a soldier's battle. And I don't regret a minute of it. I'm thirty-two—not so very old, but my body doesn't seem to remember what my mind feels."

"I hid my surprise poorly. Forgive me. I did think you closer to John's age."

She smiled. "They didn't allow nurses younger than thirty to serve. I had to be well into spinsterhood in order to qualify." She patted my arm. "But you needn't worry yourself. I remember after I saw Fredrika Bremer, whose books I loved, I was so upset that my sister Nan and I went into the closet and cried though we were great girls of sixteen and eighteen."

I couldn't help but smile, already seeing past her aging face to her spirit within. I placed my hand on her arm. "I can't imagine all you've been through. Ultimately, it's strength of character that counts, and you have no short supply of that."

She studied me a moment, rested her hand on my own. "I think we are to be good friends."

I nodded. "I hope so." I squeezed her fingers once before pulling away. I couldn't help contemplating that this was the same hand that last knew my brother's. Dear John, who used to lift me upon his tall shoulders so I might scurry up into the loft when I was a girl. Dear John, who always encouraged me when I shared my poems with him. I gave a sidelong glance to Louisa. I had never told her I loved to write. I didn't want her thinking I wished anything from her except friendship and employment. And yet I couldn't help but wonder in coming to this quaint town, so close to Boston, if cultivating a relationship with a real author like Louisa could open doors for me that wouldn't have been possible in Pennsylvania.

I thought of the family farm, the small church we attended each Sunday, Bryant ever faithful in the left pew closest to the window. He'd been upset when I'd left, but the thought of going through another harvest season instead of exploring what the North had for me left my legs shaky and my middle trembling and desperate. I'd never encouraged him, had no reason to feel guilt at going away. In fact, I felt if I didn't leave, Pennsylvania itself would strangle me. I longed to be free of it all at the same time that I longed to find the place I belonged.

Now I gazed with hunger at the bustle of the main thoroughfare as we passed through the center of town. Reynolds's apothecary, Holden's grocery, a boardinghouse, and a plethora of other businesses. A new hope bubbled up within me, warm and pleasant and full of anticipation.

"It is not much now, but when it gets stirred up, Concord

can be quite a sight to behold. You will love the festivities held on the Fourth—the children make the streets hideous with distracted drums and fifes. Everyone wears cockades wherever one can be stuck, flags flap overhead like colored birds of prey, and everything in heaven and earth seems to be consigned to red, white, and blue."

"It sounds marvelous." I inhaled the stuffy air of the carriage as if I could experience what she spoke of merely by breathing the words still lingering in the air. "I am beyond thrilled to be here. Oh, and I must say, I gobbled up *Moods*."

She raised an eyebrow at me. "Did you truly?"

I couldn't meet her gaze, though I hadn't lied when I said *gobbled*. I'd read it in one sitting. "Absolutely."

"And what did you think?"

I couldn't begin our friendship with untruths. "It was interesting."

"Interesting how?"

We'd only just met. Need she pinion me with such questions? Perhaps I shouldn't have initiated the topic anyhow.

"Interesting in that it's bold, unlike anything I've ever read before."

She leaned back in her seat. "But that is not a good thing."

"That's not what I meant—"

"The reviews have been coming in for a couple months now. They are not all wonderful."

"I'm sorry," I whispered.

"I bent a lot for the sake of my publisher. I believe the real message of the story was lost as I attempted to free my mind upon a subject that always makes trouble—love, of course. What did you not like about it?"

"Are all New England women as direct as you?"

She laughed, and the act took at least five years off her features. "Most certainly not. May's always reminding me to be more tactful. Perhaps we can have this conversation another time?"

"Yes, at least let me unpack my valise before you start drawing criticism from me, else I'm afraid you'll have your brother-in-law turn this carriage around and send me on a train south once more."

We laughed together, and it relieved some of the tension in the air. "Agreed. Now tell me in more detail why you agreed to my proposition. I was under the impression you were quite fond of your brother George. Is it his wife who rankles you?"

It seemed I could not escape her direct manner no matter the topic. I stared out the window as the quaint town dissolved into a lush forest of trees. When I spoke, I didn't look at her and my words were quiet. "Have you ever felt there's something . . . missing?"

I expected her to ask me to elaborate, but instead I heard a long, drawn-out, and very unladylike sigh. "Yes. Though I'm not certain you will find it cooking and cleaning at Apple Slump."

I let a soft smile form on my mouth, for I was quite sure she was wrong. "Perhaps Europe will be your adventure, Louisa, and perhaps Orchard House and Concord will be mine."

～～

I stomped the dust of my boots on the front stoop before following Louisa into the place she affectionately—or perhaps not so affectionately—called "Apple Slump."

Compared to the small, but well-lived and well-loved farmhouse I grew up in, Orchard House was grand. Just off the main road where the Revolutionary rebels chased away the King's army, the brown, gabled house sat proudly nestled at the foot of a steep hill, a massive chimney crowning its center, fruit trees, overshadowing elms, and a happy garden beyond. To me, it seemed quite large for only three people, though I found some relief in the fact that there must definitely be enough room for me.

We entered the foyer and I doffed my bonnet, hanging it alongside Louisa's on a hook on the wall.

"Mother can no longer do all she once did. We are looking for help with the laundry, the cooking, and the cleaning. The only other task that is dear to Mother's heart is the feeding of the vagrants."

"The vagrants?"

"The poor wanderers who are often pointed in our direction. We never turn anyone away." She stopped short at the base of the stairs. "I never mentioned that. I didn't think it a problem . . . is it?"

"No—no, of course not. We fed many of the injured soldiers traveling through our town."

I followed her into the parlor, a quaint room with plentiful windows and a shelf of books.

Louisa's mouth tightened. "The war left behind a path of destruction for many of us. It may be over, but there is much unfinished business—not only in the country but in our minds and hearts as well."

I nodded, acknowledging the pull within me to be a part of it all—the repairing of our country, the serving of others.

If I could do it in ways that used my mind, rather than just my hands, all the better.

"We will have much time before I leave. I do hope we can talk more. My sisters and I used to . . ." She shook her head. "Never mind."

"Anna is still close by, is she not?" I knew from Louisa's letters that she had two sisters.

"Anna is in Concord and often takes meals here during the week while John is at work in Boston. But she has her hands full with two small boys and keeping her own home. As I mentioned in my letters, May is in Boston taking art classes. Anna and I miss her but think it well she is pursuing her talent and passion."

We walked into the dining room and my gaze fell to the small piano and the portrait above it.

As always, Louisa didn't miss my glance. "Do you play?"

"Yes. When I have the time."

Louisa reached out her hand and straightened the oval sketch of a young girl above the piano. "I suppose that will suit, though I must check with Marmee first." She swallowed, and for the first time I noticed a foreign vulnerability pass over her. She ran her fingers over the wood of the piano. "This was Elizabeth's, my sister. She never lived here but we brought the piano. She died eight years ago."

"I'm so sorry, Louisa. I think I can understand."

"Of course you can. Before I met John, I may have argued over that. There's something special about a sister, you know?"

"I'm afraid I don't. I've only been blessed with brothers."

"John . . . he was special, though—I could tell. Perhaps the only man better than a sister."

I wondered if she said that to make me feel better. Really, it didn't matter. I had to agree.

She continued showing me the rooms downstairs. When we came to her father's study, she knocked lightly upon the door.

"Come in!"

Louisa opened the door and I saw a spry, elderly gentleman lying on his back on the rug. I gasped. "Is he unwell?"

Louisa laughed. "He's probably healthier than the lot of us put together! Father, won't you stand up? Johanna, the girl I spoke to you of, is here."

Mr. Alcott stood, his silver hair on end, and held out his hand. "Lovely to meet you, dear girl. We're so glad you could come to help while Louisa goes off to have her adventure."

"The Welds are paying me, Father. I'd rather like to think of it as work."

"Most pleasant work, I daresay. And what's wrong with that?" He winked at me and I wondered not only how we would get along, but if I imagined the peculiar tension between father and daughter.

"Is Mother resting?" Louisa asked.

"Yes, thankfully. Now if you'll forgive me, I am due to visit Mr. Emerson. I will return for dinner."

He donned his hat and exited the study. I noted the many books along the room. The paintings and gadgets and contraptions. It seemed to hold a sort of eccentric order about it which fit Mr. Alcott well.

"Father will keep to himself, and Mother spends most of her days resting, as she should. She's worked for most of our growing-up years and I always said that I wanted to be the one to make sure she never went without." Louisa got a far-away look upon her face. "Well, that hasn't happened quite yet, but there's still time, yes?"

She showed me the wood room and the kitchen, then led me back outdoors. Once outside, she stared at the hill beyond. A long driveway led up the hill and I caught the fading scent of lilacs on the breeze. "Who can guess?" she mused aloud. "I may just miss this place when I'm gone. Do you miss your home, dear?"

"Some, but mostly I miss Mother and George." I missed them at the same time that I associated them with home. At the same time that I realized home had become a place I associated with boredom and predictability. A place I must run from or else stay bound.

I felt lighter here, in Concord. Was it the new, the distraction, or a power in this historic New England town? A town that was drenched in the notion of freedom—first in our fight against the Crown, and now in the fight for the equality of the African. Looking at Louisa, thinking of her words of preferring liberty to marriage, and remembering the message of her novel—a novel that I didn't love but that forced me to think on what the role of being a woman meant.

I closed my eyes against the warm sun, and Louisa didn't seem to mind my pause to soak everything in, to saturate myself in the moment. What was it about this place that made me feel alive? Was it the possibilities, the freedom? Or perhaps it was the undeniable hope that maybe this was the place I truly belonged.

CHAPTER SEVEN

I can't do much with my hands; so I will make a battering-ram of my head
and make a way through this rough-and-tumble world.

~ LMA

Taylor

April 2, 2019

Dear Taylor,

It has been some time since I've written. I've tried not to be bitter about your lack of response, and even wondered if you could respond—if you were on some secret news mission in the Middle East, perhaps, or worse, had fallen sick and weren't able to write.

That's what I've wondered, all these years. Until we decided to hire another investigator to find you. Turns out you never moved from California. I can only assume you still want nothing to do with us.

I'm sorry about that day, Taylor. If I could change it, I most certainly would. Over and over again I've replayed it in my head, punished myself for how I hurt you.

I know what I ask is monumental, and yet for Mom's sake, I write anyway. Please, Taylor, is there any way we can put this behind us? I truly believe we are sisters, and while friendship might be something that can be cut off, the bond of sisterhood is not. And our mother needs you.

We found out last month that she has stage three breast cancer. She's being treated in Boston, and I have no doubt she will beat this thing. But she needs you, Taylor. She needs all of us. Together. You are still a fourth of our family, and we miss you. Mom dreams about you, more since her diagnosis. I feel she has a hole inside of her—we all do—that won't be filled until you come home.

I don't mean to guilt you. For once it seems I'm at a loss for words. I used to know you so well, used to know what would make you feel better—if I'm truthful, I even used to know how to get you to do what I wanted. I realize all that has changed, that we're near strangers now. But it doesn't have to be that way. Come home, Taylor. We love you.

Victoria

P.S. It may not be my place, but when I saw the investigator's report that YOU are the person behind one of my favorite authors, I couldn't help but feel a surge of pride. Maybe that will offend you, but I hope

*it doesn't. I'm cheering you on, Casey Hood. I truly am
glad one of us is reaching her castle in the air.*

~~

I was doing it for Lorraine. Well, for Lorraine and my conscience.

That was it, and nobody—including myself—should
expect anything more.

I brushed my bangs out of my face at the stoplight, caught
a quick glimpse of myself in the rearview mirror, met my
own challenging gaze. I was no longer the awkward, unsure
girl I'd been the last time I was in Massachusetts. And while
I'd earned a few extra lines around my thirty-seven-year-old
smile, I was proud of them and proud of all I'd accomplished
since I'd left the Bennetts.

Being alone had a way of wringing every ounce of life
from you. At least it had for me. But it not only wrung me
out, it made me stronger. Instead of making me cower in
defeat, that last day at the Bennetts' had bestowed a driving
force upon me. A driving force to succeed, to not be stopped
no matter the costs. Forget that hazy thing called hope—the
only thing I could rely on was myself.

I'd written my first novel in a beaten-down studio apartment in Cambria, California. I'd gotten a job waitressing
at nights—never pondered the journalism job I was supposed to get after finishing college. Instead, I wrote. Like a
madwoman.

And amazingly enough, the words came. The incident in
front of the Bennetts' garage had released a wealth of words.
It was as if my life in Concord, my life with the Bennetts,

had been the Hoover Dam that was holding the waters back, and now they finally flowed free. I might have been alone, but in some ways I'd found where I belonged. And it wasn't with people; it was with pages. Pages and pages of *fictional* people. People I could tame. People I knew would never betray me.

I wrote beach reads. Literally. Fiction set in small towns along the Pacific coast. I often took a few days off to visit the towns I wrote about for inspiration. In my books, the characters always behaved. They did as I told them. And if they cheated on my heroine with their sisters, it was because there was a plan in mind, a greater good I would work out in their lives by the end.

I found freedom in this sort of control, and for the first time in my life, I couldn't get enough of it. I didn't think about Will; I wrote. I didn't think about Victoria; I wrote. I didn't think about Will and Victoria; I wrote. And after I was finished writing, still clinging to the crazy thing that had propelled me to drive cross-country and possessed me to write my first novel, I submitted to agents.

Kathy Sullivan wasn't an A-list agent back then. But after *Monterey Winds* came out, that changed. Readers gobbled up my seemingly simple story of a summer romance gone wrong against a backdrop of Steinbeck country. It stayed on the *New York Times* bestseller list for six months, and I quit my waitressing job, upgraded to an upscale condo overlooking the Pacific.

The victory was short-lived because I had no one to share it with. So I flung myself into my next novel, then my next. I started saving like crazy, and after careful calculations to add up all the money the Bennetts had spent on me, I sent them a bank check through my lawyer, finally putting aside the heavy guilt—the feeling that I'd stolen from Lorraine and Paul. Stolen their time, their love, their home—even their name.

I met Kevin while writing novel number six. He threw me for a loop, that's for sure. A journalist and chaser of stories, I was okay with his low-maintenance, low-commitment attitude. He came and went as he pleased, and I didn't demand much from him, was always happy to walk into my home after a research trip to see his gym-toned physique standing in my kitchen in nothing but boxer shorts.

We didn't go deep. He tried a couple times, but I refused. I was satisfied to simply have a companion, someone to share dinner and a glass of wine with, someone to watch a movie with, spend the night with, and bounce story ideas around with.

He'd once tried to tell me he loved me, but I would have none of it. He took it okay, actually. Seemed to accept that, although I had feelings for him, I would probably never acknowledge them, much less confess them.

My Bluetooth sounded out the ringing of my phone. The object of my thoughts popped up on my display.

"Hey. How's Washington?" I asked.

"Don't know, I'm not there. I'm in Denver, remember?"

"Oh, right. Sorry."

"You there yet?"

"Driving the rental from the airport."

"I just wanted to wish you luck, Taylor." His voice got serious.

I wasn't a fan.

"Thanks. Have fun in Denver."

"Call me tonight, okay?"

I tried not to sigh too loud. He was a decent guy. He was worried about my emotional state. Why did I resist?

"I will. Thanks, Kevin."

We hung up, and I tried not to wonder why he stayed with me all these years. He'd asked me to marry him once, not long after he'd tried to tell me he loved me, after we'd been together about three years. When I'd said no, he hadn't run away, hadn't assumed that this was a closed door for us.

I'd been young back then. Young enough to go to my yearly checkups and not have the doctor give her annual it's-now-or-likely-never talk about having children. Young enough to not have a few silvery strands of hair at my temples. Young enough to still dare to build those blasted castles in the air, to be naive enough—or maybe stupid enough—to think I had all the time in the world for my life to get back on track.

I groaned as I took the Concord exit, inhaled a deep breath to calm my quaking nerves. This wouldn't be easy. Being here, back in Concord, back at the Bennetts'. Seeing Lorraine, sick. Seeing Victoria, period. Seeing the man I knew to be her husband.

I pulled into the Colonial Inn, just up the street from my destination. I slid my hat low over my head, hoping to avoid any familiar glances.

After I'd settled into my room, I decided a walk was in order. I wasn't due at Paul and Lorraine's until later tonight for dinner. A walk would be a perfect way to still my jittery stomach. And Sleepy Hollow Cemetery would be the perfect destination.

~~~

No note lay at Louisa's grave, proving that I wasn't the only one who had changed, who had exchanged new habits for old ones.

I didn't feel peace when I walked among the old stones. Instead, it seemed that ghosts haunted and whispered to me, chasing me among the paved paths and through the towering pines, though I couldn't be sure if they were real ghosts or the ghosts of my past.

Perhaps I had committed a major grievance against God, or against the dead, in opening Victoria's letter that day. Perhaps our downfall had begun with me, with imposing myself on some hazy communication between the living and the dead.

I didn't stay at the cemetery long. Instead, I walked along Bedford Street and turned toward Lexington Road and Orchard House. The sun shone bright in the sky, but the wind bit my skin just a little, as I was used to the warmer California weather. I zipped up my sweatshirt and within twenty minutes, Orchard House stood before me, looking just as I remembered it.

Strange to stand there, at what was in many ways the symbol and center of the bond Victoria and I had once shared. Stranger still how I didn't cringe at the welcome sensation.

More than once, I thought to write a book set in this town, to pay homage to Louisa Alcott instead of John Steinbeck or

Joan Didion. But every time I sat down to create characters, the memories of the Bennetts and of that last day came forth. As time turned and years went by, I realized it wasn't so much the reason I left that was painful, but the fact that I'd ignored their attempts at reconciliation. That I hadn't gone back. Hadn't forgiven.

What was more, I knew *that* book—a Louisa book—was the book Victoria had wanted to write. No matter if I had the authority to accomplish it, in many ways, it felt like stealing.

I imagined such a book on the shelves of the Orchard House gift shop, a deep, dark part of me relishing what that would do to Victoria. How it would be one last blow to her dreams. Just in case the softball bat on her laptop hadn't accomplished it that day.

I adjusted my purse over my shoulder, my muscles suddenly tight with the remembrance of my sister's bat in my hands.

Truth be told, I'd never understood rage and revenge until that day, and its possession frightened me. In that moment, I was not in control. And every moment after that, these last sixteen years, I fought to make sure I was in control.

I wondered why Victoria hadn't mentioned what I'd done in any of her letters—she'd only asked me to forgive *her*. I wondered if she rewrote her stories or simply started new ones. With the way ideas came to her, it probably hadn't taken her long to pick herself up and begin again.

Begin again with Will.

I walked up the side path to the gift shop, shaking my head at the painful thought, surprised that it still had the power to singe after so many years.

I noted the banner on the door announcing the 150th anniversary of the publication of *Little Women*.

Huh. That's right. The first part of the successful novel was published in 1868, but the public quickly insisted on a second installment, girls across the country demanding to know if Jo and Laurie would find a happy ending.

Louisa had refused to let Jo settle for her rich, handsome friend—one she loved like a brother. Instead, she'd introduced Professor Bhaer, along with the many pains of growing up—parting from her sisters, Meg's domestic troubles, Jo being denied a chance to tour Europe, and the heartrending death of Beth, all introduced the following year, 150 years ago.

I opened the gift shop door, imagined Bronson Alcott carrying wood into this part of the home—then the woodshed area. I breathed in the scents of books and history, and my stomach relaxed. It might have been hard to be back in Concord, but here, at Orchard House, I could think of only one word and surprisingly, it felt pleasant: home.

A group clustered in front of the door to what I knew was the Alcott kitchen, a tour guide speaking about the many ways Bronson Alcott sought to improve the house, including the door before them, which swung shut so that he could push it open without hands when carrying wood into the home, allowing it to close behind him.

The older guide pushed through the door, followed by the group. I glimpsed the soapstone sink below the kitchen window, the walls a deep yellow. Once the door closed, the young woman at the desk smiled at me. "Can I help you find anything?"

"No thank you, I'm just looking."

I meandered through the gift shop, perusing the many books on the shelves. I picked up *March* by Geraldine Brooks along with a sweet-smelling soy candle that I would give to Lorraine later.

I ran my fingers over a copy of *Little Women*. The book was small and fat, the cover green with what looked like holly vines upon it. Four little women, almost cartoonish, adorned the front, one clearly blonde—Amy. It looked nothing like the copy my birth mother had given me, the copy I'd left behind at the Bennetts' all those years ago.

I picked it up, thought a brief second about purchasing it for Victoria, a small token of truce. Surely enough time had passed for us to lay aside old hurts, to at least acknowledge one another if for no other reason than for the sake of Lorraine.

What happened—the pain—had been real. Maybe it still was. But we'd been so young. Young to love; young to the world; young, and maybe even blinded, to our own selfishness.

I'd thought many times about how it was that Victoria and Will came to find themselves in one another's arms that afternoon. I wondered if it was the first time, if the moment had surprised them just as much as it had done me. Or had such an affair been going on for a while? Had they fallen in love, planned to tell me when I came home that day, even?

I hadn't stuck around long enough to find answers. And now, sixteen years later, I still didn't know if I wanted them.

I'd loved Will. He hadn't been some silly schoolgirl obsession. He'd been the real thing. A hero born of a bathroom prayer. I thought he'd felt the same way. What had I missed?

And my best friend. My sister. The person I loved more than anyone else. How could she betray me so completely?

I walked up to the counter with my items and gave them to the girl. She flipped over the candle and typed the price into the cash register, followed by the novel.

"Twenty-six fifty."

I handed her my debit card. "Do you still do Jo March Writing Camps?" I asked.

"Absolutely. It's one of our most popular camps. Would you like a flyer?"

I shook my head. "No, I don't have any children. I was just curious. My sister and I used to come."

She smiled at me and gave me back my card. "Me too. I loved it."

The door behind her opened, and I glimpsed the foyer and front door of Orchard House as a group funneled through, ending their tour.

"Would you like to take a tour?" the girl asked, handing me my bag.

"Oh no, I don't have time today, but maybe I'll be back soon."

The last of the group filed into the gift shop and a familiar-looking woman with a name badge stopped at the desk. "You have everything under control, Nicole? I'm going to be heading out." She smiled at me, and I froze, feeling my mouth fall open even as I tried to stop it.

My gaze flew to her name badge and then back to those blue eyes.

She was just as pretty at thirty-seven as she had been at twenty-one. Her dark hair was pulled back in a low ponytail, accentuating high cheekbones and a mature beauty that echoed her mother's.

My mother's.

She gripped the edge of the counter. "Taylor . . . I—I didn't expect you here."

I dragged in a shaky breath, tried to stay strong beneath my sister's gaze, but found myself shrinking instead. "No, I—I didn't expect you here, either."

CHAPTER EIGHT

Success is often a lucky accident, coming to those who may not deserve it, while others who do have to wait and hope till they have earned it. That is the best sort and the most enduring.

~ LMA

Taylor

VICTORIA THREW HER ARMS around my neck, and I stood, my feet cemented to the floor, my arms braced at my sides, one hand clutching my purchases.

When she finally released me—well, no, she didn't really release me because she still lightly held my arms in her hands—she started talking a mile a minute, just like I remembered.

"I'm so glad you've come. I really can't believe you're here, actually. Wait until Mom and Dad see you—I didn't tell them that you were coming, you know."

"Y-you didn't?"

She shook her head. "I wanted to surprise them . . . and to make sure you were going to show up." She winked, then gestured for me to follow her through the door she just came from. "I just have to grab my purse."

I followed her, speechless, as if in a trance. I tried to shake myself out of this state. This was the old me. The timid, frightened Taylor. Not the strong, self-assured Taylor I knew myself to be. "You work here?"

She smiled back at me, and I thought she should have been focusing on honing her acting instead of her writing all these years. To so easily pretend to pick up where we left off required a certain gift of theater I hadn't known she possessed. "I'm the director. Never did publish a book, but I decided to go after my next favorite—all things Louisa May Alcott and Orchard House. I can't imagine doing anything better. I love it here."

She glowed. She did seem happy, though I wondered if my presence didn't have something to do with the joy written on every square inch of her face just then.

"I'm glad for you." I pushed out the words, even as I noted the sparkling diamonds on the ring finger of her left hand and tried to come to terms with all the emotion they suddenly stirred within me. I hadn't been able to resist a quick search of her name on Facebook. The profile picture had told me all I'd needed to know—Will had been the one to give her those diamonds. Will had been the one to get down on one knee and present her with that shimmering setting of shining perfection. To push the ribbed band onto her finger at a wedding ceremony some time later.

I wondered who Victoria had as her maid of honor, if despite the tangle of circumstances she would have asked me if I hadn't run away.

"How did you know I was here?" She opened a small cupboard in the hall and reached for her purse.

"I—I didn't."

She stopped short. "Oh. I thought—" She waved a hand through the air. "Never mind. Doesn't matter."

"I was taking a walk and ended up here."

She smiled. "Of course."

I couldn't hold her gaze. "Of course."

"I could give you a ride to Mom and Dad's."

"I think . . . well, you think you and I should catch up first?"

She blinked. "Yeah. I'd like that."

I shook my head, not wanting her to get the wrong impression. "I mean, so you can fill me in on Lorraine. How's she doing?"

"Mom, Taylor. Please don't call her Lorraine. She won't take it well."

I swallowed, knowing she was right but hating to be chastised by Victoria all the same.

She bade the young clerk, Nicole, goodbye and we walked past Bronson Alcott's School of Philosophy to the steps at the base of a hill that led to a separate building. I knew the Orchard House offices and classrooms were kept there. Victoria waved to a man with a baseball cap who was trimming the hedges around Bronson's school, and he returned the gesture.

She mounted the stairs. "Mom's had her first two rounds of chemo so far and is keeping her energy level up. She's doing better than I expected, quite honestly."

"Well, that's a relief." This was stable, even safe ground. Our common concern for the woman we both loved. "How is she emotionally? Mentally?"

Victoria finished climbing the last stair to the office building and stopped, scrunched up her face. "You know what? She's good. At first, not so much, but one of her friends invited her and Dad to church and . . . well, they've always been so skeptical of organized religion, but I think it's helping her through this time. I say, whatever works."

I agreed, even as I thought of Victoria's letters I'd found at Sleepy Hollow. Had writing to a long-dead woman worked for her? And what of her long-ago claim that she believed in a God she could call a friend? That He had given her the desire and creative ability to write? Were those beliefs challenged with age and circumstances? Worse, had I contributed to knocking down any faith she'd once had?

She pressed a button on her key chain and a shiny gray Honda Pilot beeped. She dumped her things—a purse and a lunch box—in the backseat. "You want to take a quick walk before heading over?"

I shrugged. "Sure."

I placed my things beside hers, noted a pink soccer ball and a Nintendo Switch case lying carelessly on the backseats.

Yes, I'd seen photos of kids when I looked up Victoria and Will online. But something about seeing that pink soccer ball set reality firmly before me. My sister had a life all her own now—one apart from me, one I had chosen not to be a part of. The thought caught me off guard and an ache of something that felt an awful lot like loss niggled its way into my chest. But loss over what? Over the fact that I would likely never have my own children—or any family where I truly belonged? That while I'd fooled myself into thinking I was the victor with the *New York Times* bestsellers and the coastal beach property and sexy boyfriend, I hadn't really won at all? Victoria had.

How a soccer ball and video game case could elicit all these feelings within me, I wasn't quite sure. I was thirty-seven years old. My own woman. I needed to stop being jealous of my sister. My friend. Whatever she was these days.

We walked down the hill, but I couldn't get the family car and soccer ball and video game case out of my head. Maybe it wasn't so much that I was jealous of Victoria. Maybe what I felt was more like sorrow that I didn't know these children— the closest thing I would ever have to a niece and nephew.

I opened my mouth to outright ask about her kids but stopped myself. I didn't want to know just yet. I didn't want to know if her son's smile mirrored Will's in its crookedness. I didn't want to know if he was her daughter's soccer coach or liked to rough out a few video games with his son on the weekends. I didn't want to know. Ever.

Victoria widened her gait to a peppy step. "So what have you been up to? You know, besides writing all those runaway bestsellers?" When I took a second too long to answer, she grabbed my arm. "Oh! Do you want to know which one was my absolute favorite?"

I smiled, but it felt ten kinds of awkward. "Sure."

"*Long Beach Nights.*"

I wrinkled my nose. "Really? I hated writing that one, thought it would never make it to print even after I edited it a gazillion times."

"Are you serious? The mother/daughter relationship you portrayed . . . the hurt, the hero . . ." She sighed. "It was beautiful. Will found me sobbing over it one night."

My breath hitched.

She couldn't miss my thoughts, suddenly heavy with the realization that she and Will shared an actual life together, that their betrayal had not only culminated in a complete, three-hundred-sixty-degree circle of perfection, but that it had sparked something real, something authentic— something more lasting than anything I'd ever known.

I cleared my throat, knowing I needed to speak, sensing that Victoria wouldn't be the first to do so, to acknowledge that four-letter word that had first come between us more than sixteen years ago.

"So . . . how's he doing?"

I'd come here vowing to be strong, and yet I'd ruined whatever fortress I intended to erect with that single sentence, for it stank of old hurts and vulnerability, of past regrets and second-place ribbons.

"I'm so sorry, Taylor," she whispered. "What happened back then was . . . I mean, it was a complete mistake, a fluke thing, but then . . . after you were gone for so long . . . I just wish we could have handled it all better."

Yeah, a whole lot better. Like not falling for one another at all, for starters. Like not giving whatever feelings they had for one another a chance to grow. Like stifling and stomping it out before it had a chance to fan into flame and keeping one's lips to one's self.

I bit off the bitter words that wanted to pour forth from my mouth, tamed them instead. I'd learned to keep my acrimonious words to the page—my stories were often more interesting because of them.

I started slow. "I suppose . . ." I began again. "I guess I can understand how it would happen . . . I mean, he was Will." Perfect, handsome, smart, funny Will. "And you were you." Perfect, beautiful, petite, brilliant. Really, a much better match for him from the get-go. "I guess I just don't understand how you could *let* it happen."

About a thousand things were wrong with this conversation, but that I couldn't keep those bitter feelings over my sister's marriage to myself stuck the deepest. I shook my head. "You know what? Forget it. It's water under the bridge, really. All for the best. Tell me about your kids."

"No, it bothers you. We should talk this out. Taylor, I know you didn't come here for us. I know you came for Mom, but when you sent word you were coming back home, I couldn't help but hope that we might make amends. That we could be . . . you know, sisters again."

I couldn't speak, couldn't formulate thoughts or coherent words that I could trust enough to thrust between us.

She continued. "I wouldn't expect it to be the same relationship we had when we were teens or even in college. I wouldn't expect anything, Taylor, except what you wanted to give. I just . . . I want you in our lives again. I miss you." We walked for a minute, and when I didn't respond, she dragged in a deep breath. "I suppose I also realize we have to wade through some of the ugly past to get there. Would you—well, don't you think you could wade with me?"

I stopped walking. This was too much, too fast. I came here for Lorraine. She and Paul had treated me as their own child the best they could, giving me food and my own room and braces and an education and as much of their love as they could manage. And when I left, in some ways, it felt as if I'd stolen it all from them, as if I'd taken what they'd done for me and treated it like it didn't matter. Like they didn't matter.

But they did. And now I wanted to show them.

But none of that had to do with Victoria. Not really. And making amends with her wasn't on my list of things to do now and maybe not ever.

I glanced back the direction we came, leaving her vulnerable question to hang in the air between us. "I think . . . I think I'd like to go see Mom now."

Defeat darkened her pretty features, but she nodded, gave me a tight smile. "Sure, Taylor, sure. She'll be happy to see you."

We walked toward Orchard House and then up the hill to her car in silence, a mountain of unspoken regret between us. For me, at least, it was too much to climb.

CHAPTER NINE

All the philosophy in our house is not in the study; a good deal is in the kitchen, where a fine old lady thinks high thoughts and does good deeds while she cooks and scrubs.

~ LMA

Johanna

"Blast this wretched wind!" I shoved a clothespin on the line, ordered it to stay put upon the handkerchief I was attempting to wrangle into submission beneath the afternoon gale.

I heard a laugh behind me and turned to see Mrs. Alcott at the door of the kitchen. "She won't listen, you know. Is known to have a mind of her own, that wind."

My face colored at the thought of the elderly woman hearing me use such poor language. "Forgive me, Mrs. Alcott. Is it always so blustery in Massachusetts?"

"Not at all, dear. And don't worry too much about apologizing—both Lou and I are no strangers to an occasional tantrum, though we're trying to improve upon ourselves."

I nodded. "Are you feeling well today?"

"Very, dear. I was going to help with dinner as well. Anna's bringing the babies over. There's nothing like some grandchildren to lighten the heart."

"I'll be in soon as I finish hanging the rest."

She closed the door and I went back to my laundry. I had taken a special liking to Mrs. Alcott. While at times she seemed confused, there was something that sat in her spirit—something that old age or hard times or war hadn't been able to snuff out. I saw the same thing in Louisa, and though I couldn't quite grasp it, I knew it wasn't something that possessed my own mother. Not that I wanted it to possess her—or me for that matter.

The Alcotts were a different sort. A week with them was more than enough time for me to understand as much. I gathered Mr. Alcott did not have steady work, and besides teaching and giving what he called *Conversations*—lectures on his ideas about education and philosophy, which I understood were highly unorthodox—he did not bring any income. Mrs. Alcott had been the one to go to work when Louisa was younger, helping the poor of Boston. They had been a wandering family, moving often until eight years ago when they finally settled on this piece of earth not far from their dear friend Ralph Emerson. Now Louisa had taken her place as the provider of the family, largely through her writing, which seemed to be slowly gaining success.

"The trouble is that I don't know enough of life to write," she'd told me the night before as we both sat doing handwork in the parlor by the waning summer sun streaming through the windows.

"Don't you? What of your experience in the war? Of staring death in the face and coming out victorious?" If this lady had nothing to write about, how was I to ever hope to pen something of meaning myself?

"I suppose . . ." Her fingers never stopped moving, weaving needle in and out of cloth with grace. "Though I think Europe will be just the inspiration I need. It must be a capital place to let a story simmer."

"You will have a marvelous time. What do you think you will write upon your return?"

"Certainly something grander than a 'book for girls,' which is all my publisher can talk of me writing."

"How lovely! Why don't you give it a go?"

"I refuse to spend my time writing moral pap for the young. Such drivel."

I couldn't help but laugh. If I had a publisher asking *me* for a story, I'd see to its writing even if it did contain some pap.

I'd never known anyone quite like this woman, and though sometimes I found myself appalled at her outlandish behavior, at the same time I couldn't wait to know what notion she would turn on its head next.

"And how do you think you will manage here? Are you satisfied with your work?" she asked.

"Most definitely." And I was. It was good work, yet it left me with some time for myself—to walk into town or read one of Louisa's many Dickens books or fiddle around with a poem or two of my own.

"I feel better leaving Father and Marmee knowing you are here."

"I will do my best by them, and you."

She placed her handwork on her lap. "I am truly glad

you've come here, Johanna. And if it's not too presumptuous of me to say—I believe that if John were alive, he would be right proud of his sister for having an adventure of her own."

Tears pricked the corners of my eyes. Though I knew it behooved her for me to be here, I also knew the genuineness of her words—couldn't imagine a false bone in her body, in fact. "Thank you."

"Now, don't you think it's time we spoke of the problem you had with my novel?"

"Louisa!"

"I'm in earnest, dear. Kindly criticism never offends but to me is often more flattering than praise, for if anyone takes the trouble to criticize, it seems to prove that the thing is worth mending."

I thought on that for a moment before I spoke. "The story was very interesting. Bold, which I liked, though I didn't find comfort in it."

She waited.

I sighed, figuring I had best be out with it. "At some points it felt as if you were writing the story as a means to express disapproval of marriage . . . or worse, condone a free sort of love."

Her mouth tightened, and she nodded. "I have heard that criticism, though that was not my intent. My intent was to show the moral shortcomings of a moody nature—one guided by impulse—and their disastrous results. The end result was not what I meant to have it, for I now believe I followed bad advice and took out many things which explained my idea and made the characters more natural and consistent."

I didn't know what to say to that. She'd asked for my opinion.

"Yet I agreed to the changes. There really is no excuse." She exhaled with a huff. "I only wish I had done better justice to my own idea. In the end I heartily believe it, am willing to be blamed for it, and am not sorry I wrote it."

"You made me *feel*, that much is certain. I couldn't decide which I wanted—Sylvia and Adam to live happily ever after or Sylvia and Geoffrey. Even so, I feel you did give us a happy ever after for Sylvia and Adam in a sense, and that is what upset me."

"You didn't wish for them to be together, even in death?"

I swallowed.

"Don't be bashful now, Johanna. I can only respect you if you come by it through an honest means. Now is a perfect opportunity."

"Very well, then." I smoothed a stray piece of hair behind my ear. "I felt you cheated us—and your characters—by selecting the solution of death to let them be together. It was entirely too Shakespearean for my tastes. You let them all grow in the story into their most noble selves, and yet in some ways, I felt Sylvia and Adam had the simple way out in death."

"Death is simple now, is it?"

I widened my eyes at her. She'd asked! I refused to back down now. "Not simple in reality, but a means of a simple solution for your story. Poor Geoffrey is who I felt sorry for. How much more authentic for Sylvia to persist in honoring her marriage vows despite her tangled feelings for Adam? What if the happy ending was not death, but the finding of a true love within the bonds of marriage?"

Louisa had grown quiet, and I grew uncomfortable.

"I have hurt you," I said.

She exhaled. "Just my pride, and that has been hurt before."

"Forgive me. I should have insisted on staying quiet."

"I asked, and I think at the heart, you are right. Entirely too romantic, but right."

I smiled. "Is it marriage in general you are against or simply how it can lead to a lifetime of sorrow if too hastily enacted?"

She straightened. "I am a hearty proponent of a smart marriage that is thought and prayed upon. But I fear ladies as a whole are too insistent upon making a match for superficial reasons or for the *simple* fact that it is their expected course."

"Was Geoffrey not a worthy man for Sylvia to be married to? If one were to follow the fickle heart, would not one be constantly questioning the vows one has made?"

"So you do not believe in a single, true love for a woman's heart?"

I leaned my head back in the chair, looked out the window. I thought of Bryant, who had pursued me throughout school. He helped his parents run their farm, attended church every week, had grown into an upright and godly man. Yet was that enough of a reason to succumb to his advances when my heart was not drawn to him? Was there a man out there intended just for me, and if I didn't find him, would my one chance at true happiness forever be lost?

"I suppose I don't. I suppose I believe in true love, but more so I believe in the perseverance of two hearts to unite as one despite the obstacles that oppose their union."

I wondered if Louisa had ever loved a man. I wondered if she believed her chance at love had been taken from her or if she simply wrote to justify her stance as a single woman. Despite the passion I felt from her, I also felt a barricade—a vulnerability and likely a past hurt that she wouldn't share.

I decided it best to let the subject lie dead.

"Are you upset with me, then?" I asked.

"Quite the contrary, in fact. I appreciate your honesty. Was there anything else? I do welcome it."

I shook my head. "No . . . I found the story captivating. I suppose it just didn't sit well with me for some reason."

We continued on with our handwork before she spoke. "Why don't we turn the tables, Johanna? Tell me of your castles in the air."

I grasped my needle tight. "Pardon?"

"My sisters and I used to dream up what we wanted for our futures. Our castles in the air. Tell me, what is it you dream of?"

"I . . . I'm not accustomed to voicing such thoughts aloud."

"And why not? Why is it that the men should have all the dreams and we should be nothing but their encouragement?"

"Is it such a terrible thing to support one's husband?"

"Of course not. But is it such a terrible thing to have our own ambitions and goals? Come, there must be something that calls your heart."

I inhaled a great breath of air, sucked it in all the way to my belly. "I admit I was excited to come to Massachusetts, a place of such high esteem in the literary community, because I'm quite fond of poetry."

Her mouth fell open just a bit. "Are you? That is wonderful! I've always been a better patriot than poet myself, but when I was at Fruitlands—Papa and Mr. Lane's Utopian society— and all of us being much tried and stretched, living on unleavened bread, water, apples, and discontent, I would get to sleep saying poetry. I enjoyed Phillis Wheatley a great deal."

"Oh yes, I as well. Such an inspiration she is!"

"Have you tried your hand at some?"

I nodded. "Please know I don't expect anything from you, Louisa. I didn't come here to be taken under your wing or any such thing."

"Fiddlesticks! I don't care if you did. I should be glad to help. And you will help me, won't you? Iron sharpens iron. And if ever I am tempted to allow a publisher to change my works when they are not within my heart, I expect you to talk me out of it."

I expelled a great breath of air. "I—yes . . . of course."

She shook out Mr. Alcott's breeches, which she had been mending. "It's settled then."

Now I grabbed up another handkerchief to hang on the line, thinking that I had just under two weeks until Louisa left for her grand adventure. She'd asked to read my poems, and I told her I would think on it. I had given her criticism, and she had taken it well. I wasn't certain I could do the same.

And yet something about our agreement—an odd sort of partnership—made me feel all the more welcome, as if some strange sort of destiny or perhaps the Lord Himself had led me to this place, this time, this family. They were an odd bunch, but miracle of miracles, I felt at home among them, as if I belonged. At the same time I felt the freedom to explore who I could become on my own. It was one of the greatest feelings in the world.

A gust of wind ripped the handkerchief from my hands and sent it flying across the gardens. "Oh!"

I picked my way around orchids and chrysanthemums and tomato plants. The handkerchief had settled on a patch of clover, but when I stooped to pick it up, another squall of wind skirted it away.

"Blast!" I took off running again. This time I spotted a young man walking down the drive on the adjoining property. The handkerchief traversed the wooden gate. The man's gaze met my own and he held up his hand in greeting or as if to say, *"I'll get it."*

I smiled in gratitude, watched him jog a couple of easy steps to where the piece of disobedient laundry sat at the bottom of a pine. He scooped it up. I brushed my hair out of my eyes and crossed the remaining distance to him.

"Thank you, sir."

He doffed his hat, revealing a head of blond curls and eyes the color of the bluest lake. "It is my pleasure." He held the handkerchief out and I took it, even as I tried not to be taken aback by his charming good looks.

"I don't believe I've had the pleasure, miss."

I dipped my head. "I've only just arrived at Orchard House, sir. My name is Johanna Suhre."

"Miss Suhre." He bowed to me and I felt my face color. He straightened. "My name is Nathan. Nathan Bancroft. I live just up the way." He pointed to a large house set back from the road a bit. "Are you here for a visit?"

"Long-term, as far as I can tell." At the words, an ache

for home and Mother and George and our nights before the fire started in my chest. I was happy to be on my adventure, but no letter from Pennsylvania had reached me yet. For the first time I understood what John felt when waiting for word from home while in the army. "I'm employed at Orchard House while Miss Alcott travels abroad."

"That woman doesn't approve of staying still much, does she?" He winked at me, and I felt my face flush again. A desire to defend Louisa came upon me, though I wondered if there was even cause for it. Certainly Mr. Bancroft only wanted to make conversation.

"I—I don't know. I suppose she wants to live life."

"And what of you, Miss Suhre? Do I detect a hint of an accent? Are you a wanderer like our Louisa?"

Our Louisa. He was familiar with Louisa and the Alcotts, then. Quite familiar, it seemed. "I am from Pennsylvania. Louisa met my brother in Washington during the war."

He nodded, and though I had decided to put my guard up when it came to Mr. Bancroft, I couldn't help but study his fine features and gentlemanly dress, so unlike the farming boys I knew back home.

"It seems you do not approve of standing still much either, then, Miss Suhre. Are you 'living life,' as you put it?"

I lifted my chin. "I suppose I am, the best I know how."

His gaze fell to the handkerchief in my hand, and for a reason I couldn't quite pin down, I felt ashamed.

"If I can ever be of any assistance in helping you live your life, say in the form of a walk into town or a carriage ride to Walden Pond, please do not hesitate to flag me down with your laundry again." He tipped his hat and was off.

I stared after him, holding the handkerchief tight, something in my belly stirring. I wondered about Mr. Bancroft, if the opportunity would indeed come for me to take a walk or a carriage ride with him, if I would enjoy doing so. I wondered what his interests were, if he lived alone in the big house up the drive. He seemed like no other man I'd ever known. I couldn't help but think of kind, unassuming Bryant. Of his hand in one pocket of his overall, sun shining on his sweaty brow, his question stretching between us, feeling out the possibility of a life together.

"You think you could ever love me, Johanna Suhre?"

I hadn't answered. Instead, I'd sent Louisa a letter agreeing to come to Massachusetts.

I walked around the gardens and back to the clothesline, where I finished hanging the rest of the laundry. I took the basket into the kitchen. Mrs. Alcott stood over the stove boiling potatoes while Louisa pulled a loaf of bread from the oven.

I imagined the simple fare we would partake of shortly—potatoes, bread, perhaps some strawberries from the garden. My stomach rumbled. By far, the thing I missed most about home was eating meat—something the Alcotts did not partake in. Though I was only beginning to grasp the edges of Mr. Alcott's many beliefs, I knew that he was a transcendentalist, that he believed the state of human perfection possible and something to be pursued. The pursuit of this state involved many things, one being the absence of meat at the table. He did not believe animals should be oppressed, and considered killing them violent.

I could understand this philosophy in my head, and yet when dinnertime came and only an assortment of vegetables and potatoes filled my plate, I found my understanding slipping.

A knock sounded on the kitchen door and Louisa peered out the top half of the screen. A mother in a threadbare cotton dress with a babe on her hip stood staring in at us. She couldn't have been much older than I, but something in her eyes told me she had tenfold more life experience, and perhaps even wisdom, about her. I watched Louisa smile and greet her by name before turning to the golden loaf that was to feed five adults and two babes and cutting a generous portion—nearly half—for the woman at the door.

Not without some shame, my stomach twisted. The same happened every night, and Louisa never ventured to make more bread. I could only surmise that the family, while not in such a needy state as the beggar woman at the door, was not so well-off as I had first assumed. I couldn't help but wonder if Louisa had used the last of her proceeds from *Hospital Sketches* to buy my fare here so that her mother would have help whilst she was away.

Even so, my pay, though meager, came at the end of each week, as regular as the grandfather clock in Mr. Alcott's study.

I didn't realize I was staring at the warm bread Louisa gave the beggar woman until she spoke. "Perhaps you'll work on these green beans for us, Johanna?"

I shook my head into straights, admonished myself for begrudging the bread given to a needy, nursing mother. "She's come every day. Does she not have a husband who will provide for her?"

"He was wounded in the war. Lost an arm. He hasn't been able to find suitable work since he came home."

Guilt pierced my chest. How could I think only of my own rumbling belly when those so much more needy than I came to the Alcott home for help? As far as I could tell, they had never turned any away. Seemed to follow the late President Lincoln's encouragement to "bind up the nation's wounds, to care for him who shall have borne the battle and for his widow and his orphan."

Charity for all.

In short, love for all.

I'd never seen it lived out as I did in the Alcott home. And while I knew part of the reasoning was that this was a way to Mr. Alcott's state of perfection, I saw also how it was more than that—how Louisa and her mother cared for this woman and her family on a more personal level.

I pondered Mr. Alcott burrowed away in his study at that moment, perusing his many books and coming up with his ideas. He wouldn't emerge until dinner, and yet I couldn't help but wonder how the family might be better off had Mr. Alcott pursued regular work instead of whiling away his hours in his study. For the first time, I glimpsed marriage through Louisa's eyes. I was beginning to see why she might be so set against it—to her, even a marriage of love might very well be a sort of bondage.

I looked out the window to the large house up the adjoining drive. I snapped a green bean and then another. Did Mr. Bancroft sit in a study most of the day? What business did he attend?

"I met Mr. Bancroft this afternoon," I ventured.

Mrs. Alcott raised her brow from where she stood, poking a knife into a potato boiling on the stove. "Did you now?"

I nodded.

"I suppose he tipped his hat to give you a good glimpse of his curls?" Louisa said.

My mouth fell open.

"Louy!" her mother implored.

Louisa shrugged her shoulders. "He possesses a tendency to do that, is all."

I turned back to my green beans. I shouldn't have brought up the neighbor apparently.

"So he did, didn't he?" Louisa appeared at my side, stuck her face in view of my green beans, a playful look upon it.

A smile crept onto my lips, and then a giggle escaped.

"I knew it!" she said.

"I'm sure he only meant to be friendly in doffing his hat." I snapped a green bean and placed the ends on a dish towel. Later, I would dump the refuse into the compost pile in the back of the yard.

"Oh, I'm certain," she said in such a sarcastic way that it got me to laughing again.

"Don't you like him?"

"I like him fine enough as a neighbor. As a friend I've found him a bit too cocky for my tastes."

"Are there any men in existence of which you approve?" I asked, only half-teasingly.

Louisa sliced the bread on a wooden cutting board. "Of course there are—unfortunately they seem too few and far between. Take your brother. My regard is high when it comes to him, for it was well deserved. He was filled with humility and grace, and though ten times more handsome than Mr.

Bancroft, not one smile or dimple was wasted in attempts to charm the nurses."

I swallowed. She spoke truth about John. A better man I would probably never know. In some ways, I'd realized he did not belong of the earth to begin with. I oft wondered if that was why the Lord had chosen to call him home so soon. Better to think such things than to think my brother a mere casualty of war.

"As for others," Louisa continued, "I think tremendously much of Mr. Emerson, who has always been generous with me and allowed me to borrow from his grand library. I adored Mr. Thoreau also, bless his departed soul. He helped me think in different and new ways about our world—he showed me the depths of true creativity. My dear friend Alf, who used to help us perform our plays but has since moved away, is another. And now that I've somewhat forgiven him for stealing our Nan away, John is an absolute love. And Father, of course."

I noticed how she hadn't thought to include her father until the end. While there was no question she loved the man, I had quickly discerned a myriad of feelings she held toward the patriarch of the family—pity and gratitude mixed with a disguised dose of annoyance and frustration.

"I see," I said.

I wanted to ask more about Mr. Bancroft but decided that to express my interest would not be wise. And then Louisa's sister Anna—or Nan, as they often called her—came bustling in with her two-year-old Frederick and her newborn babe, John, and I was entirely immersed in the serving of dinner, the ensuing conversation on the idea of "recess" for children during a school day, and amusing ourselves with little Freddie's tiny antics at the table.

By the time the dishes were cleared, I'd very nearly forgotten about Mr. Bancroft altogether.

Very nearly.

CHAPTER TEN

Saw Nan [Anna] in her nest. . . . Very sweet and pretty,
but I'd rather be a free spinster and paddle my own canoe.

~ LMA

Johanna

"DO HAVE A GRAND TIME, Louisa, and please write often." I enveloped my friend in a hug and surprised myself by having to sniff back a few tears.

"Dear, you needn't remind me to write—seems I can do little else of late." She gave me her familiar smile, then picked up her valise from where it sat on the path.

Mr. Alcott waved his hand at us from the driver's seat of the Alcott carriage. "Come, Louisa, you will miss your ship!"

Her jolly expression grew somber, but her eyes remained light, and I could see what this trip—this seeing the world— meant to her. "I can scarce realize that my long-desired dream is coming true! Now, you mustn't hesitate to write of any problems. And as far as it is within your control, do discourage them from using any sort of credit while I'm gone, lest we have to dress in newspapers and live on potatoes when I return."

I nodded, though in truth I hadn't the slightest idea how she thought anything I could say would sway her strong-minded parents. I was little more than the maid. Why should they listen to me, particularly about such delicate matters as money?

I grabbed for John's ring at my neck as I watched Mr. Alcott drive Louisa away. I didn't turn from the road until the carriage was out of sight, and then I sat on the front stoop of Orchard House, realizing how empty it already felt. I wondered then if I had depended on Louisa too much. If, in trying to find a new adventure and freedom and a place to settle and call my own, I had latched on to her as a means of doing so.

I released a hefty sigh. I would write Mother a letter tonight. Perhaps a long one. Perhaps for the first time, I would include one of my poems. Louisa had said they were quite good, had encouraged me to keep writing and even submit them to publishers.

The last thought frightened me witless. It had taken days for me to work up the courage to show a few of my poems to Louisa, but to show them to a publisher, a man who had the power to stomp on my dreams with just a word?

I had decided to take this year to continue improving my poetry, to work up the pluck to begin submitting to maga-zines or newspapers. Surely one of them might take an inter-est, especially if my work improved.

The clap of a horse's hooves upon the dirt of the road drew me from my musings. A smart one-horse shay pulled by a gleaming chestnut mare stopped before Orchard House. From the driver's seat, Mr. Bancroft alighted, tying the reins to the Alcotts' carriage post.

I stood as he approached, doffing his hat slightly but not quite enough for me to get a full view of his lustrous locks. I tried to hide a smile. Surely Louisa was mistaken about why he performed the gesture.

"Miss Suhre, could I interest you in a carriage ride this fine morning? Have you had the pleasure of seeing Walden Pond yet?"

I hadn't, though I still wavered. I didn't know this man but knew Louisa didn't think much of him. Was it wise to spend time with him and without a chaperone? Mother would forbid it.

But the thought of a day in the lonely house intimidated. Mrs. Alcott rested upstairs. The laundry and cleaning had been accomplished yesterday with Louisa's help. Dinner would take little time to prepare—as the simple fare always did in the Alcott home.

I could accept Mr. Bancroft's invitation. I was now a woman of my own means . . . a bit like Louisa. Why should I not seize what the day had brought?

The scent of honeysuckle. The singing of robins and the cooing of doves. A blue sky and summer sun. Now an invitation to the pond, which I had wanted to see for some time, to explore more of this town that had captured my interest. Perhaps it might even spark a stanza or two?

"I think I should like that very much. Will you excuse me while I fetch my bonnet?"

Mr. Bancroft nodded, and I ran up the stairs, peeked in

on Mrs. Alcott, who dozed soundly, and went to my room—May's room—to get my bonnet. I'd only met the youngest Alcott once, but I appreciated her gracious ways and debated in my mind how two women raised by the same parents could be so incredibly different and yet so obviously fond of one another.

I tied my bonnet securely beneath my chin and bounded down the stairs, found Mr. Bancroft waiting for me. He helped me into the shay, and when the nerves in my hand tingled from where he touched my skin, I tried not to pay it more mind than a silly girl should.

Once I was situated, he tapped the mare's sides and the carriage lurched forward. My body bumped into his, and I tried to slide away, but there was not so much room in the one-horse shay, and Mr. Bancroft seemed entirely comfortable in taking up more than his share.

"I must admit I've come down my drive every day since we met hoping you might have a stray piece of laundry for me to fetch, and I've been disappointed every time."

I laughed, and the wind carried the sound in a manner that made me wonder if Mr. Bancroft thought it pleasant. "I am sorry to disappoint you, sir. I've kept a good hold of the laundry since that most unfortunate incident."

"Was it so unfortunate, now?" He looked at me sideways, and after glancing over at him, I quickly averted my gaze, silently cursed the color rushing to my cheeks.

"Meeting you wasn't unfortunate. Chasing one's laundry into the neighbor's yard, however . . ."

His grin was a teasing one. It pulled at the corners of his mouth and cast his features into a flattering display of light and dark beneath his hat. "I'm glad to have *that* cleared up, then."

We rode along in silence, a slight breeze rustling in the trees beyond before approaching to cool my face.

"How is your employment with the Alcotts getting along?"

"Quite well. I'm happy with the arrangement."

He nodded. "You are a brave woman to have traveled so far from home."

"My family's circumstances were changing. I must admit I was terribly jealous of John, my brother, being able to leave home and do something noble. Though I wish he hadn't had to leave us so permanently in doing so." I felt again for his ring at my neck. "After he passed, home wasn't the same. We were to move in with my brother and his new wife. I felt if I didn't break free now, I never would."

"I'm sorry." The sincerity in his deep voice caught me off guard.

I shook my head. "Forgive me. I share too much. You didn't ask my life story."

He chuckled—a pleasant, baritone sound that mingled with the clop of his mare's hooves on the road. "I'm quite interested, I assure you. What, Miss Suhre, did you feel the need to break free from?"

I shifted in my seat. Indeed, what was it I longed to break free from? For surely that was what I felt back at home, at least since John had died. Chained. Discontent. As if life was too short and fleeting and flighty for me to simply stay put where I was born and accept the way of things. Accept monotony.

I thought of Bryant's question—the one I had never answered. I should have talked to him. But how could I explain that I considered a life with him one of tedium? I could not be as straightforward as Louisa.

And yet how, in claiming I wanted to break free, could I explain this absurd need to feel as if I belonged? To find my place in this rough-and-tumble world, no matter the costs?

I chose my next words carefully, unsure of them myself. "I suppose I wanted a say in how my life should go."

"It sounds as if I'm tangling with a suffrage supporter."

I studied him, unable to discern his tone.

Not until I'd come to Concord had I given the suffrage of women much thought. My time in Pennsylvania had been one of growing up, of helping Mother after Father's death, and then of praying for John's safe return home. With the war among us, women's suffrage seemed fanciful, unimportant. But in the Alcott home, it was a favorite topic, right alongside the plight of the African. Even Mr. Alcott ardently supported the right of a woman to vote.

At first, I had simply accepted this passion as another sweet oddity at Orchard House—like their refusing to serve meat at the table and ministering to the many beggars who came to their kitchen door—but all the musings had prompted me to reflect on the subject. Why *shouldn't* women have the right to vote?

"And what would you say if I were, Mr. Bancroft?"

"I'd say I'm a proponent of the movement, though I think it will be a long while before it is realized."

I blinked. I'd expected resistance. Apparently Massachusetts men thought a bit differently than the men of my own small town. Or perhaps I had not made my way out of my four walls often enough to know what men of my own small town truly thought. What did Bryant think? And why did I care?

"You are surprised?" Mr. Bancroft asked.

"Yes, I suppose I am. I hadn't realized many men supported the notion. I know Mr. Alcott does, but he is . . ."

"An enigma, that is certain."

"A good enigma, I should state, lest you think me ungracious for their hospitality."

"Of course not."

I tilted my face to the sun, knew it would bring out the splattering of horrid freckles across the bridge of my nose and cheeks, but found myself not caring on such a splendid day, accompanied by what I was coming to think of as splendid company. "So why is it you support a woman's right to vote, when so many other men do not?"

"I believe giving women the vote would be to the general good of the people. Women are, as a whole, more righteous and moral than men. Therefore, I think it logical that they be allowed to voice their opinion, so that all of society might profit."

I kept silent, weighing whether to let my true views pour forth or keep them to myself. I could stay quiet, let Mr. Bancroft think me the righteous and moral woman he believed me to be, or I could open my mouth, set him quite to rights—and perhaps ruin my good standing in his eyes in the process.

Louisa would speak.

But I was not Louisa.

"You disagree with my logic, Miss Suhre? Come, tell me your beliefs. Am I so intimidating?"

I granted him a smile, then looked away. Through a thick copse of pine, I glimpsed the blue shimmer of water. "I'm not certain I wish to soil your view of me."

He directed the mare toward a carriage post but did not descend to tie her, rather waited until I voiced my response.

"I suppose I've seen enough of both sexes to know that neither are all good or all bad. I think it unfair to say to a woman, 'You are good just because you are a woman.' Or to a man, 'You are morally inferior because you are a man.' My brother, God rest his soul, was the best person I ever knew—not only because he was willing to make the ultimate sacrifice for the freedom of others, but because he knew compassion and integrity and kindness. I feel his heart was quite a bit purer than mine."

Mr. Bancroft stared at me, the curve of one side of his mouth tilted upward. I shifted in my seat, felt suddenly warm, wanted him to get down from the shay and tie his mare. Or perhaps, better yet, take me home.

"I've rendered you speechless, I see. Please feel free to see me back home if you find my company too forward."

"On the contrary, Miss Suhre, I find your company fascinating."

I stared at the rump of his mare, thought to ask, *Do you?* but decided that would be coy, and I did not wish to play a coquettish girl.

He alighted from the shay and held his hand out to me. I took it, permitting him to help me down. When I went to release his hand, he did not allow it. "I am sincere when I say I appreciate your forwardness. For a woman to not only speak her mind but to admit that she possesses as many flaws as her company does my heart good. Very good, in fact." He released my hand and offered his arm. I slipped my own around the fabric of his coat, tried not to notice the solidity of the muscles beneath.

"I'm not sure why Louisa doesn't care for you."

He laughed a loud, jolly laugh. "Louisa and I have some history between us."

I gave him a sideways glance as we descended a dirt path toward the pond. "Oh?"

"Nothing half as amusing or romantic as you might think, I assure you, Miss Suhre. Only business. My uncle—and my employer—is a publisher out of Boston. He's been urging me to find a good editor for his youth magazine, *Merry's Museum*. I was quite certain it would benefit both him and Louisa, but I think now I was too confident. Louisa rejected the idea outright, saying she wouldn't get behind such moral drivel. I've yet to accept her rejection, so I take it she thinks me muleheaded, is all."

"I see." That was all? Louisa didn't care for Mr. Bancroft because he wanted to offer her a job? I knew her to be moody, but this seemed beyond rationale.

I sighed. Louisa was often beyond rationale, and it was one of the reasons I respected her. She thought differently, was bold, unafraid to share her opinions. Thinking back to my conversation with Mr. Bancroft, I wondered if her ways hadn't rubbed off on me a bit. It felt good to share my views openly, to be encouraged by them, even.

We reached the shore of the lake, and I closed my eyes and

breathed deeply of pine and water and mud and honeysuckle. When I opened them, I noted how the sunlight danced off the pond, how the wind played a melody on the leaves of the trees, sweeping across the breadth of the water until it reached where I stood with my hand on Mr. Bancroft's arm, then continued past us.

"It's beautiful."

"I have not come enough. This place centers me when I get caught up in the world or my work. I tend to take life too seriously. This helps me see the big picture."

I murmured an agreement. "What is the big picture to you, Mr. Bancroft?"

A small smile again played on his mouth. "That I am but a speck in this big world. That it has gone on long before me and will continue long after me. But although I am a speck, I have a story to live. A journey. A duty to better it, even in a small way."

Something stirred within my heart. "That is very noble."

"It is, isn't it? If only what I long for in my heart could translate so perfectly to my life. You are certainly not the only one with flaws, Miss Suhre."

"But that is part of the journey, no? Struggling with our moral shortcomings and wrestling with our sin, striving to improve oneself with God's help and guidance?"

He looked down at the wet sand at our feet. "Perhaps." Seeming to shake himself from his thoughts, he gestured toward the right of the pond, to a path within the pines that wound its way along the lake.

"You work in publishing, then?" I asked.

"I do. My uncle got me started, but it did not take much

persuasion on his part. Books have always been a big part of my life."

"Me too. It must be wonderful to have a life's work with words."

"It's a blessing, that's certain. Right now, I'm trying to get a boys' magazine off the ground, something filled with heroic and moral tales, perhaps a few suggestions for a boy's adventure. What do you think?"

"It sounds marvelous and should help promote literacy in our youth, which is indeed a favorable thing. With the war over, it is noble to build not only the country, but the minds of our children."

He smiled at me again in that way of his that had me thinking he truly did think me fascinating. He truly did enjoy my company.

The thought caused a thrill of pleasure to swirl through me and for a reason I couldn't quite name, I felt important— perhaps more so than I had in all my life.

We walked along the entire body of water, speaking of our favorite books and authors—Dickens and Irving and Brontë and Whitman and Poe, along with Concord's own Emerson and Thoreau. We looped our way around the pond, and I acknowledged to myself that this was the most perfect day I could have ever imagined.

When Mr. Bancroft helped me down from the shay and walked me up to the front door of Orchard House, I felt a heaviness in my spirit that our time had come to an end.

"I'm to leave for Boston tomorrow. I won't be back until next week. Perhaps I could enjoy more of your company then?"

My heart ricocheted around my insides. "I would very much like that."

He bowed, raised my hand to his lips, where he pressed the slightest of kisses upon it. When he rose, he gave me a bold wink and then was off. I watched him drive up the lane to his house and I did not move until he was out of sight—not because I wanted him to see me staring, but because quite of a sudden, my legs felt no stronger than Mother's rice pudding.

CHAPTER ELEVEN

Places have not much hold on me
when the persons who made them dear are gone.

~ LMA

Taylor

THE BENNETT HOUSE hadn't changed much, and I found that both comforting and disconcerting all at once. So much had happened in sixteen years—it seemed that should be represented in the home before me. But besides a few extra cracks in the driveway and the boxwood grown in a little too close to the siding, the home which represented the only family I'd ever known looked just about the same.

In Victoria's passenger seat, I tucked my hands beneath my thighs to still their quivering. My rental car was still at the inn, and I regretted allowing her to bring me to Paul and Lorraine's. I could have used a few minutes to gather myself.

She parked in front of the garage, and I tried to block out the deplorable images of the last time I was there, of Will and Victoria in front of those very same garage doors, of the nervous breakdown I'd had, the honking of the horn, the virulent tears of disbelief washing my face in what would be the beginning of a long grief.

I swallowed down the memory. "You sure it's okay that I'm here?"

Victoria took the key from the ignition. "Of course it is. They're going to be so happy to see you. You *belong* here."

If that were true, I wondered why I didn't feel it. If I really did belong, wouldn't I have made my way back sooner? Wouldn't it have bothered me more to be so far away for so long?

I opened the passenger door, clutched the bag I'd just purchased from Orchard House. I followed Victoria into the house.

The first thing that hit me was the smell of banana oatmeal cookies. It was mixed in with the scents of tomato sauce and garlic bread, but I picked it out right away. It wafted through the air and into my nostrils, where it seemed to tease forth every single pleasant memory that had made up my time at the Bennett home.

We hung our purses on the hooks in the entryway and I followed Victoria to the kitchen. "Hi, honey." I heard Lorraine's voice. "Are the kids taking the late bus—?" She stopped short at the sight of me.

I stood at the threshold, taking her in. She'd stopped dyeing her hair and it was a gorgeous, sharp gray, cut just at her chin, making her look sophisticated and beautiful at the same time.

I hadn't realized how much I'd missed her until this moment, hadn't realized how being here—seeing her—might quite likely be my undoing.

"So I brought home a surprise . . . ," Victoria was saying, even as it must have been apparent what the surprise was.

I gave Lorraine a sheepish grin, and her face crumpled. She placed a hand on the counter as if to hold herself up. That's when I noticed her painfully obvious flat chest.

Victoria rushed over to her, but she held a hand up. "I'm okay. I'm okay."

She straightened, stumbled forward a step, but seemed to gather herself. "Taylor . . . it's really you?"

I hadn't expected my presence to mean so obviously much to her. The fact that it did sent my bottom lip quivering. I bit it, hard. "It's me." I forced one side of my mouth into a smile, but it didn't hold.

Lorraine put her arms out to me, and for a moment, I couldn't comprehend that she meant for me to step into them, to come to her.

Seconds must have passed before I realized the arms were intended for me. And while a part of me was scared to drop into them, another part couldn't bear leaving them waiting, her pale forearms hanging above the counter, veins translucent through skin much looser than I remembered.

I should have come home years ago, when the thought was nothing more than fancy. But as the years had passed, it seemed crazy to return home and hope for anything. And the possibility of defeat had been too dark of a shadow I couldn't get out from beneath.

Now I stumbled forward and fell into the welcoming embrace, tucking my own arms around her, careful not to press too hard lest I hurt some part of her. I closed my eyes as I perched my chin above her shoulder, tried to contain my tears.

I had once thought an embrace was risky, and in many ways I still did. But here, seeing my mom, knowing her life was threatened, I couldn't think of a better risk to take. "I'm sorry," I whispered. Sorry for leaving without a word all these years, sorry for taking all she'd done for me for granted, for stealing it and then trying to pretend I could pay it all back with a single bank check.

She shushed me, and I sank farther into the warm embrace, the scent of her Elizabeth Arden perfume once again taking me back many years.

"I should have done this all along." She clutched me tighter also, rubbed my back with her hands.

A tear meandered down my cheek, warm and vulnerable. All at once, I knew that this was the missing link in my life. All those years ago, I hadn't realized what I had—I was too busy doubting my place, doubting my rights to such a life.

Instead, I should have been grateful for the love the Bennetts offered.

Behind me, Victoria sniffed, and I slowly released Lorraine.

I swiped at my tear. "I should have called, written, visited, even. I wasn't angry at—"

She cupped my face with her hand. "I know, Taylor. I know."

I felt Victoria draw back. But I didn't regret what I said. I wanted Lorraine to know. I *hadn't* been angry at her. I'd been angry at Victoria. At Will. At God for bringing an angel into my life and ripping it out so violently, at transferring guardianship to my sister.

Lorraine wiped the bottom halves of her lids with the

backs of her thumbs and straightened. "We have a lot of catching up to do. I hope you plan on staying for supper?"

I glanced at Victoria, who nodded but didn't look quite as peppy as before. "Of course she is." She opened a utility closet on the other side of the wall and grabbed two aprons, threw one at me. "What needs to be done?"

Lorraine beamed. "Just the salad and setting—"

The creak of the front door and loud footsteps pounding down the hall interrupted her. "It's vacation! Woo-hoo!" The footsteps barreled around the corner until I caught sight of their owner—a towheaded boy of about nine who practically plowed into Victoria, throwing his arms around her waist.

Victoria laughed, ruffled his hair. "Happy vacation, kiddo. How was your day?"

"Great! We did an obstacle course in gym and I was the fastest!"

"That's wonderful, honey. Here, I want you to meet someone very special." She turned her son around and for a second I felt as if someone had punched me firm and swift in the gut. This kid was the spitting image of Will. A young Will, anyway. I recognized it from one of the slides his parents had shown me when we were dating. I still remembered the snapshot, young boy Will at the top of Mount Washington, hands on his hips as if he'd conquered the world.

Had Victoria seen the picture? Did she realize the resemblance?

I shook my head. But of course she did. A wife would know those things.

Victoria held her other arm out and I forced my attention away from the boy to look at a beautiful young girl of about thirteen. Her features—from blue eyes to prominent cheekbones—were so obviously Victoria's, but if possible, she was even prettier than Victoria had been at her age. "Maddie, come here, honey. I want you to meet your aunt Taylor."

I cringed at the name, saw the girl named Maddie do the same. I stepped forward, even as Victoria's daughter did not. "Just Taylor's fine."

Victoria couldn't thrust me on her kids like this and expect them to slap a label in front of my name as prominent as "Aunt," to force some sort of relationship that wasn't there. And these kids . . . these beautiful children . . . Victoria and Will's children . . .

Victoria's smile grew tight. "Of course, I'm being too hasty. Taylor, this is Maddie. And this is Caden. Guys, this is my sister I was telling you about."

Huh. I wondered how that conversation had gone. *"Hey, kids, guess what? You have an aunt I never told you about or talked about. Well, not really your aunt and maybe not really my sister, but she lived with us for a bit when I was growing up and after I stole her boyfriend—your dad—I never saw her again. But now we'll be one big happy family."*

Right.

I stepped forward, thrust my hand out to Caden, who was closer. "Nice to meet you."

Caden took it, and something sticky nearly glued our palms together. I fought the urge to snatch my hand back and wipe it on my pants.

"Aren't you the writer? The one Mom's always reading? We saw your books at Target, you know."

"Did you?"

"Yeah, right on the end. Mom says they save that for the best books."

Hey, what do you know? Cute kid. Suddenly I didn't quite mind his sticky hands as much and even tried not to imagine what the mystery substance was that pulled slightly at my skin when we released the handshake. It was probably foreign and not bodily. One could hope.

I turned to Victoria's daughter, offered a handshake. "It's nice to meet you, Maddie."

My hand hung in the air and I looked at the young teen, arms crossed, leaning against the doorway with smoldering eyes.

"Maddie Rose . . ." Victoria's tone held a warning, and her daughter dropped her arms with a sigh, reluctantly held her hand out to me.

She clasped it for the shortest possible amount of time, then drew away, looked at her fingers, and wiped them on her pants. "Your hands are dirty," she said.

I scratched my brow. Throwing her brother under the bus for getting my hands sticky would probably not win anyone over. What did she have against me anyway?

I decided to try one more time. "You look so much like your mom when we were your age."

She shrugged and turned around. "I'll be upstairs," she threw over her shoulder.

Wow, what a peach.

Victoria patted Caden's back. "Go wash up, then take some cookies outside while we finish up supper, okay?"

Caden didn't have to be told twice. In no time, he was

shoving banana oatmeal cookies into his pockets and the screen door was slamming behind him.

Victoria smoothed her hair. "I'm sorry about Maddie. She's going through a . . . stage."

I tried to brush it off. "I'm sure trying to thrust a new family member onto a teenage girl isn't easy." If anyone could relate, it would be her.

Victoria washed her hands, then reached for a cutting board. "Yeah, but she didn't have to be so rude. I'll talk to her later."

Lorraine poured a cup of tea, then offered it to me. I accepted. "Tell us what you've been up to, Taylor. And don't leave anything out. Once Victoria found out you were Casey Hood, I bought every last one of your novels. They're wonderful. You truly do have a talent. I'm so proud of you."

I couldn't help but bask in the words, soak in the fact that the woman I knew as "Mom" was proud of me, that I had in fact found approval from her. I looked at Victoria's back, seemingly stiff as she attacked a head of lettuce with a long, sharp knife.

Good. Let her feel. Let her feel pain, if necessary. Enough of this pretending to want a perfect, sisterly relationship. Enough of this "wade through some of the ugly past" stuff as if it were no more than a small stretch of salty water with a few unpleasant pieces of stringy seaweed. No, this was hard stuff. Real stuff. And I wanted her to see that, even if it took a little bit of jealousy to get there.

"Thanks . . . Mom. That means a lot to me."

She glowed. "We've missed you, honey."

I smiled and nodded but couldn't quite find my voice to

communicate the same sentiment. Maybe because I wasn't ready, maybe because I still felt I had some penance to pay before I was let back into the Bennett family, maybe because I didn't know if I even wanted to be let back in, or maybe because in some crazy way, I thought that it might hurt Victoria's feelings to see Lorraine and me fix our relationship so easily, and maybe I didn't want to hurt my sister after all.

Again, Lorraine tucked an arm around me, another around Victoria. "It's so great to have both my girls under this roof again. Wait until your dad comes home."

From within the embrace, Victoria and I caught one another's gazes. I smiled. We needed peace. At least here, in front of our mother. Whatever simmered beneath could stay there awhile longer or maybe forever. As long as Lorraine didn't see it.

CHAPTER TWELVE

The home-making, the comfort, the sympathy, the grace,
and atmosphere that a true woman can provide is the noble part,
and embraces all that is helpful for soul as well as body.

~ LMA

Taylor

I LOWERED MYSELF to the dining room chair, took in the five faces surrounding the table. Paul sat at the head of the table, fully bald but in a striking, Mr. Clean sort of way. He'd been surprised to see me but, like Lorraine, had welcomed me without questions into his strong arms, the scent of Old Spice and leather more comforting than I thought it would be.

I shouldn't have been surprised by this unmerited grace from them, and yet I was. For it was one thing to forgive past hurts and move on—it was another to *actually* move on, to cling to gratitude and to one another's hands around a dinner table where so much history mingled between us all.

I didn't question the holding of hands during a short prayer before the meal. It was like nothing we'd ever done while I stayed at the Bennetts' as a teen, but it seemed fitting, nice. Paul's husky voice filled the room as he thanked an unseen God for the food, the gift of life and family, and even specifically for me. When he was finished, I released Lorraine's and Caden's hands—no longer sticky—and passed Caden's plate for Victoria to dish out a piece of lasagna.

Maddie looked sulkily at the empty place beside her. "Isn't Dad coming?"

I'd wondered the same thing but admitted relief when we'd sat down without Will. I supposed I would have to face him eventually. Just like I had to face Victoria and Lorraine and Paul. But Will was different. Sure, I'd seen him that last day in front of the garage, but the night before that we'd walked downtown, grabbed a couple sandwiches at Main Streets, reminisced about the night we first met—a date gone wrong, a sign on the back of a bathroom door, an angel latte.

How would things have been different if I'd never seen that sign? Would I never have left Concord? Would Victoria and I still be close? Would I never have written eighteen bestsellers? I certainly never would have met Kevin.

Would things have been better? Or worse?

I truly couldn't say.

And really it didn't matter.

But I'd learned one thing: never depend on something good coming from a bathroom prayer. Any prayer.

"He's working late." Victoria dished out some salad beside Caden's lasagna. He wrinkled his nose and I hid a smirk. He caught my amusement and wrinkled it again, obviously enjoying being the one to elicit a smile from me.

"Again? On a Friday night?" Maddie slumped in her chair, picked up her fork to spear a piece of romaine.

"He has that big project due soon, right? For the city?" Paul asked.

Victoria nodded. "There was some sort of snag last week that set them back. We'll all be happy when it's done."

I studied Victoria's rigid shoulders, her downturned mouth. Funny how despite our time apart, I could still read her better than one of her beloved Louisa May Alcott books. And right now I knew—something bothered her. And I didn't think it had to do with Lorraine being sick or her and me *wading* through the past. It had to do with whatever was bothering her daughter. If I had to guess, I'd say it had to do with Will.

I took a bite of lasagna, ricotta and mozzarella and sauce and sausage all melting in my mouth in a display of esculent perfection. "This is fantastic," I said after chewing. "I—I don't cook much. Neither does Kevin, but there's something about a home-cooked meal. Especially one of *your* home-cooked meals. Thank you so much."

Lorraine smiled, finished chewing carefully. "I hope you'll stay for many more. There's always room at this table for you, got that?"

I gave an awkward smile but averted my gaze, grabbed for the honey mustard dressing.

"Who's Kevin?" This from Maddie.

I looked up in surprise. "He's my boyfriend."

"You should have brought him," Lorraine said. "We would have loved to meet him."

I shook my head. For some reason the thought of my two separate worlds meeting caused no small amount of anxiety. "He's in Denver on business. Maybe some other time." Before they could ask more questions, I turned to Maddie and Caden. "So what grades are you guys in?"

Caden wiped his mouth, full of orange French dressing and mozzarella, on his sleeve. Victoria handed him a napkin.

"Third! And I'm the fastest kid in my grade."

Maddie rolled her eyes.

"How about you, Maddie? Middle school?"

She nodded. "Seventh."

I caught Victoria's gaze. We'd been in seventh grade when I first moved in with the Bennetts. "Seventh grade can be tough," I said.

Maddie shrugged and sighed, twirled a piece of stringy mozzarella around her fork. I wondered if the girl was always this moody or if perhaps she had something specifically against me. Did she harbor resentment over the fact that I'd never been around and upon arrival her mother wanted her to call me "Aunt"? I wouldn't be so fond of me, either.

We chatted quietly over the rest of dinner, Caden talking about his plans to build a clubhouse over vacation, Victoria cautioning him that Will would be busy at work and probably not able to help.

Once our bellies were full and our plates empty, Paul insisted on clearing the table with the kids, leaving me, Victoria, and Lorraine to talk over our decaf coffee.

The hazelnut roast warmed my insides. I directed my next words to Lorraine, asking what I'd wanted to ask all through dinner but had felt wouldn't have been tactful. "So what's the plan for your treatment?"

She dragged in a deep breath. "Chemotherapy for probably another five months, followed by radiation, with tons of prayer in between."

"How do you feel?"

"A little tired, but more emotionally than physically. It does my heart good that you're here. Will you be able to stay for a while?"

My mind scrambled to think of an answer I wouldn't later regret. "I booked three nights at the inn. I have a deadline in July, so I do need to make time for that, but . . ." I didn't want to offer to stay longer if I wasn't welcome. But I didn't want to run away too quick again either.

I caught Victoria smiling at me. I scrunched up my face as if to ask, *"What's so funny?"*

She shook her head. "I just can't get over the fact that you actually have real deadlines now . . . and you *make* them."

We laughed, all of us, and it felt good.

On a whim, Victoria grabbed for my hand. I stilled beneath her touch, tried to stop myself from pulling away. "Hey, why don't you stick around the next week or so if you can? The three of us can hang out, maybe you can get some writing done, and we're having Jo March Writing Camp over April vacation. Maddie's attending for the last time. I could use some help and who better to teach a bunch of young writers than Casey Hood?"

"I—I'm flattered, but I'm not sure—"

This time it was Lorraine who grabbed for my hand. Her skin felt cool compared to Victoria's, more loose around the bones than my sister's. Would she survive? I'd wasted so much time. Blocked out what the Bennetts had meant to me.

"I'd love it if you'd stay in your old room, Taylor. There's no need to be at the inn."

I swallowed the lump in my throat. "I don't know . . ." This was all happening too fast. Yes, I was glad to be here, relieved for the warm welcome, but to sleep in my old room tonight? "I think I'll just stay at the inn. I'm only right down the street and—"

Lorraine squeezed my hand tighter and I felt a desperation in it that scared me. "Please, Taylor. I—now that you're here, I don't want to lose a moment. Give me this much. Don't you owe it—?" She stopped, but it was too late. The words were already out in the open.

I owed her.

And she was right. I slid my hand from hers.

She shook her head. "I'm sorry. I shouldn't have said—I didn't mean . . ."

But she did. And didn't I deserve the words?

"It's okay," I whispered, dragging in a deep breath. "I suppose I could get some writing done here . . . and it might be fun to do some teaching . . ."

Victoria smiled, but it seemed guarded. Surely she had her own doubts about me staying here too. "The kids will be excited to have you. And I found something the other day that I want to show you." She shrugged, gave me a look forced with hope. "Who knows? Maybe it will be just like—"

She seemed to catch herself, and I was glad of it.

Because we couldn't fool ourselves into thinking it would be just like old times. It wouldn't. And I needed to remind myself of that more than anyone.

I was here for Lorraine. Maybe now I was here to write a book.

End of story.

CHAPTER THIRTEEN

I like to help women help themselves, as that is, in my opinion,
the best way to settle the Woman question.

~ LMA

Johanna

NOVEMBER 17, 1865

Dearest Johanna,

I was so very glad to receive your long scribble, to
hear that Marmee and my dear old Plato are doing
well. Please do not fret over my parting comment about
keeping on top of their spending—it was wrong of me
to make it. I will settle things when I return, which I
am not quite ready to think upon yet!

Still, it touches me to see how they miss me, think
of me, and long to have me back. I begin to realize
how much I am to them in spite of all my faults, and
knowing this sort of love lightens my spirit all the more.

The boredom I felt at Schwalbach is gone. I think
I've had enough of spa life to last me quite some time.

I try to be patient with Anna, but we are an amusing match—she who can't stand the thought of books and spends her time doing nothing but playing backgammon and cribbage. I am not even sure the patience of an angel will be enough to see me through the rest of my time with her.

Ah, but Vevey! This small spa town should not be underestimated. The Alps stand tall and proud, white spectral shapes towering above the green hills and valleys they lie between. Lake Leman was beyond comparison, and the Pension Victoria houses not only comfortable rooms, but a cast of characters fit for any book I might write—and I find myself again quite amused, even as I know that I, a thirty-three-year-old Yankee spinster, am but one of them.

There is a Frenchwoman who offered me French lessons but grew most impatient with me after two lessons. I am not as discouraged as I perhaps should be. A pleasant Englishwoman and her daughter have been a welcome distraction, and two Scottish ladies who have met Sir Walter Scott have refreshed me.

If there was to be an evil character in this play of Vevey, it would be Colonel Polk. A Confederate commander, he travels with his family but turns his nose up at Anna and me—two Yankee women who certainly disgust him, though I can't say I wouldn't like to pluck a feather or two from his cap if I had the chance, either.

The last character is one who has completely intrigued me—Ladislas Wisniewski. Don't fear on the pronunciation—two hiccups and a sneeze will give you the name quite perfectly! He insists we call him Laddie, and I have to admit it hasn't been since your brother that I've come to admire a man so. He is young, a Polish refugee who fought against Russia in the insurrection. He has come to Vevey to attempt to heal his failing lungs. The poor thing cannot seem to get rid of a brutal hacking cough, but ah, when he plays the piano and has a peaceful break from his coughing fits, there is nothing more lovely.

Listen to me—a spinster turned into a simpering girl! But you know as well as anyone, that I like boys and oysters raw—and Laddie is just so. He does not put on airs, and when I once asked him to play the Polish national anthem, which Polish villagers had sung while under the attack of the Cossacks, my dear friend hesitated, fearful to offend any Russian guests at the boardinghouse.

I insisted. "I should rather enjoy that insult to your bitter enemy," I said.

And do you know what he returned? "Ah, mademoiselle, it is true we are enemies, but we are also gentlemen."

I am not sure I will ever learn what it is to be noble and good, but I feel blessed to have angels in my path—such as your brother and Laddie—to show me the way. We enjoy ourselves by taking long walks, sailing on the lake, and giving one another English and French lessons, to which Laddie often becomes frustrated, slapping his forehead and lamenting, "I am imbecile. I never can will shall to have learn this beast of English!"

I feel both young and old when I am with him. He brings me flowers at every dinner and tucks sweet notes beneath the door of my room, and I look forward to our long conversations in the evening. If I were in my right mind, I would burn this letter before I send it. I've spoken of him to such extent not even with May, for I know she will think me foolish, having feelings for one so much younger. Soon I will have to put them in my pocket, as it is a romance that is never meant to be, but for now, they are flying free.

I suppose I haven't much of a right to caution you about Mr. Bancroft, as I've thrown caution to the wind these last couple of months. I see now how the heady feelings of love can do that to us, and yet I wish we could better heed the lesson of my Sylvia in Moods *and not be ruled by them. How hard it is, though!*

You are a grown woman, Johanna. My opinion of Mr. Bancroft—Nathan, as I noticed you called him in your last letter—should not matter. I only wish you to not be hasty in making any future plans, especially without your family close by. I imagine you may feel lonely, and Nathan has filled that longing, as I feel the same when it comes to Laddie. I know Concord must be preparing for husking parties about now, and I trust you will enjoy yourself with the company, the cider, the dancing red ears of corn. Please send my regards to all.

I've an idea for a new novel, and though it is a bit sensational, I cannot keep it from my head. It's about a young girl who is duped into marrying a less-than-worthy fellow and who comes to regret it. I think it will take place in Europe, for I feel I can further enjoy this time if I can conjure up characters in my head who will bask in this beautiful setting along with me.

Give my love to the family, as I know the letters are sometimes few and far between.

Yours,
Louisa

January 7, 1866

Dearest Louisa,

What a pleasure to receive your letter and hear of your adventures! Vevey sounds breathtaking and your companions—particularly Ladislas—most delightful.

Orchard House is well. Christmas was warm here—not warm in temperature but in spirit. A simple affair in which your parents invited the many needy into their home for cider, pumpkin pie, and gingerbread. Nathan joined us, and though he seemed a bit taken aback by the company kept, he ended up having as jolly a time as the rest of us and even sang as I coaxed some carols from Elizabeth's old piano. Your mother said that if Lizzie could have looked down from heaven, she surely would have been pleased. I do hope so.

Nathan continues to court me and has even read some of my poems and is showing them to his uncle to see if he can use any in his publications. He is away in Boston much and it's a wonder that he doesn't permanently reside there, but he says he likes to get away from the city and rest in the country. He certainly does have much on his plate and does not seem to enjoy the shorter winter days. They can be trying, though when he is home, we have a capital time jingling about in his sleigh or ice-skating on Goose Pond. We even rode about on horseback before the snows came and enjoyed the cattle show, which I found very pleasing.

Your new idea sounds fascinating, and yes, sensational. Can't you write a sweet little love story just one time? Always such heavy subjects with you! But I know you have heavy thoughts—they must come out best in a story. I will look forward to reading it.

I can't wait to hear more of your adventures, my dear friend. Write soon.

Yours,
Johanna

CHAPTER FOURTEEN

I found one of mother's notes in my journal. . . .
I often think what a hard life she has had since she married—
so full of wandering and all sorts of worry!

~ LMA

Taylor

I CAME OUT OF THE SHOWER to hear my cell phone ringing. I entered the bedroom and lunged for the phone on the bed. My old bed. In my old room. Funny to be here now, in this place where I'd spent so much of my teen years.

It looked different now. Maddie stayed here often on the weekends and had painted and decorated it to her liking— lots of pictures of the ocean and soccer players I didn't know. And yet my heart had near leapt from my chest when I perused her bookcase, seeing my old tattered copy of *Little Women* on the top shelf.

I'd slipped it from its place with care, noted how the binding was looser than ever and wondered if Maddie had read the book as voraciously as I had. Strange how that thought warmed me.

I tapped the green button and put the phone to my ear. "Hello?"

"Hey, beautiful. Where you been?"

I breathed out in relief. "Kevin." It was nice to hear his voice, and for a moment I felt guilty for not thinking about him more these past couple of days, for not missing him when I went into Boston for dinner before seeing *Les Misérables* with Lorraine and Victoria, for not thinking to call him after I ran the trail through Minute Man national park while Lorraine and Paul were at church that morning. "I'm sorry. I've gotten wrapped up with everything here."

"That's okay. You'll be home tomorrow night, right? I'm flying in too. Let's meet up for a romantic dinner. I had the best stuffed shrimp here and I think I know what the secret ingredient was. What do you say I try it out on you?"

"Oh, that sounds wonderful . . ."

A second of strained silence. "But . . . ?"

"I've decided to stay around a little longer."

"What? Really? When were you going to tell me?"

I fumbled through my suitcase for a pair of jeans. "When I talked to you, which I guess is now."

There was a moment of silence on the other end. "I don't get it, Taylor."

"What?" But I knew.

"I don't expect your world to revolve around me—I think you know that by now. But I would like to think I matter enough to keep me in the loop."

I closed my eyes. He was right. I was being inconsiderate. Yes, I wanted my independence, but Kevin was part of my world in California, part of where I belonged. And somehow all of that felt ten times safer than being back in Concord.

I couldn't take it for granted. I wouldn't.

"You're right. I really am sorry. I should have called sooner."

A long sigh on the other end of the line. "How long will you be staying?"

I pulled on jeans, sponged up my wet hair with a towel. "At least through the week. I'm helping Victoria out with some classes at Orchard House. I'll work on my writing while I'm here."

"Maybe I could fly over Tuesday morning."

I felt suddenly hot, my just-showered skin sticky and flushed.

You know the fight-or-flight response theory? Well, in my books, I always made my characters fighters. Face their situation, no matter how unpleasant, and deal with it. It's because I had a lot of respect for that ability. It's because *I* wanted to be like that.

But I'd known ever since that day I saw my boyfriend's lips all over my sister's that I wasn't a fighter. I was a flighter. Because I didn't think smashing Victoria's laptop in a fit of fury exactly qualified as fighting.

Now, talking to Kevin, I couldn't bear to face his question head-on. I couldn't bear to face the reality of what we were, of what we were likely never to be.

"I don't know, Kevin. Things are . . . strained. Hey, I actually have to run. Victoria's picking me up for Jo March Writing Camp and I just got out of the shower." My sister had offered the ride, and I had accepted. I figured it'd be less awkward than arriving in the middle of a bunch of young kids by myself and not knowing where to go, what to do.

"Yeah. Okay. Great. Have fun." He hung up, the silence speaking his frustration better than a sad, crooning love song ever could.

I threw the phone back on the bed and pulled a light sweater over my head. Was it my fault that every relationship I had was fraught with some sort of dysfunction? Scientific probability would say yes.

Why, then, couldn't I own it?

I scooped up my brush and began yanking it through my hair with vigor. Large clumps caught in the bristles, and I released the tension, started again, pulling harder, almost savoring the sting on my head which distracted me from the emotional pain I didn't want to dwell on.

Kevin had asked me to see a counselor once with him. I'd denied him right away. Maybe though . . . maybe I should revisit the possibility. I was thirty-seven years old, for pity's sake. I couldn't live like this forever.

I worked a tiny amount of mousse into my hair, blow-dried it until it was presentable, put on a small amount of makeup, then scooped up my cell phone, laptop bag, and the book Victoria had given me last night, *Aunt Jo's Literary Lessons*, that served as part of the instructional writing time at Jo March Writing Camp. Victoria had told me I could use the book as a guide, or I could wing it. She was leaving the entire instructional writing time up to me, and I wasn't quite so confident I should be trusted with it.

The scent of coffee lingered in the kitchen, but when I entered the large area, bright with morning sun splashing on clean, white cabinets, it was empty. I opened the cabinet to the right of the refrigerator, found the travel mugs there, just as I'd remembered, and poured freshly brewed coffee into one of them.

I heard the side door open, thought to yell and let Victoria know that I'd be right out, but didn't want to wake Lorraine or Paul if they still slept.

I looked around for sugar, couldn't find any, but opened the fridge and settled for a dash of creamer, then screwed the lid on top of the mug. Victoria didn't like to be late. I might not be ready to make amends with my sister, but I didn't need to start off our week together by annoying her, either.

I turned but stopped short at the sight before me.

Not Victoria, but her husband.

"Will." I regretted speaking his name the instant it left my lips. It sounded too . . . personal. Too wrong.

"Taylor, hey. I didn't expect—I mean, Caden left his glove somewhere around here. I'm dropping him off at baseball camp this morning."

I hated to admit how good he looked. Too good. His hair still full, his jaw clean-shaven, he looked to have aged only about half the amount I knew he had—and every year fit him. His shoulders had only grown broader, his presence doing the same thing it had done to me all those years ago.

Only this time, he was a married man. My sister's man.

"Victoria told me you were back in town. It's good to see you. Real good. You look great."

"Um . . . yeah, you too."

That should have been it. He had a glove to find, I had a

teaching gig to get to, but we both just stood there, the world seeming to stand still with us.

He rubbed the back of his neck, and I tried to suppress the feelings pouring through me, feelings that spoke of regret and jealousy and hurt over what my sister and Will had done to me all those years ago. Standing with him there across the room, I didn't even want to ignore it. Just once, I wanted to bask in it. Bask in the hurt and shame and rejection, in all the unholy feelings coursing through me.

He cleared his throat. "I tried to call you. Kind of a lot, actually. When I came back from Iraq, I didn't know where you were . . ."

I shook my head. Iraq? He'd joined up after all? Gone to war?

I tried to fit this new reality in my head, tried to piece together Victoria and Will with this new slice of information. I wanted to ask but thought better of it. Instead, I decided to pretend I already knew. "I changed my number. Listen, none of this matters anymore, right? We're good, okay?" I smiled, a little too brightly maybe, to indicate that everything was fine. That the past could simply be swept under the proverbial rug and all would be well.

"I'd like to talk with you sometime. Clear the air a bit. You think that'd be all right?"

I laughed—more like snorted. "You sound just like your wife. You remember her, right? I don't think it's a great idea for us to talk or clear the air." My words were fighting words, surprising even myself.

"Victoria thinks it's a good idea. And so do I."

I rolled my eyes. "Whatever."

"Okay . . . maybe tonight?"

I rubbed my temples. "Tonight? No, Will, not okay. I'm sorry—I just can't do this. And don't you have some big project due that's taking all your time?"

"This is more important. You're more important."

The young woman inside me wanted to be flattered at his words. But the more mature, life-hardened woman wasn't fooled.

"I need to go. I'll be around for the week." I brushed past him and he didn't move out of the way. My shoulder skimmed his arm and I clamped it to my side, as if I'd been burned.

The side door opened and Victoria appeared. "Oh, hey." She looked past me at Will.

"You know where he left his glove?" Will asked her, more than an edge of impatience in his tone—one that changed completely when speaking to his wife.

"Um, might be upstairs."

He went toward the stairs, Victoria's gaze following him, something cold—or maybe just sad—within her eyes. Was she mad we'd been alone, or was it the same thing that I caught the other night at dinner, the thing I heard in Will's hard tone, that feeling that something wasn't quite right between the two of them?

She turned to me, put on a sunny expression. "Ready?"

I looked back up the stairs, to where we'd last seen Will, and blinked. "Yeah. I was just getting some coffee."

I didn't think there could have been a more peculiar situation if I pulled it from one of my books. I followed her out the door to her car.

"Victoria, are you guys all right? I mean, if me staying here is going to create—"

"Everything's fine, okay?" She gave me a tight smile. "Let's just have a great day. This is my favorite week at Orchard House and Maddie's excited. Let's have fun."

I slid into the passenger seat, said hi to Victoria's daughter, who nodded at me but didn't bother taking out her earbuds.

Victoria put the car in drive. "So what did you think of the book? It's basic, but I think it works for our purposes."

"Yeah, I think it's perfect, but I have to admit I've never taught kids before. Only adults. I'm a little nervous."

There. I'd admitted vulnerability. Surely that was some sort of healthy relationship marker. Maybe I didn't need to keep seeing a counselor after all.

"Oh, you'll be great! The staff is so excited that *the* Casey Hood is going to teach, and I know the kids will be floored as well."

"Floored, huh?

She gave me a guilty grin. "I'm a dweeb, yes. Some things never change."

"So who usually teaches the classes? I don't want to usurp anyone."

"That would be me, so no need to worry about that."

I wanted to ask her if she still wrote or if she'd traded in dreams of publication for those of marriage and children, but I couldn't bring myself to voice the question.

She stopped at a light. "I'm serious about not imposing on your time, though. There are two classes. One first thing in the morning and one after lunch. If you want to borrow my car, you can go back home, or . . . well, I had Luke set up a little something special for you in the school."

"School?"

"Bronson Alcott's School of Philosophy?"

"Really? Wow, that'd be great. Who's Luke?"

"The groundskeeper."

She pulled into the driveway beside Orchard House and drove her van up the hill. When she parked it at the top, we grabbed our stuff and the three of us trooped down the stairs. When we reached the school, she turned to Maddie. "Go on inside, honey. We'll be right in."

Maddie obeyed, though she didn't seem happy about it.

I followed Victoria to the school, where she pushed open the door. We climbed the stairs, and a chill from the barnlike structure raced up my legs. "I wish we could find you a quiet place inside the house, but I thought this might do." She gestured to a corner on the back side, where a fire burned. A small desk and swivel chair sat atop an area rug. "I thought it might be neat for you to write some of your book here . . ." She shook her head. "But don't feel like you have to. Maybe it's a stupid idea. Something I would have liked to do, but we never were the same in that—"

I stopped her words by putting a hand on her arm. "It's perfect. I can't wait to write here."

She slumped over in what appeared to be relief, smiled at me even as her bottom lip trembled. "I'm glad."

There was more to say, and for the first time I wanted to say it, but she turned and led us back outside, then on the path toward the Orchard House entrance.

True, I didn't understand all that stood between me and

Victoria, both the good and the bad. And true, I'd come here thinking if I gave Victoria anything, it would be the cold shoulder. But there, in that old room that represented so much of what had brought us together in the first place, seeing all the effort she was going through to make me comfortable, something small changed within me. As if a piece of the hard exterior I'd buttressed around my heart got chipped away.

I didn't want to wade. I didn't want the ugly. But like it or not, it seemed it wanted me all the same.

CHAPTER FIFTEEN

I live in my inkstand, scribble, scribble from morning till night,
and am more peckish than ever if disturbed.

~ LMA

Taylor

"DID YOU KNOW that Louisa May Alcott moved to Concord when she was just about your age?" Victoria addressed the small group seated around the classroom. "That's the first time she had her own room, and that meant so much to her because she finally had a place of her own to start writing. You see, you are never, never too young to write. Or too old for that matter."

Her gaze caught mine and something passed between us, though I couldn't say what it was. Did Victoria think it was too late to revisit childhood dreams?

She skimmed through Louisa's publishing history, ending with the publication of *Little Women* one hundred fifty years ago. Then she put her hands together. "Now, I have a very special guest for you today. While we may not be able to talk to Louisa May Alcott in the twenty-first century, we have other authors who know a thing or two about writing a good story. This is my sister, Taylor, and she writes under what we sometimes call a pen name. Her pen name is Casey Hood, and chances are you've seen her books around. And today she's going to be your teacher and tell you a little bit about what it takes to be a writer."

The group clapped, and I rose to stand beside Victoria. A sea of young faces and eyes looked expectantly up at me, and I dragged in a deep breath. I'd done plenty of public speaking before, but never in front of my sister and niece, never with such a young audience.

I greeted them and thanked Victoria. "This is a special place. I remember coming here as a girl and sitting in the very bedroom where Louisa May Alcott wrote *Little Women* and thinking, 'Wow, I better write something great here.' But you know what? I learned something since then. Writing . . . in a way, it's all great. No matter what other people think of it, no matter how many times it doesn't win you a contest or get you published, every word serves a purpose. And none of them are bad."

I dragged in one more deep breath, tried to think what I needed to hear as a young girl, a young writer. For so long, I'd felt trapped, not good enough, as if I didn't fit in. What had set me free?

"Louisa May Alcott felt strongly. She had a little bit of a temper, and she was known for doing things other girls didn't like doing—like running. I think I didn't learn to write until I allowed myself to feel. It's when I unleashed that thing inside of me that I was always stuffing down—when I became honest in my writing . . . that's when things started happening."

I met Victoria's gaze, and she nodded encouragement. I took it, opening the book. "So let's start our time by talking about what every good writer needs to do—read!"

I finished out the lesson, and we led the young writers back down to Orchard House.

Victoria squeezed my arm. "You did great."

I wasn't completely sure she wasn't just being nice, but I decided to take the compliment at face value.

We ushered the campers through a quick tour of Orchard House, my own limbs tingling at being back in the same rooms where the Alcotts lived and breathed. Then, up to Louisa's room, where they sat on the same carpet with their notebooks. I stood near Louisa's desk, letting Victoria encourage them to release their pens to their imaginations.

I closed my eyes, soaking in the room that had always represented something magical to me. I remembered that long-ago day of Jo March Writing Camp, how Victoria and I had reinstated the Pickwick Club. She'd always been twice as determined as me. What had happened?

The room quieted as the kids began to write, and Victoria came beside me. "We'll be here for a little while. I like to give them a lot of time. Feel free to get to your own writing."

I nodded. While part of me could have stayed forever in that room with all that young enthusiasm and creative juices flowing, another part of me longed to tuck myself away and hide within black words and white screen and make-believe people.

I slid around the children, felt Maddie's gaze heavy upon

me, but stopped at the raised hand of a little blonde girl who couldn't have been older than eight. I crouched beside her.

She leaned close to whisper into my ear. "What if we don't know what to write?"

I tucked my hands around my knees, looked at her blank page. "Sometimes, one word will do it."

She looked at me, her brow furrowed.

"What's your favorite time of day?"

Her gaze darted sideways at the rug before dragging back to me. "Morning, when Mommy makes me pancakes."

"There's your word . . . *morning*. Or try *pancakes*. Make one sentence out of that and see where it takes you."

Her face lit up and she thanked me, started writing her sentence. Truthfully, I didn't know if it was the best advice, but she was writing.

I went down the stairs, glimpsing the portrait of Louisa's niece in red—May's daughter, nicknamed Lulu. Not for the first time, I thought about Louisa's relationship with her youngest sister—the one portrayed in *Little Women* between Jo and Amy.

No doubt, like many sisterly relationships, it was a complicated one.

"I detest rude, unladylike girls."

"I hate affected, niminy-piminy chits."

I smiled at the long-ago memorized exchange between Amy and Jo but sobered at the thought of Amy throwing her sister's beloved book into the fire. I remembered reading it for the first time, feeling the horror of all Jo's hard work . . . gone.

Without some shame, I recalled the softball bat I'd used

on Victoria's laptop that day sixteen years ago. At the time, I thought the punishment just and well deserved. Now, with each day that passed where Victoria didn't mention my last transgression, with each day that I realized she didn't intend to guilt me over what I'd done, a sharp sense of shame grew in the pit of my belly. My time with the Bennetts—and Victoria—seemed to water it.

There'd been hope for Jo and Amy and for Louisa and May. After Amy fell into an icy pond, in part because of Jo's neglect, Jo realized how much her sister meant to her. The real Jo and Amy—Louisa and May—had grown up to support one another in their creative endeavors. May even named her only child after Louisa. And weeks after the youngest Alcott gave birth to her child in Europe and realized she would not survive, she had requested her husband send their daughter to her sister back in New England, that Louisa might be the small girl's mother when May could not.

Yes, there'd been hope for the two sets of sisters—both real and fictional. But what of Victoria and me? Our bond was different, the fracture that had separated us seeming more severe.

I thought of Will in the Bennett kitchen that morning. Seeing him had stirred a million things inside me, and yet, in the end, none of it mattered. He was my sister's husband. Maddie and Caden's father. Wasn't it selfish of me to come back into their lives, harboring a sixteen-year-old grudge? Their betrayal hurt, but like it or not, it had produced a marriage, a beautiful family.

I thought of Laurie marrying Amy, how despite Jo's insistence that Laurie not love her, she was still hurt over his love for Amy. The thought made me feel a smidge better. Healing would take time. Still, Jo had met her Professor Bhaer, and I had yet to meet mine.

I slid out the door of the gift shop and up the path to Bronson's school, tried to correct my thinking. Kevin. Kevin was my Professor Bhaer. My perfect match. We suited one another. No matter if I couldn't admit vulnerability to him, if I couldn't give him my full heart. This was real life, not fiction. Sometimes love wasn't perfect. Best to save perfect for the novels.

I opened the door of the school. The fire, though beginning to die down, still gave off a toasty warmth into the cool April morning. I rubbed my hands together and approached the corner Victoria had arranged for me.

I used to think this place—Orchard House and its grounds—held some sort of mystical power for writers. Now I knew. It wasn't so much the place as what we brought to it. If Louisa Alcott and *Little Women* hadn't already captured the hearts of those who visited, the place wasn't half as meaningful.

What did I bring to this place all these years later? This place that in many ways felt like home to me?

I lowered myself to the office chair, grateful for the rug under my feet instead of the hard wood boards that lay beneath it. I slipped my laptop from my bag and opened it to the document I had begun last month.

I looked at the words, at the characters I'd created that now echoed back at me flat and lifeless. Sudden panic seized me.

Leaving this place, clinging to my anger, was what had enabled me to write and write well. What if, in coming back to Concord, in slowly mending the rift between me and the Bennetts—maybe even me and Victoria—what if I was giving up my ability to write a great story?

I looked out the window to the steep slope in the back of the school.

Feel deeply.

That's what I believed made a good writer. Perception. Honesty. Authenticity and feeling. If anything, coming back to Concord should make me a *better* writer.

I dove in for the next half hour, forcing words onto the screen because that's what I did—I wrote. Even when I wasn't inspired, even when I felt like the words were no good. Wasn't that what I encouraged that little girl in Louisa's room to do?

But for the first time, the words—the story—felt all wrong. I sat back, pondering how I could fix it. If I could fix it.

A knock came at the door.

"Come in!" I yelled, almost welcoming the distraction.

A man pushed through the door, his arms laden with wood. "Thought you could use some more. It's cold out there for April."

"Oh!"

I went to help him, but he shook his head. "I got it."

"I don't mean to be any trouble. But thank you, I appreciate it."

He laid the wood beside the fireplace, took up a poker, and stuck it into the glowing coals. "Boss's orders. Besides, you're helping the kids without pay—it's the least we can do."

I discreetly studied his profile beneath a black-and-yellow

Bruins hat. Specks of gray danced at his temples, faint but pleasant lines hugged his eyes. He stood after adding a log to the fire, and when he backed up a step, I noticed a slight limp.

"You're Luke, right?" I held out my hand. "I'm Taylor."

He grasped it and I noted how calloused and worn his hand was. So large it enveloped my own. I couldn't help but think of Kevin, of his soft hands. Not that I cared. Kevin used his brain for work, probably never mowed a lawn in his life. It suited him.

"Nice to meet you." He stood there relaxed, slipping his hands into his pockets.

"You too." I gestured out the window. "You do a great job. The place looks beautiful."

"I do what I can." He nodded toward my laptop. "Hear you're some big-name author. How's the writing coming?"

I scrunched my nose in the direction of the screen. "There's things being written but I'm not so certain they're good things."

"What do you write?" He adjusted his hat, giving me a better glimpse of his face, his still-full head of hair, definitely beginning to gray in a distinguished sort of way.

"Fiction. Small-town romances, that sort of stuff."

"What's your last name? I'll have to check some of it out."

I flopped down in my chair. "I'm not sure it'd be your sort of thing . . ."

"How do you know? Maybe it's just my sort of thing." The corner of his mouth twitched, and I couldn't help but find it charming.

I raised my eyebrows. "You read a lot?"

"I'm not part of a book club or anything, but yeah, I do my fair share. Mostly classics and nonfiction. Reading Lord of the Rings now."

I was intrigued. "Yeah?"

"Yeah. So what's your last name so I can look you up?"

I dipped my hand in my bag, searching for a bookmark. "It's Bennett, but I write under a pen name."

With sharp clarity, I remembered Lorraine coming to me sometime in the middle of the adoption process. She needed to know if I wanted to keep my birth mother's last name or change it to theirs.

"What do you think?" twelve-year-old me had asked, lifting my quivering gaze to where she sat beside me on my bed.

"Honey, we'd be honored to share our last name with you, but we understand if you want to keep your mom's."

I'd thought for a long time, all too aware that I was taking her time from making cookies or working in her flower beds, all too aware that she had already spent more time than she should have with lawyers and social workers and paperwork on my behalf.

"You can think about it awhile if you'd like," she'd said.

But I shook my head. When I spoke, it was with a slow start. "When you adopt me, then . . . you would be my mom, right?"

I couldn't be sure, but I thought Victoria's mother's eyes were especially wet and shiny in that moment.

"That's right. Is that okay?"

I bit my lip, nodded. "Then I guess I should have the same last name as you?" I tried out the thought on her, didn't want to appear presumptuous that I could share such a special thing as a name with people providing me with so much undeserved acceptance already.

She smiled. "I think that would be fitting."

"Okay, then."

She touched my face, cupping it in her cool hand. "Okay, then."

I had a new name. A name that meant I belonged with a special unit of people.

A family.

Little did I know that truly fitting in, truly belonging, would require so much more than a simple name.

I sighed, looked at the bookmarks my publisher had printed for me, my pseudonym prominently displayed on my newest release. *Casey Hood.*

I'd told myself it was to keep my privacy, to keep from being found out from those in my old life. Now I wondered if the attempt to change my name, even on my books, hadn't been just another way to break from my past.

I blinked and gave Luke the bookmark. He looked down, holding it slightly farther from his eyes. I imagined him poring over Lord of the Rings in an easy chair at home, a pair of reading glasses perched on his nose.

"Casey Hood . . . I think I've heard of you."

I shrugged, gave him a small smile. "My books are around."

He leaned against the windowsill, crossed his arms over his broad chest, the Framingham Police initials bold on the front. "So what's giving you trouble about your story?"

Something in me wanted to put a wall up then. Some sort of barrier. Who was this guy—the maintenance man—to come in and start asking me all these questions? He was being entirely too nosy.

And why didn't I mind?

I dragged in a deep breath, decided I had nothing to lose. "You want to know what I just told those kids up there?"

He nodded at me, encouraging.

"To be honest in their writing. To feel it, deeply. Only now I don't think I'm following my own advice."

"Why not?"

"Because . . . I'm here. This place, I grew up here. There's a lot attached to it. I suppose a lot that I don't want to feel. I think it's interfering with the writing."

"So you have to face it."

I squinted up at him, shrugged. "Maybe."

"But you don't want to."

"Maybe," I whispered.

He scratched his cheek, where the shadow of growth started. "Sounds to me like you got two options."

"Have."

"What?"

I winced. "Sorry. Bad habit—correcting a stranger's grammar."

He smiled, and it was definitely worn around the edges. But there was something solid there, too. Something that spoke of security. "As I was saying . . . sounds to me like you *got* two options . . ."

I rolled my eyes. "Those being?"

"You can face whatever's bothering you, whatever scares you about being here."

Scares me? I hadn't said that, had I? "I'm really looking forward to hearing what option two is."

"You could write about it. Work it out in your story. Don't writers do that sometimes?"

I studied him. "I suppose they do."

He pushed off the windowsill. "Anyway, it was nice to meet you. Guess you'll be around for the rest of the week?"

I nodded. "Thanks for your help."

He raised his bookmark. "Thanks for this."

"Really, I'm not sure if I can quite compare with Lord of the Rings—you may be better off skipping out."

"I'll be the judge of that." He winked at me. "Let me know if you need anything. It was nice meeting you, Taylor."

"Nice meeting you." I watched as he exited the building, then headed over to the office building.

The school felt suddenly empty. Too quiet. I stared at my computer screen. I'd written twenty-five thousand words—a quarter of the book. Yet I could no longer deny it wasn't working.

I closed the document and looked out the window. A few feet in front of the sharply inclined slope stood a large pebbled rock. It would be perfect for sitting on a warm and sunny day, and I wondered if Louisa had ever done so.

I hummed quietly, turned back to my computer, and opened up a new Word document. The blank page waited before me, more inviting than intimidating.

"You could write about it. Work it out in your story. Don't writers do that sometimes?"

New characters, a new setting. Victoria's long-ago words

after our first day at Jo March Writing Camp echoed in my mind.

"Write it. Write your story. Like Louisa did in Little Women. . . . *Write your story, and make something good come out of it."*

Maybe I would finally take that advice to heart. Both Victoria's and the mysterious groundskeeper's. I would write out my story—or one similar to it—and in it I'd find my solution. Words could be tamed, sorted, controlled.

Surely in this story I could find some semblance of peace over the troubles that had plagued me for the last sixteen years. Maybe I could find *myself.* If not myself or peace, then maybe I could brave the waters of optimism and at last search out that dangerous, elusive thing I'd feared too long . . . hope.

CHAPTER SIXTEEN

I felt God as I never did before, and I prayed in my heart that I might keep that happy sense of nearness all my life.

~ LMA

Johanna

I STARED AT THE PRECIOUS PAPER on my lap, the ink on the end of my pen drying as I tried to summon up that tenuous first line. It often only took a couple of words strung together to set off more swirling within me, but today, they did not come.

I raised my head toward the January sun, uncommonly bright and warm. The rock I sat on was a marker of sorts. Mr. Alcott spoke often of his plans to one day build a school on the property. A school of philosophy. I could only fathom how interesting it might be to attend such a school, to share ideas with learned men and perhaps even women.

I breathed deep, pulling air into my lungs, moving my booted feet along the still-hard earth of winter. I stared at the blank page again but couldn't summon up an ounce of inspiration. Instead, my thoughts turned to Nathan, as they were wont to do of late. He'd traveled home from Boston just yesterday and was to leave again tomorrow, but he hadn't yet called today.

I had purchased some sugar in town out of my own pay just two days earlier. I planned to make him some of my lemon cookies. He could bring them along—something sweet to remember me by.

Giving the paper one last look of longing, as if words would pop upon them merely by will, I stood. Perhaps some baking would stir my creative muse to life.

Going inside, I hid away my writing supplies before returning downstairs. Orchard House lay quiet, as Mr. and Mrs. Alcott were gone for the day to visit Anna. I set to work making the cookies, then cleaned the kitchen with care while they cooled. I placed them on one of Mrs. Alcott's plates and walked up the long drive to Nathan's house, enjoying the sunshine, toying with a jumble of words that had the potential to become the first line of a poem.

Still, nothing came. What would I write of, and why did I feel suddenly drained of words?

I approached Nathan's grand home and held the plate of cookies against my middle with one hand so I could knock with the other. I waited a minute, but no one answered. Strange, for it looked as if his carriage was in the barn and even if Nathan wasn't home, usually his butler, Ivan, was puttering around. I knocked again and again waited, then one more time for good measure. I turned away, disappointed that I had used so much sugar for what seemed to be a waste, for if Nathan had already left, the cookies would be hard and stale upon his return.

Behind me, the door creaked open, Nathan's tall, silver-haired butler eyeing the plate I'd brought. "I'm sorry, Miss Suhre. He is not feeling particularly well. Perhaps you could return tomorrow?"

"He is off for Boston tomorrow, is he not?"

"Yes, but—"

From behind him came a low, unrecognizable growl. "Who is it?"

Ivan stepped into my line of view, closed the door to block me. I couldn't understand his secrecy and leaned to the side so that I might see inside the home. I heard Ivan's low voice, then a louder one I recognized as Nathan's.

Reluctantly, it seemed, Ivan opened the door and allowed me entrance. I stepped inside, clutching the plate tight in my hands, not sure what was about or why I should be nervous over it.

Nathan stood in the hall, his suit a rumpled mess, his blond curls on end, his eyes weepy and bloodshot. I rushed to him, put a hand on the side of his face. "Nathan, are you unwell?"

He pulled from me with a jerk and went unsteadily into his study. I followed, tried not to be hurt over the slight.

"I made these for you."

He glanced at the plate, gestured to an empty table by the window.

Not exactly the reaction for which I hoped.

"How was your day?" I asked. I knew he was tired from all this travel.

"Rotten as eggs, if you must know."

I looked at him, his normally erect posture slouched, his

hand a bit shaky as he reached into a cabinet behind his desk and poured himself something. Alcohol? Was this what was wrong, then? Was my Nathan drunk?

I went to him, placed a hand on his arm, and tried to guide him to a chair. "Come, let us talk about our problems instead of drowning them in whiskey."

He pushed me away again. This time, hard enough to send me bumping into the small table where I had placed the cookies. I saw the table teeter back and forth, knew I must stop it, but was still in such shock over Nathan's rough treatment of me that I could not gather my wits enough to do so.

As if time paused, I reached a hand out, but too late. Mrs. Alcott's plate fell to the ground, shattering with a sound that echoed throughout Nathan's large study. Cookie bits and wholes fell among the shards of porcelain, rendering the entire batch inedible.

"Now, look what you did!" Nathan stood above me, gesturing to the plate, and I could not fathom who this man was. Yes, I knew alcohol could spur men to act in abominable ways, but I never expected Nathan to be one weak enough to entertain it.

I stood, raised my chin to him, looked in his bloodshot eyes with something like a challenge, then removed myself, leaving the mess.

He did not follow me, and once safely in Orchard House, I attacked the kitchen floor with a scrub brush and a vengeance, the tears adding to the suds of my efforts. Without warning, an intense homesickness came over me and I could not imagine bearing another five months in this cold Concord town, the reality of who Nathan was taunting me in my head.

I'd let love rule me, and I had fallen weak. Louisa was right after all. Better to keep one's liberty—and keep one's head about love, lest it ruin one's heart.

After I'd exhausted my muscles on cleaning, I retrieved my inkwell and paper, sought the rock at the back of Orchard House once again.

This time, the words came, as I knew they would, for something about the stir of emotions—hurt and anger and loneliness—fed them.

> I am small
> But a flood starts with one
> Drop of water
> And a forest starts with a seed
> As does a civilization
> Or a disease.

I stopped and read over the words, my heartbeat calmer at the cadence of the lines I'd crafted. Perhaps foolish, they seemed to give me some sort of power—order in my otherwise-orderless world.

Nathan was wrong to act as he did. I might be little more than a servant, not much of anyone according to this world, but I was *someone*. I deserved to be treated as such.

I remembered riding home from town one day in our carriage alongside my brother John. I'd been no more than twelve, all of us still adjusting to life without Pa. John had popped down from the carriage, given me a small bow, and held his hand out to me.

I had scrunched my nose at him. "What's that for?"

He'd grinned. "Well, I figure with Pa not being around anymore, I better start being nice to you so's you know how a man's supposed to treat a lady."

"Are you serious?" I'd asked, frightened to take his hand lest he pull me down in the mud or frighten me with a toad in his pocket as he'd been known to do.

"Afraid so, little lady. It's a tricky job, but someone's got to do it."

Tentative at first, I took his hand, trying not to show surprise when he did help me down and even offered his arm for our short walk to the house.

"Now, Johanna, you're growing up fast and you're pretty as those there wildflowers in spring. Soon boys will be knockin', and I might not always be around to tell you which are the good and which are the bad, got it?"

"I suppose . . . ," I said, though in honesty I couldn't imagine any boys seriously courting me.

"So it's up to you. Don't ever settle for anyone who doesn't treat you like a lady, you got that?"

I giggled. "But I'm not a lady."

"Don't matter. If a boy loves you rightly, he'll think you are—and he better treat you that way, too."

I didn't understand what John had been talking about then. But I did now. And if I were to go by my departed brother's advice, I should be running long and hard away from Nathan Bancroft.

Despite the ache in my heart.

Though I'd begun to hope I'd found my place here in Concord, first with the Alcotts and then with Nathan, perhaps I'd been wrong. Perhaps I should depart for home after

Louisa's return, be content to scribble my poetry by night and milk cows by day.

Truly, there could be worse things.

I went to bed that night trying to brush the sadness from my spirit. Instead, I wrote by candle- and moonlight, sneaking into Louisa's abandoned room, for it contained a half-moon desk by the window. There, I finished my poem and felt a strange sort of wholeness in the midst of the dark.

~~

Nathan called the following day. I was feeding the stove with wood when a knock sounded on the kitchen door. I opened it to see the man I knew and loved, despite his horrid actions and secrets. He was back to his well-put-together self, suit crisp and straight, curly hair tamed. And his eyes . . . his eyes were clear and dry. And pleading.

I shut the door upon him.

He knocked and did not stop. "Johanna, I beg of you. Please, dear. Open the door. I must apologize for my actions."

"I do not wish to speak with you," I yelled through the closed door. And yet his shadow lingered.

A moment later he was again knocking on the door.

Mr. Alcott appeared from his study, a look of sincere puzzlement on his face, for the Alcotts never refused entrance to anyone—beggar or stranger—and most definitely not neighbor.

"Johanna, is that Mr. Bancroft?"

"It is," I answered, closing the door of the stove.

"Best you answer it then, dear?" He spoke the words so innocently, I wondered if the man could even understand a sharp disagreement with another human. I decided I must go out and speak to Nathan then, though I had little desire to do so—and the part that did do the desiring, though small, was the part that frightened me most.

"Yes, sir."

I grabbed my cloak and muff and slipped out the door.

When Nathan saw me, he sucked in a deep breath that looked something like relief. "Johanna," he breathed.

I crossed my arms in front of my chest.

"I only have a scarce recollection of my abominable behavior yesterday, and even that is enough to scare me witless. Ivan has provided the rest. Please know that is not—that is not who I am. It is not who I long to be."

I shivered against the cold, tried not to let my heart warm at his sincerity. "Clearly it *is* who you are when you drink."

He nodded, looked at the ground. "It is."

"Then knowing so, why do you continue in it?" I softened my voice, for even though one could not argue the error of his actions, I did not wish to feel haughty.

"I was troubled, and it was a weak moment. I did warn you I had moral shortcomings, did I not?" He attempted to inject jest in his latter sentence, but I did not find it amusing in the least.

"Could you not come to me with your troubles?"

"I did not wish to burden you."

"Burden away, if it would spare you from that evil!"

He rubbed the back of his neck, nodded. "You are quite right, of course. Is there any way you can forgive me?"

I looked at him, the pitiful expression seeming to hint that my answer would denote whether his life was worth living or not. He was a man of passion. A man who felt. And I'd known for some months now that I was at the heart of his feelings. But what of that split moment of yesterday? When his feelings were of unbridled anger? When whiskey consumed and blinded and sought for release?

I must be cautious. I was without family, and while Mr. and Mrs. Alcott were certainly my advocates, I did not wish to trouble them with bad news of their neighbor. I visited Anna often, but she was busy with her brood and we hadn't quite the connection I shared with Louisa. I was sure Nan felt the same, for we were both too reserved, too quiet, whilst Louisa served to unscrew our honest thoughts. I also had an inkling that Nan, with her increasing deafness, got tired of using her ear trumpet when I spoke. And I often tired of yelling.

"While I don't feel I have a right to impose stipulations upon you—"

He stepped closer, scooped up my hands with his own. "Impose, dear Johanna. Impose away, if it means there's hope for us."

I wrenched my hands from his passionate grasp. "I cannot abide men who befriend their liquor. I am unsure if you see a future . . ."

I was being too forward. And yet I had allowed him to kiss me. More than once. Glorious, passionate moments that spoke of elation and promise. He had even spoken words of love. Yes, our relationship was a bit on the outskirts of the norm. I had no father to approve of a courtship, and Mother was too far away. Though I hadn't a penny to my name, and Nathan was quite well-off, something about me had captured him. But was I enough to keep him from his drink?

He lifted his hand to my face, ran a thumb along my cheek. "I do."

I swallowed, not pulling away from him this time. "I cannot be with you if you insist on taking to drink when life ails you."

"I will be an angel, Johanna. I promise it. When I realized all I have to lose . . . it is a small sacrifice for a greater prize."

I couldn't help the tiny smile that crept to my face. Forgetting John's warnings, I thought instead how everyone deserves a second chance, a balm of grace. Was it not a worthy thing to be the one supplying it?

I nodded, and he bent to kiss me softly upon the cheek. When he held my hands, this time I did not pull away. "I want to make up for my poor behavior by taking you to Boston for the day. On your next day off, perhaps?"

I agreed, and when a box of beautiful new dishes arrived the next week to replace Mrs. Alcott's broken one, I felt Nathan had proved his sincerity above and beyond what I could ask of him.

CHAPTER SEVENTEEN

I honor marriage so highly that I long to see it what it should be—
life's best lesson, not its heaviest cross.

~ LMA

Johanna

"SHE'S HERE!" Louisa's sister May, normally poised and grace-ful, flew wildly about the lawn as I stood with Anna and her two boys at the gate. Little John pressed my hand, apparently anxious over the commotion. From behind, I heard a stifled sob from Mrs. Alcott.

I forced my lips together, noticed Louisa's beloved "Marmee" anew. She would no doubt look different to Louisa since she had last seen her a year earlier. Pale, weak, often withdrawn and sad. Her back was bowed, as if she'd finally stooped under the weight of all her hard work and good deeds. Selfishly I hoped Louisa wouldn't blame me for her mother's failing health. When it came to her mother, my friend could be quite protective.

I hung back as she alighted from the carriage with Mr.

Alcott, allowing her family to swarm around her, bestowing hugs and kisses in unabashed affection. The tender scene was enough to make my own eyes smart as I thought of my family and how it had been over a year since I'd seen them. I grabbed for John's ring at my neck and smoothed the metal beneath my thumb.

George and Mary were expecting a wee one next month, and Mother seemed in her glory. More than once, she hinted in her letters that Bryant was still a bachelor in need of a respectable wife.

It was her way of saying she missed me, I knew, but it was not the bait to see me home. Especially now that Nathan occupied so much of my time.

Louisa stooped to plant a kiss on little John's cheek and then straightened and held her arms out to me. She looked wonderful—much healthier than when she departed—and I wondered if it had been all the spas she went to or her time with Laddie that had something to do with her improved constitution. We embraced, and for just a moment I felt I belonged, that I was a sister to this woman, a child of this family.

It only lasted a moment, and then it was gone, as fleeting as a summer shower. But it left a fresh gentleness to it, which I chose to pocket for another time.

What was it about this family that drew me? They were like nothing I grew up with, and yet their deep beliefs—how they felt and acted upon those beliefs—called to me. I followed them all into the house, a foreign heaviness sitting upon my chest. What might happen to me now that I was no longer needed at Orchard House?

~~

When Nathan came to fetch me later for an evening carriage ride, I withdrew myself from the merry conversation in the parlor with some bittersweet feelings. Louisa sat in a chair, describing Europe with all the skill of the accomplished writer she was, successfully holding us spellbound. When Nathan knocked, I went to the door and invited him in, certain the Alcotts wouldn't mind.

But his face was shadowed in storms, and I knew at once that he had had a trying day and wished to be alone with me.

I tried not to show my disappointment. I enjoyed being with Nathan immensely. He hadn't faced the grumps in some time, particularly now that the warm weather was upon us. But the laughter and chatter of the family within called to me as well.

"I was hoping to catch the sunset at Walden Pond with you," he said, and I could not turn down such an offer of romance.

So I excused myself to the family, allowing their pleasant chatter and the scents of strawberry rhubarb pie to follow me as I grabbed my shawl and walked up the path to Nathan's now-familiar shay.

He tapped his mare a bit harder than necessary, and the shay jolted down the drive. I placed a tentative hand on his arm, felt the muscles clench beneath, and drew my fingers away, remembering the mood of his I witnessed last January.

True to his word, he had been a perfect angel since. Jolly, even. At least in my presence. I admired his resolution to keep away from his drink and to win my heart. Still, rebuilding trust took time. That moment when he pushed me in his study, though forgiven, would not be so easily forgotten, it seemed.

It wasn't until now, in his one-horse shay, as he tapped his jumpy mare, prodding her to go faster, that I recalled that Nathan hadn't exactly promised he'd never take another drink. I wondered if he did when in Boston. Even so, I was not his keeper. As long as he never treated me in such a poor manner again . . .

"What troubles you?" I asked.

He hunched over, gripping the reins, his expression a surly one. "Uncle and I are in disagreement, and he refuses to hear me out."

"Whatever over?"

"I feel *Merry's Museum* is better suited to be a girls' magazine. I proposed a new boys' publication opposite of it—one with me as editor."

"Sounds like a brilliant plan to me."

His posture relaxed then, and I could see how he desperately needed someone on his side. He needed *me* on his side. I didn't know much of his parents, except that they had died when he was young. I wondered if he had not flung himself into the world and beneath his uncle's protection, racing toward success but missing the acceptance and love that a healthy family could bring.

In many ways, I longed to fix this. To rescue him, even. Maybe to rescue the both of us. Silly, perhaps, to think that I, a small girl of nineteen, could rescue a grown man, but I felt my love might just be enough to save him. Why couldn't it be done? One might think Nathan Bancroft had all the world could offer, and yet I suspected that very deep, he didn't possess some of the most important aspects of life—family, unconditional love, faith.

I wanted to help him. I wanted us to grow. Together.

"Uncle did not think it such a brilliant plan."

"Would it not broaden your readership—to have two magazines geared to two different audiences?"

I saw him relax again, was grateful I could have such an effect upon him. "Uncle does not think we can afford the start-up costs for it yet. I believe we cannot afford *not* to do it." He sighed. "In the end, it is his company."

"That bothers you."

He shrugged. "Nevertheless, it is the way of things."

"What if you were to start your own publishing company?"

He looked at me with something like a half-frozen grin. "You're serious?"

"Maybe not right away, but eventually. I don't see why not. You know the trade. You are a good businessman, and you are willing to try new ideas." I couldn't help but think that maybe, if our future stayed this course, I might help him. Imagine . . . a life filled with both a man I loved and our shared passion for words. I couldn't imagine anything more worthwhile, more exciting.

I thought of the poem I'd recently finished, tucked away in May's room at the Alcott home. Many times I'd brought it down to show Nathan, but it never seemed the right time. He, distracted by work or so tired of it that he didn't wish to speak of it at all.

Soon, though . . . soon I would show it to him.

He looked ahead, occupied with his own thoughts, pensive, no longer concerned that his mare had slowed to a more comfortable pace. "I owe everything I have to Uncle. He is the only family I have. I cannot leave him."

"I understand." Though I didn't mean that he should abandon his uncle suddenly. Only that he should not be chained to something that kept him from his dreams.

We reached Walden Pond and he tied the mare and helped me down. The sun hovered above the horizon and the earthy scent of sand and pine wound around me. It was good that I'd come. Nathan had need of me, and I felt a help, which suited me greatly. Not to mention the night proved beautiful. Perfect, even.

We walked a bit, and when we reached a grove of pine trees tucked out of the way, Nathan turned to me, presenting a glittering ring in his hand. I gasped, backed away a step.

He gazed softly at the shining adornment. "I've been carrying this around in my pocket for some time now, knowing I was going to ask you and yet not certain I'd ever work up the courage to do it." He planted one knee on a patch of dried pine needles. "Johanna, my life has taken on a new color since you first lost your laundry in my drive." He smiled, revealing the dimple on his cheek that I hadn't seen in too long. I loved that it was there now, for me. "I know you have nothing of worldly means, and still I find you have everything I want. I would love for us to continue coloring one another's worlds. Together. Will you be my wife, dearest?"

My stomach trembled. Though I'd hoped for a proposal sometime in the future, I hadn't expected it quite so soon.

But why not? We loved one another, had shared this past year together, both the good and the bad. Now that Louisa had returned from her trip, I would no longer be needed. And I knew that Mr. and Mrs. Alcott had borrowed money whilst Louisa was away. They could not afford to keep me on, and I could not stay unpaid.

The family was dear to me, yet what of my future? One where I had my own family? I thought of sweet John, gone at such a terrible young age. Life was indeed too short. I must seize it when it presented itself. And here, with Nathan on one knee holding a glittering promise of our future, it appeared it had. He wanted me. I would really and truly belong to someone. We could begin our own life, together.

"Yes," I said on the end of a breath.

He stood. "Yes?"

"Yes, you silly man!"

He slipped the ring onto my finger and kissed me so wonderfully I felt as if I were in a Brontë novel. I melted into him—his arms, his mouth, his desire, for it stirred a foreign one within me, and as it deepened, I'd never felt so content, so sure of the path set before me.

CHAPTER EIGHTEEN

In everyone's life there comes a waking-up time
and it's well for them if it comes at the beginning and not at the end
when it is too late to mend the past.

~ LMA

Taylor

"KNOCK, KNOCK."

I looked up from my laptop, tore myself away from the story that had suddenly captivated me, to see Victoria with her brown paper lunch bag.

Three days had passed since I spoke to Luke. Since I opened that new Word document and explored characters that were maybe a little too close to me and Victoria. Since the story came alive with its Concord setting. The words were coming—most of them born of my own experience. For once, I dove into the hurt. Looking for answers, searching for healing, even. Funny thing was, I didn't think the story was half-bad. Maybe even one of the better ones I'd written.

My problem was getting consumed in it. Yes, I had a

deadline to make, but my priority was Mom. She was tired this week and seemed to be happy I spent time with Victoria—in some capacity, at least. But the story was threatening to take me away. I had to remind myself constantly that this was not real life—it was my career, it was important, but it wasn't the *most* important.

Right now, Mom was. Maybe even my time with the Bennetts as a whole.

I'd never had this problem—real life competing with my stories. Probably because I didn't have much *real* in my life.

"Hey," I said to Victoria as I reached for my lunch bag. She'd made this a habit so far this week—eating lunch together in Bronson Alcott's school. We'd kept it to small talk mostly—chatting about the kids or how Mom was feeling or plans for dinner that night. Surface stuff, which was fine by me.

I was saving the nitty-gritty for my story.

"How's it coming?"

"It's coming."

She sat on one of the hard chairs, opened her lunch bag, and pulled out a sandwich. The light scent of tuna filled the space between us. "You're doing an amazing job teaching the kids. And while Maddie might be the last to admit it, I can tell she's getting a lot out of what you have to say."

"It's . . . nice. Being here, pouring a little bit into them."

"Seems like we were just in their shoes, doesn't it?"

"Sometimes it feels like yesterday. Other times it's like a lifetime ago."

She stared at the wooden boards at her feet, tuna sandwich still untouched in her hand. "I know what you mean."

I would miss this. Teaching, being here, maybe even eating lunch with Victoria. It was Thursday. We hadn't spoken about what would happen after the week was out. Mom had chemo treatments next week. I thought about offering to take her, to stay on another week, but I hadn't worked up the courage yet.

I popped the lid off my salad, poured dressing onto the green leaves. Silence hung between us, and I felt a new—or maybe old—heaviness. It was that barricade again, the thing that kept us from reconciling.

"How come you stopped writing?" I whispered the words, even as I regretted them once they were between us.

She lifted her gaze to mine. "Do you really want to know?"

No. No, I supposed I didn't. But I couldn't take it back now. "I—I don't know. Do I?"

She laughed, but it wasn't an amused laugh; it was a bitter sort of laugh. I definitely shouldn't have asked.

"I stopped writing after you left." She let the sentence hang there, and though I felt she wanted me to ask more in order to draw it out from her, I refused. Was it my fault she stopped writing?

She bit into her sandwich, chewed slowly, and swallowed. "At first, I thought it was temporary. I thought after I got over the laptop thing—I never did back up those stories—that I'd write again."

There it was. All those years ago, I'd wanted to hurt her. And I had. I'd known she didn't back up her stories. At the time, I'd been counting on it.

Even now I owed her an apology. She'd apologized for her part in our separation. Now it was my turn.

Only her apology didn't seem to be enough, and I doubted mine would be, either.

"But you didn't? Write again, I mean?" I asked.

She shook her head. "A few months went by, then six. We didn't hear from you. You didn't answer our calls. Will had enlisted, was gone for a year. One day on leave he showed up at our doorstep. He was a wreck. Iraq really messed with him. He was hoping you'd come home, but you hadn't. He found me instead."

Was I the reason Will had enlisted? I wondered how something like war could change a person, how it changed him.

Victoria blew out a long breath. "We started writing to each other. A lot. After his tour he started coming around more. In many ways, we grieved together."

"How sweet," I ground out. I could put up with a lot of things, but her trying to convince me that she and Will fell in love because of some tragic twist over my departure . . . I wasn't buying it.

"You're right." She put down her sandwich. "It wasn't sweet. It stunk big-time. You have no idea how guilty I felt— how guilty both of us felt. It was one minute of weakness, one minute of wrong that I wished over and over I could have taken back, and it cost us all."

The information felt like overload. All this time, I'd wondered if they'd been sneaking around behind my back. I wondered if I'd been completely blind. To know that their betrayal had been a onetime—maybe even a one-minute— thing didn't exactly make me feel better, but it did put things in perspective.

"I guess . . . I mean, it was just a shock, you know?"

My statement felt petty at this point. Will and Victoria were married, had been through and weathered ten times as much as Will and I had during our short dating period. It wasn't so much that Victoria stole my boyfriend; it was that the two people I cared about most in the world had stabbed me in the most painful possible way—in the back, when I hadn't seen it coming.

"It was my fault." She stood, paced to the far window facing Lexington Road, and looked through the glass as if seeing that long-ago day. "I'd just gotten home from class. I should have been on top of the world, but I felt . . . lonely." She sucked in a gulp of air. "You'd been distant since you started dating Will, but you seemed so happy—like he gave you something that me and Mom and Dad couldn't, no matter how much we tried, no matter how much we showed our love."

I let her vulnerable words sink in even as I wanted to stop up her mouth and keep them from pouring forth. But I knew what she said was true. The Bennetts had given me the world, and yet deep down I never felt as if I belonged. Then, after Mom started pulling away, clearly relegating me to second place in order to spare her real daughter's feelings . . . well, I'd pulled away even more. It had seemed like our makeshift happy family simply wasn't meant to be.

At least that's what I thought.

"I knew you were going to leave. You were going to go off and get married and have kids and I would probably have a great career, but that's it. A career." She turned to me. "I was jealous of you, Taylor. Crazy jealous of how you had been dealt the worst circumstances but came out on top. You had a *story*, an interesting one with what seemed like the perfect Hallmark ending. And all I had were my castles."

I licked my lips, didn't want to break the spell by talking. My sister, jealous of *me*? How crazy was that?

"I got home that day, sat near the garage, and just cried. I don't know, maybe I was PMSing or something, but I couldn't get myself together. I didn't even see Will pull up. You know him—of course he was concerned, thought something was really wrong." She brushed her hair out of her face, shook her head. "I shouldn't have poured my heart out to him. It sounded like such a sob story even to me, probably sounded like I was looking for attention. I guess I kind of was. Will . . . he reassured me that my future looked bright, that I was your best friend, all that; then . . . he hugged me. I'm sorry, Taylor. I swear it was innocent, but I should have stopped it there.

"Only I didn't. It felt good—even for a minute—to know what you knew all the time. To know that comfort, that acceptance. And if I'm going to be honest, it felt good knowing that for just a second I was taking your place." She sniffed. "I'm the one who kissed him. It was my fault."

I breathed in deep, my heart hammering against my rib cage, longing to break free. Even now, I longed to run out of the school, race through the hills Louisa so often ran to as a child and then a young woman. But I didn't. Adults didn't run. They stayed.

We were quiet for several moments before I got up the courage to speak words that didn't completely blame and condemn. "It's not really fair to take the full responsibility. It didn't look like he was exactly fighting you off when I got there."

"You're right. I was surprised when he didn't. Surprised,

and I'm sorry to admit it, just a little bit thrilled." She pressed her lips together. "I'm so sorry. I'm sorry for my selfishness, my jealousy."

"He stayed away for a long time after you left. We couldn't find you, had no idea where to look. After he got home from the war . . . well, it almost felt like we were different people. We'd grown, and when we finally accepted that you weren't coming back . . ."

"You found comfort in one another."

Victoria nodded. "Sure, I felt bad about what happened, but as the months passed, I got angry at you too. You didn't even give us a chance to explain. You didn't give me a chance to say I'm sorry. You didn't give *us* a chance, Taylor. We were family, and you ran out of our lives without a second glance."

I stood, fire in my belly. "That's not true. You have no idea what I went through, how lonely I was. I couldn't come back, Victoria. I didn't want to find what I expected all along—that if I came back, I would just mess things up for everyone—including myself."

"Family sticks together, even when it's hard."

"There's only one problem with that concept," I said.

"What?"

"By that time I'd convinced myself I'd never really been a part of the family."

"How can you say that?"

I rubbed my brow, figured since we were being open and since I was already wading, I might as well wade deep. "Mom started pulling away from me after you two argued about that date at Main Streets. Remember, the night I met Will?"

She nodded. "It doesn't mean she didn't love you, though."

"You used to write letters to Louisa, right?"

"What?" But the look on her face said it all. I saw the betrayal, the hurt, and I knew there was no turning back.

"At Sleepy Hollow. I found them."

She lowered herself to the nearest chair, hunched over in it, and wiped her forehead. I figured now was about the time she regretted asking me to come back to Concord. "How . . . ? That was private."

"Why leave it for anyone to see, then?"

"Decent people don't go fishing through things left at burial sites," she snapped.

"I never claimed to be decent," I shot back with just as much venom. "I only read one, but it was enough. And you know what you wrote, Victoria?"

"Those were private thoughts. I was a young teen. You can't possibly—"

"You wrote that you wished I wasn't your sister after all." I shook my head, my chest on fire. "I hated feeling like a charity case. Hated it even more knowing that we could never be true best friends again. I'd always be wondering if, deep down, you wanted to get rid of me."

"Taylor, we were sisters. It's only natural to feel what I felt. You shouldn't have read the letter."

"I wished I hadn't, but by then it was too late."

"How could you cling to that? It was a rough patch, something sisters go through." Victoria rubbed her temples.

Lunchtime was almost over. We'd have to go back in to face a room full of eager writers. I'd have to teach, pretend like this conversation never happened.

"I stopped writing those letters after you left, too."

"Are you trying to make me feel guilty?"

"No! Taylor, will you just get over yourself for one second? I'm trying to explain, to do the hard work in repairing our relationship because despite everything, I still love you. I never, ever stopped thinking of you as my sister. Through the good and the bad, in the end you are the only one I have."

My bottom lip trembled, but I couldn't tell if it was from lingering anger or some other emotion. I didn't speak, thought I'd only mess everything up more—if that were possible.

"I stayed away from writing after you left. When Will and I began dating seriously, I vowed to never write again." She shrugged. "Now it sounds kind of stupid, but back then I figured it would do as my penance—taking your boyfriend, in some ways taking the life you'd planned for yourself."

I wondered if it made her feel better. And now did she expect me to release her from this self-inflicted guilt?

"I think you did your time." I felt her gaze heavy upon me, and I acknowledged the hollow feeling inside my chest— disappointment, not in her, but in myself. I needed to give a little here. Yes, I'd been wronged, but did I truly intend to cling to one minute of betrayal for the rest of my life?

It had rocked my last sixteen years. What did I want my next sixteen to look like? Who did I want to be? Would I let the continued fear of betrayal and disappointment ruin a possibly beautiful thing?

I thought of Mom and the cancer trying to eat away her body. I thought of Dad and Maddie and Caden and all of us holding hands around the dinner table. Of Victoria's declaration that she loved me, that I was the only sister she had.

If I wasn't careful, I might throw it all away again. For me, there was only one shot at this family thing, and it was here, now.

I tamped down my doubts and opened my mouth.

"Victoria, you were a *great* writer."

She shrugged, wiped at her eyes. The light from the window shone upon her dark head, highlighting a few gray hairs at her roots. I was reminded of how we grew older, how this part of our life could be a sweet time if I only opened myself up a bit.

Sisters.

I hadn't wanted to think it was possible. But here, now, I wondered if new beginnings were indeed possible. If *family* was possible.

That idea I'd been so frightened of filled my chest. *Hope.* But this time it seemed attractive, near foreign after I'd stifled it for so many years.

I breathed deep and plunged. "I . . . I'm sorry about your laptop."

She nodded, and I took it as a sign of forgiveness. But it didn't seem enough. What would be enough? And why, suddenly, did I want it?

Then I had an idea. An idea I didn't think through quite fully, but an idea I felt might heal a big part of us. I didn't ponder, didn't deliberate. I leapt.

"You should write again. Maybe . . . we should write together again. Think we're too old for the Pickwick Club?"

Her mouth fell open. "You—you're serious?"

"I think I am."

She laughed, but it turned into a sob. Tears wet her cheeks, and the backs of my own eyelids burned.

"I don't know what to say."

"You better say something before I change my mind."

"Yes. Yes, of course I'd like that."

I swallowed down a lump in my own throat. "Good. We can start tonight."

"But I haven't written anything."

"We can write together, if you want. After supper. Maybe Maddie can join us." I didn't know if the girl would be open to the idea. Truthfully, I didn't know if *I* was open to the idea. Was I ready for any of this?

Victoria swiped at her eyes again. Nodded. "I think that would mean a lot to her. It would mean a lot to me." She glanced at her watch. "I've been meaning to show you something." She got up, went to the bottom drawer of the desk, and slid it open. "I admit I was half-hoping you'd find this and ask me about it, but I guess you're not as much of a snoop as I would be."

I stared at a small book of papers, bound with string. It was yellowed, fragile. "What is it?"

"A book of poems. By a woman named Johanna Bancroft. I didn't have a chance to read them all. I wanted to come back to them when I had time and could really think about what it means." She pointed to the fireplace. "In the fall we noticed some of the mortar was crumbling. When the workers went to repair the bricks last week, a couple were so loose they took them out . . . and found this. But the crazy part is, it's dedicated to Louisa. There's a note in the front and everything."

"No way."

She handed me the little book. I took it carefully, almost

frightened to handle such an old document, the edges of the paper crumbly.

The front simply read *Poems by Johanna Bancroft*.

I opened to the first page, squinted at hazy script at the top, written in weathered ink: *To Louisa*. "How'd you manage to even read this?"

Victoria smiled. "Remember that class I took on rare manuscripts? It came in handy."

I gave the book to her. "What's it say?"

"'To Louisa. You didn't just give me wings; you gave me a voice and a space to use it. You are the sister I never had. John would be pleased. Johanna.'"

"Did you look into it at all? Who is she?"

Victoria shook her head. "I've read every Louisa May Alcott biography and I don't remember a Johanna Bancroft being mentioned once. But I didn't spend too much time on it yet. I've been . . . distracted."

I couldn't tear my gaze from the page Victoria had just read, couldn't focus on what exactly she was so distracted with.

"Well, we definitely need to get to the bottom of it," I said.

She beamed at me. "I was hoping you'd say that." I realized then that somewhere in the space of the last half hour, I was letting walls crumble. They weren't anywhere near disintegrated. Somehow I didn't know if I wanted this relationship with Victoria again. Did I want the hassle of caring for a sister again? A best friend? Did I want the aggravation of trying to build trust again?

I looked at the little bound book in her hands, a creative

collection of something between two women. How had it found its way behind the bricks of the fireplace, tucked away for all these years? Who was this Johanna, and how had Louisa made a difference in her life? And what, if anything, did it mean to me and Victoria?

"You might think I'm crazy," she said. "But I feel like it's more than coincidence that this came to me the week before you came home. As if Someone bigger wanted us to discover this."

I fought from rolling my eyes. Either Mom's newfound religion was rubbing off on Victoria, or she had written one too many letters to Louisa. Maybe Victoria's willingness to believe in the supernatural hadn't disappeared as I thought.

But I knew better. The one time I believed in an angel had eventually turned into the biggest disappointment of my life.

I looked at the little book, at the careful writing that dedicated the book to Louisa, and I couldn't deny the draw of it. Whoever this woman was, she had known Louisa Alcott. It had landed in Victoria's hands, and she had chosen to share it with me.

For the first time in a long time, I felt I was part of something special. I couldn't describe it or explain it, for certainly I'd been a part of unique projects before. Each book that I wrote and worked on with my publishing team felt special. But this . . . this discovering of something that held so much meaning to Victoria and me for so long—this was different. Especially now, when we'd just started connecting.

I wondered if she would have shared the book with me if I hadn't reinstated the Pickwick Club.

The door behind us opened, and we both jumped. Luke stood at the top of the steps. "Did I interrupt something?"

Victoria stood, indeed looking guilty. "Luke. Not at all."

"Nicole asked me to check on you. The campers are getting antsy."

Victoria glanced at her watch and cringed. "We're late." She handed the book to me. "Think you can find a safe place for this while I get them started?"

I tried to protest, but she was gone before I could form the words. I stared at Johanna Bancroft's book, wanted it out of my hands in the worst way.

Luke's footsteps came up behind me. "You okay?"

"Yeah." I placed the fragile book carefully back in the bottom drawer of the desk, straightened, and smiled at him. "Nice day out, huh?"

His gaze lingered on the drawer, but to his credit, he didn't mention it. "Beautiful." He nodded toward the laptop. "How's the writing going?"

"Good. Really good. I think I just may have you to thank for that."

He cocked his head to the side in an endearing sort of way. "Yeah?"

I stuffed my hands in my pockets. "Yeah . . . you know what you said about facing my problems in my story? I tried it, and funny thing is, I think it's helping my real-life issues."

He smiled, the gesture revealing straight, but not perfect teeth. "I'm happy I could help. But you know, I just finished reading *Monterey Winds*. I'm not sure I should have messed with a good thing."

"You're joking."

He scratched his freshly shaven jaw. "I kid you not. It was amazing. Helps that I'm a Steinbeck fan, of course."

I laughed. "Of course."

An awkward silence passed between us, a strange sort of tension seeming to ping-pong across the room. "I better get to the kids," I finally said.

"Oh. Oh, sure. I'll see you around."

I slid my laptop in my bag before opening the drawer one more time to see Johanna Bancroft's mysterious book. I wondered why I felt so very much alive when just a week earlier, I'd considered everything in this town dead to me.

CHAPTER NINETEEN

I find it impossible to invent anything half so true or touching
as the simple facts with which everyday life supplies me.

~ LMA

Taylor

"How are you two doing?"

I looked up from my laptop screen to see Mom standing at the threshold of the dining room, a cup of tea in her hands.

Victoria blew a piece of hair out of her face. "It's been a while since I've written anything besides promotional materials for Orchard House."

Mom's smile warmed the room. "It will come, honey. I can't tell you what it means to me to see both of you together again, doing what you love."

I tried not to make my grin too tight, too forced. This, writing with Victoria, was a bit of a stretch for me. I'd thought it could be a way for us to start rebuilding broken bonds, but this Pickwick meeting was nothing like our old ones. I glanced at Victoria, saw the same forced smile on her face, which in a strange way made me feel slightly better.

"I'm heading up for the night. You girls enjoy."

We responded with our own good-nights, but I didn't go back to my computer screen. "Maddie didn't want to join us?"

"She has a project due Tuesday she has to work on."

I shrugged. "You all are staying here again tonight?"

Victoria bit her lip, nodded.

"You've changed," I said.

She leaned back in her chair. "How so?"

"You've lost something . . . a fire. I feel like it's still there, but it's as if time and life have buried it."

She huffed. "Well, you've pegged that one right."

"I'm sorry," I whispered. Though I couldn't say exactly what I was sorry for. For pegging her so well? That I had spoken it or that she had changed in the first place? Certainly not that I hadn't been around to be by her side through whatever life had thrown her way. And if I was honest with myself, was I sorry? Or did I secretly think she deserved the hard turns life had dealt her?

"You know, I'm not the only one who's changed."

I raised my gaze to hers, met it with an openness that I knew held a bit of a challenge. "I know I've changed. And I'm okay with it." I was weak before, too dependent on others. Somehow breaking away had freed me. For too long I'd locked myself up, forced myself to behave lest I be loved less. Escaping to California had set me free at the same time that it locked me in a prison of resentment. How was that possible? How could I be free yet yearn to belong? Why was it I so desperately wanted to depend on only myself yet still longed for another to bear my burdens?

She looked at the table. "Will and I . . . we're taking some time apart, Taylor."

While I'd sensed that something was wrong—maybe even between her and Will—I never guessed it was this serious.

"You're . . . separated?"

"Temporarily, yes. Maybe permanently. I don't know."

"What happened?"

"I wish I knew." She sniffed, and her bottom lip trembled.

"Victoria . . . I'm so sorry." And I was. No matter what had happened in the past, it felt small compared to this—the potential ruin of a marriage, the potential devastation of a family.

"It's not your fault. Will's not the same person he used to be . . ." She shrugged. "I'm not sure he'll ever get past whatever happened in Iraq. I'm not sure he'll ever open himself up to me."

I thought to get up, to put my arms around her, but I couldn't summon enough strength in my legs to stand. "I—I wish there was something I could do to help."

She let out a derisive snort. "Do you really?"

"You can't think I'm happy about this."

"In some weird way I wonder if I didn't have it coming."

"You mean because of . . ."

She nodded. "I gave up writing, thought that was penance enough. But it wasn't enough. Maybe nothing would ever be. Maybe Will felt it too."

Something within me broke down then. I went to her end of the table, crouched down, and put an arm around her. "I don't know a lot about penance and God and how all that works, but I do know that you have a beautiful family, that no matter the circumstances surrounding its beginning, at one time you and Will loved each other. And I know by watching Mom and Dad that love isn't always easy, that it might take work. Maybe you and Will should go talk to someone."

She blinked, and a tear fell from her wet lashes. "I suggested that a long time ago. Now . . . I don't think I even want to bother with the work. What he's done . . . what he's doing . . . how he's hurting not just me but the kids . . . well, I hate him. I wish he would just go. Far, far away."

I didn't know what to say. I wasn't an expert on marriage, but I could listen. Try to understand.

But Victoria didn't say anything more. Just dried her eyes. "I'm sorry. This is *not* what Pickwick meetings are for."

"Oh, I don't know about that. Remember when Andrew Landry kissed Monica Greenleaves behind the middle school bleachers? It took a few Pickwick meetings to get through that one."

She smiled. "I had fallen head over heels for that kid. What a wreck I was." She sighed. "If only my problems were so small now."

"How are Caden and Maddie handling things?"

"Caden can sense something is off, but he doesn't really know yet. Maddie seems to know all too much, and she's chosen to blame me."

I opened my mouth, but again words failed me.

Victoria closed her laptop. "I'm sorry. I can't write right now. Maybe never."

While the stresses of life had broken the dam for my words, it appeared they did the opposite for Victoria. I thought of Johanna Bancroft's book of poems. "I'll be right back." I ran upstairs to my room and scooped the book off my desk. I'd packed it carefully in my bag before leaving Orchard House for the day, planned to look at it before bed. Now, though, it seemed right to revisit it with Victoria.

She blinked when I came down the stairs with the book in my hands. "You took it with you?"

"I did feel kind of nervous, but you told me to keep it safe."

Her mouth tightened into a thin line. "I suppose I did."

I slid my chair over to hers. "Read me the first poem."

She carefully flipped past the dedication we read earlier to the first verse. The paper was decently preserved, just a bit brittle at the edges. When she opened to the first poem, she dragged in a quivering breath, though I couldn't be sure if it was lingering emotion over our talk about her marriage or the expectation of reading the words within the little book.

TRUST

Standing on the edge
Of the pier,
Years and tears aching
to flood the bay,
Asking—no, begging God for a sign,
Should I leave or should I stay?
A sailless boat drifted by,
"Trust me" on its side.
I unfolded myself, and
what was there spilled out and

Splashed against the side of the boat.
I was sucked underneath,
Dark and drowning and unable to shout,
The light of the surface out of reach.
A hand reached down
And held my own and
Whispered, "Trust me," to me alone.
Was I lost and now am found?
Who am I that I did not drown?

"*A hand reached down . . .*"

"Sounds like she's been through a lot," I said when Victoria had finished reading.

"Or it could have nothing to do with her. Does every story you write reflect your life?"

No, I supposed it didn't. But every story I wrote had a piece of myself contained within. Readers usually couldn't guess which part it was, but it was tucked there, within it all. I wondered what part of Johanna Bancroft's self was tucked within this poem.

I went to my laptop, googled Johanna Bancroft's name. No results that would have indicated a historical Johanna caught my eye in the first couple of pages. I tapped my fingers on the table. "Hmmm . . . didn't the dedication say something about a John? It sounded as if both Louisa and Johanna were close to him or at least knew him."

Victoria pulled her legs up onto the chair, crisscrossing them. "The only John I can remember is Louisa's brother-in-law, Anna's husband. John Pratt."

"Maybe this woman was involved with him somehow?"

"Involved? Let's be careful what we're insinuating here. These were people—real people, no matter how long dead. We don't have any reason to assume that John was unfaithful to Anna. From what I read, he was one of the few men Louisa truly admired."

I thought to defend myself. Seemed to me Victoria was being a bit too touchy about my word choice. Again, I wondered if what she and Will were going through was beyond fixable. With some effort, I let it go.

"Maybe a sister, then? Surely we can trace John Pratt's ancestry?"

Victoria nodded. "I have entire files at work. Anna and John's ancestors are still in town, too. I'll look into it tomorrow." She stretched. "I'm beat right now. Think I'll call it a night."

I tried not to show my disappointment, tried not to *be* disappointed. How had I gotten wrapped up in all of this, anyway? I'd come here to see Lorraine, to give myself some sort of peace. Instead, I was getting drawn back in. I was letting things like Pickwick Clubs and mysterious old books take precedence above my deadline, my boyfriend, my whole life in California.

I thought of my brief conversation with Kevin before supper. There'd been nothing wrong with it, on the surface anyway. He didn't seem to be holding any hard feelings over my not wanting him to come to Massachusetts, was already planning his next trip surrounding a big story his editor had in mind for him.

He seemed great. And I was great without him. Why, then, did that bother me?

I never wanted to be tied down to another person. After Will, after the Bennetts, I didn't want to depend on needing anyone that much again. And I thought I'd gotten past it. And yet, had I? I was here, home, feeling like things were heading in a decent direction. I was actually enjoying my time here, felt it was good for something deep inside me. Why was I so against Kevin playing a part in all of this?

I said good night to Victoria and turned back to my computer screen.

The dishwasher running in the kitchen sounded familiar. Too familiar. I stood up, a sudden need to run taking over. I slipped my laptop into my bag and grabbed my purse and keys. A little distraction would be good. A change of scenery. I needed inspiration, and I wasn't sure I could get it here.

～～

I drove into downtown Concord and parked at one of the meters. The library closed in half an hour, so that wasn't an option. I found myself wandering toward Main Streets Cafe. I told myself it wasn't on purpose, but it was.

The story I was writing was close to home, maybe too close, and for the first time I was letting myself go there. For some reason, I knew being *here* would help.

Again, Luke's and Victoria's words jumbled in my mind, making a peculiar hodgepodge of inspiration.

"Work it out in your story."

"Write your story and make something good come out of it."

I entered the café. They'd done a few updates, and it suited the place. I went to the counter, ordered a decaf coffee, then found an out-of-the-way corner table and settled in.

Within minutes, the words were flying onto the screen with little effort. I couldn't remember the last time my fingers had trouble keeping up with the story in my head. What was more, the story was good. Very good. And I didn't usually feel that way about things I wrote, at least on the first draft. But this, giving myself fully over to whatever had been stirring within me for sixteen years now, maybe longer . . . there was a strange sort of release I felt within my being. A release I found surprisingly satisfying.

"Well, I guess some things definitely change."

I looked up, blinked, forced my mind from the story I'd been completely enthralled in to see someone who too closely resembled one of my characters.

"What are you doing here?" I asked.

"Same thing as you, I guess." I noted the small workbag Will held. "Was just finishing up, actually, grabbing a coffee for the road when I saw you over here. The words come a lot easier than they used to, huh?"

I shut down my computer. "Yeah. I guess they do."

He shifted from one foot to the other, Styrofoam coffee cup in hand. Being with him in this place after I'd just been totally immersed in all the emotions this story brought up within me was too much. Too strange.

"Could we take a walk?" he asked. "I mean, if you have more writing to do, I can wait a bit, but I thought this might be a good chance for us to catch up."

I tapped my long-empty coffee mug on the table. "I don't really think that's a good idea." Considering our history, considering I was finally making some progress with Victoria, and considering what she had just told me about her and

Will being on unstable ground, I didn't think it wise to spend time with her husband—my first love.

"Taylor . . . please?" He looked so vulnerable then, so entirely innocent. With the single look I remembered why I had fallen for him in the first place. His many faults seemed to fade against the many good qualities I'd known him to have. I wondered if maybe Victoria hadn't been simply looking for sympathy earlier. He'd been to war after all. Quite likely I was the one who had sent him there. Marriages had rough patches. She could be difficult. Maybe she was just as much at fault over the divide as he was.

I released a long sigh and closed my laptop. "Maybe just a short one."

He grinned. "Great. Thank you. I don't take this lightly, believe me."

I shouldered my bag, placed my mug in the spot for dirty dishes, and followed him outside. The cool night air nipped at my skin and I zipped up my sweatshirt as we headed farther down Main Street. In the distance, the library lights had dimmed. My laptop bag gently slapped my side as we walked in silence. I refused to be the first one to break it.

"Victoria told me you're a hotshot writer now. *New York Times* bestseller list and all that."

I shrugged. "It pays the bills and apparently it's something I'm good at."

"I'm happy for you, Taylor. It's awesome your dreams came true."

I kept quiet for a moment. Really, I didn't want to feed into the conversation at all. Better to discourage him, to end this time together.

But he didn't speak anymore, and I began to feel rude. As much as I hated to admit it, I wanted this time, small as it was. While I didn't allow myself to daydream about Will often, there'd been moments in the weeks after I'd left that I had done so. I'd imagined him finding me, explaining away what I'd seen with my own eyes. Years later, I would imagine a conversation that went something like what we were having now.

"How about you? Victoria said you're a hotshot engineer. Are all your dreams coming true?"

I gave him a sidelong glance and a small smile, an attempt to keep the conversation light. He returned the look, but the intensity of his gaze beneath the streetlamps was anything but light. "Almost all of them."

Fire erupted inside me, threatening to scorch my insides. I couldn't pretend his words meant anything other than what they did. There was no mistaking the intention behind them.

But whatever he wanted to imply, it didn't matter. For their sake, I would not hurt Victoria—or myself—something I wished she had spared me all those years ago.

I did an about-face. "I have to go."

He grabbed my arm. "Taylor, no, wait. Please. I'm sorry. I have things I want to say to you, and that—it didn't come out right."

I crossed my arms in front of my chest and he released his desperate grip. I rubbed the place where his fingers had dug into my skin. His rough touch felt as foreign to me as his presence, as the desperation clinging to him. He *had* changed. Better to get this over with, then. Let him have his say and be done with it. "Okay, go for it."

He forced a hard, determined breath into his lungs. "I wish I had looked harder for you back then. I should have hired an investigator, tracked you down, tried to explain. But I was . . . scared."

I ran a hand over the side of my face, could hardly believe we were having this conversation. "What were you scared of, Will?" I couldn't keep the sarcastic bite out of my tone, the impatience.

"Scared you'd turn me away, never forgive me. I know it sounds lame, but it's true. So I decided to run too. Only it turns out the Middle East was a bad place to do it. It messed me up, Taylor. When I finally got back, I was sure you'd have come back home by then. I couldn't wait to see you, to start new. Only you were still gone."

But Victoria was very much here.

I dipped my head, closed my eyes, imagined him waiting, hurting. My heart thawed just a little. "I should have kept in touch with all of you. I realize that now. I'm sorry for whatever happened to you over in Iraq, I really am. But what's done is done, and you have a beautiful family, a great job. I think . . . well, maybe it all turned out how it was supposed to in the end. Maybe we're better off."

Did I believe that?

"Are we?" he asked, echoing my thoughts. "I've never forgotten about you. I tried to move on, and in some ways I did, but what if . . . ? I mean, Victoria and I haven't been doing good for a while now, and I can't help but think that the root of our problems was our beginning. We were a mistake—I'm realizing that now."

"I can't believe you," I whispered.

He swallowed. "I'm not happy, Taylor."

My emotions swirled within me. This was so low—like nothing I expected from the man I used to love. And at the same time, a horrible part of me relished his words. That he regretted his decisions, that he really had loved me all along.

I stomped that part down. I was an awful human being. Victoria . . . poor Victoria.

"There's more at stake here than *your* happiness," I said. "You think we can go back and undo all these years, pretend there's a second chance? Will, I don't even *want* a second chance. I have my own life now. A life that, for the most part, I love."

He stepped closer, undeterred. "But something's missing for you, too. I know it is, because I know you. I can see it. I saw it right away in the kitchen that morning."

I tried to tell myself he was wrong. That my life was complete, that nothing was missing. He was trying to manipulate me—something I never remembered him doing but something he seemed to be skilled at now.

And maybe he was right. Being back in Massachusetts did make me realize that there *was* something missing. I'd thought it was family. But being in this place with Will, remembering what we had, the realness of it . . . was that what I'd been missing all along? Had that entire day—him kissing Victoria and then me running away—simply been one horrible mistake?

He stepped closer, his presence taking up every space and corner of me, if only for a moment.

No. Even if this was some awful mistake, there was no way something good could be birthed from it at this point.

We weren't kids anymore. Even if I wanted to—and I wasn't entirely sure that I didn't—we couldn't ignore the misery we left in our wake. We couldn't cling to selfishness.

"I have to go," I said, turning.

Again he grabbed my arm, but this time he pulled me against him, pressed his mouth to my own. It was a desperate, hungry kiss and it left me shocked. I pushed at him, frantic.

When I finally broke away, I slapped him across the face. Hard. "That was so out of line, I don't even know where to begin."

He held his face with his hand. I found it hard to believe he could be as surprised as he looked by my reaction. "I—you're right. I'm sorry. I just . . . I don't know what to do anymore, Taylor."

I pointed a finger at him, anger bubbling within me. "Fix yourself. Then—if you're lucky and Victoria doesn't have the sense to leave you—try to fix your marriage." I left, walking with forceful steps, praying he wouldn't follow behind me, glad when there was no sign of him.

When I got in my car, I started it, locked the doors, and put my bag on the passenger's seat, my hands shaking. I buried my face in them, didn't bother stopping the tears that came forth.

He'd messed with my emotions, that was for sure, but more than anything I felt terrible about that kiss. Was I at fault? While I hadn't been the one to initiate it and even did my best to stop it, if I hadn't agreed to the walk in the first place, it would have never happened. I let him open up to me. I never should have allowed vulnerability, for either of us.

I'd have to tell Victoria. There was no way I could keep this information from her. Right when things were starting to look up between us, too. It would hurt, and she might not even believe that I was innocent, but it didn't change the fact that I hadn't made anything better by coming here.

It was a single kiss, all those years ago, that had changed the course of my life. How would this one change the course of Victoria's? Victoria, who was in a marriage with two children? I had to admit, the long-ago transgressions of my sister looked paltry beside what I'd done this night—potentially propelling a marriage and family into ruination.

I put my car in drive and headed toward the Bennetts', thinking that the sooner I went back to California and Kevin, the better.

I wiped away the last of my tears as I pulled into the Bennett driveway, trying not to see ghosts of sixteen years past in the shadows my headlights formed in front of the garage.

I did not wish I was with Will. This night had cemented that in my mind. While old regrets had tormented me for years, the last hour had closed out a very long chapter of my life.

Will was not the same man I'd fallen in love with. And even if he weren't my sister's husband, not for one minute would I choose to be with him today.

CHAPTER TWENTY

The love of one's neighbor in its widest sense [is] the best help for oneself.

~ LMA

Johanna

I stayed in bed longer than usual the next morning. I was certain the household would sleep off their excitement over Louisa's arrival, and I chose to lie awake in the cot beside May's bed, musing on the night before and the future that would soon be mine.

In truth, I was a bit frightened to face my friend. It was no secret that I admired Louisa, that I cared for her as the sister I never had. But while I could share my thoughts freely on paper and in a letter, I wondered if I would be able to so easily communicate them face-to-face.

Though she had written of her acceptance of me and Nathan, I wondered if she would approve of a marriage. Fiddlesticks! I got out of bed and began my morning toilet, careful not to wake May, who still slept. This was my life, not Louisa's. Liberty might be better than love in her eyes, and yet I had never been more independent in my life. More at *liberty* to choose love. And that meant I needn't anyone's approval.

I heard a soft snore coming from Mr. and Mrs. Alcott's bedroom across the way before I descended the stairs with light steps and stopped short upon finding Louisa at her desk in the parlor. With the creaking of the bottom step, she looked up and smiled.

I suddenly didn't know what to do with my ringed hand. Putting it before me felt too showy; putting it behind me felt as if I was trying to hide something. "You're up early," I said. "I thought for certain you'd sleep late with all the festivities last night."

"I couldn't sleep too late, for my curiosity over the account books woke me with the first ray of dawn." She looked at the ledgers before her. "Things have, as I expected, fallen behind when the moneymaker was away." But her smile softened her words, and she didn't seem cross. "Lucky for me I have plenty of offers waiting. There is sudden hoist for a meek and lowly scribbler who was told to 'stick to her teaching,' it seems. I will have to become like a spider once more—spinning out my brains for money."

I smiled. Maybe it was good we spoke now. She seemed in a jolly mood. I could tell her of my plans to marry Nathan, allay any fears she had of turning me away. "I am making plans . . . ," I began.

She turned toward me fully. "Johanna, you've been quite dear to me and my family. And we could still use your help unless you are ready for a new adventure."

Yes. An adventure. That's what marriage to Nathan would be. A beautiful, engaging adventure.

"I think I am."

The corners of Louisa's mouth turned downward. "I see. Well, I suppose you miss your family. No doubt they miss you."

"I do, though that is not my plan." I fidgeted with the ring on my hand, then tentatively, showed her my fingers.

She grasped my hand, her mouth falling open. "Johanna! I had no idea you were quite so serious."

I breathed deep, relieved to be out with the news. "We are."

She leaned back in her chair. "It's beautiful. And you are happy and at peace with the future you have decided for yourself?"

I nodded. "Very."

"Then I am happy for you." She stood and embraced me, and I tried to fight off the emotion bubbling in my throat.

We pulled apart. "Thank you," I said. "For being happy."

"Have you written your mother?"

I shook my head. "Not yet, but I aim to today."

"Please know you are welcome to stay here until the wedding." She grinned. "I admit I'm glad you will be close by."

"Me too." I knew I should let her get back to her accounts but could not leave without voicing one question. It was a question I hadn't let myself think of until now, a question that might be ridiculous to ask, even. And yet, imagining my wedding, imagining George walking me down the aisle when I wished John could be the one to do so, propelled me to voice my thoughts. "Louisa, do you think John would be pleased?"

She looked at me steadily then, and I almost regretted the

question at once. For Louisa was nothing if she wasn't honest, and I didn't know if I wanted her honest answer.

"I believe he would be pleased you are happy, dear. And I've no doubt you are a good judge of character. That you have spent adequate time with Nathan to know what type of man he is, that you haven't one doubt he will treat you well to the end of your days. That you have thought long and prayed hard about your decision, that you are not merely being swept away by emotions like my Sylvia in *Moods*."

No doubts. Yes, of course I hadn't any. But like a rooster crowing at an ungodly hour of the morning, the memory of Nathan shoving me aside, of the fallen and broken plate of cookies, clamored for attention. I thrust *it* aside. He had apologized, had shown himself a man of upright character these past several months. All was well. And as far as thinking and praying, wasn't love about more than thought? Wasn't it an instinct of sort, a knowing? Surely God directed my heart in this matter. *This* was where I belonged. I'd felt it the moment I'd come to Concord, and now that I had the entirety of my life with Nathan to look forward to, I felt certain that this was where it was all to lead me. To the man I loved. A man who wanted me forever and always by his side. A man passionate about the very same things as me—the rebuilding of our country through literature and writing. We would work together, be a team not just in marriage but in benefiting society through our words.

I wanted it so badly I could nearly taste it on the edge of my tongue, as sweet as a peppermint drop and ten times more satisfying.

Why should Louisa have to ruin it by comparing me to

one of her characters? And that flighty girl Sylvia, no less. She had learned a hard lesson in *Moods*. But I was not some fictional character. This was real. This was life.

Still, I had opened this line of talk with my own question. I must affirm Louisa's statements that I did indeed, have no doubts.

I nodded. "Of course I am certain of this. With all my heart."

Louisa turned back to her ledgers. "Then I am quite certain John would be pleased."

～

We decided upon a September wedding. Nathan sent fare for Mother and George's little family and invited them to stay at his home the week of the wedding.

The ceremony proved a small affair. Mrs. Alcott had been ill of late and Louisa hired another girl, devoting herself to her marmee as she spun away at what she called one of her "sensational" tales dubbed *Fair Rosamond*.

Louisa alone made her way up the drive to Nathan's backyard to watch the minister marry us. George, proud and tall, gave me away while Mother dabbed her eyes with her handkerchief. A modest crowd of Nathan's friends, many whom I'd just met for the first time, along with his uncle and a few acquaintances from church, also joined us in the celebration.

Mother and George's stay was all too short, however, and soon Nathan and I bade them goodbye at the station and were off to our brief seaside excursion.

Life as a married woman proved to be bliss. I'd never seen Nathan happier and for once he seemed at peace with his uncle and his career. We settled into his home, where I enjoyed keeping house and cooking for him, always encouraging him to invite his friends whenever he chose. He did not go to Boston as much and many times we acted as silly as two children, chasing one another around the house, laughing and teasing until we ended up in the bedroom in one another's arms.

One night I came to him as he sat on the outside porch. The sun bade good night earlier as the year waned, and I snuggled into the crook of his waiting arm where he sat in the porch swing. I held a few papers in my lap. An important piece of myself I wanted him to have. Papers of vulnerable words I wished to share with him. My poetry.

I'd hoped he'd ask about them, but he just kept pushing his feet to move the swing, staring off at the lingering sun as the gentle chirp of crickets sang it to sleep.

"I wanted to show you some of my writing. My poems." I quelled my anticipation. There was so much that could be lost in this moment. He could read them and think less of me. He could think them nothing more than silly sentimental scribbles. Or he could pretend to like them to spare my feelings.

He closed his eyes, leaned his head back in the chair. "I'm tired, Johanna. Might we look at them together tomorrow?"

I didn't answer straightaway, for surprise stopped me from doing so. "Yes . . . yes, of course."

But the next day was busy, and Nathan never asked after my writing in the weeks to come. Every time I thought to bring it up, fear of being brushed aside kept my mouth closed.

~~

Like any young wife, I vowed to be a light in my husband's world—to try to please him in every way, to keep home a pleasant place. I insisted that Ivan was no longer needed as I had nothing to do but see the house ran smoothly. Quite honestly, I did not want to share the duties—or the house—with the older gentleman, and once he left and Nathan saw how cozy it was with just the two of us, he was pleased.

As was normal with most anything, the newness of our marriage began to wear off after several months. The playfulness settled to what I believed was something realer, truer. But the "truer" thing came with that familiar shadowed look of Nathan's as Christmas came and went and the doldrums of winter settled upon us. He resumed his Boston trips and sometimes at night, he would lock himself alone in his study for hours while I sat by the fire mending clothes or carving away at a poem or two by candlelight.

I once left a poem on his dresser. A gift to him, certainly, but a relatively simple and lighthearted endeavor that bared my heart and feelings for him all the same, disclosing this part of myself that I longed to share but that he persistently neglected to see.

I read it over one more time before leaving it with a few brilliantly colored autumn leaves.

KISSING IN THE KITCHEN
The kitchen door opens,
Expectation enters.
She holds her breath.

He passes her
and places his lunch pail
on the corner counter.
His scent is of winter
when it's warm inside.
She longs to go there.
The moment lingers,
her breath still holding
inside her heart.
A step closer he comes.
She feels his warmth.
Inevitable embrace
awaits,
while she inhales
him and hates that he
is so far away.
Then it goes,
the moment
of too-far distance,
and he folds
her inside his
strength.
She no longer waits
or wants,
for there it is,
kissing
in the kitchen.

When he came home later that day and placed his lunch pail on the counter, he came to me with surety, kissed me with enough passion to create a small, crackling fire within me.

"Thank you for the poem," he said.

I smiled up at him, my heart singing. "Did you like it?" I asked, sure he must have with a response like that.

He tapped my nose. "It is adorable. Just like you."

Adorable.

The word was meant to be a compliment. Why did it feel an insult? Did he think my verses nothing more than childish musings to fawn over? Did he not see any literary promise in them?

That night, he hid himself away in his study again. When I knocked upon the door and entered at his call, I did not miss the shining glass of liquid sparkling by the firelight. It couldn't be. He'd promised, after all . . .

"I wanted to check in on you. See if you need anything."

Such as my company.

He shook his head, his eyes glassy as he stared into his drink. "I am to be the one to take care of you." He seemed to do battle with something within himself, only I did not know how to give him what he needed for victory.

"Leave, Johanna. Now, please."

I did, going to my cold bed, feeling an intruder in my own home. I had such high expectations about our future together, our marriage. Had I been blind?

CHAPTER TWENTY-ONE

Life is my college. May I graduate well, and earn some honors!

~ LMA

Johanna

I STRAIGHTENED from where I was picking currants from our bushes and wiped my sweatied brow with the backs of my berry-stained hands. The warmer weather seemed to bring hope to our household. I had decided to foster that hope with one of Nathan's favorites—currant jam. He'd given me enough money in the household account to order jars and sugar, and I had spent the last two days gathering the ripe berries.

I knew if Nathan saw me, he would insist on hiring a boy. It seemed to bother him when I did what he considered "common" work, and yet I thought it healthful for my mind and body, and it did not bother me. I did not tell him that I often visited the Alcotts to help when I could, as both Louisa and her mother had recently suffered the rheumatic fever. The last I visited, Mrs. Alcott was half-blind, Mr. Alcott seemed to have aged tremendously, and Louisa herself seemed weak and a bit nervous—not at all how I remembered her.

She insisted on paying me what she could when I helped, and only to soothe her pride did I accept. I often wondered if it were easier for her to think of me as "the help" rather than a friend who simply wanted *to help*.

I lugged the currants into the kitchen, smiling as I thought of Nathan's reaction to seeing a stock of jam in the pantry that night. I donned my checkered apron and opened my copy of Mrs. Cornelius's book with all the determination of a runner set for a grueling race. I imagined Nathan slathering the jam on my fresh bread, how he would look at me with surprise and pleasure when he tasted the sweet spread upon his tongue.

I had seen Mother make jam plenty and had even helped her once, but to my dismay, and despite my ardent efforts to boil, strain, and sugar it, the mixture proved too runny and would not for the life of it become a beautiful, smooth concoction.

And still I did not give up, trying to reheat and resugar and scold the liquid into jelling. The sun began its slow descent, and I knew I should be cooking the mutton, for Nathan was to arrive any minute, and yet I could not release the thought of all those beautiful currants gone to waste.

Finally, looking at the mess of a kitchen, runny currant mixture all over my new jars and pans and stove, I slumped onto the floor, admitting defeat, and sobbed into my checkered apron.

I had opened the window to allow the burnt sugar smell

to clear out of the kitchen, and above my sobs I heard a carriage mounting the drive. My tears flowed all the more, for I liked to be waiting for him on the porch, the scents of a simmering supper wafting to greet him. Still, would he not understand? Surely, as soon as Nathan saw me in such a state, he would take me in his arms and assure me that all would be just fine in the end. That he didn't care about jam as much as he cared about being home with me.

I heard the carriage stop and then . . . voices. One was Nathan's. The other, a man's voice I didn't recognize.

Of all days! He'd brought company home. In my early days of housekeeping, when I was certain that being a wife and having dinners on the table would be a feasible task, I had told him to invite guests whenever he saw fit. And he had beamed at me as though I were the sweetest girl in all the world. Only now . . . oh, he should most certainly have sent word!

I fell further into despair and did not even bother getting off the floor or fixing my hair or wiping currant juice from my face. What did it matter?

The voices again, then footsteps in the house and Nathan's voice. "Dear? Are you home?"

"I'm here," I answered weakly. I didn't bother to lift my head, for I didn't want to see the shadow of disappointment cross his face at the untidy kitchen, at the mess I had made.

Did I imagine the foul word that came from his mouth upon entering?

I waited for him to come to me, to kneel on the floor beside me and wrap me in his strong arms, to call me "dear" again and ask what was wrong. But he didn't, and I lifted my head. "I'm sorry, Nathan. I've ruined it all."

His chest puffed out in a deep breath as he surveyed the kitchen again, his gaze finally landing on me. "I've brought Charles home. Charles Inglewood. I invited him to stay for the night. We're to talk of the possibility of a new venture. What I've been wanting to do . . ."

I swiped at my eyes. "I'm sorry. I didn't know."

He paced the kitchen, raked a hand through his hair. "He can't stay. Not like this. Not with you . . ." He looked at me again, and I'd never felt so inadequate before him. Yes, sometimes he came to bed late and seemed to avoid me. Sometimes he could be withdrawn or surly, but he had never, never looked at me as he did in that moment. Such displeasure, even disgust, that I felt certain he regretted marrying me.

I didn't know what else to offer, what would improve the situation, if anything.

"I will drive him into town and put him up in the boardinghouse. We will fetch dinner and do our business there. Perhaps by tomorrow morning, you could be presentable for a breakfast."

"Yes. Yes, of course." I wanted to help him. I would redeem myself.

"Very well."

And he was gone. Without a peck on the cheek or a kind word.

I heard him explaining away the change of plans by claiming me ill, and a rebellious part of me wished to pop out of the house in my currant-stained checkered apron and prove him a liar. He had been gone for days! Hadn't he enough time to talk business? Why must he bring it home and then desert me when I felt such a failure?

I sank to the floor again as the horse clopped back down our driveway, and I let the tears come.

Much later, when they were dry, I got to work cleaning the kitchen. More than anything, I wanted to run down to Orchard House, to pour my troubles out to Louisa. But she was in one of her writing spells, composing fairy tales for a Christmas book that Mr. Fuller had requested.

I could not bother her with such a trifle as jam. And I knew she would take my side—say that Nathan should not have given me such a great burden and surprise when we had not spoken for days about such affairs as dinners.

And her defensive words would not serve my marriage well. For I would believe them true, believe that I was in the right and my husband in the wrong, and it would only create a further divide between us.

Instead, I prayed as I worked to clean the mess I'd made, tossing out the ruined currant liquid and scrubbing splatters of red goo from the stovetop, counters, pans, jars, and floors. Again, despite having failed me once, I looked to Mrs. Cornelius's book for a simple breakfast that might redeem me in my husband's eyes and Mr. Inglewood's.

I cleaned myself last, settling by the waning light of the large parlor window to write a letter to Mother. Though we seldom mentioned him, I couldn't help but write of John, of how he loved Mother's currant jam. Then, because she was far away, and it felt safe, I told her a bit of the afternoon's events and felt better for it, though I knew I would probably not mail the letter in the end.

It grew dark and I lit the candles, falling asleep in the parlor so I might not miss Nathan when he came in.

There was no fear of that. For he made every sort of ruckus when he entered, slamming the door so that I jumped awake from where I slept upon the sofa. I rose, gathered a guttering candle, and brought it to the foyer. "Nathan?"

"Leave me." His words were slurred and I knew what that meant, though I hated what it portended for us.

Still I tried. "How was your dinner?"

He took off his hat and hurled it at the coatrack, missing by many feet. "How the deuce do you think it went? How can someone be expected to invest in a man who can't keep order in his own home?" Anger frayed the edge of his words as he headed for his study. Words that seemed to pinion me in the pit of my belly and thrust the blame of the world upon my shoulders.

For a small moment, I believed it. I did feel bad about the jam and my part in Nathan's distress, really I did. But he needn't be so angry. He'd known I was not perfect from the beginning, and I knew that he wasn't. Yet part of marriage was bearing with one another, was it not? And that meant forgiving when we witnessed those shortcomings.

Shortcomings. As if my attempting to make my husband currant jam were a shortcoming.

For a moment all the layers I'd wrapped around myself since I'd met Nathan unraveled, and I saw what I was becoming. A shadow of my former self. But who had I been to begin with? I'd come to Concord looking for a place to belong, a place to find my independence and pursue my passion for literature. I'd thought that Nathan was a part of that plan. I loved him, perhaps to a fault. But was I allowing myself to wither away, to be choked and snuffed out in the name of that love?

I dragged in a long breath, wanting more than anything to make peace. With both Nathan and myself.

"I am preparing a beautiful breakfast for tomorrow. Mr. Inglewood will come, won't he?"

"No," he snapped. "He's leaving first thing in the morning."

"Well, if a simple misunderstanding put him off so, perhaps he is not a wise partner to begin with."

He went to his cupboard, pulled out a bottle of whiskey. Something hard knotted in my chest at the sight of the alcohol. Yes, I had long suspected. Maybe even known after seeing the shining glass beside him that night in this study. But to voice it seemed to breach the trust we had established as husband and wife. How many times had I dusted that cupboard, wondered if it contained what I feared, yet chosen not to open it? Not to let suspicion taint our new marriage? Now, though, I couldn't argue with the evidence. And he wasn't even bothering to conceal it.

I stepped forward. "You promised."

He ignored me.

I placed a hand on his arm. "Nathan, this is not the answer. There is a better way for us to work—"

"I said leave me!"

I did not see his hand coming. Nor did I anticipate the power behind it. Black came over my vision, and I fell to the floor, partly from the force of it, partly because it put me in a state of shock and my limbs simply gave out.

I reached out a shaky hand to steady myself on the side of his desk.

"Johanna . . ." I felt his arm on my shoulder, but I flinched. "If you did not persist in harping on me . . ."

I couldn't dredge up words to defend myself. What's worse, I felt the start of an apology on my lips. Something. Anything to make it right between us again.

He helped me to my feet as if it were a chivalrous act. And once I regained my balance, I left the room to hide myself away in the bedroom, pathetic tears soaking the pillow.

I had known better, hadn't I? I had seen his true form once before, had chosen to ignore it. I thought I'd been extending grace, but perhaps I'd only been extending my own naiveté. Believing what I wanted to believe. Hoping for something beyond what I knew to be real.

Now it was too late. And I hated myself for it.

The next morning Nathan was gone when I woke. One glance into the looking glass proved the horrors of the night before, and I collapsed back into my bed and chose to sleep away the day. Night came, and I rose to walk around the moonlit house, sat on the porch for an hour or so, listening to the crickets and owls chanting a melody just for me.

Words swirled in my head, something like a poem forming, nonsense trying to create sense from some well deep inside me. I prayed. I asked for wisdom. And then when the grandfather clock struck twelve, I went back up to bed.

My last thought before I dozed off was the very acute feeling that I had somehow let John down.

"I'll fix it, John. I promise," I mumbled, half-asleep, into my pillow.

I would. This would not be the course of my life. I would be a better wife, not harp on Nathan so, try to be more understanding. I would fight for what was mine.

Everything would be fine.

CHAPTER TWENTY-TWO

Work is such a beautiful and helpful thing, and independence so delightful,
that I wonder there are any lazy people in the world.

~ LMA

Taylor

"Hey, I was hoping I'd catch you." Luke stood in the door-way of Bronson Alcott's school, his now-familiar form shadowing the frame, something in his hand. "Can I come in?"

"Of course." I shut my laptop, ending my final writing session on the grounds of Orchard House. It had been . . . inspirational and confusing all at once. In some ways, my time here seemed cut short. Much too short.

"I didn't know if you'd be back, it being the last day of camp and all. I saw this and I thought of you." He held out a vintage book, no words on the front. I took it from him, recognizing the picture—the automobiles holding families, the mountainous backdrop.

"No way." I flipped it open to the title page. A first

edition John Steinbeck. *The Grapes of Wrath*. "Where did you get this?"

"I was at my favorite antique shop the other day and it was just sitting on the shelf. A good price, too. I thought of you."

"I—thank you." I stood, thinking to give him a hug, but for some reason it felt too forward. Maybe it had something to do with my time with Will the night before, maybe it was something more, but I simply touched his flannel-clad arm instead. "This is beyond sweet. I love old things."

"I thought so after I saw you hiding that old book the other day."

I laughed. "You weren't supposed to see that."

"I know."

I gestured to one of the chairs near my desk, and we both sat down. "So if it's not too intrusive to say, you don't strike me as the antique-shopping type."

"And if I recall correctly, you didn't think I'd enjoy your novels, either. But I'm on my second one."

I scrunched up my face. "You're kidding."

He shook his head. "*Long Beach Nights*. Kind of steamy for me, but I'm getting into it."

I smiled. "You have plans this weekend?"

I'd just been trying to make conversation, but as soon as the words were out, it sounded like an invitation.

"I'm thinking about taking Chloe for a walk on the beach and probably church on Sunday, but other than that, nothing. You?"

Church and a girlfriend. Or a wife, though he didn't wear a ring. Another unexpected twist.

"I guess I have to think about heading back to California."

"You don't sound like you want to."

I shrugged. "Still feels like a lot of unfinished business here, you know?"

"Like that book you and Victoria were hiding the other day?"

"That among other things. Many other things."

"Well, there's plenty of extra wood to keep this place warm if you decide to stay another week."

I looked at my computer, set below the window, and stared out to the steep slope behind Orchard House, the pebbled rock seat just below it.

I sighed, taking in the way the sunlight played off the leaves of the trees, creating pockets of light and dark in the woods beyond. I wouldn't mind staying here. But was that what was best for Victoria and her family? After last night, I couldn't see that my staying would help matters. But Victoria and I had just started mending things. There was so much left undone and left unsaid, the least being the mystery behind Johanna Bancroft's poems.

"Thank you. I guess I'll have to decide soon."

"Well, you've been great for the kids. Heard more than one talking about you as if you hung the moon and the stars."

"I enjoyed them." I cleared my throat. "What about you? Have you done work like this always?"

He shook his head. "I was a police officer. Got shot on a shift one night." He gestured to his leg. "It's why I don't walk so well. But I like to stay busy, even if I can't do that sort of work anymore."

"I see." The small glimpse into his life served to endear

him to me all the more. Who was this guy? I couldn't help but compare him to Kevin, who was as fast-paced about work and life as I was, or to Will, who seemed bent on his own wishy-washy feelings of late.

I looked closer at Luke, saw the weathered lines around his eyes and mouth again, and for the first time appreciated them. He'd been through a lot of life, and I longed to know his story, though I couldn't understand why.

"You and Chloe have kids?" I asked.

His face colored. "Now that'd be kind of awkward considering Chloe's my chocolate Lab."

A laugh gurgled up from my belly. He caught it, and we both let the humor of the situation saturate us. When it finally died down, he stood. "Well, I hope you stay. I mean, I hope this isn't goodbye." He held out his hand.

I grasped it, and the warmth shot up my arm and straight through to the end of my toes, surprising me with its intensity.

"Thank you so much for the book. I plan to display it on my coffee table when I get home."

He winked at me. "I signed up for your newsletter, so I suppose I'll be hearing from you again soon, regardless."

I shook my head. If we were in another time, another place . . . if there was no Kevin or California . . . this guy might be a danger to my long-guarded heart. "You definitely will."

"Okay then. See ya." He walked toward the door.

I opened my mouth to say something, anything. To ask if I could join him on the beach and meet Chloe. But the words fell off my tongue. Probably better that way. "See you."

He left and shut the door, but I heard his deep voice

talking to someone just outside and I looked out the window to see Maddie on the steps of the school. They chatted for a moment and then he was gone.

I opened the door, settled myself on the steps beside Victoria's daughter. The spring sunshine soaked through my sweater and I pulled my Converse-clad feet up to the step below the one I sat on.

Maybe I wasn't welcome here. But I didn't want this coldness between me and Maddie. "Hey," I said, glancing at her profile, so much like Victoria's when we were Maddie's age.

"Hey."

"I loved your first page."

That morning, all the campers had chosen a piece of their writing to share. Maddie's was the best by far. Yes, she was one of the older kids, but she had that certain something—the same thing Victoria had had at her age.

I wondered if it were possible for my sister to find it again. I wondered if there was a way for me to help her find it.

Maddie squinted up at me. "Really?"

I nodded. "I know good writing when I see it. You remind me a lot of your mom." I smiled. "Maybe you don't want to hear that, but it's true. Your writing . . . it's authentic, honest. Your mom used to write like that too."

"What happened?" she asked, surprising me with the first real avenue of communication between us.

"I . . . don't think it's my place to go into all that."

She sighed, blew out a breath that fanned her dark hair. "I actually kind of know what happened. She told me when she told me about you."

I searched for words to respond to this revelation but was

at a loss. Did Victoria tell her daughter everything? Or did she leave out details?

The scent of woodsmoke wafted to my nostrils. "I must have been a bit of a surprise. I'm sorry I wasn't around more to see you and Caden."

She shrugged. "It's not like I knew any different. Mom and even Grandma and Grandpa kept quiet about you. Dad too."

Her last sentence lay heavy between us, pregnant with meaning. This was why Maddie was hostile to me from the beginning. She knew about the history between me and Will. To her, I was a threat to her parents, a threat to her family.

"I saw you two last night."

I almost missed her whispered words, thought to ask her to repeat them but couldn't get over the shock of what they might mean.

"I want to hate you, but I don't." She pulled her knees up to her chest. "I saw you pull away and slap him, and I feel like . . . like you wanted to do the right thing. I know I'm just a kid, but I feel like I understand." A tear ran down her cheek and I wanted to put an arm around her, comfort her somehow, but was afraid she'd push me away.

"How did you . . . ? I thought you were home."

"I snuck out, rode my bike downtown. Mom would kill me if she found out. I was texting Dad and he said he was working at the café. I just wanted to talk to him alone, but then I saw him talking to you. I followed you guys."

"Maddie." I rubbed my temples, felt the very adult temptation to lecture her about how dangerous it was for a young girl to be out at night alone riding her bike. Yet what right did I have over Victoria's daughter's life?

"Are you going to tell Mom?"

"I don't think my tattling on you will do much for whatever sort of aunt/niece relationship we're going to have, will it?"

"I meant about you and Dad. Last night."

Oh. That. "Yes. She needs to know. I only wish it hadn't happened."

"I know. I—I saw. He's different than he used to be. Or maybe he's not. Maybe I just can see more. It's like he's running from something."

"You are far too intuitive for a thirteen-year-old."

She gave me a sad smile. I squeezed her arm. "It's probably why you're such a great writer."

She stood. "I'm going to tell Mom I snuck out. But I thought you should talk to her first about . . . you know."

"I'm sorry, Maddie. I wish things weren't like this. Maybe it would have been better if I hadn't come, I don't know."

"If it makes you feel any better, their problems started long before last week."

I watched her walk away, back into Orchard House, probably to look for Victoria.

It was time for me to talk to my sister.

CHAPTER TWENTY-THREE

If we did not love one another so well, we never could get on at all.

~ LMA

Taylor

"I AM STUFFED." Victoria leaned back in her chair, the barest remnants of asparagus and mushrooms left on her plate of seared scallops. "Thanks for suggesting this. It's nice to get out with just us, though I wish Mom were up to it."

White tablecloths and rustic wooden chairs combined to make 80 Thoreau a cozy but elegant place to relax and eat. "She's been tired. Do you think she's up for her chemo next week?"

"She doesn't really have a choice." Victoria lifted her pinot grigio to her lips. "I don't want to pressure you, but I think it would mean a lot to her if you stayed a little longer."

I blew out a long breath. "I'm not against it, but before you go inviting me to stay, we need to talk."

"Okay, but first can I show you what I found today?" She took out a few folded sheets of computer paper.

"Uh, yeah, sure." Telling Victoria her husband kissed me wasn't ever going to be easy, but I was grateful for another delay. I slid my empty plate to the side and looked at the papers she put between us.

"So I looked into John and Anna Pratt's genealogy and found no Johanna. I was sure there would be something; then I got to thinking that there must be a clue in at least one of the biographies written about Louisa May Alcott. I searched my favorite—you know, the one by Madeleine Stern? There were several Johns in the index, and I thought I'd just write them down and we could research them one by one, you know? But one—John Suhre—stood out from the rest." Her eyes sparkled, and for the first time since I arrived, I saw a glimpse of the passion that had flowed from within her as a teenager. A passion for writing and history, a passion for all things Louisa May Alcott.

I found myself catching it. "Is this our John? What did you find?"

"I thought he might be it because from the sound of Johanna's dedication, the John she referred to was dead. This John seemed to fit the bill. I remember reading about him years ago. Stern doesn't say a lot about him, though, besides that he was a stoic blacksmith Louisa took care of during her time as a Civil War nurse."

I held up a hand. "She was a nurse?"

Victoria rolled her eyes. "How do you not know that, living with me for nine years?"

I stifled a laugh, shook my head. I'd never been as obsessed as she was about some of these things. "Go on."

"Well, I went to my copy of *Hospital Sketches* and read

about him again. There was something there, Taylor. Something I hadn't seen reading all those years ago as a teenager. Louisa . . . she didn't think much of many men—but this one, this John, she seemed to think a lot of him."

"She loved him?"

Victoria looked out the window. "Maybe. Or maybe she just respected him. Like she recognized there was substance to him. An honor that so many other men around her seemed to lack."

Honor.

I thought of Will and what I needed to tell Victoria. For some reason Luke's image came to mind—him walking, slightly crooked, through an antique shop, spotting the first edition *Grapes of Wrath*. Him handing it to me.

I shook the picture from my head, tried to replace it with one of Kevin, who made me dinners and was most attentive to my every want or need—but who would never see potential for a meaningful gift in an old book.

What was honor, exactly?

It was unfair to compare any of these men, for they each walked different stories. Maybe that had been Louisa's problem to begin with—comparison. In some ways, how could any man compare to a man dying with honor for his country? Impossibly high standards weren't realistic. And yet expecting faithfulness was.

"What are you thinking?" Victoria asked.

"I was wondering if Louisa's expectations regarding men were too high, if love should trump all else and see past mere imperfections and faults."

"Love." Victoria practically muttered the word.

While it was a perfect opportunity to confide to her about last night, I instead chose to stick to our historical conundrum rather than our present-day one. "Was there anything in the book about a Johanna?"

"No. Not in the book. But I did find this online." She flipped to a few pages she'd printed out. The writing was small and hard to read, but I saw the heading: "Finding Private Suhre: On the Trail of Louisa May Alcott's 'Prince of Patients.'" It was taken from *The New England Quarterly* and written by a John Matteson, author of *Eden's Outcasts*.

"This article traces the idea that Louisa fictionalized some of her experiences in *Hospital Sketches*. Or perhaps she simply wanted to protect her identity and those of the soldiers she met. She didn't first publish the book under her name even and calls herself 'Tribulation Periwinkle' in the book."

"Huh."

"She seems to have fabricated John's age, where he lived, and even his siblings' names, Jack and Lizzy."

"Why keep his name, then?"

"She didn't give his surname in the book. That was found later, in her journals," Victoria said. "I don't know . . . there's something sacred about a name, don't you think? Maybe, if she really was close to him, she wanted to honor the true him with that much—his name and good character."

"Okay. And this article proves she fabricated some of these other things?"

"Pretty much. The author found convincing evidence of who John was from a variety of sources—a book by a military historian about the Battle of Fredericksburg, John's own letters home to his family, and a genealogical search. It all falls into place, and you'll never guess who he found John Suhre's sister to be."

I lifted my gaze to hers. "Not Johanna Bancroft."

She nodded excitedly. "Well, she was Johanna Suhre at the time, and I suppose we can't be 100 percent sure, but it seems likely. I don't see that Louisa knew any other Johannas, and being that someone named John meant an awful lot to both of them—it would make sense that it be someone like his sister and the nurse who grew fond of him—maybe even loved him—as he lay on his deathbed."

I leaned back in my chair. "Wow. I can't believe you found all that."

"It's kind of up my alley." She winked at me. "But I'm dying to know more of Johanna's story and how Louisa played into it all. I didn't find anything online, but we have the book of poems. I say we dive in and see if we can find any clues."

I reached into my purse and pulled out a sandwich bag with Johanna's book tucked within. "But poems can be fictitious. Just as Louisa threw us off by fictionalizing her Civil War account, Johanna could have written about fictitious feelings or characters in her poems."

Victoria tapped her fingers on the table. "You yourself said there's a piece of honesty—a piece of yourself—in every writing, fiction or not. I don't think it's outrageous that we try to find it."

I flipped through the book, glimpsing titles of various poems, trying to catch one that might give us a clue. My eye caught the word *marriage*, and I gave the little book, opened, to Victoria. She read.

TILL DEATH DO US PART
UPON THE MARRIAGE BLOCK

In anger,
I hear crowds inside my head
yelling words of untruths.
I block my ears
from the jeers
and instead
think memories of you.
Love, or rather marriage,
is like a block of wood—
like the trunk of a tree
sturdy in its youth,
silly with leaf,
but later hewn to only a few feet.
At first you carried me in your arms,
spoke with charm, and
swore me no harm.
Placed me above you
on a pedestal of solid wood,
that should the years have told,
you'd chip away
with words bone cold.
I became withered and old—
but then came spring—
and again I'd open and bloom
and sow your seeds
ignoring the weeds
that occasionally choked
out my reasons for loving you.

Years and tears . . . and
the wood in which I stood,
and understood, to be our love,
cracked and chipped,
and
I lifted
to my toes
for there was no room.
I choked and screamed
and tried to lean
on you.
They tied my hands
though I didn't understand,
but then I understood
all about this block of wood.
I heard the words inside my head
of the crowds and what they said.
And then I saw myself
toppling upon our love
that you chipped and kicked
and left me hanging
like the witch
I never was.

Victoria's voice near trembled as she finished the poem.

"Um . . . I think I know why her poems were never published back in the nineteenth century."

She swallowed, nodded. "And you're telling me this is fictional? I may not be the author here, but those words are coming from some place of authenticity. I—I understand them."

I opened my mouth to suggest it could be a nod to the Salem witch trials which happened so very close to Concord, but I knew Victoria was right. No nineteenth-century woman would fictionalize such a poem for fun. There was feeling in the words, there was fight, there was confusion, and there was anger. I wondered if Louisa Alcott had ever read them, if perhaps she'd helped Johanna in a marriage gone wrong.

I closed my mouth, couldn't help thinking of Victoria's own marriage.

She didn't seem far behind. "I know how she feels. Like everyone thinks you're married to the perfect man, but they don't see what you see. They don't see how you try and you do love, but it's never enough. They think the problem is you. *You* think the problem is you."

I slid my hand across the table to cover hers. "I'm so sorry, Victoria."

"It's not your fault," she whispered. "It's mine. Only mine."

The waitress dropped our bill on the corner of our table, but we both ignored it. I started slow. "I have something to tell you that won't make any of this easier, and yet you need to know."

She put her head in her hands, and although she didn't speak the words, I felt how the gesture admitted defeat already—as if she couldn't handle one more piece of bad news.

There would be no easy way to do this. "I went to Main Streets to do some writing last night. I saw Will there."

A small sound, almost like a whimper, came from somewhere behind Victoria's hands, where her shining wedding rings did little to hide the raw hurt behind them. I hated that I had to do this. I'd come here bitter. All these years, I'd told myself I didn't care about Victoria, that she wasn't really my sister and definitely not my friend. But I couldn't ignore the bond that held us even when I hadn't wanted it to.

She'd hurt me in the past, yes, but seeing where I could have been if things had gone how I so badly wanted them to all those years ago . . . in some strange way I couldn't help but think that she'd saved me from the hurt she was going through now.

I wasn't sure that was forgiveness exactly, but it was something that felt an awful lot better than resentment.

Only now I'd have to continue. Go deeper into this pit.

"I shouldn't have agreed to walk with him. I thought he had some things to get off his chest, thought it'd be healthy for us to have some closure after all these years." I watched Victoria slowly lower her hands from her face. "I felt I owed it to him to at least listen.

"He said things. Honestly, I couldn't believe they were coming out of his mouth. I walked away from him, but not before he kissed me."

Victoria stared at the remnants of her wine in the bottom of her glass, her face frozen and emotionless.

"It was half a second. I was surprised—you have to believe me, Victoria. It didn't last. I didn't let it. I didn't want it. I know he wasn't think—"

"Don't make excuses for him. Or you."

I whispered, realized I was begging, but not able to help myself. "I didn't come here for any of this. I came for Mom." I sounded defensive, maybe guilty. Was I?

She stood, fumbled for the papers she'd just been sharing with so much excitement. She tucked her pocketbook under her arm and left.

"Victoria, wait. Please." I grabbed up Johanna's book, the sandwich bag, and my own purse, went after her before remembering the bill. I stopped a curse from slipping out of my mouth, went back and slid enough cash into the bill book, along with a hefty tip because I didn't have time to wait for change.

I left the restaurant, looked toward my car. No Victoria. I saw her then, walking in the direction of home. It wasn't far, probably a twenty-minute walk, but that wasn't the point.

"Victoria!" I tried again. "Victoria!"

I growled under my breath about how muleheaded she could be, thought about taking the car but then decided against it and ran after her instead. My tennis shoes pounded the pavement; my pocketbook fell off my shoulder. I picked it up, felt sweat gathering at my palms where I held Johanna Bancroft's book.

I should stop, put the book—which should be in some museum instead of within my sweaty palms—in the sandwich bag. But Victoria was getting farther away, and right then all I could think about was getting to her. I had hurt her, and surprisingly, that thought hurt me.

I realized then that I still loved my sister. Running after her now, I imagined never being able to get to her. Was this how she felt all those years ago when I'd left?

We weren't perfect. Our relationship was a mountain range of highs and lows and scrapes and bruises with a little joy mixed in. Really, shared blood had very little to do with it. She was the only sister I had. And like it or not, right now I was the only one she had.

My breaths came fast by the time I caught up with her. I grabbed her arm. "Please, we need to talk."

She jerked away from me. "There's nothing to say." Passersby gave us sidelong glances.

"Come to the car. I'll take us home."

"I need a walk."

"Fine, then. I'll walk with you." I could be stubborn, too.

"I should have never asked you to come."

The words hurt, but I refused to let her see that. "I should have never come."

"It would have been easier if you kept on being your selfish self, wouldn't it have? Just let Mom think you didn't care that she was going through the hardest trial of her life, is that right?"

"I was not—am not—asking to start anything between me and Will. You have to believe me. I am more than over him, and the last thing I want to do is hurt you like I was hurt all those years ago."

She stopped walking. "It's just like you to make this about you, isn't it? What happened back then, it was wrong, okay? I already told you that. But this is ten times wrong. He's my husband and—and—" She made a loud sound of annoyance—half-grunt, half-scream. "Just go. I need some time to think."

"I want to help."

"You've helped enough."

CHAPTER TWENTY-FOUR

Helped start a temperance society. Much needed in C[oncord].
A great deal of drinking, not among the Irish, but young American
gentlemen, as well as farmers and mill hands.

~ LMA

Johanna

I WOKE TO A POUNDING inside my head, realized it was some-one at the door, and chose to ignore it, tried to fall back into slumber once again. The caller would eventually give up and depart.

"Johanna?"

My eyes flew open. Louisa.

It had been some time since I had seen her. I knew Mrs. Alcott was not well, that Louisa was busy with her stories, and though I liked to help, I had found myself busy with my own pursuits of late. Jam making and all that.

"Johanna, are you home?"

I burrowed further under the covers, hoping to hide the evidence of my shame.

Her footsteps sounded up the stairs and then to the

threshold of my door. "Dear, are you unwell?" She came in, drew one of the curtains aside.

"I am fine."

She drew open another. "Then why are you abed in the middle of the day? You're not like my poor Sylvia, are you?" she asked, a slight tease in her tone as she referred to a scene at the beginning of *Moods*.

"I am only tired. Please leave."

I felt the weight of her hand on my shoulder. "Johanna, it's unlike you to succumb to the doldrums. Please, tell me what troubles—"

I knew then that she saw my face. I had not raised the looking glass to it since the other night, but I could tell by the pain that healing would be slow. Could I hide from the world for so long?

I refused to look at her, could not fathom how I had gotten myself into this situation.

"No. Johanna, Nathan did this?"

"He was drinking. I made the mistake of harping on—"

"If you made any mistake, it was in marrying the monster who would raise a hand to his wife. This is inexcusable." She paced around the room. I couldn't remember seeing her this fired up about anything for some time. When she stood still, she put her hands on her hips and faced me fully. "You must come away at once and stay with us again. I won't hear otherwise."

"I can't, Louisa. I just—can't. I've made a complete mess of it all." Then I let it all pour out of me. How this was not the first time I had witnessed his unkind hand unleashed by drink. How I had ruined the currant jam, how I truly had encouraged him to invite guests over at any time, how I had called him out on his faults when he was not in the proper mind to handle them.

Louisa sat on the edge of my bed, listening to me without speaking. She looked unwell. I knew the past winter and spring had been trying for her, that she forced the stories from her mind to provide for her family, that in many ways she had never truly recovered from the typhoid she'd suffered while nursing John. This—I—was not a burden she should have to bear.

With that in mind, I finished my story and threw back the covers, rose for the first time in many hours, and tried to force a bright countenance upon myself. "All will be well. I am certain Nathan will be home anytime, that we will both see the fault of our ways, that we will begin under the light of a new day. Thank you for listening to my whining, dear. I am sorry to have troubled you."

"Johanna," Louisa started, and it came out more gentle than I'd ever known from her, which alarmed me of itself. "You cannot stay with him. The fault lies with him, not you."

How could I heed the advice of this woman? This woman who chose to paddle her own canoe and insisted that for many, liberty was better than love? This woman who could name only a handful of men whom she admired? Her standards were high. But what about marriage? Would she have me discard my sacred union at the first sign of marital trouble? Of course I believed it wrong for Nathan to hit me. But was the just action to leave him altogether?

"He is my husband," I whispered.

"And you are worth more than to be treated this way by the man who vowed to love you above all others. I was there, do you remember? This is *not* love."

I opened my mouth to defend myself, to defend my husband and the life I'd chosen, but no words came forth.

Louisa rubbed one temple, then let her hand fall. She dragged in a breath. "When President Lincoln first called for the seventy-five thousand volunteers, Father agreed that no greater calamity could befall a people than that of deliberating long on issues endangering liberty. Mr. Emerson, also, said that gunpowder smelled good, for bad as war might be, it would be safer and better than a peace without freedom. Johanna, if you do not take up the call to change the course of things, you *will* live to regret it."

I allowed her words to sink in, pondered their possible truth, their possible consequences. Deep down, I hated how she spoke to me, as if she knew more, as if I were a child. I didn't want her pity or advice—I wanted her understanding and friendship.

I smoothed my dress, straightened my posture. My friend was older, and though I respected her, I had to claim my life as my own. My marriage as my own. If I did not do so now, when would the time present itself?

Like it or not, *this* was where I belonged. I would not skulk away in shame when troubles came upon me.

"I thank you for what I'm sure you believe is sound advice, but this is my marriage. My life. And I'm not entirely certain you can relate all that well to either."

My words came out sharper than I intended, and they caused her jaw to fall open, her brows to rise.

I was a coward. I couldn't abide her concern, and so I feigned strength. And at the same time, I wanted to fix this myself. To prove to her and anyone else that it was only a bump in the road of a normal marriage—a down of the many ups and downs. This was not failure.

She dragged in a breath, and I tried to guard my heart from feeling pity for her, for her heart was genuine. I successfully did not budge.

She stood. "Very well, then. Since you seem to think yourself entirely capable, I will leave you to it. I can't abide by dishonorable men, but neither can I abide by women who can't recognize the power of their own worth within them. We just fought a war to free the slaves, do you recall? A war for which your own brother gave his life. If you allow your marriage to shackle you in this manner—if you choose to allow this ruination of body, mind, and soul—then you are in the same position as those Africans who know they are free yet are still yoked to their former masters."

She left then, and once I heard the door shut, I screamed out my frustration, fought against the urge to throw a brush at the door where she last stood with her haughty words.

This was *my* life. My marriage. And I would not run from it. I would fight for it. And I would save it.

～⁓～

Nathan came home the next day. Before I saw him, I heard him walk to his study, and then I heard the clinking of glass against glass. He came into the kitchen with an armful of what I saw now was a large collection of glass bottles—liquor—from his cabinet.

I stood aside as he placed them on the counter, watched as one by one he unstopped each and dumped the contents down the sink. The glugging sound of the liquid was the only thing that could be heard.

Only after all were drained did he turn to me. "And that is the last time there will ever be liquor in this house again, Johanna. I promise it."

He had made a similar promise before, but I hadn't the heart to voice my doubts with his eyes so alive with determination. He put a finger to my face, and it took every effort within me not to cringe at his touch. The pad of his skin just grazed the edges of what I knew to be a fierce black-and-blue mark. So gentle, so caring. The complete opposite of how I had seen him last.

I wanted to believe this. To fall into his arms and forgive and move forward. Wasn't that why I hadn't run to the Alcotts in the first place?

And yet the trust I held for him had been torn, like a worn shirt shredded for the rag bin. I wondered if it would ever be whole again.

I didn't speak. Didn't know what to say.

"Johanna, please forgive me. I know I don't deserve it—I hate myself just looking at what I've done. That wasn't me. Please, dear, please say you'll forgive me or I shan't want to live another day."

I nodded and even welcomed his lips when they bent to mine. It felt good in his arms, good to be whole. He had made a grievous mistake and recognized that. We would move forward and start anew after all.

Lord willing.

~~

Three days later, Nathan and I had settled back in and seemed to appreciate one another anew. I even planned on bringing up the subject of my poetry once again. While I was making a glorious oyster pie to smooth over any of my husband's still-ruffled feathers, a message boy came to my door with a large package. I recognized the writing immediately as Louisa's.

After the boy left, I sat on the porch and unwound the ribbon from the thick sheets of paper. It looked like an entire book.

The first sheet held a letter, and when I spotted my name at the top, I found myself grateful that the package was meant for me, that Louisa hadn't completely cast me off over our disagreement the other day.

Dear Johanna,

I understand you are cross with me, yet I hope this is not the end of our friendship. I wrote this last year, but Elliott would not have it, saying it was too long and too sensational. I've since worked to shorten Fair Rosamond *to make it a bit more palatable for the public. Please share with me your opinion, for I value it greatly still.*

If not, please send it back and we will continue on with no hard feelings.

Yours,
Louisa

I thought it odd that she would not come and speak to me about this, that she would send me a story and ask for help after our frosty parting.

In truth, it was easier to stay mad at Louisa for suggesting such an abominable thing as leaving my husband. It was easier to stay isolated from her.

But holding the heavy manuscript in my hands, I simply could not bring myself to ignore her request.

I started as soon as I finished the pie and read the first half of it in one day. Nathan came home that night and spotted it, asking what it was, and after I told him, he didn't quite successfully hide the roll of his eyes over one of Louisa's *manuscripts*. But he left it alone and I finished reading it over the next two days.

It was good. Still very sensational, but good. Still, I couldn't quite ignore why Louisa had asked me to read it in the first place. Yes, I'd given her my opinion before, but something about the manner with which she asked this time felt urgent, personal.

I knew why after reading the novel.

It featured a distraught heroine—Rosamond—living alone with a sullen grandfather on an English island. Rosamond longs for escape and freedom, even makes the bold and foolish proclamation that she often feels she would sell her soul to the devil himself if it meant a "year of freedom." Shortly after, her grandfather is visited by Phillip Tempest, a man who resembles Mephistopheles, a demon borrowed from German folklore.

Rosamond falls in love quickly, and though she realizes Phillip has his own moral struggles, she believes that her love is powerful enough to save him. A year later, her husband admits that Rosamond has stolen his heart, but their happiness is not to last, for Rosamond begins to suspect that Tempest's evil streak runs fouler than she could have guessed. Her suspicions are confirmed when she finds that Phillip already has a wife and a son—and that he has fooled her into becoming his mistress. Rosamond escapes right away, but Tempest chases after her, finding her again and again, in some ways enjoying the perverse chase and the many disguises Rosamond attempts.

With the help of a handsome Father Ignatius, a priest she has met while hiding within a convent, Rosamond finally— years later—returns to her grandfather's island where a tragic end awaits them all.

As I read, I found myself cheering Rosamond on, wanting her to find freedom from the man she thought she had married. While the ending echoed *Moods* just a bit, I didn't find that the disastrous conclusion bothered me so much this time.

Yet something else did.

There was a message here, and I knew Louisa meant it for me. Though I doubted she had tailored the story specifically for me, I did know how passionate she was toward women in situations like Rosamond's. Women who were oppressed.

And I hated that she viewed me that way.

Yet even through this, I could see she only wanted my best. She wanted me to recognize myself in her Rosamond, to understand her plight, admire her, and perhaps take up one of my own.

But I had not married a man who already had a family. Nathan *was* my husband. And he had not oppressed me. He asked for my forgiveness. He loved me.

I was *not* Rosamond. Or Sylvia. Or any fictional character of hers. Truthfully, I tried not to let it irk me that she felt I needed to learn through her stories. Could she not simply be my friend?

I did not wait in returning the manuscript. Despite my still-healing face, I walked down to Orchard House and knocked on the kitchen door.

The hired girl answered. "Hello," I greeted. "Might Miss Alcott be in?"

"Yes, she told me to fetch her if you called." The girl bustled up the stairs and I made my way into the parlor, wondered on Mrs. Alcott and how she fared, if she was abed this day.

Louisa came down the stairs, gave me a bright smile.

"I'm sorry to interrupt your writing."

She shook her head. "I'm glad you've come." Her gaze fell to the manuscript in my hands. "You do not wish to read it?"

"On the contrary, I have read it."

"Oh. Thank you."

She didn't ask for my thoughts, though I knew she wanted them.

"Please, sit." She gestured to a chair and I couldn't help but think how formal we suddenly were, how the tension of our last encounter had followed us. "You're healing well." She gestured to her own face.

"Don't," I ground out. I couldn't ignore it altogether, but I didn't want to go down this road right now.

She straightened. "Very well, then."

Oh, I hated how this *thing* was between us! Couldn't friends disagree and remain amicable?

"Your story is amazing. I could hardly put it down," I began.

She inched to the edge of her seat. "That's wonderful to hear. I am curious what you thought of the end."

"It reminded me of *Moods*, but this time I found it . . . appropriate."

"And what did you think of Rosamond?"

"I thought her foolish at the beginning, though I ended up pitying her and wishing for her escape from Tempest."

Louisa swallowed, seeming to choose her words carefully. "I have always had a heart for a woman's freedom—you know that. It's why I wrote the story."

I looked down at the front page. "And yet you will not submit it under your own name?" For it read A. M. Barnard, not Louisa May Alcott.

She leaned back in her chair again, looked out the window. "I have worked hard to gain the readership I have. This is one of the tales I wrote for me. I am not certain my current readership will find it to their liking. If a publisher even wants it, that is. But I did not just write it for me or for readers. I was thinking of you as I reworked it, Johanna. I thought of John and how I wish I could have done more for him in his last days. Perhaps I am trying to make up for that."

"For all your talk about liberating women, you seem to claim a stake in my own freedom."

She looked at me, hurt in her eyes. She shook her head. "I only wish to help."

"Please, Louisa, let it lie. Can we continue our friendship as it once was, without this thing between us?"

She didn't answer right away, and I wondered if she might refuse me. "Yes, dear," she whispered. "I will always be your friend."

~~

With tentative steps I approached my husband where he sat near the fireplace, reading the newspaper. I held my poems in my hands, clutched them tight enough that the slight dampness from my palms moistened the paper.

I stood before him and he placed the paper aside, attentive as he had been for days on end since he emptied his liquor bottles. "Hello, my dear."

I relaxed at his words. "I was hoping to speak with you."

He shifted in his seat, patted his lap. Part of me wished to sit on his knee, to be close in that way, another part of me thought I should stand, for I wished to talk business.

In the end I chose his lap, knowing his mood would sour should I spurn his invitation. But I could not look into his eyes once there, so very close as we were. I near crinkled the papers in my hands. "I was wondering . . . if you might be willing to use some of my poems in any of your publications? Miss Alcott thinks them quite good and I . . . I long to be a part of your work in some way."

The knee opposite the one I sat upon started jiggling, beating out nervous energy. I hated what it seemed to portend.

"This is important to you, isn't it?" he asked.

"Yes, Nathan. Very much. I want to be alongside you in

this way, to share this with you. I always thought we would, but life got busy. Now . . ."

He placed a gentle finger on my lips. "Hush, dear. You needn't explain. Of course I will read them."

He took them from me and laid them atop his paper. Then he lowered his mouth to my neck, began kissing just below my jaw, causing shivers of pleasure to chase along my spine, though I couldn't be certain if the source of pleasure stemmed from his warm lips or the prospect of sharing such an important, intimate part of myself as I had poured out into my poetry.

When I tidied up the parlor the next morning, both newspaper and poems were gone.

Two days passed without Nathan broaching the subject. When we sat down to dinner on the third day, I waited until he finished chewing his first bite of dumpling before opening my mouth.

"Did you have a chance to look at any of my poems, dear?"

He took his time swallowing his water. "I did. They are . . . well done, my love. I shared them with Uncle, but he is not certain he can find a place for them just now."

My shoulders slumped. "Oh."

"Don't despair, Johanna. Publishing is a consistently changing phenomenon. We'll see what comes of it."

I nodded, licked my lips, preparing myself to ask whether he thought my poems worthy of publication.

But I couldn't push the words forth, so fearful of more rejection. If he thought them good, he would have said so.

He would have highlighted a certain line or stanza that he thought particularly beautiful, he would have praised my use of imagery or asked the source of my ideas.

Yet he did none of these things. And I was left clinging to the hazy hope that my poems would be remembered sometime in the future for one of his uncle's publications. I thought of them in Boston on some desk, open and exposed, visible for any wandering eyes to see.

And I wished I had never asked Nathan to read them in the first place.

~~

A year passed and we got on well enough. I did not see Louisa much, though I tried to explain that away due to Louisa's living in Boston for most of the winter, as the new editor for *Merry's Museum*, a magazine for both boys and girls—just one of the many things Nathan seemed much afflicted with.

Our marriage and home were peaceable by anyone's standards, though I secretly longed for more. For an intimacy that went beyond the mere physical, for a deeper connection to my husband. And yet he didn't hesitate to pour out his heart—only it often came in the form of grumblings and complaints about circumstances I wished he had the courage to change.

Though the liquor was not in the home, the shadows that plagued Nathan never quite left him. Even when I announced that I carried his child, the momentary happiness did not linger long.

He stayed in Boston often, and I secretly wondered if he drank his liquor there. Though I never once voiced my misgivings. Instead, I turned to my writing, finding solace in the storm of words that stirred my heart, in pouring my troubled soul out to the waiting arms of a blank page.

The blank page never turned away from me or spurned my advances. Always it welcomed.

One day, Louisa came to my door. I embraced her, as I hadn't realized she'd returned home. She looked at the small bump of my belly, plain to see under the summer dress I wore, and beamed. "Why didn't you write?"

I blushed. "One hardly writes of such things. Though I am certain you wouldn't hesitate."

We laughed. It felt real and so very good.

"It is wonderful to see you," I said. "I look in on your mother once in a while and know she ails often. How did you find her?"

"She grows feeble but at least has her comforts, now. And my time in Boston has allowed me to keep the hounds of care and debt from worrying her. For that I am grateful."

I gestured to the chairs on the porch, and we sat, both preferring to be outside on such a beautiful day.

"And your work in Boston? Does it suit you?"

"Very well. I get much work done while I'm away and can find a bit of rest as well. I much prefer the city. You should come with me sometime. We could see a play and they always have stimulating talk at the new women's club."

"That sounds wonderful." Nathan had taken me once, when we courted. But never since.

"Let's plan it, then. For the fall perhaps? I plan to go back at that time. After I write this confounded girls' book that Father has told Mr. Niles I will write."

"Oh, I'm so glad, Louisa. Have you begun it?"

"Only just. We will see if it makes a go, I suppose."

We visited awhile longer, and when she stood to leave, she eyed me carefully. "You look well. Are things . . . ?"

I wished she hadn't raised the subject, but this time I could alleviate her fears over my well-being in good conscience. "Yes, things are near perfect."

Though I saw something of doubt in her eyes, I chose to ignore it. "And you, though I know you will be in a writing whirlwind for the next few months, please do tell me if you need anything."

"Just strength enough to write it."

"Then I will pray God give you it."

CHAPTER TWENTY-FIVE

When tired, sad, or tempted, I find my best comfort in the woods, the sky,
the healing solitude that lets my poor, weary soul find the rest, the fresh
hope, or the patience which only God can give.

~ LMA

Taylor

I DIDN'T GO HOME. Back to the Bennetts', rather. Instead, I drove past Victoria on the road and headed to Walden Pond, feeling that some time alone might soothe my spirit.

When I glimpsed the calm body of water, I felt something within me relax and subside like a wave retreating upon the shore. I walked to a grove of trees just above the sandy beach area, out of the way of the scattering of people, and sat down. The scent of pine tugged some sort of calm within me.

Coming to the water often did this for me. I wondered if it wasn't why I'd driven all the way across the country to California. Back then I'd wanted a different ocean—one that would be a world away from my problems. Only my problems hadn't stayed behind. They'd followed me, even if I hadn't realized it.

Still, sitting here below the blue sky and the setting sun, the gentle peck of a woodpecker sounding on the tree behind me, my problems—however real—seemed just a bit smaller. As if the turning of the world didn't depend on my small struggles.

I wondered about Lorraine's newfound faith.

"This spring, I'm feeling it more than ever," she'd said the other morning. "As much as I've always loved nature, now I seem to see God Himself in it all. Maybe because the possibility of death seems more real than ever, or maybe because this winter felt long and spring is giving me hope. New life from darkness. That's what I'm clinging to."

I knew she'd been trying to share something that was important to her, and so I had listened, tried to understand, but ultimately wrote it off to a desperateness that cancer would create in anyone.

But now, sitting here, soaking in the sun and examining the pink buds on the trees, I came just up to the edge of what she'd been trying to tell me. I couldn't plunge in, couldn't grasp it fully, but I felt . . . something. Some sort of hope. Assurance. And it didn't scare me as I thought it would.

I slid Johanna's book out of its sandwich bag, flipped toward the beginning, trying hard to make out the old words.

OF YOU STANDING AGAINST THE SUNSET

Of you standing against the sunset
I will never forget
the way it wrapped you up tight
in its orange light
and set you free,
inside yourself,

inside me.
You bared your soul
with a story untold
that crept under your skin
like a festering sin
within the walls
of what withheld
you from me.
And then you were free.
I held your hand
to have you understand
and walk into liquid light
of a promised land.
To lick your wound
and soothe the fool
you thought you'd be.
But you would not go.
Your fear undisclosed.
Those tortured ghosts
of who you thought
you should be.
Kept you from sight.
Kept you from light.
Kept you from me.

Who was this person she wrote of? Was he the same man she married? This poem was at the beginning of the book. Had their love—and marriage—taken a turn for the worse after this was written? Or did it have nothing to do with her actual life?

I sighed, put the book back, and looked toward the beach, where a man threw a ball to his dog. A chocolate Lab.

I squinted against the sun, thought I might be imagining things. But no. I recognized the build, the slightly crooked gait. I stood, waved my hand. "Luke!"

He adjusted his hat. "Well, ain't this a surprise."

I scrunched up my face. "For a guy who likes to read the classics, you have absolutely *abominable* grammar."

He shrugged, but it didn't dim his smile. "Can't be good at everything, I guess."

The dog—Chloe, I remembered—ran up to me, dropped the soggy ball on my right foot, then excitedly rubbed her nose against my leg.

"Chloe, sit," Luke said.

She obeyed but looked at me as if she couldn't wait for me to pet her.

"It's okay. I love dogs."

He made a motion with his hand, and Chloe again stuck her muzzle in my thigh, her tail wagging furiously.

"You have one?"

"No. I . . ."

Why didn't I have a dog? Kevin had mentioned it once, us getting a dog together. But that seemed like just a step away from having a child together, and I had balked.

"I don't," I finished.

I patted Chloe for another moment, then grabbed the soggy ball, threw it down the small stretch of sand.

Luke watched the dog dash along the beach. "What brings you here?"

"I needed to get away. Victoria and I were arguing."

He nodded. "About whether you should stay longer?"

"Not exactly. I had to tell her something. Something she didn't want to hear. Something I didn't want to tell. Now she wishes I never came at all."

I expected him to speak some reassurance. Something like *I'm sure that's not true*, but nothing came from him. Only silence.

I couldn't take it. "Have you ever felt like your presence—even if you don't intend it—is harmful to someone else?"

He looked at the sand at his feet, nodded. "You want to walk?"

"Sure." I put my pocketbook strap across my chest and buttoned my sweater against the slight chill of the open water.

Chloe came back to us, dropped the ball at Luke's feet. He scooped it up, threw it again. She ran after it with enthusiasm, her legs kicking up sand.

"I didn't tell you how I was shot."

I didn't speak. I didn't want to break this connection, the small bit of himself he seemed about to unveil.

"It was a young kid. Drugs were involved. It was the most intense chase I'd ever been part of, ending with a shoot-out, just like the movies. There were a few of them shooting at us, but the one who shot me was eighteen. He's still in jail. Might be for a good long time." He pulled his baseball cap lower and I wished he'd take it off so I could see him more fully.

He didn't. "His aunt wrote me. She had raised him, felt awful bad about what he'd done. Maybe it was a mistake, but I started spending some time with her. At first, it seemed like we were helping one another grieve. She was mourning her nephew; I was mourning my leg and my career. But after a time, it became apparent she still had some complicated feelings about what happened that day. We decided to part ways." He lifted his gaze to me. "So yeah, I know what you mean about trying to help but just making things worse by being around. But that doesn't mean that leaving's the answer."

"It was for you."

"For us, tragedy brought us together. You and Victoria . . . you're family. That's different."

"The Bennetts adopted me when I was thirteen. Sometimes I think what Victoria and I are is more complicated than being sisters or family."

He nodded, and though he didn't ask more, I found myself spilling my heart to him, telling him everything. Maybe it was that he'd shared a piece of himself with me, or maybe it was some unseen force that drew me to him, but I told him about growing up with the Bennetts, about falling in love with Will, about finding him and Victoria that day in front of the garage.

I'd never voiced what had happened to anyone, not even Kevin, not even my counselor. Speaking it all out into the open gave me a surprising sort of release, a freedom I hadn't known I needed.

Luke listened, nodding once in a while. When I ended with what had happened last night between me and Will and how I had just told Victoria that afternoon, he grimaced, and I felt his sympathy and understanding—something else I hadn't realized I'd needed—or wanted—so badly.

For a long moment, he said nothing. We reached the end of the sand and, without discussing it, continued along the wooded path around the pond. Chloe clung to her ball, setting it down now and again to sniff out trees along the edge of the path.

"So you think you should go back to California so you won't be in the way of your sister and her husband."

I inhaled deep through my nose, let out my breath on a long sigh. "I came here thinking how hurt I'd be. Now I feel like I'm hurting everyone else."

Luke gestured for me to go ahead of him as the path narrowed. "Seems to me your sister's problems didn't start when you came to Concord. It's likely they're not going to end when you leave. I understand she's angry now, but my guess is she's going to need you. Soon. Let her cool down, then talk to her."

"You make it sound so simple."

"I saw the way you two worked together this week. Even when you were in the school, hiding that old book. You have something together. Keep searching for it."

I couldn't help but smile at his simple wisdom. I opened my mouth to tell him about Johanna's poems but stopped short. As far as I knew, Victoria hadn't disclosed what we'd found to anyone. In some ways, this discovery felt like the last thread that held us together. I closed my mouth, suddenly unwilling to share it.

Yes, history and the Alcotts had always been more Victoria's obsession than mine. But maybe it was my turn to find out more about Johanna, to show Victoria I cared about what we'd found. That I cared about her.

CHAPTER TWENTY-SIX

Respect and esteem must be the foundation, but above and beyond must be an abiding love that makes all things possible and without which no marriage is a true one, no household a home.

~ LMA

Taylor

I DIDN'T MAKE PLANS to return to California. Instead, I gave Victoria her space and accepted Lorraine's invitation to go to church with her and Paul on Sunday morning.

I wasn't sure what I expected. I'd been to church here and there for funerals and weddings, but standing beside Mom with this group of strangers singing about a God they'd given their hearts to, a God that was both just and loving all at once, I couldn't quite take it all in.

In some ways, I felt like I didn't belong. And in some ways, I wished to give myself over to it, for just a short amount of time, even. Forget myself and sing from a place deep within, a place that threw all my insecurities and fears aside and fell at the feet of this mysterious Being whom Mom seemed to be so certain existed in the midst of her trials.

On the way home, she reached behind her from the passenger seat. I placed my hand in her own smooth, cool one and squeezed.

"I'm glad you came this morning. And I'm glad I haven't heard anything about you leaving just yet."

I couldn't see her face as she spoke the words, and I thought that somehow it made it easier for her to speak them.

I wondered if she often wanted to speak words to me when I was growing up in the Bennett home, if she just didn't know what to say or how to say it. I sure hadn't. There was no rule book about fostering and adopting your daughter's best friend. Or in my case, your best friend's mother.

"I'm glad, too," I said. And I meant it.

When we pulled into their driveway, I didn't see Victoria's car. Again. I didn't miss the look Lorraine and Paul gave one another.

"Did she go back home?" I asked.

Lorraine nodded. Paul clenched his jaw.

"That's not good?" I asked. Wasn't it good that she and Will work things out, talk things through?

"It never seems to be." Dad got out of the car, nearly slamming the door behind him.

Mom and I didn't move from our places.

"It's hard on him," she started. "Seeing one of his daughters hurt like this. Will's . . . changed. We want our grandchildren to have a father, our daughter to have a husband. But at what cost?"

There were lines I couldn't clearly read between, but I didn't prod further. Instead, we went inside, enjoyed a light lunch of chicken salad. After, I went upstairs to my old room and flopped on the bed with Johanna's poems, ignoring my story and deadlines and all other obligations.

Why I thought this was the thing that would bridge the divide between me and Victoria, I didn't know. But there had to be something—some clue as to Johanna's story and her connection to Louisa. Could it help Victoria and me heal our own relationship?

I read through the entire book of Johanna's poems without finding one more trace of evidence to point me in the direction of who this woman was. The poems were largely about lost love. They were sad and deep, and though I was left feeling emotion, I didn't feel especially uplifted or inspired after reading them. If only I'd found something to bring to Victoria—some new piece of information for us to share once again.

Who was Johanna Bancroft?

I tapped my fingers on my stomach, wondered how to go about finding more. Victoria had shown me John and Anna Pratt's family history on a printout from ancestry.com. I opened my laptop and pulled up the website. After signing up for a free trial, I got to work, searching Johanna Bancroft's name.

The problem, it seemed, was finding the *right* Johanna Bancroft. After no definite leads, I tried Johanna Suhre instead. Minutes passed as I went down rabbit trail after rabbit trail, eliminating each possibility by time frame or location. When I had exhausted all the search results, I stood and stretched, feeling the need to be free of the tiny room.

I grabbed my keys and wallet, wondered if Luke might be at Walden Pond again this afternoon. As I drove south, I tried to think of other avenues I could explore to unravel the mystery behind Johanna. Victoria hadn't found anything in her biographies, but there must be something *somewhere*. Whoever had hidden the poems—be it Johanna or Louisa or someone else—had wanted to hide them for some reason. But why?

Nothing in the biographies, but what about letters? The idea gripped me with ferocity and I pulled over, tapping the steering wheel of the rental. I'd seen a book at the Orchard House gift shop this past week. Something about Louisa's letters. In less than five minutes, I pulled into the rather crowded parking lot of Orchard House. Strange how I'd only been away from it for a day, and now, being here, I realized I'd missed it.

I entered the gift shop among a crowd of tourists and searched for the book I'd seen. There. *The Selected Letters of Louisa May Alcott. Selected* meant far from complete, yet maybe somewhere within I would find a clue. I noted the book beside it, similar in cover. *The Journals of Louisa May Alcott.* I scooped that one up too and purchased them both.

It was likely a long shot that I'd find anything. Victoria knew the details of Louisa's life better than I did, and she hadn't remembered anything about Johanna. More so, if there was something, a Google search online would have fleshed it out. I was likely wasting my time, but doing something—in a way, I realized, trying to reach out to my sister—was better than doing nothing at all.

I continued to Walden Pond, but this time I just sat in my car, poring over the books. I searched both the indexes for a Johanna Bancroft or Johanna Suhre but found nothing and decided to settle in with the journal, thinking if our mystery woman was in any way important to Louisa, it would be within the journal.

I was a fast reader, and the sun rocked near the horizon when I finished it. While it had fostered a renewed appreciation for the woman who had written *Little Women* and her continuous struggle to improve and master herself within her lifetime, I hadn't found one clue or reference concerning Johanna. Realizing I was short on sunlight, I opened the book of letters.

I was a quarter of the way through when I found it. I sat up, blinking, wondering if my brain was playing tricks on me. I read the sentence again, nearly squinting in the fading light.

It was a letter from Louisa to her younger sister May while she was in Europe. It was dated November 1865. It appeared May was in Boston, and Louisa was cautioning her sister to be mindful of their parents.

Johanna does well with them, but I fear a time is coming when I will not be able to pay her. I know your art is important to you, as it is to all of us, and I know you care for Papa and Marmee, but I beg of you to see to them more often than you do.

I dog-eared the page even as I remembered how Victoria used to cringe when I did this very thing. I dialed Mom's number.

"I hope I didn't wake you," I said. I knew she often took naps in the afternoons.

"No, not at all. Was just making supper. Should we expect you?"

"I think so. Is Victoria there?"

"No. I tried calling, but she didn't answer. Dad was going to head over to check on things."

"I wanted to show her something. You think she'd mind if I show up on her doorstep?" As soon as the words were out of my mouth, I wondered if my plan wasn't a mistake. I didn't want to barge in on her space, her family, especially if Will was there, especially if they were trying to work things out. But she couldn't ignore me forever. And if Dad thought there was reason enough to check on her, then maybe it wasn't such a bad thing if I was the one checking.

"I don't see why not." She gave me her address and simple directions.

I pulled up to Victoria's home ten minutes later. A blue colonial with a farmer's porch and attached three-car garage. It suddenly hit me that Victoria hadn't yet invited me to her home. That perhaps I wasn't welcome here. That perhaps me showing up this soon after our argument was the worst thing I could do for our relationship.

I looked at the passenger seat, at the dog-eared page from *The Selected Letters of Louisa May Alcott*, and opened the door. The interior light came on and I glimpsed the name of Madeleine Stern, one of the biographers Victoria had mentioned the day before. Surely this discovery would mean something to her.

I clutched the book at my side, made my way up the neatly landscaped cobbled path. Solar lights shone on either side, the scent of fresh mulch lingered in the air. I climbed the front stairs, noted a porch swing in the far corner.

How many nights had she and Will sat out here, swinging, enjoying the home and family they'd made together? Surely my arrival hadn't ruined all that. Surely they could work things out.

I rang the doorbell. Once, then again. Maybe they weren't home after all.

I was about to turn around when the porch light came on. The sound of a door squeaked open. I turned and saw Maddie behind the storm door, her face tight behind the tiny lattices of the screen.

"Hey," I said. "I hope it's okay I stopped by. I wanted to show your mom something."

She opened the door and I stepped in. One look at the girl's puffy eyes told me something was wrong.

"Should I—should I leave?" I asked. "I don't want to interrupt anything."

She bit her lip, shook her head fast.

I stepped closer. "Maddie, what is it?"

"I think you should talk to Mom," she whispered.

"Where is she? Is your dad home?"

"No." She pointed up the stairs.

I saw a faint bluish light coming from the living room, heard what sounded like a video game. "Is Caden okay? I can take you guys to your grandma and grandpa's if you want."

She nodded. "Can you talk to her first? I don't . . . I didn't know what to do. It's never been this bad, and . . . I'm only a kid." She crumpled against me, sobs wetting my shirt.

I stood for a second, shocked. Then my arms came around her and I stroked her hair, murmured that everything was going to be okay, even though I hadn't a clue if that was even a quarter of the way true. Still, for the first time I felt like a real aunt, felt that I was doing something right in comforting, in caring. Maybe I did belong here, in this house I'd never set foot in. Maybe I was needed, even.

After a moment, I pulled away from my niece. "What happened?"

"She's upstairs. Please?"

I squeezed her to me one last time. "Of course."

Still clutching Louisa's book of letters, I climbed the dark stairs, felt I needed to approach Victoria like one might approach a wounded animal hiding in an obscure corner, without throwing on bright lights and scaring her away.

The last rays of the setting sun shone through several doorways upstairs. I passed what looked like Maddie's bedroom, then Caden's, then a bathroom. At the end stood a closed door.

I knocked.

Nothing.

"Victoria? Can I come in, please?"

Still nothing.

"Victoria, are you okay?"

Sudden fear gripped my chest. What if she was in there and something terrible had happened? While she didn't strike me as the suicidal type, maybe whatever Maddie spoke of had been the last straw. Or had she slipped some sleeping pills? Maybe she was out to the world. Did Victoria have a drinking problem or addiction I didn't know about? And why should I? I hadn't been a part of her life for sixteen years.

Still no answer. I raised my voice. "Victoria, open up." I tried the handle, but it was locked.

"Go away, Taylor."

I breathed a long sigh of relief. She was alive. Even sounded coherent.

"Can I come in? Please? I—I have something to show you." Though I doubted she'd be interested in anything— even anything Louisa Alcottish—I had to show her in that moment.

"I don't want to talk. Go away."

I thought about leaving then. Victoria was a big girl. She didn't need me to take care of her. But the thought of going downstairs and telling Maddie I had failed in talking to her mother made me stand my ground.

"Maddie asked me to come up. Dad's going to be on his way over soon if you don't answer Mom's calls."

Silence.

"Please, Victoria. I'm sorry about what happened the other night. If I could take it back, I would. I just . . . I didn't realize I do, but I want things right between us again. I—I want us to be sisters again."

I didn't hear movement behind the door, so when it unlocked, I jumped. She didn't open it, though, so I twisted the knob and went through, then closed it behind me.

Faint rays from day's end came through a large bay window with a seat below it—just the sort of place Victoria used to dream about reading in. The room smelled faintly of Will's still-familiar cologne and my gut twisted, but why, I couldn't tell. I saw her shadow on the floor alongside mounds of scattered books at the foot of the king-size bed. Her hands were tight around her knees, pulled up to her chest, but I couldn't make out her expression.

Tentatively, I sat beside her on the cool hardwood floor,

brushing aside a copy of Louisa's *Eight Cousins*. A chill raced up my legs. I'd demanded to come in, but now that I was here, I found myself at a loss for words.

She sighed. "What'd you want to show me?"

This wasn't how I'd pictured this moment.

"It's nothing—well, it's something, but it can wait. What happened? Did you talk to Will? Did you guys fight?"

"I don't want to talk about it." She sniffed, and I felt that her brokenness, her vulnerability, lay just below the surface. That if I could just say the right words, it would wiggle its way to the open, perhaps toward healing.

"Maddie's worried about you."

"Are they okay?" she whispered.

"I—I don't know. Yes, for now I guess. Victoria, what happened?" This time I put some demand in my voice. This had to end. Something needed to be done.

Again she didn't answer, and I stood, went to the door, and swished my hand along the wall, searching for a light. Enough of this—this hiding.

"Taylor, no—"

But it was too late. A pool of light shone upon her. She was surrounded by a smattering of books. *Little Women. Jo's Boys. The Inheritance. Under the Lilacs. Little Men. A Long Fatal Love Chase.* All Alcott books. I noticed the top shelf of her nightstand, empty of all but two of Louisa's books—*Moods* and *Jack and Jill*. I searched her face and body for signs of injury, certain that Will had somehow hurt her physically. I remembered his rough hands from the other night, thought that was why Victoria hid in the dark—that she was physically hurt. But aside from a shiny face, wet with tears, and a slew of scattered books around her, I didn't see any evidence that she was hurt. Physically anyway.

Did that mean the wounds weren't there? No. I of all people knew that some of the hardest hurts to heal were invisible to the eye.

In some ways it would have been easier to speak if I'd seen evidence of violence, easier to condemn Will and champion Victoria. But what could I say that would support my sister?

Finally my tongue loosened. I moved it against the roof of my mouth, trying to work up enough saliva to speak. Still, no words came forth.

"I thought he was going to hit me. He never came that close before." My sister's tone spoke not only of facts, but of an intense, intense sadness that I would likely never be able to touch, that I didn't *want* to touch because it just scared me too much.

"He was shouting at me, so loud I'm surprised the neighbors didn't call the cops. Swearing at me. Throwing my books at me. Calling me words I never thought would enter this house." When she told me exactly what words those were, I fell in a heap beside her.

"Will? Will said those things?"

I just couldn't make sense of it. Despite his foolish proclamation of affection for me the other night, despite his uncharacteristic forceful grip on my arm that had left small bruises I'd seen in the shower. Not big enough to hurt or bother myself over, but a remembrance of the emotional destruction he'd left in his path.

"Yes." She started to sob, curled up on the floor in a fetal position. "He said he wanted to hurt me. That I deserved everything, deserved to die even. I don't know what I did to make him so angry. It was almost like he was somewhere else, another time, another place. The way he spoke . . . in such detail . . . The kids heard everything. Everything. I can't take this, Taylor. I can't take this."

I leaned next to her, rubbed her shoulder, shushed her as if she were a baby. "It's going to be okay, Victoria. It's going to be okay."

But was it? How could I be so sure?

"Has this happened before?"

"Not this bad, but it's becoming a new habit it seems." She swallowed, and her face looked wan in the dusky light. "I brought up what you told me yesterday. I was angry, and it made him angry, too."

"Will you listen to yourself?" I couldn't believe this was Victoria. My strong sister. She didn't take anything from anyone. She was confident, secure, well-adjusted, came from the best family I knew. How had it come to this? And at the hands of a guy I thought was one of the best men I knew? "Victoria, this is *not* your fault." I breathed deep, tried to gather myself, but it didn't work. Instead, I got to my feet and paced back and forth before her, my mind spinning. "If there was ever a point in history that women should be empowered to stand up for themselves, to realize that there is never a reason for this, it's now. It doesn't matter that he didn't hit you. You do not deserve to be treated like this. No one does."

She sat up, clenched her fists on top of her bent knees. "You think I don't know that? But you are not in my shoes. You do not have a family depending on you. You don't understand what it's like to want to make it work, to hope for better every single time. You don't understand—you can't understand."

"I could if you told me. I could. I want to." I did. Maybe not exactly about this, but about hoping and being disappointed.

More silence. I wondered if Maddie and Caden heard our raised voices. I tried again. "Kids are not a reason to endure this. Maddie's a wreck downstairs. Do you think that's healthy?"

Her bottom lip trembled. "I feel like if I stop trying, I'm throwing it all away. Do you know how scary that is?"

"Do you know how scary it is to know he's verbally and emotionally abusing you—throwing *books* at you—and you're trying to fool yourself into thinking it's okay?"

"This is not your marriage, Taylor. This is not your life."

"What is wrong with you?" No, I wasn't in her shoes, but I couldn't understand why she wasn't running as far and fast from this situation as she could.

She crumpled back to the floor, and I fell beside her, alongside the bent spine of *Under the Lilacs*. I'd said I wanted to help, and I was doing a lousy job. "I'm sorry," I said.

She didn't say anything.

"Has he . . . has he ever hurt the kids?"

"No," she snapped. "I'm not completely stupid."

I tried not to argue with that statement in my head. What had happened to the strong Victoria I knew?

"Do your parents know?"

She shrugged. "They suspect things aren't great. Though I don't think they realize how not great." She groaned long and loud. It ended on a hiccupy sob. "I don't know what to do."

I didn't know either. To me, a virtual outsider, it seemed obvious. Leave the idiot. But to Victoria, it apparently wasn't so simple.

"Start by breathing." I inhaled an exaggerated breath, let it out, then repeated until she copied me.

"What's this going to accomplish?" she said between breaths.

"I don't know, but it's the only thing I could think of."

She cracked the smallest of smiles and I considered it a victory.

"Where'd he go?" I asked.

She shrugged, picked up *Eight Cousins*, and smoothed a bent page. "I don't know. He stays away a lot now." She licked her lips. "I should tell you . . . him kissing you, him cheating on me . . . it's not entirely new."

I rubbed my temples. "What?"

"I thought I was being noble trying to tough it out, you know? In a way, I thought he was even doing it for my sake. To make me realize how much I don't want to lose him. It almost feels like a game sometimes. He's always saying he's sorry, that he wants to start new. And for a while, we do. And I hope. But then . . . something happens. This time it was you."

I ground my teeth together. "This is *not* my fault, any more than it's yours. You have to see that. This is crazy is what it is. You don't treat people you love like this."

She nodded. "I know. I know."

"I just don't understand. I mean, I saw his volatile side a couple times but nothing like this."

"He's angry. In some ways it's grown with him. Angry his

life didn't turn out different, I guess. Angry about whatever happened in the Middle East."

He looked so good on the outside. Good job. Clean-cut. Defender of our country. He'd been my angel when I was faced with that nasty date. Now Will *was* the nasty date.

She swallowed. "After we had the kids, things got harder. I think . . . well, I think he thought he made a mistake in marrying me, in not looking harder for you. He blames me. Easier than blaming himself, I guess."

I thought of him standing on Main Street the other night, confessing that he still loved me. "Family is hard. But you don't give up; you don't treat the people you're supposed to love most in the world like this."

Victoria swiped her wet lower lids. "You just run, is that it?"

I gritted my teeth at the jab. I was pointing too many fingers when I had faults enough of my own.

"He's not all bad. He has a lot of good qualities. We've had some amazing times together. Both alone and with the kids." She clenched her eyes shut. "Two years ago we hiked Mount Washington. All of us, even Caden. It was hard. And we had to encourage one another, work together as a family. I remember reaching the top, linking hands, looking over at Will and thinking we could accomplish anything with our love. Anything. I never would have guessed this was where we'd end up."

I filled my lungs. "I know it's easy for me to come in here and tell you a simple solution, but you cannot live like this. It's all kinds of wrong. If he's not willing to get some sort of counseling or psychological help—and keep up with it—you *need* to leave. And even if he is, I wouldn't blame you for leaving."

She looked down at the hardwood floor at her feet. Her hair was pulled back in a ponytail and she looked small— young and fragile at the same time that she looked old and worn. Nothing like the woman I knew her to be, the woman I desperately hoped was still alive somewhere in there.

"I'm tired of it all. I am, but part of me keeps hoping maybe this is just another bump in the road, you know?"

No wonder Maddie had seemed so desperate. I understood what she felt and that this situation could not be solved with the two of us alone, in her bedroom, especially if she couldn't see past the truth of my words.

I looked at the mess of books around me, imagined Will yelling, throwing my sister's precious possessions across the room with her as the target. "What would Louisa say?" I whispered. In some ways, it felt ridiculous to try to get to her by asking such a question. But in other ways, I realized it might be the *only* way to get to her—this teenager who wrote letters to a long-dead author in hopes of finding a historical connection. The woman who found her career in running the place where Louisa wrote her bestselling novel. The woman who poured her life into informing others and inspiring young kids who loved to write.

I remembered something I'd read just that afternoon. "Never mind. I'll tell you what she'd say." I picked up the book I'd brought to her house, took a moment to find the page, for I hoped the words would hit my sister the way they had hit me. "'Painful as it may be, a significant emotional event can be the catalyst for choosing a direction that serves us—and those around us—more effectively.' Victoria, maybe this is your painful time, a time that will foster change for you and your kids. But the ending doesn't have to be bad."

"This isn't one of your stories, Taylor."

"I—I get that. But you're not alone. You have Mom and Dad. And you have me. You cannot stay with him right now. For your sake, for the sake of your kids. What if next time he does hit you?"

She gulped, her face pale beneath the recessed lights of her bedroom. "I know. I just—I don't know if I have enough strength to do what I have to do."

I held out my hand to her, remembered something I'd heard in church that morning about God being our strength when we felt weakest, about how He stepped in for us when we couldn't do the work ourselves. I wondered if I could do something similar for Victoria.

"You don't have to. I'm going to be strong enough for both of us."

It was a lofty promise, and I wasn't sure I could fulfill it, but for the first time I felt like the older sister. Like Louisa might have felt taking on the responsibility of caring for her aging parents, her widowed sister and nephews, and later May's daughter. I felt purpose and an assurance that it was a good thing I'd come to Concord when I did.

Victoria put her hand in mine and squeezed. She didn't say anything, but she didn't have to. Her accepting my hand—accepting me—was enough.

CHAPTER TWENTY-SEVEN

A great sorrow often softens and prepares the heart for a new harvest of good seed, and the sowers God sends are often very humble ones, used only as instruments by him because being very human they come naturally . . .

~ LMA

Taylor

VICTORIA TOOK THE NEXT DAY off from work, and I brought Mom to chemotherapy. By the time we'd gotten her and the kids settled in at the Bennetts'—for good this time—it had been late.

Mom and Dad had done a lot of hovering when Victoria brought the kids over. Still, she didn't confide in them what had happened, only said she and Will were taking a break. She insisted this was her problem, that she only needed some time to get away from the situation.

While I wished she would tell them, a small part of me was honored that I was the one she chose to confess her secrets to, even if they were the ugly ones. Maybe *especially* because they were the ugly ones.

I spent most of the night reading up on domestic abuse.

It turns out I'd done almost everything wrong when I'd spoken to Victoria. I'd practically called her stupid, practically bullied her into leaving her home. Really, was I any better than Will?

I should have been more supportive. I should have listened better and been nonjudgmental. But after reading, I felt I had a healthier handle on how to help. The domestic violence hotline website advised concerned loved ones to help their victim come up with a safety plan, to encourage my loved one to participate in activities with family and friends outside the relationship with the abuser, and lastly, to remember that I couldn't "rescue" anyone, no matter how much I wanted to, no matter how determined I was to do so.

It was going to be a long road, but at least now Victoria and the kids were safe.

I looked at Mom, sitting in her chair, the drugs that were intended to kill the cancer within her dripping from an IV into her veins. These drugs were going to help her, going to save her life. But in killing the cancer, they were going to kill a lot of the healthy cells, too. It was going to make her feel sick. I wondered then about the worth of the bad stuff. The stuff in our lives that we had to suffer through, that didn't add up—could it possibly produce something good in the end?

She caught me staring at her IV bag and smiled. This was the last thing she needed right now. Stress wouldn't help her heal, and yet how could we keep her from it?

I shifted in my seat. "I'm sorry you're going through so much right now."

She took a long, shaky breath. "It hurts to see Victoria

suffering. It hurts to wonder if we've been betrayed by the man we gave our daughter to—one we thought was honorable. But, Taylor, I cannot tell you how grateful I am to have you here, especially now. Not just for my sake, but for your sister's."

"I wish there was more I could to."

"You just being here is enough." She studied me then, and I tried not to avert my eyes from her probing ones. "It really hurt when we received that check in the mail from your lawyer."

I couldn't hold her gaze. At the time, I thought it had been a good thing to do, a worthy thing. Now I could see it for what it was—in some ways, the cheapest way to fling my guilt as far away from myself as I could.

"I—I see that now. I'm sorry."

"And I forgive you. *We* forgive you. And I have to ask for your forgiveness, too."

"What?"

"I wasn't always the mother I should have been to you. I admit I was insecure about my place in your life. I was insecure about showing you my love, fearful Victoria would feel cheated. After that day she accused me of preferring you to her, I wrestled with myself a lot. Even wondered if on some level, it was true. You were easier to love, always thanking us, always grateful. She was—well, a normal daughter, I suppose. Half the time I felt I juggled both of you, only I could never keep up."

I swallowed, felt her words knocking at the lingering remains of the chain link around my heart. This time I wanted to give myself over to it. "I thought sometimes you regretted taking me in. It's hard being the outsider, you know? You and Dad did so much for me, but I guess I thought you felt obligated. It doesn't change the fact that if I had been able to choose, I would have chosen you. I love both of you so much."

She blinked and swiped at her tears. "You girls both mean so much to me. God answered my prayers when He brought you home, and now that you are, I feel like no matter what— even if I don't beat this thing in the end—all will be okay."

I went to her and put my arms carefully around her body. "I'm not going anywhere, Mom."

~~

I tried not to wince when I saw Kevin's name on my phone. Again. I'd ignored him too many times these past several days.

I swiped left and answered. "Hello?"

"Oh, you *are* alive. I thought you fell off the face of the earth."

"Yeah . . . sorry about that. Things are a little crazy here." Still, in the middle of all this, I should have called him. I should have *wanted* to call him.

"What's going on, Taylor?"

Part of me wanted to pretend I didn't know what he was talking about. But another part of me—the part that was starting to become accustomed to this open, honest thing and even found it freeing—wanted to throw caution to the wind.

I took my phone onto the front porch, out of earshot from where Mom and I had been reading in the living room after her treatment. "I don't know."

"I'm flying over tomorrow."

I panicked. "No. No, please don't."

"I'm getting the feeling you don't want me around, Taylor."

"Of course not." Kevin was perfect. Almost as perfect as I thought Will had been. I shook my head. That was ridiculous. I'd been with Kevin for too long not to know him well. He would never hurt me. So why was I refusing to fully open myself up to him?

"I can't live like this anymore." His voice was heavy on the other end, and something within me scrambled to make sense of it.

"Wait, what do you mean?"

"This, Taylor. I thought I was okay with it—you, having your space and all that. But I'm not. I think we should call it quits for now."

I waited to feel heartbroken, sad. Something. But the only thing I could summon up was relief. Which wasn't saying much for my compassion. "I—I think you might be right."

"Really?"

"Yeah."

Silence on the other end, and I knew I'd hurt him. Even though I hadn't been the one to initiate this separation, I realized he was looking for me to swoop in and save us. Tell him to fly out East, tell him I couldn't live without him.

But I couldn't tell him.

I wouldn't.

"Okay, then." Something seemed to catch in his throat, and I closed my eyes against my own tears. Not because we had come to this, but because I had caused him pain. "I'll have my stuff out of your place by the end of the week. I'll mail you the key."

"Kevin, I . . ."

"What?"

"I'm sorry I can't give you what you deserve. I'm sorry I wasted so much of your time."

I heard a large intake of breath. "Taylor . . . it was never a waste. Keep in touch, okay?"

"Okay," I said, though I wondered if I would.

And just like that we were over. I couldn't quite understand the peace that brought. Kevin had been the only thing tying me back to California, and right now, I felt very much as if I belonged in Concord. And yet when he'd invited himself into my world here, I hadn't wanted it.

I heard the screen door shut and I hung up the phone after saying goodbye, turned to Victoria.

"Hey."

She nodded toward my phone. "What's wrong?"

I sat on the rocking chair closest to me, and she sat in the one beside it. "Nothing. I am actually okay. That was Kevin. We broke up."

"I'm so sorry."

"Honestly, I think it's a good thing."

We rocked for a minute before she spoke. "So I guess it's just like back when we were teenagers, huh? At Mom and Dad's, without men in our lives."

I laughed, but there was little humor in it. "Yeah, just like it." I turned my chair to face her. "How you doing?"

She shrugged, and her bottom lip quivered. "Hanging in there."

I remembered what the domestic abuse website had said about doing things with Victoria that had nothing to do with Will. "You want a distraction?"

"You're not going to make me cook, are you?"

I laughed. Real this time. "I wanted to show you something yesterday, remember?" From her expression, I saw she didn't. "I'll be right back." I ran upstairs to grab the book I'd dog-eared and handed it, open, to Victoria. I pointed to the sentence in Louisa's letter to May that mentioned a Johanna. "There."

She read it and I didn't think I imagined the slight uplift in her posture. "No way. This must be her, right? Our Johanna?"

"It has to be."

"From the sounds of it she was a house helper while Louisa was in Europe."

I nodded. "Maybe they communicated after John died, or maybe Louisa even reached out to the family of her 'prince of patients.' I just wish I knew where to go from here."

Victoria squinted up at me. "Don't you have a book to write?"

"I'm thinking of incorporating all this into it—if it's okay with you. So I'm considering this research."

"You don't need my permission to write your story. You haven't had it for the last sixteen years."

"This one's different. It's about two sisters. They're not us, but you might see us in them."

"Oh, boy." She leaned back in her rocker. "Does it have a happy ending? You know I'm a sucker for happy endings."

I grinned. "I think it might, but I haven't written it yet."

"Okay. As long as there's a happy ending."

~~

I took the keys Victoria gave me. "You sure this is okay?"

"If anyone asks, just tell them you're picking up some stuff for me to work from home. It's the truth. I just don't feel like going out quite yet."

I tucked the keys in my purse and set out on my quest, landing at Orchard House once again. A few cars were out front, but overall it was much quieter than last week with Jo March Writing Camp. I parked at the offices and was relieved to see no one around. I let myself in and headed to Victoria's office. Once inside, I used the key she'd given me to get into the bottom drawer of the file cabinet.

She told me she had a copy of the complete letters of Louisa in here—those in the book I'd bought, but also those not included. Victoria told me there were over six hundred letters in existence, but that not even three hundred had been published. She had obtained the copies years ago, and though they were officially the property of Orchard House, she insisted this was important—that this one time they could be taken off the grounds.

I ran my finger over the carefully labeled folders, some of them financial records for Orchard House, others information about programs offered, and others historical records. Finally I reached one marked "Letters" and jiggled the thick folder out from its tight spot within the cabinet. I placed it on my lap, opened it to the first page—a copied cursive letter from Louisa to her mother. This must be it.

I heard footsteps behind me and jumped up, feeling guilty even though I had every right to be there.

"Luke."

He adjusted his hat. "Taylor. Thought that was your car."

I lifted the folder. "Victoria asked me to get her something."

"She feeling okay?"

Why did it feel wrong to be anything but 100 percent honest with this man? Yet blabbing Victoria's business wasn't my place. "I think she'll be back soon. Everything running well?"

"As far as I can see." He gestured to the bottom cabinet, still open with the key hanging out.

"Oh." I shut it, locked it, and straightened. "How's Chloe? I really enjoyed walking with you two the other day."

"Yeah, me too. Maybe we can do it again sometime, if you're planning on staying a bit longer."

"I am."

He raised his eyebrows, the brown of his eyes deep. "Definitely now, huh?"

I grinned. "Definitely."

My family needed me. And I was starting to realize that maybe I needed them all along, too.

CHAPTER TWENTY-EIGHT

Much talk about religion. I'd like to see a little more really lived.

~ LMA

Johanna

NATHAN DID NOT AGREE to me traveling to Boston with Louisa alone. But he did agree to take me so that I could spend time with my friend while he worked.

My babe was scheduled to arrive in less than two months, but I carried small and could hide my growing womb beneath the large talma I now wore, though it was a bit out of fashion beside the bustles and hoop skirts of the women around me.

Louisa and I walked on the cobbled streets toward the Tremont House, where the women's club met. The ladies in their beautiful dresses and hats, the gentlemen in their finery, all swarming through the streets intent upon their destinations, the scents of food from a nearby dining establishment, the colorful display of candy in a shop devoted to confections, a jeweler's, flower stores and bookstores . . . it was all too much for me to take in. And to think my husband practically lived here. What adventure!

I heard Louisa laugh beside me. "You haven't heard a word I've said, have you?"

I shook my head. "Forgive me. I am in awe of this city. But that's no excuse for my inattention. Please tell me what you were saying."

"Mr. Niles wants a second volume for spring."

I stopped walking and placed a hand upon her arm. "Of *Little Women*?"

She nodded. "The first edition is gone and more are called for."

I had to stop myself from jumping up and down, bursting at the seams with excitement for not only my friend, but for myself—that I would get to read more of the March sisters.

Louisa's *Little Women* had quickly become a huge success, and I could see why. It was my own favorite of hers. Domestic, honest, and even simple, it was as far from Rosamond and Phillip Tempest as one could get. And it was winning new hearts every day, including mine.

"I will begin in November. I'm finding a little success to be quite inspiring, am now even finding my Marches to be sober, nice people and not quite the bores I feared the Pathetic Family would seem."

"Far from it." I adored her "Pathetic Family," both in real life and in the pages of her book. "Oh, you will have Jo marry Laurie, won't you?" Jo March had especially captured me with her fierce independence. I loved seeing my friend in fiction. For to me, Jo wasn't fiction at all. She was Louisa.

And all of America was proving to find her a breath of fresh air in the literary community.

She made a scoffing sound. "You are just as hopeless as the girls who write me."

"But Laurie is so . . . perfect. And he loves Jo, doesn't he?"

"What of what Jo wants? Whom she loves?"

"There is no one else."

She raised her chin. "Not yet, perhaps, but I refuse to marry Jo to Laurie to please anyone, even you, Johanna."

I could tell I had gotten her dander up and thought it best to not take offense.

"Jo should remain a literary spinster, but I haven't the heart to disappoint all the young ladies who write me. Out of perversity, I plan to make a funny match for her and expect vials of wrath to be poured out upon my head. I can't help but enjoy the prospect."

"You are dreadful!" I teased.

She smiled. "Dreadful or not, know that I think of your brother as I write my honorable heroes. He inspires me to write them, along with all the other good men I've had fortune to cross paths with in this life. The same will be true for the match I make for Jo."

Tears pricked my eyelids. "That is beautiful, dear. And you are brilliant." I paused, thinking of those we'd lost. "It was so nice to know your Lizzie, even if it was in the pages of fiction."

She didn't speak right away, and I knew her to be thinking. "Beth is the character I have kept the most true, though in life she was ten times as sweet, never caring much for this world beyond home. She was such a dear little saint. I believe

I'm better all my life for those sad hours I spent with her." She looked down at my middle. "Do you need a rest?"

"No, I am splendid."

"What of your writing? Did you bring any poems to share with me? Have you any news of them being published with Nathan?"

I shook my head, not wanting to spoil our time with talk of continued rejection. "No poems, no news. Besides, I've been too preoccupied preparing for this little one." In truth, I had continued at my poetry, felt it a magnificent way to empty myself of anxious thoughts surrounding Nathan so that I could better pour myself into my marriage and my coming babe. I had accepted that publication might never come. Perhaps my poems were not all that good, anyway. I mustn't bother Louisa or my husband with them any longer.

She smiled. "You will be a most excellent mother."

"Tell me, how are Anna and the boys?"

"Nan is depending on her ear trumpet more than ever, but very well. Oh, and little Johnny! He's a heavenly sort of fire to warm and comfort us with his sunny little face and loving ways. She is a happy woman indeed. I sell my children; though they feed me, they don't love me as hers do."

I placed a hand on my growing stomach, understanding the truth of her words. I'd dreamed of writing, but beside the promise of this child, such castles in the air paled in comparison.

We arrived at the hotel and entered the grand establishment. I followed Louisa to the back, where the ladies' ordinary was located. She ushered me into the club, a venture that was little more than six months old but seeming to gain popularity. She introduced me to Mrs. Cheney and Mr. Higginson, Mrs. Robinson, Mrs. Severance, and Mrs. Howe, all names I knew either from their writings or Louisa's praise of them.

We settled in to begin the meeting and I listened to the minutes of the last, felt pride over being part of such an official thing in the middle of Boston. One of the ladies stood to read a paper she'd written on women's suffrage. My tiny babe kicked heartily within my belly as the words were read, and I wondered if the unborn child sensed something stirring within me as the speaker eloquently argued for the right of a woman to vote.

"Can you all please recall the first line of the Constitution? Not even the first line, rather the first seven words! 'We the People of the United States.'" The speaker, a Mrs. Weiss, spoke with such poise and confidence, I couldn't help but be entranced by her words.

"I have to wonder about that line. Why then, if our forebears did not wish women to vote, did they not write, 'We the white males of the United States'? Here, in our very own Constitution, we are given our rights and yet they are ignored. We—men, women, blacks, Jews, we are all *people*! It is a matter not only of our rights, but of divine justice, that we claim this cause and fight for a voice—both within our personal futures and in the future of our country!"

All applauded as she finished, and I remembered my long-ago talk with Nathan by Walden Pond when we first began courting. We had ceased talking of controversial issues together, largely because I didn't broach any contentious issues any longer. Things went along fairly well, and I didn't see it wise to throw a stick in a finely running carriage wheel.

But listening to the chatter following the talk and finding my heart stirred for a passion as it hadn't been in a long while, I vowed to speak of such things to my husband again. To pull at his thoughts—and perhaps his heart—once more. When was the last time I'd been moved to action, moved to care? And I longed for Nathan to be beside me in this. Men were at this club. Some men cared. Perhaps Nathan would as well, as he once said he had.

We'd forgotten such small things as meaningful conversation. We'd forgotten adventure. Had we ever worked together for a worthy cause? If it couldn't be in literature and writing, perhaps something else. I only wanted to feel a part of him, to change the world for the better, even a small bit, for the sake of our little one.

After a lively conversation which served to further inspire, we bade the members of the club farewell, and Louisa led me east.

"How I wish Marmee could have been here for that!"

"It was absolutely splendid. My heart is on fire. Tell me, how is your mother getting on?"

"Achy and old, I'm afraid. The last she came to Boston, she broke down in King's Chapel, poor dear. Several old ladies came in who knew her and she got to thinking of the time when she and her mother and sisters and father and brothers all went to church together. Still, she says she will live to get the vote, even if her daughters have to carry her to the polls!"

I smiled. "I've no doubt that she will."

We continued chatting about the meeting, me asking many questions and her answering them and seeming to enjoy the role of teacher immensely.

The sun shone bright, the leaves in the trees above Granary Burying Ground vivid with autumn color against the blue of the sky. Louisa told me she wanted to show me as much of Boston as time—and our energy—would allow, including the Old Corner Bookstore, which housed her publisher's office on the second floor. "How about an early dinner before the theater? Do you think Nathan would mind if I spoil your appetite? I'm not one for extravagance, but we simply must stop at the Parker House Hotel and order a chocolate cream pie. It is the most delicious thing you will ever taste."

I couldn't argue with that. We walked a block or so, then allowed the doorman to grant us entrance into the hotel. My jaw fell open at the extravagant interior—plush carpets, elaborate wainscoting that rose all the way to the ceilings, where golden chandeliers lit the place with cheery brightness. Louisa bustled over to the entrance of the dining room and greeted the attendant.

I followed her, a bit self-conscious in the room full of mostly finely dressed gentleman. I put my hands in front of my burgeoning belly as the man led us to a spot by the window.

"Are you certain it's fit for us to be here?"

"Of course it is! Were you not inspired by any of Mrs. Weiss's speech? Are we not people like the rest? Besides, we are not the only women."

I thanked the waiter as he handed us each a menu, then looked around with discretion to assure myself that we were indeed not the only women in attendance. Louisa might have felt fine forging ahead into the world of men, but I was most definitely more cautious by nature. Thinking to enjoy a meal *and* pie in front of so many gentlemen seemed a bit assuming, even for me.

But yes, there was a scattering of women about. Though I didn't see any others dining without men, or alone, like Louisa and me. My eye caught a table of two couples enjoying themselves over sumptuous plates. I wondered why Nathan hadn't brought me to Boston more often. And though I knew he thought it improper that I was out so far along in my pregnancy, I secretly hoped *he* would show me around the city before we left.

I caught sight of a striking woman in a dashing bonnet in the far corner. I looked again at the man she dined with, though I was certain it was only because I was just thinking of my husband that I noticed a similarity.

I blinked. Looked again. But no. There could be no mistaking my husband across the way. The jacket he wore that I had helped him into that very morning, the one I had lovingly stitched a button on three nights prior. His strong and handsome profile beneath his noteworthy blond curls, the hand holding his wineglass, the smile—the very same smile with which he favored me when we were courting and in the first few months of our marriage. Only now he smiled at the beautiful woman before him.

The cut of her dress wasn't immodest . . . exactly. And yet the way she leaned over the table at my husband was. The way she put her hand out and rubbed his arm in such a familiar manner. The way he leaned toward her, the smile falling into something else—something much more dangerous. A sort of passion I recognized but hadn't seen in quite some time. He placed his hand on top of hers—the one on his arm—and I thought I might be sick right then and there as all feeling leached from my face, my arms, my legs. My stomach twisted and churned as if tossed on a violent sea of discord.

"Johanna, are you ill? Is it the babe?"

I shook my head, unable to find my voice.

"Do you wish to leave?"

I shook my head again. For leaving would mean walking by my husband and *that* woman. Risking being seen. Risking seeing more than I wished to see.

Louisa turned to where my attention was focused, seeming to search.

"Don't," I managed, though I couldn't quite understand why she shouldn't. Because it was impolite? Because she would see something that would reflect poorly upon me?

Why did any of it matter?

She turned slowly back toward me, and I could tell she'd caught the same sight I had.

Still I longed to be wrong. "Please tell me that isn't my husband," I whispered.

"Johanna, I'm so sorry."

My chest tightened as if it were being squeezed through a laundry wringer. I couldn't breathe. Suddenly my legs strengthened and I was up. I must leave. Leave the hotel. Leave Boston. I stood, settled my hand on the edge of the table to keep the room from swaying, then launched myself toward the exit.

A stronger woman would have confronted him. Gone

over and asked to be introduced to his companion. Or simply thrown the wine he was drinking in his face.

But I was not strong. Perhaps I'd fooled myself into thinking I was for a short time—when I came to Concord in the first place, when I chose to have my own life, when I sat with Louisa at the women's club among so many intelligent and capable women—but now, with the truth of my life before me, with the man I loved caught up with another woman and me about to give birth to his babe, I felt only brittle and weak. Like a piece of laundry that'd been used as a rag for so many years and long since served its purpose. Thin, weak, too easily stretched.

I did not know my way around Boston, but I did know the direction from which we came and the Common nearby. I walked hastily toward it, anxious to be away from people and tall buildings, the squeeze and press of betrayal. I heard Louisa calling my name behind but could not bring myself to stop even for her. Or maybe *especially* for her. She, who had warned me about Nathan both before marriage and after. She, who had seen me perhaps in her heroine Rosamond and Nathan in Phillip Tempest. Was I little more than a woman who had been tempted and duped by a man and would now spend the rest of my life suffering the consequences?

But no. I had seen the signs of trouble firsthand, had chosen to ignore them. Had I not in some ways brought this entire torment upon myself?

And looking back now, I saw I was a fool. The change in our relationship had been gradual, slow, like the toll of a distant bell that draws closer and closer, boding disaster. Only I stopped my ears against it. Much like I stopped my ears against Louisa's initial warnings about her neighbor, much like I stopped my ears against the doubts calling out to me when I first accepted Nathan's proposal.

I wondered how things could have been different had I heeded them. But he came with swift charm and force, much like a tempest. And I was captured by it, by the good I saw even despite the warnings. By a need to feel wholeheartedly loved. By a need to feel as if I belonged and was a part of something bigger than myself.

I thought I could save him and perhaps myself in the process. But now it was too late.

I heard fast footsteps behind me, forgot that Louisa still ran when she felt up to it, that she had few qualms about doing so in public. When she came beside me, she did not say a word. Only walked with me.

I did not know what I should say, where I should go, how I could reconcile what I'd seen with what I thought to be true in my head. I knew some men—even gentlemen—had mistresses. But I did not think *mine* would have.

I had tried to be attentive to his every want or need. Yes, I sometimes failed, but what wife did not?

When I saw a bench near Frog Pond, I sat with a huff, unable to walk any longer. Back at the Parker House Hotel, my husband no doubt still sat with that woman. Did he stay at the hotel when he was in Boston on business? Did he meet that woman often? Invite her into his room?

A spout of tears came over me at the thought of him sharing such intimacies—intimacies that belonged only to me. I knew he wasn't perfect, knew his worst side, but never in a million years had I imagined unfaithfulness.

Louisa sat next to me, did not speak into my tears or take my hand and try to comfort me. Instead, her presence was enough. For I knew the one thing that would make this moment more unbearable was to bear it alone, and she was doing what she knew best—that which she considered the "most noble thing one may be called to do in life." She had done the same for John as he prepared for death, and now she did so for me as I faced the truth of my husband's actions—she shared another's suffering.

When my tears finally died down, she spoke. "When I was a little girl, I played here often. One day I was racing so fast with my hoop, running around topsy-turvy as usual, that I did not look where I was going and I fell into the pond, right here, unable to swim."

I didn't see why she would tell me such now. Yet I couldn't be choosy over how she wished to help. If she chose to do it in a story—something she no doubt possessed skill with—then why should it bother me? Perhaps if I had been more attentive to the story of Rosamond and Phillip Tempest, I would not be so surprised by this unpleasant turn of events.

"I remember going under the water and being so frightened. I'd been completely taken by surprise. One minute my mind was on the hoop; the next all that consumed my brain was the frigid water swallowing my limbs, making my senses frantic. I saw light at the surface, but it was so far away. I couldn't breathe."

I hadn't heard this story before, and I realized then that while Louisa was generous in sharing her fiction with me, there was much of the "real" her I was coming to discover in only bits and pieces.

"All of a sudden, I felt a strong hand grip my arm and pull me up, a sopping wet girl who no doubt looked more like a half-drowned rat than a proper little Boston lady. The hand set me down on solid ground, and when I looked at it, I saw how dark it was. It released me when I saw the face that belonged to it—a large black boy with deep, somber eyes who stared at me for only a moment, and then he was gone, probably afraid to be seen touching a little white girl."

I peered into the body of water before us, the place in my mind thirty years older. The story had a way of numbing me to reality, and I let it.

"I never did know who he was, and I never got to thank him. But that set my little abolitionist's heart on fire. And it showed me something else. That sometimes when I feel very grief-ridden, very weak, God will step in and make a way." She stopped, stared at the waters of Frog Pond. "To go very near death teaches one the value of life. I think of the time after the war when I suffered the typhoid. I think of the time I had to say goodbye to Lizzie. Great grief has taught me more than any minister, and when feeling most alone, I find refuge in the almighty Friend."

Louisa and I didn't talk much of faith and religion. It was a part of us, much as it was a part of anyone. But after John died, I found myself thinking on such things less and less, on forging my own way. And in truth, I found the Alcotts' belief that one must constantly be improving upon oneself to obtain a more godly state tiring and wearying. I knew Louisa's beliefs to be unorthodox. She also had scant tolerance for religious talk, instead demanding faith in action. But here, I wondered if this wasn't a truth I could grasp—a God who was not only just, but a friend.

"I don't see what way that will be," I said. "I am about to have a child. My husband does not appear to be the man I . . ." I sniffed, muffling my unfinished thoughts. "Could I have imagined what I saw?" I knew the question was desperate, but was it wise to leap to conclusions? Could there be an explanation?

Louisa gathered a deep breath, seemed preoccupied with two boys racing fast across the Common. "I suppose there could always be an explanation . . ." My heart leapt at her words. "But you may be a fool to listen to one. If I saw John Pratt with another woman in such a state, I would be in a fit of fury for Nan's sake. Even if nothing more than what we saw occurred . . . Johanna, no self-respecting woman would stand for it."

Again she called me to something I couldn't own. For what options did I have? Go back home to Mother and George? Live in my brother's home, raise my child without a father?

"I am not like you," I said.

"And I am not asking you to be. I am only asking that you open your eyes to the facts before you. Think of your child."

"I am thinking of my child! What kind of life is it to be raised without a father?"

"What kind of life is it for a father to be away, making another life apart from his wife and babe?"

I stood. "Only you would be so bold as to speak of such things. Any other respectable woman—"

She stood, her eyes meeting mine. "Hang respectable!" I

felt the gazes of passersby upon us. "Is your husband respecting your marriage vows? Are you, if you go on pretending you didn't see what you saw back there?"

My bottom lip trembled.

Her voice softened. "I only wish to help. At least confront him. Don't sweep his actions under the rug and allow them to become worse. Our men deserve our respect, but we also deserve to be treated respectably. Talk to him now, before it goes further, if it hasn't already."

More tears at her words, and this time she placed a hand on my arm. "I would help you how I could."

"I do not wish to be another beggar at your door." I gently pulled my arm from her. "I will talk to Nathan. I promise."

"Tonight?"

"Yes," I let out before I could let fear suppress it. "Tonight."

CHAPTER TWENTY-NINE

I've made so many resolutions, and written sad notes,
and cried over my sins, and it doesn't seem to do any good!

~ LMA

Taylor

"THIS IS WHY they should still teach cursive in school." I flipped another page to read a letter from Louisa to her childhood friend, Alf Whitman, who I noticed referred to her sweetly as his "little woman." With much effort, I read through the letter, saw glimpses of Jo's Laurie in it, including a recollection of some fun the pair "had at the last ball . . . staring our eyes out at the people 'bobbing around' down below." I rubbed my eyes after reading the paragraph. "Even I'm a bit rusty."

Victoria looked up from where she sat at the breakfast bar of the Bennett kitchen. "Really? I'm not having a problem."

I rolled my eyes. "What a surprise. Why do I feel like

we're back in high school, me struggling over homework or a story and you breezing through everything?"

She laughed. "And yet look who's the one breezing up the bestseller lists now, right?"

Again I rolled my eyes, then nudged her with my elbow. "Look, from Louisa, 1862—'saw many great people, and found them no bigger than the rest of the world. . . . Having known Emerson, Parker, Phillips, and that set of really great and good men and women living for the world's work and service of God, the mere show people seem rather small and silly.'"

Victoria caught my gaze. "You are great, Taylor, but not because of your books. Because you're here. Because you care. Because you came back."

We went back to our reading. The kids came home and Victoria spent some time talking with them about their day, reiterating to them that they would all be staying at Grandma and Grandpa's for a while.

When she returned, she went straight back to the letters and didn't seem to want to talk.

I continued reading, my eyes burning from straining them against the old, copied handwriting. There were countless letters from Louisa to her mother and her sisters, to her childhood friend, Alf, and later, many to editors and publishers in Boston and New York. Though I found it interesting, I began to skim, searching for Johanna's name.

"You know, she destroyed a lot of her personal letters and journals after her mother's death—both hers and her mother's. I guess there was a lot there that spoke of how hard things often were for Abigail Alcott. Louisa didn't want things left behind."

"I can't say I blame her. I mean, would you want strangers reading your personal thoughts?"

She shook her head, looked at me pointedly. "Definitely not."

I winced. Right. "Did I mention I was sorry about that?"

"No, but I accept your apology."

I smiled, savoring her words. "Thank you."

I sat for a moment, imagining the letters Louisa had destroyed. Most likely those would be the ones of special interest, and yet it would be impossible to re-create them through any effort of imagination or speculation.

We went back to reading. I noted the common theme in Louisa's life of striving for the better. In one particular entry of her girlhood she wrote:

> *I was cross today, and I cried when I went to bed. I made good resolutions, and felt better in my heart. If I only kept all I make, I should be the best girl in the world. But I don't, and so am very bad.*

My own heart ached for small Louisa, for I could understand her plight, as it seemed a much older Louisa could as well, for below the entry was written: (*Poor little sinner! She says the same at fifty—LMA.*)

I marveled then at the plight of the human heart, the condition that none of us could escape, no matter how far we flew or no matter which ocean we sought.

What was the answer to our burden?

Another thirty minutes passed before Victoria grabbed my arm. "Wait. Here!"

I peered over her shoulder. The letter was addressed "Dear Johanna." I stood up, adrenaline rushing to my limbs. "This is it."

Victoria read out loud. "'Dear Johanna, I was not certain whether I would hear back from you, and I am so very glad I did. . . . Presumptuous as it may be, I confess that your John had become very dear to me in the short time I knew him. I still think of him often. His strength of character and bravery in the midst of the impossible will, I am quite certain, stay with me forever.'"

I pointed to John's name. "It's him. And from the sound of it this isn't their first letter. They must have been in communication about Johanna's brother."

Victoria read on, and it was like finding treasure—to an Alcott fan, at least. Louisa wrote of her time with John at the army hospital. She encouraged Johanna to write more of John, saying stories had a way of healing grief.

"They grew close through their letters."

We ended that letter only to find another and another. As we had inferred earlier, Johanna would travel to Concord to stay with Louisa's parents while she went to Europe. There was one letter while she was away, but it sounded as if there were many missing. Still, we got the gist of their relationship—one that seemed to be more than simply that of employer and employee. They were friends, and though it appeared theirs was a harmonious friendship, there was one point they most definitely disagreed upon—at least in 1865, while Louisa was overseas and Johanna was taking care of the house and her parents: Nathan Bancroft.

There was not much about him in the letters until Louisa mentioned the wedding in a letter to her sister, Anna.

Attended Johanna's wedding. Cannot say I've been saddened by the experience of nuptials this much since your own wedding—and that for selfish reasons. This time, my concern is purely altruistic. Though Johanna seems set. I have been wrong before. I pray their marriage proves a blessed one.

We searched awhile longer after that but found no more word about Johanna, either good or bad.

Victoria folded the papers back into their folder.

"Do you really think that's it? No more?"

"It seems to be. Maybe they grew distant after Johanna married Nathan."

"But that doesn't explain the poems. It's like we're missing a big piece of what happened."

She shook her head. "I'm not sure where else to search."

She looked tired, defeated, as if she was about to throw in the towel on this or maybe just life itself. Without thinking, I grabbed up her hand in mine. "There's more, and we're going to find it."

I couldn't help but be disheartened by the weak smile she gave me. "Sure."

I squeezed her hand. "Please tell me how I can help you."

She dragged in a wobbly, ragged breath. "I know you can't tell, but you being here has made all the difference. It's going to be a while before I can pick myself up from this. I don't know who I am without Will. I'm not even sure I want to find out."

I bit the inside of my cheek, holding in any lecture or scorn that would make her feel worse. "I can help you. I remember who you were—who you are. Write again, Victoria. What better sort of outlet than that right now? You should have never given it up—not out of guilt, not for Will. It's a part of you, and you can't just throw it away."

"I'm numb. I don't *want* to feel."

An idea came to me then, and it was so absurd, I questioned its validity for at least a solid minute in my mind. There were about a thousand different reasons I shouldn't pave this path. Most professionals, my agent and editor included, would probably discourage such a distraction. But in many ways, Victoria was at the heart of my story already. Why not give her a say in it?

"What if we wrote together?"

"We already tried that, remember? Our Pickwick meeting the other night."

"No. Write one story together. Our story. The one I'm on deadline for."

I could see right away that she was tempted. That, in some ways, I offered her a childhood dream on a gold-trimmed platter. But she shook her head. "I can't intrude on your deadline, Taylor. And I never understood how people write books together anyway. I mean, what does that even look like?"

"It looks like working together. You've always been brilliant with a story, and right now I need help. And I know you can contribute so much more than if I were on my own. Or what if you wrote in some of the historical letters my main character is finding? It would be fitting to have a different voice with those. Please, help me."

She looked at the folder before her. "I can try. But I'm not making any promises—"

Something in my heart lightened, and I hardly recognized it. "I'm not expecting anything. I promise. Whatever you have to give I'll be grateful for. Thank you."

"Don't thank me yet." She slid off the stool. "Now how about you helping me with something a little more concrete? Supper."

~~~

Two days passed. Victoria went to work and read my story at night, catching up on what I'd written so far. The kids went to school. Dad took Mom to chemo.

We got a good start on the story, and Victoria did write a few letters between our historical heroine and Louisa May Alcott, similar to the ones we found. But the connection between the present-day story and the historical letters didn't quite jibe.

Thursday night, my sister took off her reading glasses and put them on the dining room table to rub her eyes. "I miss him," she said.

I closed my eyes, didn't have any wisdom to handle such emotions. I wanted to remind her of the words he'd called her, of her beloved books hurled at her, intended to hurt. But really I wasn't certain if any of that would serve her well either.

I thought of Will. Of how life had changed him or rather wrung him out into a different person. Was it life, war, or was it something he was predisposed to already? Something I hadn't seen all those years ago when he told me he loved me in Boston's Public Garden?

"I've been thinking. About Johanna."

"What about her?" I tried to sound nonchalant, though secretly I counted it a victory that she'd been thinking about our story and Johanna, that we could move past her acknowledgment that she missed her husband.

"I think there's one avenue we haven't explored, and it might be worth looking into."

I straightened, leaned toward her a bit.

"She probably has family. Maybe even direct descendants. We know enough to find out pretty quickly on ancestry.com. A lot like I had done when I was searching for John and Anna Pratt's family."

"Of course," I whispered. "Now that we know her husband's name."

"It doesn't mean they know anything," Victoria cautioned. "But there's a good chance they could at least know the basics—that she worked for the Alcotts and all that."

I thought of Johanna's poem on marriage. "And yet if there was some history that they didn't want discovered, or that maybe even Johanna didn't want discovered, perhaps they've kept it hidden."

Victoria's lips thinned. "You might be right. She wrote about her troubles in the poems it seems, but then they were hidden away in Bronson's school. Someone—whether it be

Johanna or Louisa or someone else in their circle—didn't want them found. It's bad enough my kids have an idea what Will and I are going through. I'd hate for that to be passed down our family line."

I opened my mouth to force some positive words into the conversation. Perhaps tell her that good or bad, it was part of the story. The journey. That perhaps good could *come* from the bad.

But I stopped myself. It might be too early for such pep talks. Besides, did I really believe those words? It was a recent thought, one I hadn't dwelled on to much extent until coming to Concord, until singing a song in my mother's church about such things. Did I really believe it?

"Let's look into it," I said instead.

We logged on to the website and got to work. Within an hour and a half, we had Johanna Bancroft's family tree. At least one arm of it. She and Nathan had only one child, born in Philadelphia. Cora Bancroft. According to the site, Cora had had four children.

"Look!" I pointed at the screen. Cora's first child was named Louisa. "There is no way that is a coincidence."

Victoria shook her head. "If Louisa was such a big part of Johanna's life—maybe even so much that her daughter named her firstborn after her—then why isn't more mentioned about Johanna in Louisa's journals and letters? I'm voting on the name being coincidence."

I mumbled something about her raining on my parade but brushed it off quick, kept following the line which eventually led us to two sisters—an Amber born in 1986 and a

Nicole born in 1988. They both had marriage records in Maine and they both had two children each, all under the age of ten.

"So we find them, right? It should be easy enough using social media."

Victoria nodded. "Even if they didn't do the research themselves, they can hopefully point us in a better direction than we have now."

I opened another tab to my Facebook account. I only had an author page, but it would have to do. I plugged in the name Amber Macedo. A page of results came up, and after searching through the first few for clues of the Amber from the Northeast that we were looking for, I instead typed in Nicole's name. Nicole Carotenuto. Only one came up, and I clicked on it to see a profile picture of a pretty young woman with a blond man, both tan with blue ocean behind them.

I worked on composing a message that explained our predicament and what we were looking for. After Victoria read it over and approved, I sent it and closed the laptop. "I'd say that's good progress for the day. And this letter you wrote for our story—it's beautiful. Better than any of your others so far. It's coming back to you, isn't it?"

A small smile lifted one corner of her mouth. "I felt . . . freer in that one."

"I could tell."

The doorbell rang and I went to answer it. Something akin to disgust climbed up my insides at the sight of Will just over the threshold.

I stepped out onto the porch, closed the screen door behind me. "What do you want?" I snapped. I didn't care what that website said, in this moment I felt my sister needed all the protection I could give her.

Will stood, straight and sure as ever. "I want to see my wife."

"No."

"Don't let her get to you too, Taylor. I'm sure she told a crock of lies about me, didn't she? Yes, I may have been a little out of line this past week. My deadline at work, things have been stress—"

"That is no excuse to throw books at your wife. To call her a . . . Get out of here or I'm calling the police."

"Taylor—"

"I mean it, Will. Leave."

"Taylor." The voice came from behind me and it sounded smaller than it had when I'd just been talking to her. Then, she'd been animated trying to figure out the mystery of Johanna Bancroft. She'd been without chains, like her old self. Now I clearly saw what Will did to her. I saw, and I hated him for it. "It's okay. We should talk."

I wanted to disagree, but no matter how much I wanted to at that moment, I could not be Victoria's keeper. "Fine." I opened the screen door for her to come out, gestured to the porch chairs for her to sit in one. I took the other. "Say what you need to say," I said to Will, who was still standing near the steps.

Victoria crossed her arms in front of her chest. "Taylor. Please." The words were like a slap. Hadn't she just been saying how grateful she was that I was here, how grateful she was for my help? I thought I was to be part of the solution.

And yet, like it or not, Victoria was a grown woman. She

could decide to walk right back into Will's arms and there wasn't one thing I could do about it.

I stood. "Fine. I'll be right inside if you need me." I went into the house, closed the screen door, but left the solid door open so I could hear if anything got out of hand.

I heard a swear cross Will's lips. "You don't belong here, Victoria. You belong with me. Come home—now."

I thought of his words about Victoria lying to me, and I hated myself for entertaining it. This was what he did apparently, who he was now. Getting inside the head of his wife with poison, manipulating, trying to seed suspicion within me as well. Still, it plucked familiar chords of betrayal across my heart. I couldn't trust Will. But did that mean I could trust my sister?

"I'm not ready to come home yet, Will."

More muffled words. Then, "I'm sorry. I'm sorry . . ." He was crying. I couldn't believe it. The lowlife was legit sobbing.

I backed away from the door. As much as I wanted to hear my sister's response, I didn't want to impose on Victoria's privacy. We'd grown closer this last week—maybe even closer than we'd ever been. She'd tell me what happened when Will was gone. She'd tell me the truth. I was certain of it.

I went back to the dining room table, opened my laptop, and clicked onto my Facebook account. The red bubble indicated I had a message.

Hey, Taylor! I don't know a lot about my ancestors, but my mom is the one who does all that ancestry stuff. I read her your message. She encouraged me to give you her phone number. Hope that helps!

I wrote back my thanks, plugged Nicole's mom's number into my phone next to the name *Marjorie* and leaned back in my chair, straining to hear voices outside.

Mom and Dad would be home soon. I didn't know how they'd respond to Will's presence on their porch—probably much like I'd done, if I had to hazard a guess.

A couple minutes later, I heard the screen door settle in its casing. Victoria's footsteps echoed down the hall. She stood at the threshold, her arms once again crossed over her chest.

"He said he's sorry," she said.

I pressed my lips together.

"I know what you're thinking. And I know you're probably right. But I can't help but . . . hope. Is that so wrong?"

I closed my eyes. That blasted hope again. It had disappointed one too many times for my liking. "He said you lied to me about what happened."

I let my words sit between us, not wanting to ask her outright but needing reassurance.

"Taylor, how could you think . . . ? No, no, of course I didn't." She paced the floor in front of me. "He said that?"

I nodded.

She put her hands on her face, rubbed them down her cheeks. "This is what he excels at. Planting doubt. He had me doubting myself more than once after we'd gotten in bad arguments."

"And you think going back to him is a good idea right now?"

"He said he'd get help. Really this time."

"Then let him. Great. But he has a lot of proving himself to do before you accept him back into your life." I winced.

There I went again. "I'm sorry. It's your life. You have a right to live it how you want—not how Will wants you to or Mom and Dad want you to or I want you to."

"Thank you," she whispered.

I gestured to the computer. "Nicole got back to me."

She sat down. "That was fast." But her excitement was frayed, torn.

I told her what Nicole had said.

"You going to call her?" Victoria asked.

"Yes. I was just about to." Though somewhere in the space of the last half hour, my excitement had dwindled too. I looked at Johanna's book of poems, sitting on the table. At the file of letters we'd obtained from Orchard House, the books that recorded Louisa Alcott's journals. I'd put so much stock into what this search meant for us. For the book we now wrote together, yes, but also for what it meant for us as sisters. Somehow Johanna had reunited us, and I felt we had a duty to her memory to find her history.

I picked up my phone. Dialed Marjorie Pelletier's number.

She answered on the third ring. "Hello?" It was a breezy greeting, and it put me at ease.

I explained who I was and that Nicole had passed along her number. Then I launched into a shortened version of our story regarding Johanna. "So I know this might be kind of a shot in the dark, but I was wondering if you knew anything more about her. Specifically regarding her friendship with Louisa Alcott."

"My grandmother's namesake," she said quietly.

I perked up. "We saw that but we didn't want to surmise something that wasn't there."

She chuckled. "Oh, it's there all right. Gram told me many a tale while I was a toddler at her feet. It wasn't until I was older that she opened up about the entire history, though."

"We'd love to hear it if you're willing to share."

She sighed. "I suppose everyone's family has a dark spot or two they'd rather not expose. I haven't even told my daughters yet, convinced myself it didn't matter much to them what happened a hundred and fifty years ago."

I licked my lips. "I'm pretty fond of stories, and I believe they're all worth telling. The bad ones and the good. I've even been wondering if they all might have a way of birthing new life."

"Beauty from ashes," Marjorie whispered.

"Yes," I said, something light in my heart for the first time in days.

"My daughter said you contacted her by way of Casey Hood's author page. You don't know her, do you?" She sounded as if she already knew my secret.

"Casey's my pen name."

"Well, my, oh, my. You said you're in Concord, is that right? We're about a two-hour drive north of there. I'd love to tell you Johanna's history in exchange for your autograph on some of my favorite books. What do you think?"

I laughed. "I think that sounds like an agreeable arrangement."

"I could meet you halfway."

"No." I looked at Victoria. "I think a little trip up north might do me and my sister good."

She gave me her address and we arranged a time that Saturday. Then I hung up.

I grinned at Victoria. "She knows something. A lot from the sound of it."

"That's awesome. I can't wait to hear it."

"She encouraged us to bring the kids. Said her own grandchildren will be around."

Victoria nodded. "Good. Great."

"Are you okay?"

"Yes. No. I don't know. It's okay that I don't know, isn't it?"

I nodded. "More than okay."

CHAPTER THIRTY

I love luxury, but freedom and independence better.

~ LMA ·

Johanna

NATHAN CAME TO OUR ROOMS that evening earlier than expected. Louisa and I had cut our time short, as I felt a fierce need to rest my mind and body to prepare for my husband's return, to face him in his unfaithfulness.

I heard the door open from where I lay on the sofa, then soft whistling and the gentle drop of a newspaper upon the table. I opened my eyes to see him come toward me and kneel beside the sofa. He ran a hand over my forehead, and it being the gentlest gesture I'd received from him in a long while, I leaned into it even as tears welled beneath my lids.

"It is a treat to see you here, my love. Perhaps we should spend more time in the city like this, go to the country when we need rest." He kissed me sweetly, but I did not respond, for my pregnancy had served to heighten my sense of smell and I did not think I imagined the very feminine scent of rose water that clung to his jacket.

He did not seem to notice. "How do you feel?"

I moved to sit up, and he assisted me. "Rather poorly, in fact."

"Miss Alcott has traipsed you around the city, no doubt. You have overdone yourself."

"No, I was feeling splendid until we stopped for dinner at the Parker House Hotel."

I watched his expression carefully, did not miss the nervous flick of his tongue over his lips, the rapid blink of his eyes. "Did you have their famous pie, then? It is quite well done."

That sentence, more than anything else, seemed to prove his guilt. For had he been at the restaurant on business or felt no need to be ashamed of his actions, he would have surely said something along the lines of "I was there! How did I not see you?" or "I wish I had known. I would have loved for you to join us."

But he did not.

"Who were you dining with?" I whispered, trying to tame my tone for I did not want to be cross. Somewhere deep down, despite Louisa's warnings, I still wanted an explanation. Shamefully, I was fast realizing that any—even a pitiful one—might do.

He stood. "I was going to tell you tonight," he said, and I wished I believed it. "Her name is Gladys Saucier. She's the daughter of a Philadelphia publisher. We've been discussing a new business venture."

"With a woman?"

"Her father is entirely unorthodox and lets her handle details. She is in Boston often and he requested we meet."

My breaths came shallow. My explanation. Could it be so simple? But who ever heard of a woman handling such a venture?

I rubbed my temples. "If you could have seen what I saw . . . Nathan, you were entirely too familiar with that woman."

"I *am* familiar with her. We've been talking for months. I didn't want to tell you because I wanted to surprise you." He took my hands, and I found myself wanting to believe his excitement, wanting to trust his words. "I am leaving my uncle. How would you like to start a new adventure? One in Philadelphia, near your family?"

My head spun. This was too much. Was what I saw truly innocent?

"I admit I charmed her a bit in order to get us the best deal possible. But nothing more untoward than a couple of dinners and a friendly pat on the arm here and there. Johanna, I am finally to realize my dream. Miss Saucier's father has no interest in the publishing aspect, only the business and its profit. He plans to leave all the decisions to me and, with my experience, is quite willing to do so. Can't you just see us in Philadelphia, building a future for our children, building a legacy for our family? And your poems . . . Uncle never showed particular interest, but I am thinking of having an entire magazine devoted to women. Miss Saucier thinks it a marvelous idea and I've already talked to her of your interest in writing."

My thoughts churned slowly. In many ways I felt like a

little Louisa, going along in the Common with my hoop and then splashed with cold water at the course and change of my path. Only this was a pleasant change. Like a skein of yarn that unwinds into a pattern—knit and purl, knit and purl, row by row—my world seemed to right itself.

And I wanted to believe it so very badly.

Nathan had acknowledged he'd been a bit too friendly with this woman. Was that the way of things in matters of business sometimes? Was I just to accept it?

"Do you . . . you do not have feelings for this woman, then?"

"No, of course not." He said it like it was the most preposterous thing in the world, like I was a fool to even voice it. I couldn't help but be comforted by the tone. He stroked the side of my face, the same spot that had been wounded by this same hand months ago but had long since healed. Healing was possible, wasn't it? I must cling to that truth. "How could I care about anyone when I have you and our coming babe? I am a most blessed man."

He sounded so sincere and more excited and full of passion than he'd been in a long while. Perhaps this would be the beginning of good things for us.

"But she would be there . . ."

He stared blankly at me, then seemed to realize. "Miss Saucier?"

"Yes."

"I suppose, but she travels so much she would be no more than a fly on the wall here and there. Darling, please believe that you are the only woman for me." He cupped my face with his hands and kissed me deeply. I sank into it, chose to cast aside my doubts and cling to something better—love. My marriage.

"Why don't I get some dinner for us and we will have a celebratory evening together?"

"I—yes, of course." Hadn't I just been wishing for more time with Nathan? And now all seemed right with the world. All fell into place.

"Nathan?"

"Yes, dear."

"When would we leave?"

"As soon as possible. Mr. Saucier has rooms available for us and wishes to start right away. We could get settled before the babe arrives."

It would be wonderful to be closer to Mother and the rest of the family, especially when my birthing time came. But all I could think on as he helped me into my cloak was telling Louisa of this turn of events. I wondered if she would disapprove or be happy for me.

Then again, I wondered why it mattered so very much.

~~

December 5, 1868

Dearest Louisa,

It is an absolute joy to write to you of the birth of our daughter, Cora Grace Bancroft, on the very day of your own birth, this past November 29. She is a healthy, vibrant girl, and though Nathan made it no secret he wished for a boy, he has become absolutely smitten over his little daughter.

Please accept this bookmark and poem as my rather belated thirty-sixth birthday gift to you. I hope it was a pleasant one and that you had success in finishing the second part of your Little Women.

Nathan greatly enjoys his new work and talks to me much more freely about it and even seeks my ideas. I do believe this change of scenery is exactly what we needed, though I do miss you much.

Mother was here for the birth of our Cora and was a great help. She has only just left, and we are quickly settling into our time as a family of three.

I look forward to your letters when you are able.

Yours,
Johanna

December 26, 1868

Dear Johanna,

I was so pleased to receive your letter and news of your sweet Cora! Please accept this blanket Marmee made on behalf of us all as a congratulatory gift. I am certain you are a most wonderful mother, and I am honored to share a birthday with your firstborn.

It was odd to close up Apple Slump this winter, to know that you are gone also. Father goes west and Mother to Anna's. May and I took a sky parlor at the new Bellevue Hotel on Beacon Street. It was a queer time, whisking up and down in the elevator, eating in a marble café, and sleeping on a sofa bed. It did not suit me, and when a hard storm caused the steam pipes to explode, we went hungry. I am tired with all the writing this year. My brains need a rest so they might continue to work.

I have dug out my old "glory cloak" and am creeping along with the sequel of Little Women and plan to send it to Mr. Roberts on New Year's Day. I always thought the trials and triumphs of the Pathetic Family would make a capital book, and I do hope the second will do as well as the first, despite my having to marry Jo off.

I am quite looking forward to seeing your contributions to your husband's publications. Please do send them on.

I hope things are truly well with you, Johanna. If you ever need anything, please do not hesitate to write.

Yours,
Louisa

April 29, 1869

Dear Louisa,

You sounded tired in your last letter, but I am so thankful you have finally paid off all the debts of your family! I have been praying a lot lately, as I am awake with Cora a good deal. I often pray for your health—particularly for your headaches and cough.

Please do give my love to your mother.

Things are quiet here. Quiet and when Cora chooses to have a say, quite the opposite of quiet! She is a demanding little bundle, but I take her for a walk *every day, which she enjoys. I long to get out, as Nathan is busy with work and I am finding keeping up with the house and chores and dinners with a baby no small challenge.*

Nathan is hesitant to hire help around the house until he is certain his venture will prove profitable. He has lost some of his initial excitement, it seems, but I am trusting it will return with the publication of his boys' magazine, coming out next month. I write poems in my mind only, for I am often too tired to get them down on paper, though I long for a creative release and wonder if Philadelphia has a women's club. If so, I would like to join. If not, perhaps I should start one. Can you imagine me, with my baby daughter in my arms, organizing such a venture?

Now what I've been waiting to get to! I just finished your sequel while Cora napped and, dear, you have amazed and left me speechless all at once. I cried many tears over little Beth and liked your ending quite well. I could scarce believe when I read of Meg's jam incident, for it sounded so very familiar (though I liked Meg's ending a bit better, even if mine does not seem so terrible now).

At first I was heartbroken for poor Laurie, but I must admit, things wrapped up in quite a satisfying way. I did not expect him to marry Amy, and yet how very fitting it all turned out to be.

I am sorry for the affliction you suffer over your newfound fame. Being lionized, not being able to live at peace within Orchard House, is certainly a new kind of slavery that I hope you can find a way to be free from.

I pray for you often, my friend.

Affectionately yours,
Johanna

～◡～

Louisa and I kept up with our letters, though I could never quite manage to divulge the true state of affairs in my life. Even when she shared the sad news of John Pratt's death a year and a half later, how she felt responsible for her nephews now and would start a book titled *Little Men*, from which all the proceeds would be kept for their future and education, I could not open up my own grief to her.

Cora grew splendidly. A new decade turned, and though I was quite happy home with my little one, who was beginning to run me ragged with her boundless sprightly energy, that old ache started in my chest again. That feeling that life was missing something meaningful.

Nathan left the house early and often came home late. More than once I smelled the familiar scent of rose water on him, but I hadn't the heart to broach the subject. In many ways, it felt safer to simply pretend all was well. And I hated myself for it.

When he was home, he often retreated into his study. One Sunday afternoon, after I put Cora down for a nap, I knocked at his door.

"Yes," came his voice, even the one word despondent.

I saw him sitting in his chair, staring at a paper upon his

desk. I could not miss the half glass of whiskey by his side, the open snuffbox on the other.

Dejection seemed to cling to him. I hadn't the heart to harp on him about the alcohol just at this moment. Instead, I went to him, placed a hand on his arm.

"Dear, let me bear your burdens with you. Tell me what is the matter."

He picked up the paper on his desk, fisted it in his hands. I saw a list of numbers, the bottom one with a circle about it. "Saucier gave me our numbers for the last quarter today. They are not good." He crumpled the paper and threw it across the room. "I've done everything right. I can't understand why we aren't selling."

"Perhaps it just needs a bit more time—"

"We started more than a year ago now. We should at least be making a small profit." He reached for his glass, chugged it down.

I wished I could say something to help. This was his dream, and it was failing fast before his eyes. Yet he didn't share the details of the business with me as he had when we first came to Philadelphia. So how could I offer suggestions? And while he seemed all too willing to try Miss Saucier's ideas, I had the notion he wouldn't welcome mine.

"Let's go sit out on the porch in the sunshine, shall we? A little nature will cheer you."

"No."

"Remember our carriage rides to Walden Pond when we courted? The good they did you? Do you remember telling me that you had a story to live? A journey? That is still true, my dear. Perhaps we should find a spot like Walden here. Or we could fly the kite I gave you last Christmas."

He shook his head, and I thought I saw tears shimmering near his eyes. He didn't seem to hear what I'd actually said. "I will not go groveling back to my uncle."

My hand froze on his arm. "Is Mr. Saucier suggesting you do so?"

Nathan closed his eyes, and I noticed the lines around his eyes and mouth, the first touch of gray within his short-cropped curls. "He is giving me one more month to turn things around. I must come up with something brilliant. Eye-catching."

I tried to rack my brains for such an idea. Then it came to me. "Miss Alcott has become quite successful. We write often. Perhaps she would be open to an interview of sorts for your adult publication?"

"That woman has always gotten under my skin . . . but it could prove promising. And probably our best chance at boosting sales."

My heart soared that he had seen value in one of my ideas. "I could write her right away. Ask if she'd be willing to answer a few questions?"

He was already sitting up straighter. "Yes, please do. I'll ask Miss Saucier what kind of questions readers would be interested in. Dear, this just might work."

At the same time that I felt an active participant more than I ever had, I also begrudged the fact that he should have to seek out Miss Saucier for questions.

"I'm certain I could come up with some suitable

questions and have it all sent out tonight, wasting no time," I said.

He wavered but eventually shook his head. "No, I'd best run it by her. She knows what readers want."

"If that were true, then perhaps your publications would be selling more."

I knew the moment the words left my mouth that they were a mistake. But I didn't like this woman, and I didn't like the hold she seemed to have on my husband.

He clenched his fists together, and I took a step back, for I had never quite gotten over the fear that he would hit me again.

"You have one good idea and you think you can tell me how to run my company now?"

"Nathan, I—"

"Leave me."

I did. Yet despite everything, I still wished to please him, so I began my letter to Louisa. I knew she would hate the notion of an interview, for she hated anything that drew attention to herself. But I also knew she would agree to it. Not because it would sell more books or make her more famous, but because it would help me, her friend.

CHAPTER THIRTY-ONE

I intend to illuminate the Ledger with a blood and thunder tale
as they are easy to "compoze" and are better paid
than moral and elaborate works of Shakespeare.

~ LMA

Taylor

MOM FINISHED OUT HER WEEK of chemo like a champ.
Victoria and I got some writing done, and Will didn't make
another appearance, though he had called to report that he'd
found a counselor and was seeing her the following week.
Had asked if Victoria might go with him.

That seemed to lift Victoria's spirits, which I was glad for,
though I resisted the urge to caution her against getting her
hopes too high. What did I know, really?

On Saturday we drove north to Marjorie's home, Johanna's
book with us. Mom had offered to keep Caden, but Victoria
had refused, saying Mom needed her rest. We pulled up to
a tidy white gambrel house, abundant with daffodils and
crocuses. When we rang the doorbell, a pretty young woman
with an infant on her hip answered.

"You must be Taylor and Victoria." She let us in. "I'm

Amber. So nice to meet you. Mom's scurrying around trying to make everything perfect for her favorite author." She laughed.

Another woman came around the corner. "You might think we were chopped liver this weekend, right, Sis?" They grinned at each other before she held her hand out to us. "I'm Nicole."

After we made our introductions, Nicole spoke to Caden. "The other kids are playing baseball in the back if you want to join them, buddy."

Caden looked at his mom, who nodded. Without hesitation, he ran out the back door.

A stout, pretty older woman breezed into the room, holding her hand ahead of her. "I'm so glad you're here! Now which one of you is Taylor?"

I extended my hand to her. "So nice to meet you. Thank you for inviting us into your home."

"The pleasure is entirely mine. I absolutely love your books. This tickles me silly to have you here." I introduced her to Victoria, and we chatted for several minutes about which books of mine were her favorite. I thanked her for her enthusiasm as she led us to a quaint breakfast nook off the kitchen, a pleasant smell coming from the oven. From there, we could see the kids playing outside.

"I made chicken salad, spinach and artichoke dip, and tea. If that doesn't suit, I can whip up just about anything quick."

"This is perfect," I said. "Thank you so much."

She gestured to our seats, and I saw a stack of books next to my plate with a Sharpie on top. I smirked at Marjorie, who merely shrugged and said, "Just a subtle hint. I have a lunch meeting with Taylor Bennett, but I was hoping Casey Hood might make a brief appearance as well."

I grinned and happily sat down to sign Marjorie's copies, noting the well-thumbed pages on a few of them. As we all chatted over our sandwiches and tea, I noticed how Marjorie laughed with her two daughters as they told stories of their children. Their merriment filled the room, and I tried not to wonder if this could be Mom, Victoria, and me if I hadn't left all those years ago. If we had a chance of this being us still.

I looked at Victoria, a genuine smile on her face as she watched the trio. She caught my gaze and her smile widened. No, our relationship would never be Amber and Nicole's. And my relationship with Mom would never be like the one Marjorie had with her daughters. We had something different.

But that didn't make it any less special.

Maybe I was finally beginning to accept that.

Amber cleared our plates, and Marjorie poured more tea and settled into her chair. "Now what you've come for, right? I hope you don't mind that I invited the girls. They don't know this story and I thought this would be a good time for us to all share in it together."

"We don't mind at all," I said. "We're grateful for anything you can tell us."

She leaned back, seemed to enjoy the suspense she created with the pause. "Grandma Lou was quite a storyteller herself. She said she used to sit at the knee of her own grandmother Johanna, that those were some of her fondest memories. She sought to re-create that with me, her oldest granddaughter."

A slight shiver ran up my spine. We knew from the

ancestry research we'd done that Cora was Johanna's daughter. But it was still neat to be speaking with someone connected with the woman we'd been trying to figure out, the woman who knew Louisa May Alcott, the woman who had written poems that had caused us to have more questions. Would Marjorie be able to answer them?

"Grandma Lou told me a lot about her own life, but as I got older, she began to tell me about her grandmother. Your Johanna Bancroft."

Amber's infant began to fuss, and she fixed a pacifier in his mouth, propped him up on her shoulder, and jiggled him a bit until his cries turned to a contented sort of vibrating that faded as he fell asleep.

Marjorie confirmed what we already knew—that Johanna had come to know Louisa through Marjorie's three-times-great-uncle, John Suhre. That Louisa had taken care of John while at the Union Hotel Hospital, that she had guided him into eternity and went on to write about it in her popular memoir *Hospital Sketches*.

Johanna had indeed agreed to come under employment for the Alcotts. In many ways, by that time, Louisa had become the breadwinner of the family, earning income and helping to make financial decisions that had to do with her parents and two sisters.

Nicole shook her head. "So was this before or after she wrote *Little Women*? And you said two sisters. Beth had already died?"

Victoria answered this time. "This was in 1865, after the war. The first part of *Little Women* was published at the end of 1868. Louisa's sister Elizabeth died in 1858. Although *Little*

Women was set during the Civil War, Louisa fashioned the March sisters after her and her own sisters, only she made them much younger than they would have been during the war." She gave a guilty grin. "Sorry. I get a little excited about this stuff."

Nicole laughed. "No need to apologize. It's all fascinating to me. I just get a little tripped up with history sometimes."

"You know what's funny about basing fiction partly on real life and partly on imagination?" Marjorie continued. "You almost never know which is which. But as you probably realize, Louisa did write in her journals and letters who had inspired all the characters in *Little Women*, including Laurie."

"Her European friend, Laddie; and her childhood friend, Alf," Victoria said.

Marjorie nodded. "She said Alf was the sober half and Laddie the 'gay whirligig half.' And we can't much argue with that since it's in her own words. But my grandma Lou was adamant that she had another inspiration in writing Laurie—and not only Laurie, but Professor Bhaer and John Pratt and every other honorable man Louisa wrote."

I cocked my head to the side.

"Why, Johanna's brother John Suhre, of course. Louisa's prince of patients."

I drummed my fingers on the table. "I can see that being true. Often when I write a character, it may not be someone inspired from just one or two people; it may be a mix of people I've known—or even fictional characters I've met in a story. Who knows what inspires us, how our brains work. John did seem to make quite an impression on Louisa. It only makes sense she would carry that with her—not only in her memories, but in her writing as well."

"That's right," Marjorie said. "So Louisa couldn't have written *Little Women* without the inspiration of her own family, but Grandma Lou also seemed certain that the Suhre family was part of that inspiration, including Johanna."

I didn't want to express my doubts. Who wouldn't wish that a great classic such as *Little Women* was partly inspired by one's family? But Louisa had written nearly nothing of Johanna in her letters and journals. Seemed to me if Johanna was that important to her, she would have written more about her or more *to* her. Unless of course, those were some of the papers Louisa had destroyed after her mother died . . .

"There are two stories Grandma Lou insisted had to do with Johanna—one being Meg's jam story."

I scrunched up my face. "You mean when John Brooke brings a friend home for dinner and newly married Meg and her kitchen are a mess?"

Marjorie smiled. "The very same thing happened to Johanna. Only the outcome for her wasn't quite so happy."

I thought of Johanna Bancroft's poems. "She had some trouble with her husband, didn't she?"

Marjorie sobered, as it seemed did Victoria and Maddie. "She did. Nathan wasn't quite as understanding as fictional John about the jam incident. That's when Louisa tried to encourage her friend to leave the marriage. But back then wives didn't just up and leave their husbands."

Victoria seemed to shrink within herself, and I got the impression she felt like the target of our conversation, though in fact, it had nothing to do with her.

Well, nothing and everything all at once.

"What was the other story?" Maddie asked.

Marjorie put her hands on the table. "This is the part I think is the most fascinating. For as long as I can remember, Grandma Lou told me about a story Louisa had written titled *Fair Rosamond*. She wrote it before *Little Women*, and Grandma insisted it was a story Louisa finished with Johanna in mind. It was about being tied up in an unhealthy marriage." She licked her lips before continuing. "When I grew older, I searched for it, but I couldn't find it anywhere."

Victoria folded one leg beneath her, suddenly animated. "Because it hadn't been published yet," she whispered, turning to me. "No one knew about it. Remember we went to camp at Orchard House the summer it was published? Only it was released under a different title: *A Long Fatal Love Chase*. A story way too edgy for a post–Civil War readership, but perfect for readers of our generation."

"You certainly know your stuff, young lady." Marjorie smiled. "I have to admit, I sometimes wondered if Grandma Lou suffered from dementia more than I realized. Or if Johanna had told a fabricated story after Louisa had made it big with *Little Women*. It was hard to believe our family history could have involved Louisa Alcott to such an extent. And I doubted. But after *A Long Fatal Love Chase* was published, there was no questioning that Grandma had her wits about her—and that she was telling the truth. It was the long-lost story I'd heard about but that we didn't have a copy of. She was telling the truth. About everything."

"Wow," I said. "Did your grandmother ever tell you what happened—between Johanna and Nathan or between Johanna and Louisa?"

"You must understand that this isn't a part of our family

history I'm proud of—Nathan and Johanna. I wish I could say all of my ancestors shared loving marriages filled with faith and peace to pass on to their descendants."

"We understand," I said, and Victoria nodded.

"As I said, back then you couldn't simply up and divorce your husband. Louisa attempted to persuade my great-great-grandmother, but Johanna couldn't bring herself to do it."

I slumped in my seat. I hadn't admitted it, even to myself, but I'd hoped that Johanna's story would somehow help Victoria, give her the courage to complete what she must. But how would this help?

"So she stayed married to Nathan. Married to the abuse." I couldn't keep the sadness from reaching the edge of my words. I had hoped for good things. Better things for this woman who had poured her heart out in poems.

"No, not quite."

My head lifted.

"What do you mean?" Victoria asked.

"Nathan died in 1872. Grandma Lou's mother, Cora, was only three years old. Some sort of horrible accident at home."

The room was quiet. If everyone was thinking what I was thinking, which I would have bet they were, we were thinking that Johanna was not only an abused woman, but a murderer. Could we fault her? How much pain had she taken? Did she feel she needed to protect her child? Had she simply snapped?

A long, fatal love chase.

Victoria knew the story better than I did, but with *fatal* being in the title, someone must have died in the end. Perhaps this was one of Louisa's "blood and thunder" tales, one of Jo March's sensational stories, that she was not overly proud of.

"Everyone else thought what you thought, too. That she killed him." Marjorie's voice was quieter than it had been.

I remembered the words of the poem, the one on marriage, that Victoria had said she understood. Now they seemed to make sense, to point to a time when all called Johanna guilty.

Years and tears . . . and
the wood in which I stood,
and understood, to be our love,
cracked and chipped . . .
I heard the words inside my head
of the crowds and what they said.
And then I saw myself
toppling upon our love
that you chipped and kicked
and left me hanging
like the witch
I never was.

"She didn't do it," I whispered.

Marjorie's face blanched. "Grandma Lou and I never thought so either. They never did find enough evidence to convict her, but she lived the remainder of her days beneath the bitter gossip of the town. People called her all sorts of things. A murderer, a heathen, a witch—"

"But she wasn't." Victoria's voice was forceful, loud. As if she must prove this thing.

"How are you so sure?"

I opened Johanna's book of poems, flipped to the one titled "Till Death Do Us Part upon the Marriage Block" and handed it to Marjorie. All three of Johanna's descendants read it.

When they were done, Nicole rubbed her arms with her hands. Marjorie shook her head. "It certainly seems as if she wrote openly about her struggles. And yes, that she was innocent."

"But this was not given as a testimony of her innocence. It was given as a gift to Louisa, one the world wouldn't see until now. There's no reason for us to think she would lie."

"The words are steeped in honesty," Victoria agreed. "I can feel her through them."

"Still sad to think she had to live with that stigma for the rest of her life. I wonder how she survived. Or if she and Louisa stayed in touch."

"Grandma didn't know. Though she was always very insistent that Johanna had a strong faith—that she clung to God when this world disappointed her, which it seemed to do a lot."

"It must have been hard being a single mother, especially way back then."

Marjorie nodded. "She took in a lot of sewing. Louisa helped her publish some of her poems. But her most lucrative endeavor was a jelly business, of all things." She laughed. "Turned that most unfortunate incident with Nathan into a profitable business. Cora married well and happily and gave birth to my grandma Lou."

It seemed like a happy ending, so why did I not feel satisfied?

Marjorie lifted Johanna's book of poems. "I suppose you need to be taking this back with you?"

I looked at Victoria. Marjorie had given us so much. I would totally be okay with her keeping the little book for a time, but I wasn't the director of Orchard House.

Victoria glanced toward me before speaking. "Why don't you keep it for a couple days? Honestly, we should have handed it over already. A few more days won't hurt."

"I don't want to get anyone in trouble."

"No, this is your family history. You should be a part of it."

Marjorie inched out her hand to Victoria. "Thank you, dear. Thank you to both of you. I hope something I've said has helped. What you shared with us . . . well, it feels like in some ways Johanna's been vindicated after all these years."

"I'm glad," I said.

After we said our goodbyes and piled back into the car, a quiet came over us, even Caden, who seemed tuckered out with all the playing he had done. He fell asleep within ten minutes.

Victoria leaned her head back, looked out the window to the budding trees alongside the highway. "I think we did something good today."

I smiled. "I think so."

She sighed. "And yet I still feel like there's something missing. I still feel there's a piece of her we don't know."

I wondered if Victoria was looking for her answers in Johanna's story as well.

"I'm sure there's quite a bit we don't know," I said. "But I think we have enough to start a really great story."

CHAPTER THIRTY-TWO

*A few tears wrung from a man are better than a gallon of the feminine
"briny," I think, because harder to get and usually the genuine article.*

~ LMA

Taylor

ANOTHER WEEK TURNED where I didn't make plans to return
to California. Then two. Maddie had even joked that if I was
still around in the fall, maybe I could run the annual 5K to
benefit Orchard House with her and her mom.

The fall.

By then, decisions would have to be made. My book
would be turned in; Kevin's things would be long out of my
condo. What did the future hold?

Victoria and Will went to another counseling session. I
knew they talked once a day. I couldn't say I was crazy about
either of these things, though I wasn't sure why.

Shouldn't I want my sister's marriage to mend? For her
family to be whole? For victory—beauty—to come out of
the ugly?

At the same time, a part of me felt that Will was beyond trust, ever. That you only got one shot at certain things, and calling your wife unspeakable names and hurling her beloved classics at her was that one shot. Yes, forgiveness was necessary. If anyone had learned that, it was me over the past month. But there was forgiving, and there was foolishness. And right now I felt Victoria was too near the line.

I spent the days writing and keeping Mom company. We even made cookies one Tuesday afternoon—something we'd never done together, just the two of us. The next day, my phone rang. Marjorie's name appeared on my screen. We hadn't made a plan of when she would return Johanna's book to us. I figured she must be calling to tell us she'd read it through.

"Hello?"

"Taylor, it's Marjorie. I wanted to let you know I've finished."

"What did you think?"

"Definitely . . . insightful. Sad as well. I have to admit, I've never been one for poetry—for reading into it all and deciphering what it means, but it seems that hers is fairly straightforward. I wish it wasn't so plain what she was thinking at times."

I nodded, though she couldn't see. "She suffered, that was for certain."

"And yet, in some ways, I felt the Johanna who wrote these poems didn't line up with the one Grandma Lou told me about. That troubled me."

I opened my mouth to answer but thought better of it. It could be easy for me to throw out pat answers, but this wasn't my family. Johanna felt real to me and Victoria, but perhaps not as real as to Marjorie, a woman who had sat at her grandmother's knee hearing a firsthand account of her. Still, what grandchild knew her grandmother fully? By the time a second generation came along, time and age had often weathered a softer, gentler version of a woman. Perhaps this was the version Marjorie's grandma Lou had known. Perhaps Johanna's poetry reflected the younger. Neither could be discounted, but perhaps both together would give us the true measure of the woman.

I thought of how I'd changed over the years and even over the past couple of weeks. As a child I'd been shy and unsure. When I'd run away, betrayal had twisted me into a hardened version of myself—one that clung to the wrongs done to me and the rights I deserved, even if I told myself not to dwell on the past. Nevertheless, it was there, festering beneath the weight of my supposed indifference.

It hadn't softened until I'd returned. Until I'd taken off my blinders and seen with new eyes how the actions of sixteen years ago—not only Will and Victoria's actions, but mine— had molded each of us today. And each of us was a different person now because of it.

I thought of Will's seeming commitment to counseling and change, then of his words, filled with regret that night we'd met at Main Streets. I was certain that, deep down, he was not proud of who he'd become.

What version did I want to be, moving forward?

Jo March came to mind. In her character, Louisa outlined her own struggle to be that "better" version. The more patient version, the kinder, sweet-mouthed version.

Had either Jo or Louisa ever reached their ideal self? Had Johanna? Would I?

I realized then that Marjorie was still talking. "There was one line in one of the poems, though, that stuck out to me. The first poem, actually. Johanna talks about a boat with the words *Trust Me* written on its side. She's drowning, sucked under but struggling for the surface."

"Yes, I remember." It was the first poem Victoria and I had read together. Not until I'd gone to church with Mom and Dad this past Sunday, when I heard a passage about a storm at sea and a disciple foundering and a sturdy hand coming to save him did I connect the poem to a possible reference to a Bible story.

"When I read it, I remembered an object from my childhood. A wooden boat at Grandma Lou's house. She never spoke of it, but after she passed, my father kept it, said he remembered playing with it as a boy. I'd like to show it to you if you have the time."

I didn't really see how a child's boat could connect us to Johanna, but Marjorie had given us so much already, I couldn't refuse her. "Yeah, sure. That'd be great. When's a good time for you to meet up?"

～～

The next afternoon, I greeted Marjorie as she stepped out of her car in front of Orchard House. She helped her seven-year-old granddaughter, Trudy, from the car, then looked at the old gabled home, dear to so many near and far. She sighed. "It's been too long."

I noticed the package she held in her hands—a rather

bulky thing wrapped in what looked like several plastic bags. But she didn't offer to show me, and so I led her around to the entrance.

Victoria herself led the tour that Marjorie and her granddaughter were on while I waited, soaking up the sun on the steps of Bronson Alcott's school.

"Hey, stranger. Penny for your thoughts."

I squinted up at Luke, rake in hand, surprised by how my stomach did a slight flip-flop at his presence. "Hey, yourself. I'm afraid my thoughts might not be worth even that much."

He sat beside me, and I moved over a smidge. Still, his leg pressed along mine and I found it stirred something new and foreign within me. "Why don't you try me?"

I lifted my chin in a challenge. "Okay, then. I was thinking about men. And they weren't all good thoughts."

He laid his rake on the side of the stairs. "I'm not sure I'm up for defending my kind, but this could definitely be interesting. What about men were you thinking exactly?"

I shrugged. "I was thinking about Louisa Alcott and her father. I read a lot of her journals and letters these past few days, and it's got me thinking. It wasn't fair how things were, how they sometimes still are."

He didn't comment, and so I continued.

"Bronson Alcott was free to chase his dreams and try out his ideals, even though his family often suffered for it. Louisa felt a deep sorrow for her mother's plight. How she worked long days, took care of a home, and still had trouble making ends meet. In many ways, Louisa bore the responsibility for them. But she also accepted her father fully and even seemed to admire him."

Luke nodded. "Some speculate that that responsibility was self-inflicted. If she had wanted to, she could have gone off on her own and gotten married, chased her own dr—"

"Did you hear what you just said? She could have gotten married. As if that is the be-all and end-all of being a woman." I knew my words were bitter, and yet my own dubious love history, not to mention Victoria's plight, had left me so. And deep down, I wanted answers. Assurances. I wanted someone to make sense of all I was feeling.

Why I thought that job should fall to Luke, I couldn't quite fathom.

"That's not what I'm saying at all." I'd never seen him angry, but I thought this was probably the closest I'd get. "I'm saying she could have done that if she wanted. Maybe she could have lived on her own as well—didn't she, in Boston, for a time? And yes, perhaps she felt it her duty to support her family and help them, but is that such a bad thing?"

"No, of course not. But it seems like the press of it was forever upon her. As if she felt guilty about a great many things— her responsibility to her family, her temper, her inability to make money before *Little Women* was published . . ."

"And you think all of that could have been solved by Bronson giving up his own ideals and getting a regular, honest job."

"Well . . . yes."

"What is it that makes a man worthy, Taylor?"

I thought of Will, of what had made me fall in love with him, of what had made me despise him these last few weeks. I thought of Kevin, how on the surface there was no reason for me *not* to give my heart to him. But in the end, much like Jo with Laurie, I couldn't. "I thought it was the putting aside of oneself for the sake of those he loves."

"And so in your estimation, Bronson falls short."

I nodded.

"Yet if he denied the very thing that made him who he was—his passions and interests, his beliefs—he would have been lying to himself and those around him, wouldn't you say?"

I shrugged.

"What is really troubling you?"

Unexpected tears pricked the backs of my eyelids. Somewhere, I caught a whiff of a freshly budding lilac bush, and the reminiscence of childhood stirred within me.

I was thirty-seven years old. I had accomplished my dreams in becoming an author. Even being back home, building a relationship with my sister and parents, it all felt right. And yet very wrong.

"I suppose, being back here has in some ways brought me full circle. But I still feel like I'm missing something, though I haven't a clue what it could be."

I couldn't accept that it could be a man. I'd had Kevin. That hadn't satisfied. Somehow I knew that this man beside me—wonderful as he seemed—wouldn't satisfy either. I was helping Mom through chemo. I was helping my sister gain her feet and independence. I was doing my job by writing my next story. I'd even taught a group of students about writing in a town that many would consider the heart of American literature. I was doing my best in all that I could, trying to make up for lost years, for the guilt I felt pressing on my chest. I wondered why it had chosen to make an appearance now, instead of in California. What was going on?

We were quiet for a long moment before Luke spoke. "You know, I can't pretend to have all the answers, but I believe that sometimes God puts that feeling in our hearts to make room for something better."

"Better than . . . ?"

"Better than what we think should satisfy us. Better than belonging to the temporary things."

I closed my eyes. I could accept this sort of talk from Mom. Had written it off as the crutch she needed to beat cancer. But now Luke? What was it about the spiritual that seemed to be drawing everyone around me?

He tapped my leg with the back of his hand. "I better get back to work. If you ever want to talk, though, you know where to find me."

"Sure. Thanks, Luke."

He left, and not three minutes later, Marjorie and Trudy exited Orchard House, Victoria behind them. Trudy clutched her grandmother's hand and bounced up and down in excitement. I couldn't help but think how amazing it was that generation after generation of this family was sharing this special place, this special family—no matter how flawed they were in real life—that had inspired the fictional March family.

I stood.

"That was a real treat, wasn't it, Trudy?" Marjorie looked to the little girl at the height of her waist, and she nodded and smiled, revealing a half-grown-in adult front tooth.

"I'm glad you could come down for it," Victoria said.

Marjorie took her package out from beneath her arm. "I'm not sure if now might be a good time to show you this . . ."

"Of course." Victoria gestured to Bronson's school, took

out her key, and unlocked the door. Once we were all inside, I shivered—though whether it was from the chill in the large building or from the prospect of what Marjorie wanted to show us, I couldn't be certain.

We huddled around the light of one of the larger windows as Marjorie unwrapped her package. What she withdrew was rather unimpressive at first sight. The wood was worn and chipped. I could imagine some toddler hands dropping it one too many times, though the bulk of the object must have made it hard for small hands to hold.

When Marjorie held it out, I opened my arms.

I was surprised by the weight of it, which immediately set it apart not as a toy, but as a model of some sort. I tilted it to look at the writing on the side.

Carved deep into the belly of the ship were two clear words. *TRUST ME.*

I blinked, looked first at Marjorie, then at Victoria. "Just like the poem."

"'A sailless boat drifted by, "Trust me" on its side.'" Marjorie's eyes were clear as if she knew more than I could see in that moment, as if she patiently waited for the connection, but I didn't know what she wanted me to gain from the two words.

I shook my head. "I don't remember the rest. I'll have to read it again."

Victoria stepped forward. "Do you know what this meant to her, Marjorie?"

"Not exactly, I'm afraid. Grandma Lou didn't seem to know either. But she knew it was dear to her mother. I suppose a woman has a right to a secret or two in her lifetime."

"I suppose so," I mumbled, though I would have much rather had a neatly wrapped mystery than an unfinished one.

Victoria patted my arm. "We can write a story for her, remember?"

Why didn't that make me feel better?

"One thing I do know is what was kept in here." Marjorie took the boat from me and wiggled something on its side that I hadn't seen before. The top half of the boat flipped up, revealing a compartment inside not much bigger than a pencil case with a ring and an old paper.

Marjorie lifted it out carefully. "This ring has been here as long as I can remember. There's no way to know for certain, but I think it belonged to John, then to Johanna, for it's mentioned in John's letter home and even in Louisa's *Hospital Sketches*."

Victoria stepped forward. "And in a letter between Louisa and Johanna, Johanna thanked Louisa for returning the ring to their family after her brother's death."

Marjorie nodded. "And here's another letter. One she originally sent, it looks like. Though I can't be sure how it found its way back into the hands of my family."

Victoria took the letter and the ring. "Sometimes letters were returned after the death of those they were sent to. More often, though, they were burned."

Victoria tested the weight of the ring in her hand. "It must have meant something to Johanna for her to have kept it here."

"If you girls want it for a bit, if you have an interest, that is, I'd be fine with you taking a look."

I studied the ancient-looking letter, for some reason

frightened of what it held. What if Johanna hadn't learned to deal with the circumstances life brought her? What if she'd gone through life alone, ridiculed, running from gossip, never finding a place to belong? What if the letter didn't contain the answers we sought? Victoria and I could write her a happy ending. A fictitious one. One that we could count on because it was one we had control of.

Maybe, in some ways, that was better than what this letter held.

"We'd be honored," I heard Victoria say.

I smiled politely, feeling suddenly disconnected from the women in the room. As if I wanted to break free from the responsibility that family brought. Was this how Louisa felt? That she loved her family, sought belonging, and at the same time longed to be free of it?

In some ways, it was easier living three thousand miles away. Where any emotional attachments were as far away as the Atlantic is from the Pacific. Where I could more easily claim the notion that liberty was indeed far better than love. Than belonging.

It was easier, but it wasn't living. And as fulfilling as writing stories was, that wasn't all there was to living, either. In fact, I was wondering if, in some ways, my writing had taken the place of any actual living I'd done the past sixteen years. Yes, it was valuable and worthy, but too often I'd used it as a substitute for real life. A place to escape. No rejection. No constantly evaluating my worth. Comfortable, yes. But probably not healthy.

We bade goodbye to Marjorie and Trudy and stood near Lexington Road looking after their car. When they were out of sight, Victoria turned to me, the pieces of the boat still in her hands, the letter and ring inside.

"You want to take a look together?"

"I'm scared we'll be disappointed or that it will mess with the story I have in my head. I guess that makes me a wimp, huh?"

She smiled, put an arm around me. "I'm not depending on Johanna for answers to my life, Taylor. Not anymore. Or Louisa, even." She sighed. "I used to think I wasn't enough to matter, that I needed someone to intervene in my life. And maybe I still do, but I think it has to be someone greater. Greater than me. Greater than you. Greater than Johanna and greater than Louisa."

"Greater than me, huh? I don't know. That's a tall order."

She poked me for the joke, made to disguise the sudden heaviness of our conversation.

Really, though, I wanted to ask what she meant. But I didn't. I suddenly felt drained, as if I didn't know up from down or right from left anymore. As if I couldn't count on anything for certain.

"I talked to Will this morning. He sounds . . . good. He wants me to come home."

I could not make decisions for her, but this seemed beyond comprehensible. "Don't you think—?"

"I want to give him one more chance. I think the counseling is really helping. Despite everything, I want this to work. I want us to work."

I could think of a million reasons this was a bad idea, but in the end it wasn't my decision. And I loved her enough to let her go. "I understand," I whispered.

She looked down at the boat in her hands, then back up at me. "I *need* this, Taylor." She glanced at Johanna's letter again, then to me, and I couldn't tell if she meant she needed to go back to her husband or she needed to continue her journey with Johanna. Maybe on her own this time. Without me.

I didn't ask. I'd run away all those years ago, seeking escape. Now, when I wanted nothing more than to cling to my sister, I knew what I really had to do was release her.

Maybe that was part of the belonging. Not clutching so tight to those we held precious that they would break beneath our grip, but releasing them to fly free—trusting they would come back.

Maybe that's what the Bennetts had done for me all those years ago, only I hadn't recognized it until now.

I didn't know what it meant for me or for my story. Our story. My deadline. Victoria and Maddie and Caden's lives. My newfound relationship with my best friend and sister.

But I knew that if I held it all too tight, I risked shattering what I valued.

I looked at the boat, the words *TRUST ME* directly in my line of vision, and I nodded, gave Victoria a hug.

I didn't know whom I was trusting. Or why. Or what the outcome would be in this giving over of control and making myself vulnerable. But I did feel like I hadn't been led to this place, to this journey, by mistake. And I couldn't ignore the feeling that maybe, just maybe, there was more to come.

CHAPTER THIRTY-THREE

I made my fortune out of my seeming misfortunes.

~ LMA

Johanna

LOUISA'S INTERVIEW had Nathan's magazines flying off every street corner in Philadelphia and beyond. Her one stipulation was that I be the one given credit for the article. At first, Nathan took none too kindly to this, but after talking it over with Mr. Saucier, he agreed.

To celebrate, Mr. Saucier even took us out to dinner. Our neighbor Mrs. Heinrich watched Cora for us. If Miss Saucier had stayed home, it would have been a perfect night, for Nathan's eyes were shining again, and despite the obvious attentions Miss Saucier gave him, for once he didn't seem to have eyes for any besides me.

The next two months were a beautiful season of enjoying our success. For a time, it seemed I had my old Nathan back. We took Cora for long evening walks and together brainstormed future article ideas. Nathan even talked to me a bit about his parentless childhood, how it meant much to him to be a family now with me and our little daughter.

When he suggested we approach Louisa again, this time to pay her for a short story, I couldn't help feeling we imposed on my friend. I did not wish her to think I wanted her friendship only for my husband's success. I suggested he write her himself, which he did.

He came home one day and flung down a letter postmarked from Concord. "I hope you're happy," he said and stomped off to his study. I looked at my daughter, now three and a half years old, observing her father. She could be willful, and I already saw some of Nathan's temperament in her. However, for the most part, he did not take an active role in her upbringing. I couldn't help but think of Mr. Alcott. For all his faults and the pressure he might have put on his daughters, particularly Louisa, to perfect themselves, at least he was active in the lives of his girls. If we'd had a boy, I wondered, would Nathan have been around more, made more of an effort?

And yet none of these thoughts would change him. Instead, I preferred to think of my own mother, of Marmee in Louisa's *Little Women,* and of the real Mrs. Alcott. A mother could make a difference in the life of her child, particularly in the life of her daughter. And so I worked hard to instill virtue into the character of my little daughter, to correct and train but to love all the more.

She came to me now and I scooped her up, buried my nose in the hair I had lovingly washed last night, the lavender scent calming me. I picked up the letter Nathan had flung on the counter and opened the already-broken seal.

June 30, 1872

Dear Mr. Bancroft,

*I hope this letter finds you and your family well.
I am so very glad to hear that the interview did your
publication good.*

*Thank you for your offer to write a story.
Unfortunately, I have just returned home from Europe
and am a bit behind on my writing and find Mother
quite ill. I will have to decline your kind offer.*

Please give my love to Johanna.

*Sincerely,
Louisa May Alcott*

Cora grabbed at the letter after I had finished reading it, but I kept it from her grasp. I did not fault my friend for having to decline. How many favors could she do us, stretched as she was?

It was not Louisa's job to ensure the success of Mr. Saucier and his daughter or my husband. It wasn't fair he blame me, either. I supposed I could have been the one to ask her, but likely we would have received the same answer. And if we had not, well, that was not my fault, either.

I went to his study, and since the door was open, I stood at the threshold. He sulked on his chair, staring out the window. I wondered what he thought about. Mulling over ideas to save his dream or stewing in bitterness that his dream had not gone the way he envisioned?

"I know I am no Louisa," I began. "But I could try my hand at a story or two. And my poems . . ."

"Hang it, Johanna! No one wants to read *your* poems."

I flinched. In my arms, Cora began to whimper. I turned so Nathan would not see me do the same. I took our daughter out into our small yard and we busied ourselves lying in the grass, me pointing out the wispy clouds and drawing pictures in our minds of what they could be.

Castles in the air.

I'd had castles at one time. Dreams of happiness, my own family, love. Writing was a castle, also, but the real dream was a loving family. Of belonging completely to my own set of people. Being fully accepted. As Jo March said, "Families are a beautiful thing."

And I believed that. At least I had.

But what about when they weren't beautiful? When they were difficult and hard? I'd thought love could conquer it all, but perhaps I'd been naive. For I had tried to love Nathan the best I could and it all seemed for naught.

My castles in the air had tumbled from the sky, and I did not know how to begin picking up the pieces.

～～

Nathan continued in his sullenness. One day, he simply did not go to work but stayed in bed the entire day. When I called for the doctor, my husband became cross at both him and me.

I saw the doctor out. He reported my husband suffered from extreme melancholia, and if I could coax him outside or to do something that would bring joy to him, it might lift his spirits.

Despite my sincerest efforts, though, he could not be coaxed.

Two days of this, and then finally he got up, his hair rumpled. I made him a hearty breakfast, of which he ate little before disappearing into his study.

I left him alone. I cleaned up breakfast, made preparations for dinner, tidied the house, and then put Cora down for her nap. When our daughter slept soundly, I knocked at the door of Nathan's study. He did not answer and after a moment I pushed the door open. He sat in his chair as usual, a glass of whiskey in his hand, the bottle upon his desk.

"Nathan . . . ," I began. This must stop. It was one thing to be in the doldrums for a few days, but taking to drink as a solution would not solve our problems. He'd broken his promise ten times over, and yet I had long ago learned I couldn't control him. Neither did I want to. I was tired. So very tired of fretting, of feeling the full burden of our family and marriage upon my shoulders.

"Don't start your harping. It's too early in the day for all that."

"And it's a mite too early to start drinking, don't you think?" I came closer. I was done being frightened, done cowering before him. Our family was at stake. Our little girl. I must fight for us. For her.

"I said leave me in peace, woman." His words were slurred, and he said the word *woman* as if to put me in my place. To remind me that I was exceeding my station in questioning him. Yes, he was to lead us and I would willingly follow under his kind authority, but this . . . this was not what I had in mind.

Despite my anger, I chose love. For though one might

think I had learned already, I still chose to believe love could win for us. I had to get through to him.

I went to him, laid a gentle hand on his shoulder. He was still in his dressing gown. "Dear, let me help. Is it Mr. Saucier? Let us go somewhere else, start anew."

Was that our answer? Nathan seemed to thrive on new dreams and hopes. If we could live in the months of that hope, I would be willing to move again and again, to follow him to the ends of the earth if only he would look at me as he used to. If only he would fold me in his arms and tuck me close until I felt that I was truly home. If only he would love me. Love our daughter.

I put my hand to his neck, but without warning, he grabbed it and pushed me to the ground. I got up, tried not to be afraid. He wanted to push me away because he was scared. I only needed to show persistence, to show him that I was with him in this—whatever *this* was—that I wasn't going anywhere.

I went to him again. "We can start afresh, dear. I haven't given up hope."

He stood, a whirlwind of unexplained fury. "I said leave me alone!"

The blow came harder than ever before. And then another and another. Even though it had happened twice before, I found myself surprised still. I raised my hands, hated the cowering I did on his plush carpet. "Nathan, no. Please." I tried to get away from his fists, could not comprehend that he could keep on so. And then it stopped, and the sound of deep, guttural sobs came from him. In the haze of my pain, I knew this was finally it. I *was* done. I would take my daughter and go. To Mother, to Concord, anywhere but here.

The sound of metal, then the unmistakable sound of a pistol being cocked. Through my wounded eyes, I looked up to see the barrel pointed at me. What? My brain grew fuzzy. No . . . this could not be.

"Nathan, no. Please. Think of Cora." I backed away toward the door on my arms and legs, my feet tangling in my petticoats. I thought to rise and run but could not tear my eyes from his shaky hand, the small barrel of the gun aimed in my direction.

Then, slowly, he seemed to calm and gain some sort of clarity. He turned the gun from me and raised it to his own head. My breathing turned shallow, and even as I tried to scramble toward him, I heard the shot.

I screamed. Blood upon the carpet, upon my dress. And still I went to him, tried to search for signs of life among the mess, fainted straightaway, and when I woke, screamed some more.

From somewhere in the distance, crying. Small steps. I raced to the door and shut it on my little girl, tried to contain my own sobs. "Mother will be right out, dear. Right out." She must not see what had happened. She must not see.

I felt my mind slipping, knew that I needed to clean myself up before my daughter saw me.

I took Nathan's bottle of whiskey and soaked my apron with it, wiped it over my hands and face, the alcohol stinging my injuries. This was a dream. A dream. I needed help. Mother. Louisa. The police.

I slipped out of the study and hugged Cora tight. "Mother hurt herself a bit, is all. I'm sorry to frighten you. I'm sorry . . ."

My legs shook. An insistent knocking on the front door. Help.

Mrs. Heinrich, our neighbor, stood at the door. "Johanna, what's happened? I heard . . ."

I placed Cora in her arms. "Please, will you take her to your house? I must get the police. I must . . ."

She was staring at me, and I remembered my face. The scent of whiskey on me. My bloodied apron. Soon it seemed half of Philadelphia stood on my porch steps, some offering help, some to fetch the police, but most just staring. Curious stares. Whispers. They made my grief all the more real, and I felt I couldn't breathe, that I choked, that I was a tiny sapling stretching up for air but being suffocated by weeds. That each person staring and whispering held an ax, intent upon chopping me down until every last shred of me was gone, nonexistent. Until I suffocated.

And then the police came. They sat me down, asked me questions, and spent hours in Nathan's study. I told them everything. They said they would send my mother a telegram requesting she come at once. They sent for the reverend, whom I didn't want.

The days that followed were a blur. The reverend arranged a small, quiet service for my husband, and I wore a dark veil over my face, more to hide the mess that it was than in mourning.

But I did mourn. I mourned for my husband, the man I had married who had seemed lost to me for so long. I mourned for what we never had—our castle in the air that had come tumbling down upon me. I mourned for the part I'd played in his death—what I hadn't done, what I could have done. I let my anger have its way, for how could he leave me in this manner?

Sleep eluded me and I wrote an abundance of two things: letters to Louisa and pages of poetry surrounding my feelings for Nathan. The beginning of our love, the betrayal of his actions.

Mother and I worked to pack, for I would go and stay with her and George indefinitely.

At one time, I had sought my adventure away from home, away from the monotony of what I considered a dull life.

Now I could think of nothing I wanted more than monotony.

~~

Four days after we buried Nathan, the doorbell rang. Mother was upstairs with Cora packing her clothes. I cared very little if people saw me without my veil, so I opened the door.

Gladys Saucier stood there, her face pale against the black of her hat and dress, her eyes shining and beautiful. And angry.

"Johanna, may I come in?"

I did not want to see this woman. Could not fathom that anything she had to say to me would be helpful.

I gestured to the chairs on the porch, as I had become very protective of Cora. Of what she should hear about her father and his death. It was bad enough she cried in fright at the sight of my mutilated face and often ran to my mother instead of me. Miss Saucier did not sit.

"What can I do for you?" I asked, tired, not caring in the least that I was being inhospitable.

"I heard you were moving from the city, and I've come to

bid you farewell." Her tone, however, couldn't be further from a friendly farewell. She leaned close to me, and I caught the familiar scent of rose water, which reminded me of Nathan, and I hated her for it. "I know you killed him," she whispered.

My breath caught. "What?"

"He told me how you were always harping on him about providing for the family, about giving up his drink. You wore on him, you know, until he couldn't take it anymore. Until he snapped."

I gritted my teeth and stepped toward her, felt I could strangle the woman and spend my life content in an asylum knowing I had done so. "How dare you . . ."

"He loved *me*, you know. And he had a wonderful time showing me. Said I was the lover you never were."

I slapped her then, even as I knew she told the truth and even as I felt myself no better than Nathan, resorting to physical violence.

She stood rigid, her hand to her cheek, her eyes no longer cross but full of mirth. "I know you pulled that trigger, Johanna, and soon all of Philadelphia will know how you wronged Nathan, God rest his soul."

"Get out. Get out!" I screamed.

She did but smiled wickedly behind her. Passersby had stopped to watch our row, and now they stared at me as I trembled in anger. They stared at my horrid face. "What are you all looking at?" I yelled. "Leave me! Leave me in peace!"

I went back inside, felt the condemnation of their gazes upon me.

The next day, a copy of *Saucier's Social* appeared at my door, the front page a woodcut of a female hand with a gun, and the title "Marriage . . . Turned to Murder?" The subheading read, "The Tragic Loss of Philadelphia's Finest and the Surprising Hand Behind It."

I knew what was inside, and yet I could not help but read. In it, Miss Saucier skillfully painted a picture—one a bit too accurate on some levels. A man trying to achieve his dreams. A bitter wife nagging at him to be something he wasn't. Making him feel hopeless, desperate, depressed. A vicious argument, one that left him dead and me alive. She questioned my sanity. She questioned the wisdom of the police in their investigation. And while an average reader might brush it off as pure sensationalism and speculation, it was enough to sell magazines. It was enough to make people wonder. It was enough to send young boys to the front of my house, daring one another to knock on my door and then run before the crazy lady came out.

In many ways, I felt numb to it all. And in many ways, it hurt deeper than ever before. For this woman—whatever her relationship had been with my husband—and now the town saw me as the evil one. And I had a very strong inkling that either by her persuasion or by his, my husband saw me as that, too. In his own way, perhaps to excuse his poor actions, I became the enemy. The Jezebel in his life and now in the city.

I continued to write my poems, my only means of salvation. It was an amazing relief to bring Cora out to the country, to be in my small hometown again. I felt I would never leave again if only I could live in peace.

That peace didn't come right away. But it did come. Not from the outside, but in many ways, from above.

CHAPTER THIRTY-FOUR

*[I] have no special method of writing except to use
the simplest language, take everyday life and make it interesting
and try to have my characters alive.*

~ LMA

Taylor

A WEEK WENT BY, and none of us heard from Victoria or the kids. I wondered how things went with Will.

I worked on the book, trying not to begrudge the fact that I didn't hear from my sister, that she hadn't chosen to share with me what was in Johanna's letter. I could only assume it wasn't anything encouraging.

I knew Victoria wanted to make her own way, and while I couldn't fault her for it, I also couldn't help feeling abandoned. Again.

I was sitting on the porch, tapping out words on my story, wondering how it would all wrap up, when Victoria's car pulled into the drive. Maddie and Caden piled out with their bags, their faces drawn and sad. Victoria opened the door, her posture slumped, as if a fifty-pound barbell rested upon her shoulders.

She walked up to the porch. I stood on the steps, held my hand out to her.

She looked at it, her eyes glistening, then took my hand and squeezed. "It's over. For real this time."

The heart is sometimes the slowest to heal, but I vowed not to leave my sister's side while it did.

Though it didn't make sense to me, she still missed her husband—at times, still wanted to go back to him. If she didn't have the kids, she probably would have.

I was glad I was there. I distracted the kids, and Victoria. Luke and I took Maddie and Caden fishing and for hikes and to play with Chloe while Victoria worked out the logistics of separating from her husband.

Two weeks later, she found me on the porch, suffering from writer's block. She sat down, Johanna's letter in her hand.

I was quiet, knew she needed to say something in her own time.

"I read this over and over again. I thought I didn't need the past for my answers, but I'm thinking God gave me it all the same." She looked at me, her eyes bright and shining. "These past couple months have stunk. Big-time. But I think I found something precious along the way, too." She sniffed. "That last day, when I knew I was a fool to keep hoping, I had already read this letter. All I could think about was Johanna's words and the verse she had written on the back of it."

She handed it to me, and I read.

November 1872

Dearest Louisa,

Thank you for your last letter. I have since come to hear about the fire in Boston. I pray you are well and found yourself far away from the destruction.

I admit it was a great relief to unburden my entire heart to you finally. Though I hesitate to admit it, now that four months have passed, I can see that in many ways, Nathan's death has freed me. And that fact saddens me.

George and Mary made room for us in their home, their own growing brood a lively change for Cora and me. The scars of our past are still very much upon us, though I feel blessed that Cora is young enough to build new memories in place of the old. I am finding the simple chores of farm life soothing to my mind. And while I know we will not impose long-term, I feel that for now, the comfort of family is a fitting place for our healing. Here, I see George and Mary's marriage as a testament to what it should be—love and sacrifice and work, all alongside one another. The children cheer us all, as does nature. We have put up jars and jars of applesauce, and Mother has helped me perfect my—you will never guess it—jam making.

We attend the local church, and though it is a simple service with often a simple message, I find it is what I need. I have become reacquainted with a few old friends, including a young man named Bryant, who is kind to my Cora and, after noting her love for floating paper boats down the river, built her a wooden boat of her own. When he knelt down to present her with the boat and showed her the small compartment he'd built inside, I thought it the sweetest thing.

He then told her the story about Jesus walking on the water to meet the disciples in a boat. How they were so afraid of the storm, but how Christ assured them, saying, "Be of good cheer; it is I; be not afraid."

The words ignited something in my spirit.

Cora, too, was spellbound as Bryant told of Peter coming out of the boat to walk on the water to Jesus, how he began to sink, but how Jesus caught him up with His own strong hand.

After Cora ran off with her boat, Bryant held out his hand to me, and I took it. We did not say much, but I felt the promise of something new. Something full of hope.

I think perhaps that I have been looking all these years for something that was not so far away. And no, I do not mean Bryant, for he too will no doubt eventually fail in his own way.

I am talking about a bigger place to belong—in the arms of One who not only tells me not to fear, but who, in the midst of my failures, has loved me and given me a worth beyond measure. In this, I find both liberty and home—two things I once thought opposites but I now see are not so very different.

I wrote a poem about this, titled "Trust." I am sending it to you along with the others I have written since Nathan's death. I send them because a part of me wants to share them, and a part of me wishes never to

*see them again. Hide them away if you will, for I feel it
fitting they be buried somewhere in Concord.*

*I am ready to begin anew, to put the past to rest.
These poems are a thank-you for your friendship,
Louisa, dear. I am unsure I would have been able to
get through these years without you.*

*I know you are not one for traditional religion, but I
found a verse that I wish I had known long ago. Perhaps
then I would have recognized that what Nathan had
for me was not real love. But you, dear Louisa, always
seeking charity, have met every one of these standards.
Thank you, my friend, for loving me always.*

*Your loving friend,
Johanna*

*Charity suffereth long, and is kind; charity envieth not;
    charity vaunteth not itself, is not puffed up,
Doth not behave itself unseemly, seeketh not her own, is not
    easily provoked, thinketh no evil;
Rejoiceth not in iniquity, but rejoiceth in the truth;
Beareth all things, believeth all things, hopeth all things,
    endureth all things.
Charity never faileth: but whether there be prophecies, they
    shall fail; whether there be tongues, they shall cease;
    whether there be knowledge, it shall vanish away.*

I finished the letter, knowing what had spoken to Victoria
was the verse at the end. But for me, I couldn't get past
another one of Johanna's sentences.

Something stirred in my chest then, and it wasn't intimidating this time. It was foreign and yet undeniable. Beckoning and drawing me with magnetic force.

"I am talking about a bigger place to belong—in the arms of One who not only tells me not to fear, but who, in the midst of my failures, has loved me and given me a worth beyond measure. In this, I find both liberty and home—two things I once thought opposites but I now see are not so very different."

The words swirled in my heart.

What if they were true? What if I belonged because I was loved? What if that same hand that was being held out to Peter was being held out to me? Telling me not to be afraid. Telling me that while I might struggle with my shortcomings forever, there was One who was greater who had made up for them all long ago?

The prospect caused my chest to become light. Free. And suddenly I understood completely what Johanna had written.

Victoria and I met one another's gazes over the old letter. "I—this is amazing," I whispered. For once I was at a loss for words. Had to let this revelation marinate within me before voicing it out loud.

"Right?" Victoria sighed. "I knew what Will was doing wasn't love, you know? Even so, it was only that last time, when these words defining charity—defining love—were fresh in my mind, that a clearing came over my brain."

I nodded, didn't want to interrupt for fear I would discourage her from speaking.

"I used to write letters to Louisa, looking for help, for answers. But I've been thinking, maybe all along another hand was being held out to me." She brushed her hair out of her face. "I wasn't a perfect wife or even one of the best. I'm realizing how I fall short in so many ways. And I'm learning to embrace that weakness. To take the hand that God's offering me."

I grabbed her arm. "Yes. That's—that's exactly what I feel she's trying to say." Like this wasn't the end of our story. The one I was writing. Mine. Victoria's.

I thought of that long-ago entry Louisa had written as a girl, the one she related to at age fifty, the one that touched my heart, the one about her not being able to do all the good she vowed to do, the one condemning herself as "bad."

"Be of good cheer; it is I; be not afraid."

"It is I."

As if the presence were enough of a reason not to fear the future. Enough of a reason not to wallow in my inadequacy.

As if freedom wasn't found in how well I could go it alone or even how well I climbed the stairs to the lofty castles I'd built in my mind, but rather how willing I was to grab the hand offered me.

"I think I understand," I whispered. Though I wasn't sure if I was ready to take the plunge, I couldn't deny the pull of it. And for the first time, I was willing to explore it with Victoria, my best friend. Explore it with my family.

Victoria smiled, and she looked prettier and lighter than she had in a long time. "Thank you, Taylor. In a lot of ways, you've been like a Louisa to me these last several weeks." She looked out into the front yard, to the street. "You know, there's a lot of women out there like me. And I want to help them. Maybe starting with that story."

I sat up, an idea suddenly coming to me. "That's it . . . I've been stuck for days, but that's the missing piece. Our story. But your story too, Victoria." I opened my laptop.

All those years ago up in the garage, Victoria had prodded me to write my story. Write my story and make something good come out of it.

Only I never knew how. Until now. Until my story became our story. Until I entertained the thought of handing it all over to another author. The Author of Life. He was still writing the words, spinning our story. And this time I was certain that good *would* come from it.

EPILOGUE

When one cannot go away,
one can travel in spirit by means of books.

~ LMA

EIGHTEEN MONTHS LATER

I looked out over the crowd beneath the tent at Orchard House, all here for the launch of my newest book. Victoria's and mine. A book about women helping women. A book that celebrated the Alcotts and the independence of human-kind but also a book that celebrated real love and family and the blessings a marriage of teamwork could bring. A portion of the proceeds would go directly to helping women who had been in Victoria's position.

Mom stood with Dad off to the side, the hair she'd lost growing back in a lovely bob of silver, her scans taken three weeks ago clear. Luke stood beside them smiling at me. I squeezed my left fingers together, felt the newness of the engagement ring there. It felt right. Perfect, even. We'd be married in three months. The Bennetts—my family—would be alongside us when we said vows under a covenant of faith, one in which we sought to live out love for not only each other, but for God, who gave us to each other. In many ways, at the age of thirty-eight, I felt my life was just beginning.

I stepped up to the lectern, thanked the crowd for coming and Orchard House for providing the venue. "I grew up right down the street. When I was thirteen, I had the absolute blessing of being adopted into a beautiful family, but I was often filled with doubts about their love. Doubts about my worth. I ran away from them at the age of twenty-one, but I couldn't run away from the part of my heart they already had. I realized then the depth and complexities of love. How doubt can destroy, but love can give life."

Victoria came beside me, launched into her own story of being helped through a difficult time in her life by reuniting with me, by discovering Johanna's story.

"We all know the Alcotts were huge proponents of women's rights and even the independence of women. But it didn't end there, and it wasn't just about women. They fought tirelessly for abolition, hiding runaway slaves in their own home many times. They helped the poor, they put action to their beliefs, they didn't just fight for women—they fought for humankind. For the oppressed. For the underdog. It's what Taylor and I seek to do today. To continue the mission of the Alcotts and work to give awareness through the power of a story."

The crowd clapped, and I caught Maddie and Caden cheering heartily beside Mom. It hadn't been easy for them to go through any of this. Victoria had decided to not go public with all the details of her story in order to protect the kids and her privacy. They were still sorting through what it meant to be separated but still a family. Will continued counseling and seemed to be committed to change. And while he and Victoria spent time together, my sister was determined to remain cautious and take things slow when it came to the idea of possibly healing her marriage.

It wasn't always easy. Sometimes the kids resented the entire separation; sometimes they resented their father; sometimes they resented the time Victoria took to work on the book. But right now they were cheering.

I hoped this novel would be the beginning of something good for all of us.

I looked up to the sky, wondered if Louisa would have ever imagined *this* castle in the air—crowds gathering to honor her at "Apple Slump," crowds commemorating causes that were dear to her own heart.

I reached out a hand to Victoria and she slipped her cool one into mine. God had indeed cast out our fears and brought us to a new place. A place we could call home. A place where we didn't have to question our worth. A place where we put the pen in His hands and allowed Him to be the One to write our stories.

I was sure they would be some of the best yet.

HISTORICAL NOTE

IT'S BEEN MORE THAN 150 YEARS since the publication of *Little Women*, and our culture continues to be fascinated by this seemingly simple domestic tale. In many ways, its message is revolutionary. And in many ways, it is as old as time, calling each of us to our own good works and independence, calling each of us to love one another well.

As always, when writing of a true historical figure, I feel both excitement and a burden to portray them as they truly were and honor their memory. To take on Louisa May Alcott, such a fiercely admired lady and author, was a task I did not take lightly.

In preparation for this mission, I read several respected biographies as well as her published letters and journals. Though I had read *Little Women* before, I reread the beloved classic, as well as the books of hers mentioned within— *Hospital Sketches*, *Moods*, and *Fair Rosamond* (published in 1995 as *A Long Fatal Love Chase*). In my research, I gained insight into this woman—so much more than simply fictional Jo March. I gained respect for her and felt her sadness over much of the tragedy that played out in her life. Many times, particularly in dialogue and letters, I have used her own words from her letters and journals to keep a tone of authenticity within them.

Louisa was a champion of the underdog—whether it be the enslaved African, the voteless woman, the widowed beggar, her orphaned nephews and husbandless sister, or hardworking Marmee, I could imagine what this strong-willed woman's response would be to a friend in Johanna's situation.

Her experience with Johanna's brother John Suhre did happen, though she fictionalized some of it in *Hospital Sketches*. John did leave behind a brother and a sister, whose names I've kept, but the similarities end there and from then on are entirely fictionalized.

I had the pleasure of visiting Orchard House while researching, and I would heartily encourage New England visitors to take a tour if in the area. From the Revolution to the Renaissance, Concord is a town bursting with history and culture.

Though I have not witnessed domestic abuse firsthand, I have known women who have suffered its harmful effects. If you are a woman who finds yourself in a situation like Victoria's or Johanna's, or you know someone in an abusive relationship, I hope you will reach out for help. There are some great resources online at thehotline.org. No one should have to live in fear. Please know I am praying for you and that you are not alone.

I also pray the legacy of women like Louisa Alcott may continue on in our literature, minds, and hearts and that the Lord would use them to inspire hope, freedom, and most of all, love.

CHAPTER FOUR

Emma

*I am more and more convinced that man is a dangerous creature
and that power, whether vested in many or few, is ever grasping
and, like the grave, cries, "Give, give!"*

ABIGAIL ADAMS

"Ah, Miss Emma. You are lovelier than I remember." Samuel Clarke's words slid from his tongue, smooth as the silk ribbon holding the queue at the base of his neck.

I smiled, thanked him as expected, wondered how Father could think us a well-made match.

Then again, Father likely took no consideration of our personalities when deciding my future. No, mine was a match made with only monetary gain in mind.

The Clarkes' maid offered up a plate of chestnut fritters. As I raised my hand to receive one, for no other reason than to have something to do, the remembrance of Father's painful grasp after Noah's parting the other night came to the forefront of my mind. His words, like hot bacon grease, sizzled in my memory, along with the fire of his grip.

"It will be your doing if that boy finds himself on the wrong end of my musket."

I understood, didn't doubt that he would carry out his threat. If I cared for Noah, then I would stay away from him. Mayhap I had best stay away from the South End altogether. I needn't put my friends in peril.

Beside me, in a white broadcloth coat complete with silver basket buttons to match his knee bands, Samuel scooped up a mug of hot buttered rum, the ruffles at his hands perfectly positioned so as not to interfere with his reaching. "Your father tells me you spend your time minding the Fulton children. Such humdrum for the likes of yourself."

"I don't mind. In fact—"

"Now, now, once we wed, you needn't worry about such nonsense." He moved closer and I caught a whiff of sickeningly sweet cigar smoke. "I see a time soon when we will have our own brood romping around. And I will see to it you have all the help you need in caring for them so that you can concentrate on . . . other duties."

I expelled a breath—a nervous, mortified laugh coming along with it.

I cared not a pig's tooth how much money Samuel Clarke possessed nor how my parents wished for our nuptials. How could I bear to be with him every day . . . every night? To live beside him, to share intimacies with him, to be his wife?

Sarah had attested that by my own decisions, I might change the course of my life. Something that sounded so simple but was in fact the most complicated feat I could imagine. Because to find my voice meant to speak against my parents—to speak against my world.

Sarah, Noah . . . they bade me stand up for what was true and right, for my future, and yet they hadn't instructed me how to go about summoning the boldness to do so.

Mother fluttered toward us in her blue velvet trimmed with ermine, a glass of Madeira in hand. "Isn't it simply grand to have Samuel home again, Emma?" She rested her fingers on the broadcloth of Samuel's arm. "She's been just dabbling around the house, simpering over your departure. A complete pity, truly."

"Mother!"

She turned doleful eyes in my direction while Samuel leered at me with a grin that churned my stomach.

He must have mistaken my outburst for embarrassment, not chastisement toward the woman who birthed me, for he chuckled, a cocky, amused expression on his face. "Has she now?"

I searched for my voice. But alas, again, it could not be found. And what would the recourse be if I were to outright deny Mother's words?

I had chosen to remain loyal, but Noah's words pressed on my mind. Loyal to what? Loyal to whom? This woman who told untruths about me to secure her own future—did she command the price of my loyalty?

A bitter taste gathered in the back of my mouth. "Forgive me, I fear I may be ill." I left the room, bypassed Father and the elder Mr. Clarke laughing heartily over some matter, and slipped outside.

The cool sea air swept over me, settled my stomach. I breathed it in. I felt my life was fast barreling in a direction I did not wish to go. And yet 'twas the way of things. Did that mean I should accept them?

From the direction of the Town House came the sound of conch shells being blown, of whistling and stamping and shouting.

Odd . . .

The door to the Clarke home flew open. Mother appeared, eyebrows raised. "Truly, you'll catch your death out here without your cloak. Come back inside at once, dear." She stilled, the sound of the horns growing closer, raucous catcalls now mounting upon them.

"Do you hear that?" I whispered.

Mother's face pinched. She grasped my arm, pulled me inside. "Come." She walked to Father, waited patiently beside him until he directed his attention to her. Meanwhile, the sounds outside grew louder.

"Father," I interrupted.

A look of annoyance flashed across his face before he recovered, likely for Mr. Clarke's sake.

"John," Mother started, "I fear a mob is brewing."

Father and Mr. Clarke summoned Samuel and the other men present, then ordered the women to the upper chambers.

I fled toward the stairs, along with the wives and daughters in attendance. From below, the sound of the door bolt came, its echo chasing us up the stairs. The rowdiness outside rose to a deafening pitch.

"What do they want?" Mrs. Clarke sobbed into her handkerchief as she led us to an empty guest chamber.

"They're demanding your family resign their position as consignors for the tea. They want your husband and sons to refuse the tea upon its arrival," I said. How did she not know the circumstances her husband found himself in?

The clamor grew louder and more frantic. Surely they didn't mean to harm anyone. I wondered if John Fulton were among the group, but I found it difficult to believe Sarah's husband would contribute to such a fracas.

I slid toward the window, curiosity overcoming me.

"Emma, get away from there!" Mother's voice rose on edge, but 'twas so filled with terror it appeared uncontrolled, giving me the courage to ignore it.

Outside, a crowd had gathered with tin lanterns and pine-knot torches, shaking fists.

"Listen to the Body or suffer the consequences!"

"This is our town. We won't be daunted by the likes of you!"

"Huzzah!"

Additional "Huzzahs!" met our ears.

From another window upstairs, on the far side of the house, Samuel shouted down to the crowd. "You rascals, be gone or I'll blow your brains out!"

"He can't mean it," I whispered. Though I understood the fear which would make him say such words. And Father . . . he must be near insane with rage to be locked up in the Clarke home, at the mercy of a mob . . . for once, not in control.

Was a bloody fracas to start this very night, in this very home?

The crowd called back hisses and shouts at Samuel.

The fire of a pistol shattered the frozen night air.

The women behind me screamed, the gun's explosion echoing down School Street and all the way to the harbor. Though the mob grew silent, they certainly wouldn't take kindly to the shot. I sank back from the window, fearful to look down and see an injured person.

"Dear Father in heaven." Catherine Clarke whispered a quiet prayer, the scent of gunpowder finding its way to us.

Banging started then. Catsticks on the black iron hitches in front of the Clarke home. Then the shatter of glass and the sound of wood splitting. I crept closer to the window to see men throwing stones and brickbats at the first-floor windows of the house.

I clamped my hand over my mouth, wondered what was to become of us. Would they burn the house to the ground? Drag Father and the Clarkes away to be tarred and feathered? They seemed to grow mad, insensible. What might they do to the women in the house?

For once, I wished I were a man. Each day I hated this helpless feeling more and more. In Father's circles—in most of the world—women were to remain quiet and keep their noses out of politics. Yet here, now, we were in the thick of it, and without one opinion or claim to call our own.

From down the street I glimpsed the bob of torches. As they neared, my heart beat out a thrumming as fast as the cycle of a spinning wheel.

Noah. And John.

They did not know of my presence. Would I see them contribute to this tumult? I'd respected them, thought them beyond such measures, but truly, how well did I know either one? I'd heard that men often acted differently when outside the home, some of the less honorable visiting local brothels. I'd heard rumors of Samuel doing so, had wondered how I could reconcile marriage to such a faithless man.

But Noah and John? Join the fomented rabble below? To fight for a cause was one matter. But with such unruliness?

A voice rose above the crowd. John's. "Men, stop this madness." I exhaled my relief, pressed my forehead against the cold pane of the window.

A few of the men elbowed one another, quieted, nodded toward John. "Let us not indulge in violence, but act in honor at all times. Surely an agreement can be reached."

A man from the crowd waved a catstick. "I've an agreement for ya. We shall disperse if the Clarkes choose to stop aligning themselves against their country and promise to appear at our town meeting scheduled tomorrow aft. Either that, or agree to reship the tea this minute."

The crowd stomped their feet, yelled hearty assent.

Samuel laughed loudly, still from the second-story window. "Fie! We shall not acknowledge illegal and underhanded meetings beneath *trees*! Especially not those with men of low rank, who choose to ruin honest men's personal property and throw our women in distress."

The crowd grew fierce at Samuel's words. I near cursed him in my head for stirring them up again when John had attempted to dispel their vigor.

A shrill whistle pierced the night air, and Noah climbed atop the Clarkes' carriage step. "Men of Boston! I beg of you, listen to reason! Is this the way to come to a solution? Out on a winter's night, yelling at one another, terrorizing the ladies in the house?" My heart blossomed tenfold for him in that moment. I knew his beliefs, but here he stood for what was moral and right. Though unaware of my presence, he defended the ladies within. He defended Father, who had belittled and embarrassed and cursed him just days earlier. "Let us not forget ourselves in this dispute. Let us not be accused of using violence to obtain that which is honorable and right. Let us not reduce ourselves to indecorum. Instead, let us conduct ourselves with poise and grace as we demand our God-given rights as people who should have a voice within our government!"

Some cheered his words, shouting, "Huzzah," stomping their feet as a sort of applause. Yet some in the crowd turned away, mumbling, likely not impressed with Noah's speech and the impasse it brought on the entire gathering.

Nevertheless, the crowd did disperse. Father and the Clarke men came from the house to clean the shattered glass left on the walkway. Noah and John stooped to help, and when I realized they would stay and aid the Clarkes, I pushed through Mother and Mrs. Clarke to descend the stairs.

I would not be welcome outside with the men, but I made busy cleaning the glass inside the parlor, staring intently until Noah straightened from his work and caught my gaze. His mouth parted in surprise, and hiding myself partly behind the drapes, I raised my hand in greeting and gratitude.

He dipped his head, the tug of a half smile upon his face as he stared at me. I hadn't seen him since the night he escorted me home. I suspected he avoided the Fultons, not wishing to garner more trouble for me by way of my father.

Yet, to see him now . . . something bold and new burst within my heart.

What Noah took part in, what he thought worthy to fight for, who he was—titled gentleman or not—was noble. The thought made me feel at home, secure. Quite of a sudden, I longed to be a part of it.

"You there!"

Noah snapped to attention at Samuel's words.

"Do you dare ogle my intended through my father's broken windows? Off with you, now, you hear? We needn't any more aid from the likes of you."

I despised Samuel's haughty tone, the very voice of the man I was to wed.

And as Noah dipped his head again to me and then to Samuel beneath Father's glare, I knew without a doubt whose side I longed to be on.

Nay, it might not be moral for the mobs to attack the Clarke house, but neither was it moral for those of a certain station to snub their noses at others as if they were plebeians, riffraff, and blackguards. Especially the likes of Noah, who had curtailed the fury of the mob with his timely words and peaceful presence.

For the first time, I saw clearly why Sarah, John, Noah, and the Liberty Boys fought so adamantly for that which was not yet theirs.

They *were* in a sort of prison. One where the gaolers told them they mattered less than their fellow humans. One where they were denied a voice.

One where they and their families were forced to endure circumstances they didn't have a decision in, forced to bow to the whims of the so-called gentlemen of the town. Men like Samuel. Men like my father.

Watching Noah's torch bob away in the inky night, I vowed not to stand on fence posts any longer. I vowed to do what I could for the decent folk of the town—unlike me perhaps, but worthy people nonetheless. I would follow Noah's example and stand as a light for that which was noble and right.

Samuel entered the house again, disgust on his face at the broken glass near my slippers. "Your father tells me that ruffian takes an interest in you. We've decided it best you no longer visit the South End, Emma. Now that I am home, there is no need, and you have a wedding to plan and a trip across the sea to prepare yourself for. Is that clear?"

I pressed my lips together, breathed through my nose, the fierceness of a fairy-tale dragon longing to break free. Yet I must plan my steps with care and wisdom. Succumbing to feisty feelings would not do, not if I were to truly take charge of the design formulating in my mind.

"Emma. Is that clear?"

I raised my chin to Samuel, for the first time thankful that I would not be his wife in the end.

"Aye, Samuel. You are indeed very clear."

If I could grasp this newfound courage, refuse to release it to weakness, refuse to doubt whether or not I owed my parents my loyalty, then mayhap I would find my voice after all.

DISCUSSION QUESTIONS

1. In *The Orchard House*, Taylor and Johanna are both looking for a place to belong. Why do you think they feel as if they don't belong? How do they try to fill the void they feel in their lives? Are there times when searching for love might lead to unhealthy patterns or choices? What are some healthy ways to feel loved?

2. Why does Taylor feel that hope isn't always a safe option? Describe a time in your life when being hopeful about something felt like it might be setting you up for disappointment. How did you find balance between holding on to hope and not surrendering to disappointment?

3. Louisa tries to warn Johanna about Nathan Bancroft, but in the end Johanna has to make her own decision about whether she will continue to develop her relationship with Nathan. Have you ever had to have a difficult conversation with a friend regarding a concerning relationship or a decision they were making? What would you have said to Johanna about Nathan if you had been Louisa?

4. In the midst of her clashes with Louisa about Nathan, Johanna wonders, "Couldn't friends disagree and remain amicable?" How does this play out between Louisa and Johanna? Between Taylor and Victoria? In your relationships?

5. How did you feel after you found out Victoria betrayed Taylor by kissing Will? How would you have responded if you'd been Taylor?

6. After Victoria betrays their friendship, Taylor goes years without forgiving her. How does this unforgiveness affect Taylor's life and her relationships with others? What might have happened if Taylor was willing to forgive Victoria sooner?

7. As Taylor sits with her mom during chemo treatments, she wonders about the worth of bad stuff—"could it possibly produce something good in the end?" What does she conclude? How would you answer this question?

8. What consequences does Johanna find in ignoring the advice of her friend and pursuing a relationship with Nathan Bancroft? What are some of the dangers of placing all our hopes and sense of worthiness in our relationships with others?

9. How does Johanna's writing of the poems during her tumultuous marriage help her deal with the hard times she faces? Have you ever tried writing or journaling to help you when you're dealing with something difficult in your life?

10. Despite knowing that Nathan has a problem with alcohol (what we'd call substance abuse today), Johanna feels that her love might be enough to save him, to rescue him. How have you seen this pattern repeated in the lives of people you know? Why is it such a temptation to believe we can save those we love? What is it that they really need?

11. As a writer, Taylor understands the power of story—and the importance of telling both the good ones and the bad ones. What do Taylor and Victoria learn from Johanna's story? How might stories "birth new life" for someone?

12. Though living in different centuries, Johanna and Victoria face similar challenges in their relationships with abusive men. What has changed since the 1860s, and what remains the same? In what ways is it easier today for women to get help? In what ways are their struggles similar to what they have been throughout history?

ABOUT THE AUTHOR

HEIDI CHIAVAROLI (pronounced *shev-uh-roli* . . . sort of like *Chevrolet* and *ravioli* mushed together) wrote her first story in third grade, titled *I'd Cross the Desert for Milk*. It wasn't until years later that she revisited writing, using her two small boys' nap times to pursue what she thought at the time was a foolish dream. Despite a long road to publication, she hasn't stopped writing since!

Heidi writes women's fiction, combining her love of history and literature to write split-time stories. Her debut novel, *Freedom's Ring*, was a Carol Award winner and a Christy Award finalist, a *Romantic Times* Top Pick and a *Booklist* Top Ten Romance Debut. Heidi loves exploring places that whisper of historical secrets, especially with her family. She loves running, hiking, baking, and dates with her husband. Heidi makes her home in Massachusetts with her husband and two sons. Visit her online at heidichiavaroli.com.